Secrets, Lies & Chocolate Highs

Published in the UK in 2021 by Glass Frog Press

Paperback   ISBN 978-1-8384312-0-4
.epub eBook   ISBN 978-1-8384312-2-8
.mobi eBook   ISBN 978-1-8384312-1-1

Cover design and typeset by SpiffingCovers

Secrets, Lies & Chocolate Highs

Ruby Mae Winter

CHAPTER ONE

Jess Jones sat cross-legged on the floor of the tiny attic room in her late mother's beloved cottage, surrounded by small boxes which, in true Eleanor style were secured with brightly coloured metallic tape, each one neatly labelled with an ornately scrolled number in beautiful, shimmering silver. She smiled and thought they looked more like birthday or Christmas presents than boxes of belongings, but her mother would never have used ordinary sticky tape or a plain marker pen, whatever she was wrapping. Everything she did showed her artistic flair and creativity, even packing boxes.

It had taken her six long months to even contemplate starting to sort through her mother's belongings, her personal effects, her life. She had somehow summoned enough mental strength to come to the cottage shortly after her death to gather a few papers to help her deal with the essential legalities, and then, with that done, she had thrown herself back into the nursing job she loved, which helped keep her sane while she continued to try to come to terms with the untimely loss of her mother.

Jess leaned back against the wall of the attic and sighed. This most definitely was not where she had envisaged herself to be at the ripe old age of thirty-two. It was too soon to be without her mother. She wasn't prepared. She wasn't ready. And to add insult to injury, she hadn't even managed to meet any of the three life goals she had set herself. She had always told Eleanor she would be married, have her own house and a family by the time she was thirty years old. Her mother had warned her that the plan was fraught with problems, that life didn't work like that, but she had laughed it off.

But, of course, Eleanor had been right, as here she was single, with several failed long term relationships (well, okay, one to be precise, but it seemed like more), many disastrous short-term relationships, one of which ended after only five minutes when Gavin had announced he was homophobic as part of his introduction: *Hi, I'm Gavin. Thirty-five, no secret wife and no secret children. I love all sports and I dislike gay men!* It had been a blind date, arranged by a friend. She hadn't been keen right from the start, but desperate times and all that. As for his opening gambit, Jess had looked at him in astonishment. She wasn't sure if he was just trying to be funny, but if it was intended as a joke then it was in very bad taste. So she had turned on her heel and walked away without uttering a single word.

Now, sitting in the little attic, her mind drifted back to her other failed relationships. Who was next? Andy? No, it was Julian. Kind and thoughtful Julian. She had met him in the library of all places. Probably not that surprising as, to be fair, he did work there. And she loved the library. So peaceful and calm, and she'd always told herself she should read more. And although she hadn't actually started reading more at the point when she'd met Julian, she was on the right track surely.

'Are you looking for anything in particular?' he'd asked.

'Fiction. Yes, definitely fiction.'

'That's a good start, but a little more information would be helpful,' he'd said, with a look of amusement.

Then, after several library visits, he'd asked her out for a drink. And it could have been good, if it hadn't been for his mother, who rang him twice to see how the date was going. There had been three more dates, each one overseen by his mother. It had become clear that she could never compete with her, and she didn't really have the energy or the inclination to do so in any case. So it was another one to add to the list of failures, missed attempts at goal. But at least she'd started reading more, so every cloud…

Then came Andy. He was okay, quite nice actually, but had preferred the gym to her. And she certainly didn't have the energy to compete with a bench press or kettlebells. There was only one use for a kettle as far as she was concerned, and it wasn't for swinging between your legs.

But just as she was giving up hope, along came Daniel, and her faith in men was restored. He was her first proper long-term serious relationship. He was funny, considerate and kind. Tall and handsome, and always smelt gorgeous. They'd clicked immediately. He was a teacher, and they'd met in a pub when they were on respective nights out with friends. Even now she could remember his first words to her. And, unlike Gavin's, she remembered them for the right reasons: *Hi, I'm Daniel. I'm not good at chat-up lines, but can I buy you a drink?*

Not earth-shattering. Not remotely. But honest and genuine, and quite refreshing compared to some of the cheesy chat-up lines she'd been subjected to before.

After that first evening, they'd stayed together for a year. A whole year of blissful happiness. In fact, she'd been happier than she'd *ever* been. There was nothing about him she hadn't liked. Well until the fateful zoo outing.

She'd never been to London Zoo before and she had been excited. Daniel hadn't seemed quite so keen, but that's what relationships were all about, she'd told herself. Give and take. But she'd underestimated his reluctance. *Grossly* underestimated it. He'd been miserable from the start, moaning and tutting. She'd not seen him like that before.

'What's up Daniel?' She'd asked. But she hadn't been at all prepared for his reply.

'There are kids everywhere,' he'd complained. 'And I know it's going to sound strange, what with me being a teacher, but I really don't like them. Not at all.'

Unlike his chat-up line, this comment really *had* been earth shattering as (a) Could you really be a teacher if you didn't like kids? And (b) Did that mean he didn't want any of his own children?

And that's exactly what it had meant. No children, not ever, he'd confirmed. She hadn't bothered to wait around to find out the answer to *a*, as his response to *b* had not only been the final nail in the coffin but the only nail needed. She knew a life without children was not one she could entertain, not even with the man she loved.

Eleanor had told her not to be hasty. That people can and do change. But she was adamant: it was over. Finished.

Some weeks later, while flicking through a magazine in the waiting room of the dental surgery of all places, she had come across a quote:

A zoo is an excellent place to study the habits of human beings
Evan Esar

It had made her laugh, probably for the first time since she had split from Daniel. And taking the quote in its literal sense, the zoo certainly had been an excellent place. It had undoubtedly been her saviour.

Right, she told herself, that's enough thinking about past relationships. Much too depressing. But the truth was that apart from her single status, there were even more depressing facts: she was living in a room in a shared house, had no money to speak of, and had no contact with her father, who had let both Eleanor and her down so badly that she hadn't spoken to him for almost eleven years.

Then six months ago, the final body blow: her mother had died from a massive heart attack with no time for any last 'I love you's or 'goodbye's.

'Death is inevitable'. That's what her mother had said only a few months before she'd died. She was a pragmatic woman, that was for sure, but hearing those words and experiencing the reality of their meaning were two entirely different things. Death may be inevitable, but it was also cruel, excruciatingly painful, shocking and very isolating for those left behind. She had, of course, been desperately sad but had also felt so angry at times, raging at the world, at the unfairness of life, and even at the person she had loved the most in the world, her own mother.

She had been surprised at the strength of her own feelings during those first few weeks, especially as death was no stranger to her. But, quite simply, she had underestimated the difference between being involved with relative strangers who were facing death, and being directly involved on a personal level. She had learned very early on that there was little or no comparison.

At one point she had started to put her feelings down on paper, trying to make sense of it all in the form of what could only be described as crude poetry:

Oh cruel death you came so unexpectedly,
Leaving behind a trail of devastation in your wake,
The harshness of your permanency, the pain of your sting,
The fragility of life, your calling card.

Jess allowed herself a wry smile as she recalled the words she had tried to pen in those early dark days. She'd loathed poetry at school and couldn't even remember how poems should be constructed, but looking back it had been unexpectedly therapeutic. Just putting the words down on paper and then reading them out loud had been comforting, and in some ways seemed to have given legitimacy to her feelings.

She sighed as she looked around the attic and then, as happened so often, she found her mind turning back to the events of the day that Eleanor had died.

It had been a fairly ordinary early shift for her on the medical ward of the busy London teaching hospital where she worked as a registered nurse. No dramas, just lots to do, but still time to be a listening ear and, she hoped, a comfort to patients and families in her care.

She had left the ward for her lunch break and, as she always did, had gone to her locker to get her mobile phone. The ward sister had a very strict 'no mobile phones policy' for staff, and Jess always believed this was fair as they could become very distracting.

As she walked towards the canteen she saw the screen flashing with six missed calls and several text messages from Rosa Delaney. Panic had swept through her body, her heart rate quickened and a lump rose in her throat.

Rosa was Eleanor's friend and next door neighbour, and although Jess knew her quite well, she would have had no reason to phone unless there was something wrong. Without even reading the messages, Jess had phoned Rosa immediately. And she could remember her words almost verbatim: *Oh Jess darling, I'm so sorry, but you must come to the district general hospital as quickly as you can. It's your Mamma, she's collapsed, I found her this morning...*

She had rung off without letting Rosa finish and had run back to the ward. Sister was very understanding and had said of course she must go straight away, but not to rush as better to get there safely than not at all.

Sometime hence, Jess had reflected on this and decided it had been a less than tactful thing to say in the circumstances. But now she found she could laugh about it, so that must be a sign that she was coming out the other side of what had been a dark period in her life.

She recalled the journey to the hospital. It had seemed to take forever. She'd had to take the tube back to the house she shared with two other girls, in order to collect her car, and then make the slow journey out of London to the heart of the Suffolk countryside. It had taken over three hours in total, and then, when she couldn't find a parking space straight away, she'd dissolved into floods of tears. Fortunately, one of the parking attendants had taken pity on her and had let her park in a hatched area, directing her then to the Accident and Emergency Department. She had reported immediately to the reception desk, but when the receptionist checked the computer screen, she had seen the look of sympathy on her face and knew it wasn't going to be good news.

A doctor and a nurse had taken her to a tiny, impersonal room which had probably once been a cupboard, and told her the bad news. They were very kind and empathetic, informing her they had tried everything and reassuring her that Eleanor hadn't suffered.

And then, as if from nowhere, Rosa had appeared and Jess was clutching her tightly, sobbing uncontrollably on her shoulder. Rosa, in her typical comforting Italian way, was stroking her hair, saying things like: *There, there my darling,* and *Your Mamma loved you very much.*

Jess sat up straight, stretched her arms above her head and arched her back. She'd been sitting against the wall for so long that her right leg felt numb, and as Rosa would say: *This won't knit the baby an*

Easter bonnet.

Rosa used lots of sayings, many of which were either slightly wrong or said in the wrong context, but it was so endearing that it always made her smile. And, although in this case it really wouldn't knit the baby a new bonnet, Easter or otherwise, she realised that this time she had recounted that awful day without shedding any tears. And that was another step forward.

Eleanor had reminded Jess about the boxes in the attic on more than one occasion, and always with an *if I should die* comment attached to it. But, apart from the obvious paperwork and documents that everybody has, Jess had no idea what else was in them, or why they were wrapped and numbered. *Did Eleanor have some sort of cross-referencing system?* She wondered, or did she mean Jess to open them sequentially? Whatever the answer was, she decided she was actually rather looking forward to going through them; it could be quite cathartic, she told herself.

She picked up the kitchen knife and was just about to slit the tape on the box numbered 'One', when the front door bell chimed its melodious tune. She raised her eyes to the ceiling and said out loud, 'That'll be Rosa,' which didn't take much working out as she didn't really know anyone else in the lane, or indeed in the village, certainly not well enough for them to pay her a visit. She immediately reprimanded herself as Rosa had been so kind to her, and had also satisfied the home insurance company's requirements by checking on the house every week for the past six months. She put the knife back down on the floor and made her way down the steep and narrow winding staircase that led from the attic to the first floor, before calling out, 'Just coming,' and continuing down the next set of less winding, but equally narrow stairs.

She unlocked the heavy timber door and was surprised to see, not Rosa, but a tall young man standing in front of her.

'Hello?' she offered, in a way that clearly meant *who are you and what do you want?*

'Hi, I'm Will, Will Thackery. I live next door.'

'Oh right, yes, sorry,' she said quickly. 'I guessed there was someone living there from the noise coming through the walls.'

She had intended it as a light-hearted comment, but realised as the words came out that it sounded more like a complaint. She took a deep breath and looked up at his face, and to her relief his lips had parted and his mouth fell into a lop-sided sheepish grin, revealing slightly crooked but very white teeth. His blue-grey eyes twinkled as his whole face took on an amused look. They both went to speak at the same time, so Jess gestured an 'after you' signal, in order to give her some time to compose herself.

'I just thought I'd pop round as I heard noises coming from the house and I know it's been empty since we moved in next door. I wasn't being nosey, just neighbourly.'

Did she detect a hint of defensiveness in his comments? Hmm, maybe.

'Thank you,' she replied quickly. 'That's really kind of you, please come in, and apologies if I sounded cross before, you know, about the noise...'

Now shut up, she told herself, *you're overcompensating as usual.*

Will stepped inside the door and bent down to remove his boots. Jess glanced at his clothes and quickly realised that he must be doing the work on the house himself. He had paint and what looked like plaster on his clothes, and his sand-coloured hair was peppered with white dust. It was tied up in a topknot, which she thought looked rather chic, if indeed a man could look chic, of course. His off-white t-shirt was stretched across his chest, and clearly he worked out or he did some sort of tough manual job. He looked up from untying his boots and she looked away quickly, stuttering something about tea and kettles. *Not cool Jess, really not cool.*

They sat at Eleanor's small kitchen table, which was covered by a cream lace tablecloth, sipping tea from delicate bone china tea cups, decorated with exquisitely dainty flowers. Eleanor had despised mugs, and had always insisted that tea could only be properly appreciated when drunk from bone china cups. Jess poured the tea from the matching tea pot, and apologised to Will for the seeming formality.

'Mum was a traditionalist, and I suppose a bit old-fashioned in her ways for someone of only fifty-eight,' she explained.

Will looked away briefly, and then, fidgeting in a decidedly uncomfortable way, offered his condolences to her. Rosa had explained the empty cottage situation to him, he told her, when he'd first moved in around four months ago. She was relieved, at least, that she didn't have to suffer the pain of going through it all again, and relaxed back in her chair.

'Rosa.' Just saying her name made her smile. 'She's been amazing to me over the last six months.'

'Me too,' Will said.

Jess gave him a questioning look, prompting him to explain that Rosa had regularly taken meals round to him, and even done some washing and ironing. It didn't seem the right time to ask any questions, so she just nodded and smiled at him.

'I call her my Italian Mamma,' he said laughing, giving Jess another glimpse of his ultra-white teeth through his parted lips. He really was rather good-looking, she thought.

'Anyway, thank you for the tea, and it's back to work for me,' he said, pushing his chair back and heading towards the door to put his boots on.

'Did you realise that sentence rhymed?' she said, laughing.

'Erm, well yes, I guess so, but it wasn't intentional I'm afraid. I've never been known for my poetic skills to be honest,' he replied drily.

'I tried to write some poetry once. It was after my mother died.'

She immediately saw that he looked uncomfortable, and decided that she shouldn't elaborate any further. Reciting a poem about death was probably not appropriate small talk at a first meeting.

'Anyway, really nice to meet you Jess, and I feel reassured that you are not a burglar, or anyone else who might be up to no good.'

'Thank you,' she replied, and then chastised herself for (a) Making such ridiculous comments about rhyming sentences and poetry, and (b) Not being quick enough to come back with a humorous reply to his 'burglar' comment. She was hopelessly slow-witted.

As Will opened the front door, she saw Rosa coming down the garden path, carrying a large basket covered with a gingham cloth.

'Hello Will, you gorgeous boy,' she teased.

'Rosa, you're making me blush,' he replied laughing, and with that he strode off up the garden path whistling loudly.

'Jess, my darling girl,' Rosa shrilled. 'As gorgeous as ever. Bellissima,' she continued, whilst hugging her so tightly she felt she could hardly breathe. 'Goodness your Mamma would be so proud of you.'

As Rosa released her vice-like grip, she stood back and said, 'Mind you darling, you do look, and feel a little bit thin, so it's a good job I have pasta and a freshly baked cake. They will give you both energy and enjoyment.'

'Thank you Rosa. You're so kind.'

And that's exactly what she was. Kind. And warm. And loving. She remembered how her well-rounded frame had given her such comfort and reassurance at the time of Eleanor's death. Remarkably, she was never any different: she'd been a constant source of solace, a staple in her life, in more ways than one.

Inside the cottage, Jess began telling Rosa about the boxes in the attic room, and how she'd been about to start opening them when Will had arrived.

'But I guess that will be tomorrow's job now as it's getting a bit late to start and the light is not very good up there.'

'There's no hurry is there darling?' Rosa said. 'Take your time and ask for help if you need it. It must be so hard doing everything on your own. No brothers or sisters, and your father...well...' She clicked her tongue, while at the same time rolling her eyes in an exaggerated fashion.

Jess didn't think Rosa had even met her father, but undoubtedly Eleanor had spoken about him and his 'treachery'.

After Rosa had left, Jess regarded herself in her mother's full length mirror. Hmm, *a bit thin* Rosa had said, but only from the waist up, she thought. And that was *not* where you wanted to be thin. Maybe she should walk around on her hands, then the thin bit would be at the bottom, but then again, perhaps not.

She was what people would metaphorically call pear-shaped, and the truth was that her rear end and thighs were really much too big for the rest of her body. She was also quite short, only five foot and a very important half an inch, and whilst some men found this appealing, she had always yearned to be taller, if only to be able to reach the top shelves at the supermarket.

Eleanor had been a similar shape, but apart from that and, thankfully, the high cheek bones, that was where the similarities ended. Eleanor had fair hair, with hints of auburn and pale skin typical of her Celtic roots, whereas Jess had blemish-free olive skin with her hair most definitely being her crowning glory. It was very dark, almost black, with a slightly coarse texture, and had a sort of crimped look. It was brilliant for up-dos as it stayed put for hours, but looked equally stunning if straightened with irons, when it took on a gloss that looked like it had been painted on. She loved her hair, and actually her face wasn't too bad either. People often described her as pretty and sometimes even beautiful, but even though big bottoms were quite in vogue now, she most definitely was not body-confident. In truth, she wasn't confident at all.

CHAPTER TWO

At seven o'clock, Jess decided a walk to the village pub would break up the long evening ahead, and also stop her from eating too much chocolate and drinking beer on her own, which was not a good idea on either count.

She'd been to The Plough on several occasions with her mother, and so knew one or two of the locals and the bar staff, if only to say hello to. It would be a change if nothing else.

It was only a short walk to the beautiful sixteenth-century heavily-beamed building, and tonight Jess was delighted to see a roaring log fire in the huge inglenook fireplace. It was a cold evening and she hadn't worked out how to override the heating in the cottage, so she was glad of the warming welcome the pub offered. She looked around but didn't recognise anyone in the pub, not even the young girl behind the bar. So she ordered a pint of the speciality real ale and sat at the table nearest the fire. Removing her heavy winter coat, she realised she wasn't exactly dressed for the occasion, still sporting tattered and slightly grubby jeans, and a generously-sized sweatshirt that was emblazoned with the year and it wasn't a recent one either. She looked around again, and deciding that she wasn't going to offend anyone with her attire, sank back into the tub chair and savoured the crisp fruity taste of the ale.

Putting her glass down on the table, she picked up a copy of the local paper, but before she had a chance to flick through it she heard her phone beep from inside her coat pocket. Retrieving it quickly, she was delighted to see a message from her best friend and housemate, Poppy, *Hi Jess, how's things going? Been thinking about you a lot and wish I was there to help you with what must be a difficult job...*

Jess smiled, Poppy was one in a million, that was for sure. Another constant in her life. They had undertaken their nurse training together and been almost inseparable ever since. They'd even ended up working on the same ward, although they rarely seemed to be rostered onto the same shifts.

Poppy was the polar opposite to her in so many ways. She was tall, blonde and willowy, and had a smile that rendered men utterly powerless to her charms. She always knew what to say in difficult situations, and was so quick-witted that Jess was sure she could have made herself a good living as a stand-up comedian.

But they did have one thing in common. Nothing to brag about, but a commonality nonetheless. Neither of them had met anyone with the potential of being future husband material. Neither had managed to find a 'Mr Right'. Not that Poppy wanted a Mr Right, she regularly reminded Jess. She'd had plenty of opportunities, but had decided that now, at the age of thirty-two, she was going to set off on her travels. To be fair, it had always been her dream, but Jess had been devastated when she'd realised it was now a reality. She had, though, managed to hide her dismay, even helping Poppy to plan her trips.

So, maybe finding a Mr Right wasn't a common denominator after all. Perhaps it was only her own body clock that seemed to have taken on an extra loud tick.

Hi yourself, Jess replied to the text. *Things are actually easier than I thought they would be, but having said that I haven't really done much yet! Tomorrow I'm going to hit the ground running otherwise this week's holiday will be over before I've even started. How are things back there?*

Her phone beeped again, just as the door to the pub swung open. She looked up from her phone without reading Poppy's reply, and saw Will from next door standing in the doorway. For some inexplicable reason, and totally out of character for her, she waved frantically, calling him over as if she had arranged to meet him there.

That looked a little desperate she told herself, as he started to walk towards her.

'Hi again,' she said with a smile that must have reached from one side of her face to the other.

'Yes, hello again,' he replied with an amused look on his now clean-shaven face. 'Can I get you another drink?'

'Oh no thanks, one pint is more than enough for me, otherwise I'll be on the toilet all night.' She immediately cursed herself for making such a ridiculous comment. Why on earth she thought he would want to know about her bladder she had no idea, but it was typical of nurses who had a habit of talking very openly about the most personal of things. And it was also typical of how she behaved when she was feeling nervous. She was always telling herself she must learn to think before she spoke, but despite having had years of practise she was yet to master said technique.

Will returned to the table with his pint and Jess noticed his hair was newly washed, and kept from falling on his face by a thin hair band. There were no signs of any paint, dust or plaster, and he actually scrubbed-up rather well. He was wearing a pair of dark skinny jeans and a long-sleeved branded top, which accentuated his muscle definition rather well.

'Okay if I join you?' His voice broke through Jess's thoughts.

'Of course,' she replied, suddenly wishing she had changed into something a little more suited to an evening with your good-looking next door neighbour, rather than an evening at home with your housemates. But then again they would most likely have all had their pyjamas on, so it could have been worse.

'So,' Will began, and Jess was immediately back in the room. 'Tell me a bit about you and then next time, maybe I'll tell you a bit about me.'

He was grinning now, and she found herself feeling relaxed in his company, even if she had practically abducted the poor guy. And he had said 'next time', so maybe he was feeling okay about the abduction.

So she told him a bit about her life. That she was single, lived and worked in London as a nurse, was an only child, and that her father was a complete bastard, who had left her and her mother for another woman. She'd left out the bit that she was actually an adult by then, but the devil was always in the detail wasn't it? She wasn't even sure why she had told him about her father, but he already knew a bit about her mother, so it just seemed like a natural part of the potted life story she had shared with him. And he seemed interested. He asked questions and listened to what she was saying. It was a relaxed and comfortable evening. He was nice. Very nice.

Later on they walked home from the pub together, down the little lane towards their adjoining cottages. Jess pulled her coat tightly around her and joked that she might have to sleep in it if she couldn't find out how to make the heating work.

'I can take a look if you like?' Will offered. 'Although I have to confess, I'm no engineer.'

'That would be great if you don't mind,' she replied with a grateful smile, although he probably couldn't see it as the lane was absolutely pitch black.

'So where's the programmer?' he asked, once they were inside the cottage.

'Umm...I'm not entirely sure,' Jess replied sheepishly.

'Ah,' he said. 'Okay, the boiler then, I'm guessing you know where that is?'

She noticed he had a twinkle in his eye and it made her smile. 'Of course,' she replied with a tone of mock indignation. 'It's in the kitchen...obviously...' She'd seen it in there, she knew she had. She opened a couple of cupboards, and was grateful to locate it fairly quickly.

'Aha, and there's the programmer as well,' Will said in a teasing tone.

'I wondered what that was,' she replied laughing.

And within seconds the boiler had fired up and the radiators were already beginning to warm up.

'You're a lifesaver,' she said. 'Thank you so much.'

'Never could resist a damsel in distress,' he replied with a wink.

She felt herself flush, practically from head to toe and stuttering another few words of thanks, opened the door and watched him disappear up the path. Locking it behind him, she leaned against it, puffed out her cheeks with satisfaction and thought: *All in all not a bad day Jessica Jones.*

CHAPTER THREE

The next day Jess was up bright and early, and was met by a beautiful autumnal day. The watery sun was peeping through the fiery orange-coloured trees, casting shadows which looked as if they were dancing in the gentle breeze.

She could understand why Eleanor loved living in the small village of Thripton, and in particular the pretty part-timbered cottage, with its beautiful casement windows and heavy timber door, painted in a bright pillar box red.

Soon after moving in, she had planted the most wonderfully fragrant climbing rose over the tiny porch, and joked she might change the name of the cottage from No 3 Back Lane to Rose Cottage. And then, after researching traditional colours, she'd had the outside walls painted in Suffolk pink and Jess had agreed she'd done something good for posterity.

Inside the cottage, Eleanor had whitewashed the walls and scrubbed the beams. She'd bought and up-cycled some traditional pieces of furniture and contrasted them with contemporary furnishings, all made by her own fair hand. The result was the most amazing eclectic mix of old meets new, which regularly made visitors gasp with delight.

'Dressing a room is like putting the icing on a cake Jess,' her mother used to say.

And what a cake it was. A chocolate cake, with double chocolate and chocolate icing.

When Eleanor had initially announced she was going to move to Suffolk, Jess had been worried that she may be acting in haste. And when, within a week, her mother had phoned her again to tell her that she'd found a beautiful village called Thripton and a lovely cottage to boot, Jess had hot-footed it from London to meet her there, but the deal was already done. Eleanor had a tendency to be impulsive but fortunately she was rarely wrong.

The village itself was as pretty as a picture, with a beautifully-kept village green, showing off the imposing village sign, and a small pond which was home to an impressive number of ducks. The cosy village pub overlooked the green in a watchful manner, and the tiny tea rooms which also housed a small shop and a post office, looked cheerful and welcoming with their colourful bunting.

A mix of chocolate-box thatched-roofed cottages with perfectly manicured gardens, sat harmoniously alongside others built using local flint, brick and wattle and daub. The neatly mowed grass verges were interspersed with clumps of pretty wild flowers, and it was obvious that everyone took enormous pride in the village.

Back Lane itself was a quiet little lane, with the church hall and car park at the entrance, a row of terraced cottages, of which Eleanor's was one, a couple of pairs of semis, and a large detached house that was once the rectory. And then, at the end of the lane, stood the impressive Norman Church of St Peter and St Paul in all its splendour, retaining many of its original features, including the doorway with its round pillars and elaborately-carved capitals.

Although not overtly religious, Eleanor had regularly attended the village church, mainly as she loved to sing, and was quickly commandeered into the choir. And Jess had been delighted to discover that she too could sing, when out with her friends in a karaoke bar in London.

She had consumed way too many cocktails when she'd taken to the make-shift stage to sing a Whitney Houston song, but to her surprise and to everybody's delight, she was amazingly good. In fact, so good she got a standing ovation, and when she returned to the table to join her house mates, she found them searching the internet about how to enter her into a famous national talent show. She had, however, decided to settle on joining a local choir and ever since had sang regularly at events across the capital. She was a 'minor local celebrity' her friends told anyone who would listen, but although praise always made her uncomfortable, she secretly felt quite proud of herself.

Jess let out a gasp as she suddenly remembered that she hadn't replied to the second text from Poppy the previous evening. And what was more, she hadn't even read it.

Feeling guilty, she opened up the text and smiled as she read that Poppy was offering to join her at the cottage on her days off, to give her some 'help and support'. *Never cast your friends aside,* she reminded herself, and quickly tapped a reply saying that she would love a visit from her 'bestie', if she had the time. Then added truthfully, *Love you Poppy - you're the best,* before pressing the send button.

Her thoughts about her friend were suddenly interrupted by the sound of Rosa, who was singing her own version of a Kylie song in her back garden:

I wish I was lucky, lucky, lucky, lucky,
I wish I was lucky in love,
I wish I was lucky, lucky, lucky, lucky,
I wish I was lucky in love.

After listening for a few seconds, Jess decided it might be a very pertinent time to say 'good morning'. She did, of course, want to see Rosa, she always wanted to see her, but she also secretly hoped that it might serve the dual purpose of putting an end to her discordant verse.

But, on stepping out into Eleanor's back garden, her thoughts were brought into sharp focus when she saw how neglected it now looked. The grass had gone to seed and there were tall, unruly weeds everywhere. Jess sighed. Eleanor had been so proud of her little garden, and the sight of it now made tears spring to her eyes.

Once the boxes in the attic were done, she would make a concerted effort to do something about the garden, she decided. And it wasn't out of a sense of duty, it was because it mattered to her, it really mattered.

'Morning Rosa,' she called over the low picket fence that separated the two gardens.

'Good morning Jess, my darling.'

'You're sounding very *chirpy* this morning,' she said, choosing her words with care.

'Of course darling, the sun is shining and my tail is bushy,' Rosa replied with a wink.

'And do you Rosa?' Jess asked with a grin.

'Do I what darling?'

'Wish you were lucky, you know, lucky in love.'

'Good heavens no Jess. It's a Kylie song. You must know it, surely?'

'I do Rosa, yes, it's just that your version is... well... it's slightly *different* from the original version, and I wondered if that was done deliberately, or maybe it was a Freudian slip?'

'Now I'm completely lost darling and I don't even know *what* or *who* Freudian is. The truth is I am never sure of the words of these modern songs, these young people mumble so much, but what I am quite sure of is that I do not want Cupid firing his arrows anywhere near *my* bosom, or any other part of me come to that!'

'Rosa you're so funny,' Jess managed to say in between fits of giggles. 'You always manage to make me laugh.'

'Well I'm glad to see you laughing my darling. And talking about Cupid, did you sleep well after your evening in the pub?' she asked, her head tilted slightly to one side.

Jess laughed, apparently *nothing*, but *nothing*, got past Rosa, and she remembered her mother once saying that what Rosa didn't know wasn't worth knowing.

'Yes thank you, Rosa.' And then in a bid to shut down the next inevitable comment she continued, 'Will very kindly came in and sorted out the heating for me, before I literally froze to death.'

'He's a good boy Jess, a really good boy.' She looked away briefly before adding, 'Did he talk about Holly at all?'

Holly? Holly? Jess repeated the name in her head. *Who in God's name was Holly? His wife, his girlfriend, his dog?* Her mind was whirring as she tried to make sense of what Rosa had said. But, despite the fact that she felt disordered, she surprised herself when she managed to calmly reply, 'No, he didn't Rosa, you see it was all about me. It's Will's turn next time.'

But Rosa didn't seem to have noticed her attempt to close the subject down, and continued regardless. 'Such a terribly sad story, Jess. You see, Holly was Will's girlfriend, they hadn't been in the cottage very long when she was so cruelly taken from him.'

Jess recoiled in horror. 'She's dead?' she managed to stammer. 'Will's girlfriend died?'

She suddenly felt an overwhelming sense of empathy for him, and in a strange way, some sort of connection. Was that why he was so uncomfortable when she had spoken about her mother's death, she wondered? How absolutely awful for him, and how brave he was being. She suddenly felt rather sick.

'Goodness me no, darling.'

Rosa's reply brought her back from her subconscious.

'Holly's not dead, she was *taken* from him. *Taken* by another man! Goodness, your face Jess. It was like a rabbit with headlights!'

Jess immediately felt an overwhelming sense of relief, as the blood that had drained from her face and upper body miraculously began to return. She took some deep breaths and tried to regain her composure from the 'fake shock' her body had experienced.

She opened her mouth to say that someone couldn't really be *taken* from someone else, unless it was against their will, but decided better of it. Instead, she simply said, 'Poor Will', and although she realised that was something of an understatement, she felt the need to end the conversation there, and to get herself indoors as quickly as possible.

Back inside the safety of Eleanor's cottage, she made herself a strong cup of coffee, and to help her recover from the 'shock', cut a large slice of the cake Rosa had brought round the previous day. She had a strong belief that comfort food was the answer to most things, even if you were feeling sick, and this cake was the most delicious of comfort foods.

She felt relieved that Will hadn't suffered a bereavement, but nevertheless the poor man must be suffering. Perhaps she would take him a piece of cake later on.

Feeling calmer after the coffee and cake, she headed upstairs to the attic, feeling a mix of anticipation and trepidation.

Although Eleanor had always referred to the attic as a room, it was really no more than a glorified loft, although it did have the benefit of a tiny window. And, of course, it came complete with dusty rafters and the obligatory spiders' webs, which meant that somewhere hiding in the dark corners were the owners of said webs. She opened the window as wide as it would go, and smiled at the sound of the church bells ringing their celebration of Sunday in the distance.

'Right,' she said out loud. 'Where is box number one?'

Using the kitchen knife she had left in the attic the previous day, Jess carefully slit the metallic tape on the first box. She gasped, as the sight of the contents almost took her breath away. For inside, was a tiny baby tooth, a lock of hair, a pair of pink baby booties, a knitted bonnet, and the most exquisitely crocheted pale lemon blanket, that had been carefully placed between layers of beautifully soft, pale cream tissue paper. And with them a beautiful hand-penned note in Eleanor's signature italic writing:

Memories of the most beautiful baby in the world

Jess swallowed hard, as salty tears pricked her eyes.

'Eleanor,' she said out loud. 'You were the most beautiful mother in the world.'

Box number two contained several small photo albums, each displaying beautifully hand-mounted pictures of Jess, from a baby through to her primary school days. Each photograph was captioned with a memory or anecdote, again written in italics and in different coloured inks.

Box number three was similar to the previous one, with more delicately mounted photographs from the end of primary school through to secondary school. Jess laughed out loud at the pictures of her school days, but decided that some were definitely not for public viewing.

Onto box number four, which was a mixture of photographic and hand-written memories of family holidays, days out, birthday parties and friends who had come and gone, along with some bits and pieces Jess had made at school. She sat and studied each one carefully in turn. Her mother had managed to annotate many of the photos, but not even she could remember the names of some of her classmates.

Seeing pictures of her father smiling and looking, by all intents and purposes, the contented family man she had always believed he was, brought a sudden rush of both sadness and anger. But even though he had undoubtedly let them down some years later, the memories she had of the three of them as a family were still ones of pure happiness.

She stood up and stretched her body. She had been sitting for over two hours already and was feeling stiff and achy. This was going to be an emotional journey with, she was sure, both pain and sadness, but also, she hoped it would bring her some peace and happiness.

And then, as she looked around the room, she suddenly felt charged with optimism for the future. The boxes she had opened so far were filled with such important memories, not only of her, but of all of their lives together. Eleanor was very insightful, that was for sure, and she realised at that moment, that although life was fragile, memories lived on forever.

After a quick cup of coffee, and a lunch consisting of a helping of Rosa's pasta straight from the fridge, and another rather large slice of cake, Jess felt ready to continue with the important job in the attic.

Boxes five, six and seven gave her the warmest of feelings, and fond memories came flooding back to winters' evenings and weekends spent as a family playing board games, card games and doing jigsaw puzzles.

Her school friends had always loved coming to her house to join in the games, and reminiscing now, Jess realised she'd had the best possible childhood.

She was surprised at the pristine condition of most of the games considering they were so well used. Perhaps she should start a campaign to rid the world of electronic games and insist that families only played traditional games. But realising that was way too radical for the 21st century, and carried a high risk of failure, she decided to settle on ensuring her own children, should she be fortunate enough to have a family in the future, were raised in the same way as she was. She had been happy, loved and secure, which had helped shape her into the person she was today. Not that she was without faults, she reminded herself, but on balance she was a decent human being.

Box number eight was the biggest surprise yet. As she opened the top, she quickly realised it was full of beautiful rose petal confetti. She peered into the box with anticipation. What on earth was this? And then as she gently pushed her hands through layers of hand-made confetti, she quickly realised it was a wedding box, and as with the other boxes, she found a now-familiar hand written note from Eleanor which read:

To my Jess, if you are reading this, then sadly I will not be able to be with you on your wedding day. But as always I will be with you in spirit my beautiful girl. I hope you have the most wonderful day and rest of your life

Jess bit her lip as she felt tears pricking her eyes once more. She moved her fingers around the mountain of confetti and pulled out a small hinged box, which when opened revealed a gold wedding band, nestled on a cushion of navy velvet. She instantly recognised it as Eleanor's wedding ring, which she had removed from her finger the day her father had left. In the lid was a note, carefully folded several times, so it fitted neatly. It read:

Wear it, sell it, or have it melted down for its intrinsic value - the choice is entirely yours

In some ways she wished it had also said, 'or insert it somewhere very painful', but despite the upset her father had caused, Eleanor had always maintained a quietly dignified manner when speaking about the man who had changed her life forever. It had been Jess who had been adamant she would never speak to him again, and thus far she had been true to her word. But despite all of this, she understood and appreciated her mother's sentiment. It was after all, another shared memory, painful or otherwise.

In the same box, she found a sealed A5 envelope with the words 'for your dress', written on the front. On opening the envelope, her eyes widened at the sight of a bundle of crisp £50 notes, delicately held together with a strip of wedding ribbon. Without even counting it, she pushed it back under the confetti and sat back on her heels, as salty tears trickled down her cheeks.

'Marriage and children will come in their own good time Jess', Eleanor would say. 'You can't put a time limit on these things. The stars must be aligned. Be patient. It *will* happen.'

And although she was sure Eleanor was as keen for this to happen as she was, she'd never put any pressure on her. Quite the opposite.

Jess sighed. How she wished she could talk to Eleanor again. She would tell her that if she couldn't bag a decent man, then she would blow the money on other pleasures like beer, fast food and chocolate. It would have made her mother laugh and roll her eyes in mock disgust, and then she would have hugged her and said, 'Not really Mum, well actually maybe the chocolate!'

Seeing and reading the contents of box number eight had been the most emotional part so far, and Jess was in awe of Eleanor when she considered the level of thought and time she must have spent in putting the boxes together, not to mention the emotional impact on her as well.

Deep in thought and feeling emotionally drained, she startled at the sound of the doorbell, which was followed very quickly by a loud banging on the front door. Jumping to her feet, she descended the stairs two at a time, risking life and limb on the first set. She opened the door to find Will standing in front of her holding up his left hand, which was wrapped in a piece of blood-soaked material. He was looking very pale but despite this he managed to joke, 'Anyone know a good nurse?'

'Well if we can lose the adjective, then I'm your girl,' Jess replied, desperately trying to keep the conversation light, in an effort to hide the rising panic that was washing over her. She took him inside and sat him down on the leather wing-backed chair next to the fireplace.

'Had a bit of a disagreement with a very sharp tool,' he said with a grimace.

Jess raised her eyes to the ceiling. 'Well you've come to the right place. Luckily for you my mother was a very organised woman,' she said, in what she hoped was a reassuring voice. 'I'm sure I can find everything I need to do a bit of first aid.'

Will looked at her apologetically and said, 'Thank you.'

She touched his shoulder before disappearing into the kitchen, quickly returning with the mini mobile hospital that she'd fortuitously noticed in one of the cupboards the night before, when she was looking for the boiler.

'Right then, let's take a look at the damage,' she said, pulling on an enormous pair of blue gloves she'd found in the first aid box, and smiling confidently as if she was a surgeon about to perform an operation. It was important to appear confident, even if you were trembling inside, she reminded herself.

She unwrapped the piece of material from Will's now shaking hand, and realised it was a tea towel, or at least part of one. And underneath the tea towel, were several partially disintegrated tissues and a wad of something resembling cotton wool, all of which were brightly decorated with his blood.

The cut itself seemed quite deep, and so without further comment about either the amount of blood or the size of the cut, she told him that she was going to apply a pressure dressing and take him in her car to Accident and Emergency.

He didn't argue at her authoritarian approach, and maybe she would reflect on that approach later, but at this point it seemed the best course of action to take.

Within half an hour they had checked in at the reception desk of the Accident and Emergency Department, and were sitting down in the only two empty seats in the waiting room.

As Jess looked around, her mind was once again taken back to the day she had been there to learn the devastating news that Eleanor had died. But even though it was the first time she had been back there since that day, she didn't feel the need to relive the events on this occasion. She was there to support Will, who was now looking pale and repeating how grateful he was to her.

After what seemed like an eternity, but was probably more like 40 minutes or so, Will was called into the triage nurse's room, and taking account of the fact that Jess had only known him for around twenty four hours, she told him she would stay in the waiting room.

His eyes widened and his brow furrowed. 'Would you mind coming with me, please Jess? I don't mind admitting that I feel a bit scared.'

It was so endearing, that she found herself smiling warmly at him, and for some inexplicable reason said, 'Lead on Macduff.'

In return he smiled weakly, before leaning towards and whispering , 'Actually it's *lay on Macduff*. I always wondered what earthly point there was in learning the works of Shakespeare...until now that is.' His tone was light and teasing, and she immediately realised she found it rather attractive.

Back in the waiting room, Will was now in a very long queue to see the doctor. It almost certainly needed an assessment for any damage to underlying structures, and a few stitches, the nurse had told him, and then she'd congratulated Jess on her handy work. Jess hadn't mentioned that she was also a nurse as (a) She was actually rubbish at first aid and, (b) Due to her own insecurities, she always felt super pressurised when a patient or family member under her care announced they were in the same profession. She was grateful that Will hadn't said anything either but secretly she was rather relieved that she had handled the situation correctly. Medicine was her bread and butter, but accidents and trauma were a whole different ball game.

Later, much later, when she was curled up in Eleanor's huge wrought-iron framed bed, and dressed in her favourite tartan pyjamas, she reflected on the unexpected events of the day.

She had reminded Will that it was his turn to talk about

himself, with the ulterior motive of taking his mind off his hand while they waited to see the doctor, or at least that's what she'd told herself.

He'd told her he was a painter and decorator in his family business, and with a wink had said 'and a damn good one'. He'd lived in Suffolk all his life, which was why he 'spoke funny'. He and Holly had bought No. 5 Back Lane together, to turn it into their dream country cottage, but he'd quickly realised that it had been more his romantic dream than hers, and when she'd announced that she was leaving him for someone he referred to as a 'dick in a suit', he hadn't been overly surprised.

In turn, Jess had told him a bit more about herself and how her father had left Eleanor and her, almost straight after her graduation ceremony. She'd told him that her father had been having an affair, and worse still had been leading something of a double life, spending whole days and nights with the other woman.

Will had looked incredulous as she'd expanded on the story, which had confirmed that the so-called loving husband and father they had both adored, was a cheat and a liar. He'd worked in insurance she'd told him, but although she confessed to never really having known exactly what it was he did, she'd been pretty certain it hadn't entailed setting up home with another woman.

At that point in the disclosure she'd considered making a crude joke about being '*in* another woman', rather than '*in* insurance', but had thought better of it. *Keep it out of the gutter Jess* she'd told herself.

What she'd really wanted to impress on Will though, was how amazingly dignified Eleanor had been. It was somehow important to her memory. So she'd told him how, on the evening her father had packed his bags and left, her mother had quietly and calmly said, 'Thomas Jones you have deceived and humiliated your family. You do not deserve us.'

And that was that. He'd taken his dark-haired, clean-shaven, six foot and one inch frame through the door, only leaving behind the familiar scent of his aftershave. Eleanor had closed the door quietly behind him, and then had sobbed uncontrollably for several hours. She'd never told anyone that before.

Will had touched her arm then and said, 'And where is he now?'

'Still in Kent as far as I know,' she'd answered. 'After the house was sold, mum moved to No. 3, and I haven't seen or spoken to him since, although he did stalk me for quite a long time!' She'd added the 'stalking' comment in an effort to lighten the somewhat heavy conversation, but she'd not been convinced it had worked.

She turned over in bed and pulled the duvet up around her neck, suddenly feeling overcome by tiredness. But apart from the fact that, once again, Will had seen her in clothes that a charity shop would probably turn away, and that he had suffered a nasty injury, of course, she felt surprisingly relaxed and calm. It had been a strangely satisfying day and the icing on the cake was that Poppy was arriving on Tuesday.

CHAPTER FOUR

The next morning Jess woke with a start to the sound of what she could swear was her name being called, in urgent-sounding, hushed tones. She sat bolt upright, her eyes now wide and alert. And she was right. It was Rosa, who, deciding that she must have died during the night rather than just overslept, had used her key to let herself in, and was now standing at the side of Eleanor's bed, whispering, '*Jess, Jess.*'

'Good heavens Rosa, you nearly *did* have a dead body on your hands,' she said. 'You scared me half to death!'

'I'm so sorry my darling,' Rosa was saying. 'But you see, I didn't want to ring the bell as it may have startled you if you were just sleeping.'

Jess assumed there was some sort of strange logic in Rosa's explanation, and so giving her a quick reassuring hug said, 'Never mind, let's go and get you some coffee.'

'Tea for me please darling, I'm trying to be more English!'

Jess laughed and replied, 'You're fine just the way you are Rosa, no need to change at all.'

'Good, coffee it is then Jess. As I always say, it's better if you know the devil.'

'Yes Rosa, it certainly is,' Jess said with a wry smile, as the words brought to mind images of her father on the evening of her graduation, laden with bags and seemingly devoid of all emotion.

Rosa settled herself into the same armchair that Will had sat in the previous day clutching his injured hand, as Jess relayed yesterday's drama to her. She hoped there weren't any blood spillages on the chair, but if there were then at least they would be dry.

Rosa listened intently, regularly clicking her tongue and shaking her head, before admitting that she'd wondered what was going on when she'd seen them going off together in Jess's car, and then not returning until 'some ungodly hour'.

'I'm going to pop in and see him in a while before I head back up to the attic to finish the boxes,' Jess said. Adding quickly, 'Once I've showered and dressed, of course.'

'I'll come with you then darling. Italian Mammas are so much better at this sort of thing,' she replied firmly.

Jess stifled a giggle. Becoming 'more English' had seemingly been quickly forgotten.

She left Rosa drinking her coffee, while she rummaged through the bag she'd packed when she had decided now was the time to come to No.3 and face the music. But her man-radar must have been in the 'off position' when she'd chosen what clothes to bring with her, she thought, as she cast some of the items on the floor. Then again, to be fair, she hadn't really come to Thripton in search of someone who might qualify as boyfriend material. Eventually she decided on black leggings which were quite slimming, and paired them with a brightly coloured tunic with a simple round neck. After a quick shower, she applied some natural looking makeup and then dressed in her chosen outfit, joined Rosa in the lounge.

'You look lovely darling,' Rosa cooed approvingly. 'Just perfect for popping next door to see your neighbour!'

Jess smiled to herself. Eleanor had been right. Nothing, but nothing escaped Rosa's attention.

Inside No. 5, the two women found Will trying to make himself something to eat using just his functioning hand, while at the same time cursing at how difficult it was. The injured hand had so much padding and bandaging on it, that Jess thought it looked as if he was holding a club underneath it.

'Why are not your family here to help you?' Rosa asked him, shaking her head in obvious disapproval.

'I told them I could manage,' Will replied sheepishly. 'I just couldn't face my mum fussing around to be honest.'

Rosa tutted loudly and taking control of the knife Will was holding, replied, 'Well, later on I will bring you a feast. And of course I will look after everything for you. Leave it all to me, my darling.'

Jess, realising that Rosa had chosen to ignore the previous comment about fussing, saw Will's face take on a look of dismay. And so thinking on her feet, which she was the first to admit was not her forte said, 'My best friend Poppy is coming tomorrow for a couple of days, and I thought you might like to join us in the pub for something to eat tomorrow evening Will?'

But before he could answer, Rosa said, 'How lovely. Maybe I could come with you. It's been ages since I saw Poppy.'

It was a statement rather than a question, and Will looking somewhat resigned said, 'Thank you, I'll look forward to it.'

Jess turned away from Rosa and pulled a face, which she hoped Will would interpret as something along the lines of, *Sorry, I tried*.

But he was already teasing Rosa again about her being his Italian Mamma, so she guessed he was fine with it really. And most men she knew loved a bit of fuss and attention anyway.

Back at No. 3, Jess polished off the rest of the cold pasta, two packets of Maltesers (mini ones so they didn't really count) and three chocolate biscuits, before heading back up to the attic. She ran up the first set of stairs, in an effort to burn off some of the calories she had just consumed and to assuage her guilty conscience, but at the top, reminded herself that due to her unexpected lie-in that morning she'd skipped breakfast, so it would probably all balance itself out. She was a genius when it came to giving a balanced view on things.

She was now onto box number nine of twelve, and she couldn't begin to imagine what other surprises there might be in store for her.

She pulled the box towards her and realised it was quite heavy for a small box. She slit the tape carefully and then burst into laughter when she saw it contained: a copy of the Yellow Pages, a BT telephone directory, The Oxford Dictionary, a Roget's Thesaurus and an encyclopaedia. If anybody else had found this particular box it would have meant absolutely nothing, but to Jess it symbolised her mother, it *was* Eleanor Jones. It was the *Eleanor Jones* who had refused to embrace the digital world, still preferring to use these types of resources, and Jess smiled to herself when she recalled Eleanor's reaction when she had once suggested she got a social media account.

'Jess,' she had said. 'I have no wish to be poked, tagged or followed by anybody!'

And to be fair it had done her absolutely no harm. She was intelligent, worldly and smart, which was more than could have been said for her mobile phone.

She picked up the latest beautifully-scripted note from inside the box. It was something which had become a familiar sight, and it brought a smile to her lips as she read it out loud:

I can hear you laughing Jess and I am laughing with you. PS, don't forget to recycle these, unless of course you intend on using them!

Boxes ten and eleven contained some of the beautiful sets of books Eleanor and Thomas had bought her as a child. Jess thumbed through some of them, remembering how her father would mimic the voices of the characters when reading to her, and how her mother would tell her that books were the 'windows to the world'. One day, she hoped, she would be reading the same stories to her own children.

She sighed as she moved onto box number twelve, feeling a strange mix of both relief and sadness that it was coming to an end. Opening the boxes had been an emotional roller coaster, but she had loved every minute of it, she really had. It was a truly amazing legacy, left by a truly amazing person.

But nothing could have prepared her for the final box. She felt her jaw drop at the sight of dozens of blue and pink packing chips, all of which seemed to have been meticulously hand painted, and she quickly realised it was the final part of the jigsaw puzzle. It was a baby box.

Amongst the packing chips, Jess found two separate parcels wrapped in delicate tissue paper. Each parcel was tied with a coordinating ribbon, which on closer inspection revealed faint silhouettes of ducks, rattles, rocking horses and prams. They were so beautiful that she was loath to open them, but how could she not as maybe it was her destiny?

She took a deep breath and gently removed the delicate ribbon from the pink parcel. Inside was a set of the tiniest, palest pink baby clothes she had ever seen. A soft velour baby-grow with feet, a sleeveless vest, a hat, mittens and the cutest bib bearing the words, 'Grandma's beautiful girl'. The blue parcel contained identical items but in the palest of blues and the bib was printed with the words, 'Grandma's beautiful boy'.

She held the tiny clothes up to her cheek and sighed. 'Thank you Mum,' she said out loud and then leaning back against the wall, allowed the tears to flow freely and unashamedly.

She stopped off in the bathroom to splash her face with water as she headed downstairs. She'd completely lost track of time, finding it comforting to sit amongst the boxes that Eleanor had so lovingly filled.

She wondered if her mother had been ill and had kept it from her, or was she just being her usual super-organised self, wanting to ensure that Jess had lasting memories for when she was no longer around, whenever that might have been? She would probably never know, and that, she realised, was painful.

Glancing at the clock, she realised that she needed to go food shopping before Poppy's arrival the next day. Her best friend would be less than impressed if the fridge was not brimming with brightly coloured fruit and vegetables, almond milk, natural yoghurts, and anything else Jess could find that looked as if it may be vaguely healthy. And of course she would need to get quinoa, seeds, beans and pulses so she could rustle up an amazing 'Poppy-approved lunch'.

Poppy firmly believed that healthy eating was the key to her slim figure, flawless skin, shiny hair and endless energy, whereas Jess believed it was all down to genetics, and so usually filled her part of the fridge in the shared house with chocolate, junk food, and the odd bottle of beer. And after all she also had good skin and hair, so she'd easily convinced herself that all this talk of healthy eating was nothing more than a conspiracy theory.

Grabbing her coat and bag, she pulled the front door closed and decided to knock at No. 5 in case Will needed her to pick anything up for him at the supermarket. She was just being neighbourly, she told herself, although not even *she* was convinced by that.

Will gave her a list of a few essentials which she tapped into the notes section on her phone, and then with a flash of inspiration she suggested they should exchange phone numbers, for mutually beneficial reasons, obviously. That done, she headed off with a feeling of satisfaction and climbed into her slightly battered Ford Fiesta.

Eleanor and Thomas had bought the car as a graduation present for her, and although it was 'pre-loved', it had been looked after. Now eleven years on, she affectionately referred to the car as 'Rowan', an acronym for 'Rusty, Old, Worn-out and Needy'. Not great qualities for a car but she loved him all the same.

Back at No.3, with shopping tidied away and Will's 'few essentials' delivered next door, Jess slumped into the squashy sofa in Eleanor's sitting room. She closed her eyes briefly, reflecting on another busy but satisfying day. It was going to be a long and slow process sorting out the cottage, but opening the boxes had been an important part of moving forward, and probably counted as having made a start.

CHAPTER FIVE

Tuesday morning brought bright sunshine, and a sharp frost which glistened elegantly on the bare trees in the lane. It reminded Jess of a scene from a Christmas card, perfect in its own simplicity. Mother Nature at its best.

Poppy had sent a text earlier saying that she was just leaving and hoped to be with her around eleven oclock.

She had replied saying, *Can't wait to see you, drive carefully xx*

It seemed as though she'd been away from her London life, and Poppy in particular for ages, although in reality it had only been a few days. At times it had felt like she was being sucked into a vortex of emotions, a sort of weird vacuum, but she had surprised herself with her ability to be rational, to not get drawn into the vortex. Yes, there had been lows, but there had also been highs. There'd been tears, but there'd also been laughter. And now Poppy was coming. It was a relief. It was just what she needed.

She had a quick tidy round in Poppy's honour, and then sent a text message to Will to make sure he was okay. She was getting rather good at this 'just being neighbourly' business, she thought.

And then, just before eleven o'clock, she heard the unmistakable sound of Poppy's old VW Beetle trundling down Back Lane towards the cottage.

As she parked her car, Jess threw the front door open and met her half way up the garden path. The pair hugged each other affectionately and it felt so good.

'I'm so glad you've come Poppy, I've got so much to tell you that I hardly know where to start. It's been such a strange few days. Well not strange exactly, more....well I'm not really sure what the right word is.' She was conscious that the words had come tumbling out in a jumble, but her best friend knew her well enough to understand her ramblings.

Poppy smiled reassuringly. 'I can't wait to hear everything Jess, but first there's a little surprise in my car I need to show you.'

Jess looked at her friend inquiringly, but she was already, quite literally, being led up the garden path towards Poppy's car.

'Crumbs Poppy it's a bit of a cold day to have the roof down!' she exclaimed.

'Well that's the fault of the surprise,' Poppy replied apologetically. 'You see I've brought Dave with me!'

Jess pulled a face of mock horror before covering her eyes, and then putting an arm round Poppy's slim waist said, 'He's very welcome Poppy, you know I'm only teasing. I love him as well... most of the time anyway!'

The pair carried Dave's cage down the garden path and set him up by the front window of the sitting room, causing the African Parrot to bob up and down with delight, whilst squawking, 'Hello, hello, hello.'

Jess laughed. 'Hello Dave. Welcome to Thripton and your new *temporary* home. She realised she had subconsciously placed the emphasis on the word 'temporary' and really hoped that Poppy hadn't noticed.

'Thanks Jess. Sorry about bringing him but with Amber away I couldn't just leave him on his own.'

With everything going on in her own life, Jess had completely forgotten that Amber, who was the remaining third of the house share, was heading off on holiday to Greece that morning. She reprimanded herself and then grabbing her phone, quickly sent her a *happy holiday* text message, hoping to catch her before her flight took off.

Amber was an occupational therapist, based on the same ward that Jess and Poppy worked on and, in fact, was the one who'd found the lovely Victorian house where they all now lived. She'd known the landlady as she had previously rented a room in one of her other rental houses, and she'd been right in saying that Alice would be a great landlady.

The house was perfect for them. It had three double bedrooms, two bathrooms (essential when there's three girls living together, they'd all agreed), a comfortable lounge and a big kitchen/dining room. It also had parking and a small back garden just big enough for a table and chairs and a barbecue. It was a bit more expensive than they had expected, but Alice had very kindly given them a slight discount as they were NHS workers.

Jess helped Poppy carry her bags from the car and showed her to the spare bedroom.

'Wow,' Poppy exclaimed. 'This room is absolutely gorgeous, your Mum is so clever Jess...' She trailed off abruptly and a look of dismay crossed her face.

'It's okay Poppy, really it is. Sometimes I talk about her in the present tense as well. Especially when I'm in the cottage. There's so much of her in here.' Then giving Poppy a reassuring squeeze she said, 'Let's go and have lunch, I have quinoa, and apparently it's from a particularly good crop!'

After a lunch consisting of seeds, nuts, pulses, avocado and fruit, which Jess had to admit was rather good, she took Poppy up to the attic to show her the boxes.

Poppy gazed in astonishment at both the contents of the boxes and the loving care with which Eleanor had put them together. 'They are simply the most wonderful gift any mother could give a child,' she declared, and Jess could hear there was a slight crack in her voice.

'Do you fancy a game of Snakes and Ladders?' Jess asked, pointing to the 'games box'. 'It might do us both good.'

'Oh yes please,' Poppy replied. 'Let's say best of three and the winner gets to choose the next game. Just to make it more fun.'

'Poppy, I know you, remember,' Jess said, laughing now.

'Okay, you're right. It's my competitive streak rearing its ugly head again. But it'll be fun anyway.'

Two hours later and back downstairs, Poppy asked Jess what she could help with, and without speaking Jess led her to the back garden.

'Oh dear,' Poppy said, and then in an upbeat tone added, 'We've got this Jess. Gardening can't be any harder than a game of Snakes and Ladders surely!'

They looked at each other and giggled, as they both knew that it almost certainly *was* harder, as neither of them had the first idea about gardening, but it would be okay, they were together.

'Anyway, that's a job for tomorrow. This evening we are going to the pub with Will from next door and Rosa,' Jess said, trying to avoid eye contact with Poppy.

'How lovely. But you can't just drop a man's name in the conversation *Jessica Jones*, a man who you've never mentioned before and leave it at that.'

Jess laughed. There were no flies on Poppy that was for sure.

'Patience Poppy. I said I had a lot to tell you remember? All will be revealed later.'

That evening, Jess was already downstairs when Poppy came down from the spare bedroom, showcasing her long legs and slim frame in skinny jeans, paired with a beautiful floral silky blouse, which hung loosely from the waist band. Her shiny blond hair had been straightened and was tied back into a low ponytail. She pulled on a pair of black high heeled boots and smiling at Jess remarked, 'You look nice.'

'As do you, Poppy Clements. As always!'

Jess had decided on a black maxi dress which due to its jersey material clung tightly to her frame, but which also had a surprisingly slimming effect on the bottom part of 'the pear'. She'd actually picked it up in the Home and Clothing Department of the supermarket the previous evening, hoping it would be smart enough to make a statement, but casual enough not to make her look overdressed for an evening in the local pub.

She did the majority of her clothes shopping in low-cost stores, knowing that she had absolutely no chance of ever affording anything remotely designer and, in reality, the nearest she had got to this was regular wistful window shopping with Poppy.

She'd applied her eye shadow by fading it out towards the brow line to give a 'smokey eye effect' (or so she'd read in a magazine anyway), and straightened her dark hair in small sections until it laid perfectly straight around her shoulders and shone like polished ebony. Looking at herself in the long mirror she whispered, 'Not too shabby Jess, not too shabby at all.'

It was nearly seven o'clock and she had arranged to meet Will and Rosa at the top of Rosa's path.

Her phone beeped just as they were putting on their coats and she saw it was a message from Will. *Just trying to get rid of my mum. You three head to the pub and I'll join you there in a few minutes.'*

Outside, Jess and Poppy gave Rosa a kiss on either cheek and walked onto the pub, flanking her by linking arms on both sides.

'Lovely girls,' Rosa said, looking from one to the other. 'I feel like a piggy in the middle.'

Jess and Poppy hooted with laughter.

'That makes you the bacon in the sandwich,' Jess said, still laughing.

'The Rosa between two thorns,' Poppy added, making Jess groan loudly.

'Okay, you win Poppy. As usual. Too clever by half, this one Rosa,' she said, giving her friend a gentle nudge. She had a good feeling about the evening. It was going to be fun.

As they neared the pub, Poppy gasped and exclaimed, 'Wow, the pub looks stunning at night with all those little twinkling lights.'

'Let's hope they've got a lovely roaring fire going too,' Jess said. 'I'm absolutely freezing.'

'Me too,' said Rosa. 'Let's get inside my darlings.'

The pub seemed quite busy for a weekday evening, but they found a table big enough for four people close to the fire, and with Rosa settled into a comfortable chair, Jess and Poppy headed to the bar.

The young girl behind the bar approached them and without so much as a smile said, 'Yes?'

Both girls stifled a giggle as Jess asked what type of red wine they did by the glass, as had been Rosa's request.

'We only do one type,' the girl replied with a nonchalant shrug.

Jess gave a cough, which she hoped might disguise the uncontrollable chuckle that was now rising in her throat.

'And what type might that be?' Poppy replied, with a forced smile.

The girl sighed loudly, and with a look of resignation brought the opened bottle of red wine from the back shelf and placed it down in front of them. 'This one.'

Without speaking, Poppy took the bottle over to show Rosa, who decided that she'd try a 'large glass.'

Taking the bottle back from Poppy, the girl viewed the array of glasses with a look of total bewilderment, before a young man appeared next to her and said, 'Thank you Jazz, I'll see to these ladies. Perhaps you could do some re-stocking whilst there's a bit of a lull.'

'Apologies ladies,' the bar man was saying, pulling a face which resembled something between a half smile and a half grimace. 'She's new and needs a little more…um…a little more… training.' His face relaxed then and he grinned amiably at them. 'So ladies, what's your poison?'

And it was no surprise to Jess that Poppy replied almost before he'd finished the question with, 'A pint of Snakebite please, kind Sir.'

How did she do it Jess marvelled? It was as if she had a copy of the script before anybody else.

'Touché,' came the reply, and they all laughed.

Flashing a disarming smile in the direction of the barman, Poppy said, 'Seriously though I'll have a small glass of Sauvignon Blanc please. And a pint of your *best* ale for my *best* friend.'

Jess delivered the glass of red wine to the table where Rosa was sitting, just as Will swung open the door and strode towards the bar.

'Ah,' Jess said, moving back to the bar as quickly as she could, whilst trying to ensure it didn't look too desperate. 'You've managed to escape then!'

Will laughed and wiped his brow in mock relief. He was dressed in casual jeans and a navy jumper, which brought out the colour of his eyes beautifully. His hair was loose and it framed his strong-boned face rather nicely, she thought.

'Will, this is Poppy,' she said. 'Poppy is my best friend and is an expert at Snakes and Ladders. Poppy, this is Will. Will lives next door and is a dab *hand* with sharp tools.'

She was rather pleased with her 'Bridget Jones-esque' introductions, but when she looked at the pair of them, she immediately realised her newly-found wit had been wasted, as both parties were standing stock still and seemingly only had only eyes for each other.

The deafening silence was interrupted by the barman who was saying, 'Will mate, good to see you.'

'Alex... hi,' Will stuttered, in a decidedly distracted voice.

'Aren't you going to introduce me to your friends?' he asked, with an amused look on his face.

'Yes, err...yes, umm, of course,' he replied, stumbling awkwardly over his words. 'This is Jess, she errr, she kind of lives next door, kind of...And..this is...

Jess, feeling uncomfortable on Will's behalf, decided she should do the charitable thing and come to his rescue, so gave Alex an abridged version of how she and Poppy came to be in Thripton, and how Rosa fitted in the equation.

By the time she had finished, Will had composed himself, and he explained to the girls that Alex was the new landlord of The Plough. He had apparently moved in, around the same time as Will had moved into Back Lane, and as they were only a few people under forty years old in the village, they had become quite good friends. Alex laughed and said he would take that as a compliment, even if it did sound like a back handed one.

'Goodness,' Jess said. 'We should go and join Rosa otherwise she will think we've deserted her'. 'Come on Poppy,' she said. 'Let's leave the men to continue their *bromance*.'

Poppy followed her to the table as if under a spell and Jess whispered, 'Earth to Poppy, are you receiving me?'

'Yes, sorry, I'm just...well...I'm... Jess, do you believe in love at first sight?'

She knew Poppy's question didn't need a reply. It wouldn't have mattered whether she did or didn't. She knew this wasn't about her.

Rosa seemed perfectly happy with the warmth of the fire and her glass of red wine when they sat down at the table with her. Will soon joined them and Alex followed over with the menus.

'Why don't you join us Alex?' Will suggested.

Alex replied that he would have loved to, but that he only had Jazz on bar service that evening. 'As you may have noticed she needs a little supervision!' he added with a grin.

Jess was impressed by his seeming tact and thought he was probably a really good landlord.

Everyone agreed the food was amazing and that the pub was a great asset to the village.

Rosa had insisted on cutting up Will's food into bite-sized pieces and he hadn't really objected too strongly. She'd also commented that Poppy didn't seem to be her normal self, but unlike Jess, didn't seem to have picked up on the quietly flirtatious connection between her and Will. Or perhaps she had noticed and it was her way of trying to get it out in the open. She was, after all, a very perceptive woman.

With the bill paid and goodbyes said, Jess suggested they all go back to No. 3 for coffee. Will, throwing an admiring glance in Poppy's direction replied, 'That would be lovely, thank you.'

Rosa said she thought she was ready for her bed, but when mention was made of a bottle of Tia Maria, she had quickly changed her mind.

Poppy, who had suddenly re-discovered her voice chipped in, 'And I would like to introduce you both to Dave!'

Looking shocked, Rosa said, 'Good heavens darling, you should have brought him to the pub, poor man staying there all on his own while we've all been out having a lovely time.'

'Now *that* would not have been a good idea,' Poppy replied. 'He's rather too vocal for a small village pub.'

Rosa made a face and shrugged her shoulders in response, but Will, Jess noticed, was looking rather crestfallen at Poppy's revelation.

Back at the cottage, Dave was showing off his repertoire by frantically bobbing up and down on his perch and ruffling his feathers in a manic display of excitement. Every now and then he let out a loud wolf whistle and squawked, 'There's somebody at the door.'

Jess made some coffee and brought in four shot glasses filled with Tia Maria, and they all fell about laughing when Rosa raised her glass in the air, said, 'Bottoms up, my darlings,' and swallowed the whole lot in one large gulp.

Will was looking decidedly happier, Jess realised, as he gently teased Poppy about the parrot, and she couldn't help thinking that they were a rather good match.

'Anyone for another drop of Tia Maria?' she asked, holding the bottle in the air.

'Not for me thanks Jess,' Poppy answered, shaking her head.

'Well perhaps just a small one,' Will said, picking up his empty glass from the table, to the sound of Rosa's loud tutting.

'Well, you can include me out,' she declared. 'I must get home before the witches' hour.' She stood up from the chair, and appearing somewhat unsteady on her feet, Will offered to see her home safely.

'Perhaps I'll give the Tia Maria a miss after all,' he said. 'Come on Rosa, take hold of the only good arm I have left, and we can face the witches together. And may I just add, that was an excellent use of a Goldwynism.'

Rosa smiled and winked at him knowingly, leaving Jess and

Poppy looking at each other in surprise. But before either could ask any questions, Will said, 'Anyway, I have to be at the hand clinic first thing tomorrow and it takes me so long to get ready, that I'll have to be up almost before I've gone to bed at this rate.'

They all laughed, and when he added that he had visions of the hand clinic being a room full of lots of unattached hands, even Dave joined in the fun by letting out a timely blood-curdling screech.

The four all embraced each other warmly and then closing the door behind them Jess turned to Poppy and teased, 'So, you two seemed to have hit it off.'

Poppy blushed and looked away. 'What's a Goldwynism when it's at home? That's what I really want to know.'

'Now then Poppy, don't try and change the subject. As I always say, I know you too well and there was definitely some coy flirting going on this evening!'

After more coffee and discussions about the evening, and about men and relationships in general, Poppy suddenly turned to Jess with a look of concern. 'You don't fancy Will do you?'

'No Poppy, I don't. He's really not my type, but I do think he might be yours.' And she meant it. She really did.

CHAPTER SIX

Fortunately, the next day was dry and a little less cold, so Jess and Poppy ventured into Eleanor's overgrown garden, with a view to starting to return it to its former glory.

Like everything Eleanor had ever turned her creative hand to, the garden had been no exception. When Eleanor was alive, the neat lawn was always edged perfectly and the borders were an incredible mix of cottage garden plants, and flowering shrubs of different heights, colours and textures. Even the potting shed looked as pretty as a picture, painted in a sea green colour and decorated with cheerful bunting, interspersed with solar powered lanterns. It used to be a beautiful garden, but not anymore. Everything was now in such a mess.

Jess sighed and looked at Poppy despairingly, which in turn galvanised her friend into immediate action.

'Right,' she said, scanning the array of gardening tools in the shed. 'You get pruning and I'll fire up the lawn mower. I've seen a few episodes of 'Love Your Garden', and really there's nothing to this gardening malarkey!'

Jess gave her friend a grateful smile, and then picking up a pair of secateurs replied, 'Let's do this thing!'

Within a couple of hours, the garden was already starting to look better. Rosa had passed them coffee and cake over the fence, telling Poppy it was carrot cake, so counted as a healthy option, and Will had popped round after his visit to the hand clinic. He joked that he was delighted to report that his hand was still attached to the end of his arm, as were everybody else's at the clinic, and that they should all go to the pub for lunch to celebrate the 'good news'.

Not needing much encouragement to down tools, Jess and Poppy changed out of their gardening clothes, ready for the pub lunch.

Jess teased her friend at the length of time she'd taken to get ready, but was quite sure Will wouldn't be disappointed with the results. She was wearing a pair of tight dogtooth-patterned trousers, teamed with a black roll neck jumper. Her long blond hair was tied in a loose plait, and her natural looking make-up finished the look perfectly.

Jess, on the other hand, was sporting a pair of black leggings and a baggy jumper, and felt a sense of relief that she wasn't having to try and impress anybody, at least not today anyway.

When Will arrived at the door of No. 3, Jess could see he had made a similar effort to Poppy's. He was clean shaven, and looked very stylish in faded denim jeans, an ultra-white t-shirt, heavy denim jacket and loosely tied scarf.

Dave, having shrieked, 'There's somebody at the door,' at least three times, dipped his head down low at the sight of Will, and to everyone's amusement let out a loud wolf whistle.

At the pub Alex was once again behind the bar, but this time was ably assisted by an affable young lad called Jake.

'If the offer from last night still stands,' he was saying, 'I could join you for lunch, as I'm sure Jake can manage on his own for an hour or so?'

Jess found herself nodding enthusiastically, perhaps subconsciously not wanting to find herself being the third person at a couples' lunch: a gooseberry, an extra, and even worse still an unwanted extra.

They sat at the same table as they had done the previous evening and listened to Alex's recommendations for lunch. Having ordered, the conversations flowed easily and comfortably, although Jess noted that Poppy was somewhat tongue-tied when Will was talking directly to her, as she had been the evening before.

Will told Alex about Dave, and was doing a surprisingly good job of mimicking his voice and actions. He was animated and in high spirits. His eyes sparkled and Jess knew the reason why.

Feeling caught up in his exuberance, she chipped in, 'I could tell you a very funny story about Dave.' And then shot Poppy a look as if to say, *Is that alright?*

Poppy's cheeks flushed and she covered her eyes momentarily, but Jess knew her well enough to know that it would be fine to recount the hilarious, although somewhat embarrassing incident.

She took a swig of her drink for Dutch courage and began recounting the story. She told them how she, Poppy and Amber had heard a song called 'Living Next Door to Alice' at a London bar one evening, and that it had fast become their 'Anthem'. They regularly sang it in the house as a trio, with each having their own solo part, and what's more, they were word perfect.

One particular Saturday morning, soon after they had moved into the house they now lived in, Poppy had looked out of the lounge window to see their new landlady parking her car outside. She'd panicked, as the house was supposed to be pet-free, so they had quickly moved Dave's cage into the kitchen, covering it with a sheet.

The tenancy was managed by a letting agency, but they had

subsequently learned that the landlady always liked to visit her new tenants in person, just to make sure everything was okay.

Amber had answered the door and guided their visitor into the lounge, where Jess and Poppy were pretending to watch the television, which they'd put on at a very high volume.

Unfortunately, Dave had heard the front door bell and despite his cage being covered, he began squawking, 'There's somebody at the door, there's somebody at the door.'

Their landlady had asked if they had a bird in the kitchen and Poppy had owned up, explaining that it was her beloved pet parrot Dave, who she'd had since she was a child. She'd apologised for not telling her, but said she couldn't bear the thought of having to rehome him.

To their surprise their landlady had asked if she could meet him, and so they took her into the kitchen and uncovered the cage.

She'd looked at him for what seemed like an eternity, before saying, 'Wow, he's absolutely beautiful.'

'We all sighed with relief,' Jess continued. 'And then Poppy said, *Dave, this is Alice*. Now normally Dave would have squawked, *hello, hello*, but instead he dropped his head, looked directly at her with his beady eyes and shrieked, *Alice, Alice, who the fuck is Alice?*'

The punchline to the story had Will and Alex falling about laughing, as Jess explained that their version of 'Living Next Door to Alice', was the *adapted* one, with the exact same chorus line, which it seemed Dave had been storing in his memory for use at an inappropriate time.

Trying to recover his composure, Will looked at Poppy and said, 'And Alice obviously let him stay then.'

'Yes, thankfully she did, and the silly bird has never said it since. And just for the record, I was not assigned that particular line from the song.'

'I didn't think for one minute it would have been your line,' Will said, smiling at Poppy.

'Actually, and just for the record, it was the *chorus*, so technically we were all assigned it,' Jess said, rolling her eyes. But neither replied, as they were now both gazing admiringly at each other and appeared not to have noticed her attempt at humour.

Will insisted on paying the bill, as a way of saying thank you to Jess and Poppy for being such 'good surrogate neighbours', and Alex generously applied a fifty per cent discount, saying he 'knew the management'.

He had been good company, Jess reflected, and he'd told some hilarious tales about his time as a barman and pub landlord, but he'd also shown a lot of interest in what everyone else had to say. And she liked people who listened and were interested in others. In fact, she decided, it wasn't only just *people* she liked, it was a *particular person*. It was *Alex*.

Back in the lane, Will said his goodbyes as they reached the top of the garden path of No. 3. But as he started to walk towards his own path, he suddenly turned and said, 'I know you're going home today Poppy, but I hope to see you again soon.'

Jess smiled as she saw her friend blush a bright crimson colour. It was so un-Poppy like.

'Me too Will. Well, I mean not to see myself obviously...I meant to see you...'

Inside the cottage, Poppy covered her face with her hands. 'Why am I suddenly rendered incapacitated whenever Will speaks to me? I sound ridiculous,' she wailed.

Jess laughed. 'Must be love Poppy. I, for one, have never seen you like this before.'

Poppy's cheeks reddened, as she quickly tried to change the

subject. 'Oh my God, I nearly forgot to tell you Jess,' she practically shrieked. 'I've been summoned to jury duty. I start in a couple of weeks' time.'

Jess looked at her friend in surprise, as they had both always dreaded getting the call up to serve on a jury, but now she actually sounded quite excited.

'I know what you're thinking,' Poppy said, as if she had read her mind. 'But just think about it. Monday to Friday hours for a while, so I can come and help you here at the weekends, and who knows I might even just bump into Will.'

Jess laughed at her friend's cunning plan, but reminded her it was slightly flawed as she herself would still have to work some weekends with her annual leave fast coming to an end, and so would not necessarily be at the cottage.

'True,' Poppy agreed. 'But it's the start of a plan - it just needs a bit of fine tuning. And as Rosa would say, *Rome wasn't built in a day.*'

Jess rolled her eyes and hugged her friend fondly. 'Come on, let's get you and Dave packed up and on your way before it either rains or gets dark. I can't believe how quickly your days off have flown by.'

Poppy frowned. 'I know. Time flies when you're having fun, so they say. Whoever *they* are!'

Within the hour, Jess had waved Poppy off, reminding her to text as soon as she was home. It had been so lovely to see her, and now closing the front door behind her, the cottage suddenly felt very empty. She surveyed the downstairs, reminding herself that she had a lot of sorting out to do and decided that she would need to make a proper plan. She would most definitely enlist Poppy's help in the near future, and remembering what Rosa had said about taking her time, decided that she was doing okay.

CHAPTER SEVEN

Thursday saw wind and heavy rain showers, so Jess decided she would make a start on clearing out some of the kitchen cupboards. She'd remembered that Rosa had told her there was a donation box for the local food bank situated at the back of the church, so that seemed to be a sensible place to start.

She scanned the cupboards for likely items, before starting to bag up numerous tins of salmon, peas, beans and packets of rice, pasta, tea bags and several jars of coffee, carefully checking the 'use by dates' as she went.

As she looked at the stock of food, she wondered how one person could have accumulated so much, but then thinking about the actual meaning of donating the goods to people who may be struggling, realised how satisfying it felt.

With the rain looking like it was set in for the day, Jess loaded the bags into Rowan's boot and drove the short distance down the lane to the church, wondering if her good deed had been cancelled out by the detrimental impact on the environment by her using the car.

Deciding she was probably overthinking things, as usual, she walked towards the huge wooden church door and turned the heavy iron handle. Inside the church, she located the donation box and then returned to her car to collect the bags.

She began unloading the goods into the box and then jumped as she heard the heavy door handle turn, followed by loud footsteps on the stone floor. Her heart began beating faster, although she didn't really know why. It was a public place after all and anyone could come in, just as she had.

'Hello down there,' came a man's voice. It was a friendly voice with a gentle tone and she immediately felt a sense of relief.

She looked up from her squatting position, to see a smartly-dressed, dark-haired man, who was probably a little older than she was. He was smiling down at her now and she smiled back at him.

'Hi,' she said. 'I was just adding to the donations for the food bank, they're from my mum's house, she died a while back and I've just started clearing some things out...' She trailed off wondering why she was gabbling unnecessarily to this total stranger as (a) It was pretty obvious what she was doing and (b) Her mother's death or the clearing out of the cottage for that matter, was probably of no interest to the poor unsuspecting victim.

She gave him an apologetic look, but to her surprise he seemed completely unperturbed. Instead he was nodding at her, in what felt like an affirming way.

'Ah, you must be Eleanor Jones's daughter.'

It was a statement rather than a question, she realised, and so she simply nodded back at him.

'It was such a shock to everyone who knew your mother, so I can only imagine how difficult it must have been for you, and I'm sure continues to be so.' He pointed in the direction of the donation bags and she was grateful for his perceptiveness.

She stood up from her position close to the floor and gave him an appreciative smile. 'Yes, I'm Jess Jones and thank you for your kind words.'

The man smiled again and Jess realised he had what you might describe as a kind-looking face.

He offered an extended hand, and then shaking hers warmly said, 'I'm Marcus Edwards, one of the churchwardens, although I usually cover St Mary's Church in the next village.'

She smiled again and thought how different village life was compared to living in London, where if a stranger started smiling and talking to you, you would likely run a mile. 'Well I'd better be getting back as I still have lots of jobs to do, and I have to go back to London at the weekend. Nice meeting you though, Mr Edwards.'

'It's Marcus, please call me Marcus,' he replied.

His voice was soft and somehow reassuring. She nodded and started walking towards the church door, realising almost immediately that he was following her. And then quickening his pace, he moved in front of her and swung open the door. 'After you,' he said grinning, whilst gesturing towards the open door with his hand.

'Thank you and goodbye,' she replied, and as she walked away down the long gravel churchyard she heard the latched door close behind her.

But as she reached her car, she turned round at the unexpected sound of noisy, gravel-crunching, quick- paced footsteps and the sound of her name being called. It was Marcus, and he was practically sprinting down the church yard. By the time he'd arrived at her car he was quite breathless. 'I may just have had a brilliant thought,' he was saying through gasping breaths. 'Have you, by chance, inherited Eleanor's amazing singing voice?'

Jess laughed with relief. 'Goodness, for a minute I thought there was some sort of emergency.'

'Well in a way there is,' he replied laughing.

'Oh right. I see. Well as it happens I can sing a bit, or so people tell me anyway, and I'm in a choir in London.'

'Fantastic,' he replied, before she had the chance to add that she was definitely not in the same league as Eleanor. 'How do you fancy being part of our churches joint Christmas concert?'

'That's the emergency?' she said, pulling a face.

'Ok, I might have exaggerated slightly about it being an emergency. But it got your attention at least.' He looked at her apologetically and in return she shook her head in mock disapproval.

'Please,' he added softly. 'Pretty please?'

Back at the cottage she reflected on what had just happened. How had she agreed to be part of a Christmas concert when (a) She lived and worked in London and (b) Marcus, or anyone else in the choir for that matter, hadn't even heard her sing? But he had a very convincing way about him, reassuring her that they could Skype her for choir practice, and then when she was in Thripton, they could all meet up for impromptu extra rehearsals.

It might turn out to be quite good fun she told herself, albeit somewhat unconvincingly, and anyway she'd agreed to it now and she never went back on a promise.

Picking up her phone, she sent a message to Will, *Fancy a pint at The Plough?*

The reply came before she had even put her phone back down, *I've already got my coat on!*

Looking around and shrugging at the amount of work still to do, she grabbed her bag, pulled on her coat and closed the door behind her.

At the pub Jess told Will and Alex about her new role in the church choir and they too asked the obvious questions that she had asked herself.

'I'm probably going to have to wing it by standing at the back and joining in the bits I've learned at home,' she said with a half grimace.

'Well I, for one, want front row seats,' Alex replied in a teasing tone. 'And I will be asking for a refund on the ticket price if you're rubbish.'

'It's for charity you mean-spirited man,' she said, in a tone of mock horror. 'And as a local businessman my choir will be expecting a very generous donation from you!'

'Oh, so now it's *your* choir all of a sudden,' he said with a grin. 'But as you're so persuasive I will pledge £500 with one proviso. And that is that you know every single word, and I'll be watching you very carefully for any slip ups!'

'It's a deal,' she replied offering an outstretched hand for Alex to shake on the agreement.

'Deal,' he said, taking her hand and shaking it rather too vigorously.

Jess smiled to herself as she sank back into her favourite chair near the fire in the pub. Life was full of ups and downs that was for sure, but at this very moment the ups seemed to be balancing the downs rather nicely.

CHAPTER EIGHT

Next morning Will was at the front door bright and early with a card for Jess to deliver to Poppy. He was returning to work that morning and so he probably wouldn't see Jess again before she went back to London the following day, he explained.

'What's this all about then?' she asked playfully, waving the card at him.

'Oh it's nothing really, just a card.'

'Yes well I can see that,' she replied rolling her eyes. 'But if you'd rather not say that's fine, I'll get it out of Poppy anyway!'

Will shuffled from foot to foot in a distinctly awkward way, so she quickly reassured him that she was only teasing, and he went off up the garden path with a definite spring in his step.

Although she had made a rough plan regarding clearing the cottage, Jess had quickly realised that she had not been very good at sticking to it. But in truth, she wasn't very good at sticking to plans in general, so rather than changing the habit of a lifetime, she moved from the kitchen to Eleanor's bedroom, with a view to sorting through some of her clothes and taking the good items to a charity shop.

She took a deep breath, knowing that it was going to be one of the toughest tasks so far and opened the doors of the irregular shaped hand-made oak wardrobes.

Seeing Eleanor's clothes hanging neatly in what appeared to be a colour-schemed order immediately made tears spring to her eyes. There were clothes that she had never seen before, alongside some of her favourites that Eleanor had worn regularly. But the common denominator was that they were all perfectly laundered and covered with transparent garment bags. It looked more like a high end clothes shop than a home wardrobe, she thought.

Wiping her eyes and taking another deep breath, she took a handful of garments still on their hangers and descended the narrow staircase with a view to putting them straight into the car. Unfortunately, the plan was flawed as she slipped on the last but one step, turning over on her ankle and landing on the hall floor in a somewhat unceremonious fashion. Cursing loudly, she attempted to gather up the clothes which had managed to partly escape from both their hangers and their covers, and were now strewn all over the hall floor. But she quickly realised that she couldn't move her ankle as it was much too painful, and had already begun swelling up like a balloon.

As she looked around the small hallway for something to help her pull herself to her feet, the doorbell chimed loudly, prompting her to shout out, 'Help, help.'

'Jess?' came the muffled reply through the door. 'Whatever's happened? Are you okay? Are you hurt?'

Jess quickly realised, with relief, that it was Alex. 'Stop with all the questions,' she replied sharply. 'I've twisted my ankle that's all. No dramas.'

She directed him to the back door, which involved going through a small alleyway just after Rosa's cottage, and then following a path that ran along the back of the terrace of cottages. 'My gate is the second one along,' she called after him and then realised that was stating what Rosa would call, *The bleeding obvious*. Luckily she had left the back door open, so Alex let himself in and soon joined her in the hallway.

'Hi down there,' he grinned.

'Hi yourself,' Jess replied, feeling her face flush with embarrassment at her current predicament. 'And apologies if I sounded a bit cross before.' She stopped short of adding a 'but' as (a) She *was* genuinely sorry and (b) People who said sorry and then added a 'but' weren't actually sorry at all. Well that was her opinion anyway.

'Forgotten already,' he said with a grin. 'Now let's look at that injury and then we'll get you off the floor.'

Within a few minutes Jess was sitting on a chair with her foot elevated on a small table, feeling decidedly foolish.

'Have you got any ice?' Alex asked.

'It's going to sound a bit strange, but I don't really know. But it's probably unlikely.'

'Okay, I'll just pick the clothes up from the floor, then I'll make you some strong tea. To drink, I mean, not to put on your ankle,' he replied

'Thank you,' she said, managing to laugh despite the pain.

'Can't find the mugs?' he called from the kitchen.

She laughed again and relayed the story of the bone china tea cups and tea pot. She heard him chuckle and he then appeared with a tea towel folded over his arm and a beautifully laid up tea tray.

'Tea is served, Madam,' he said and she was surprised to find herself looking down with uncharacteristic shyness.'

A couple of hours later, Jess found herself sitting in the now familiar Accident and Emergency Department, awaiting the results of the x-ray on her ankle. The only difference was that this time she was with Alex, rather than Will or Rosa. And she had to admit that the company was rather pleasant.

And several hours later she was back at the cottage with the apparent 'good news' that the ankle wasn't broken, just sprained. Alex had stayed with her the whole time, despite her trying to persuade him to go back to the pub.

'It's fine. I've left Jazz in charge. What could possibly go wrong?' he'd said jokingly and then covered his face with both hands.

Jess had laughed and asked if she was improving to which he'd replied, 'Improving...umm give me a nanosecond to answer that!'

Just as Alex was getting ready to return to the pub, Rosa arrived at the front door. She hardly seemed to notice that he had let her in, rushing past him to the sitting room and throwing her arms up in the air at the sight of Jess's ankle. 'Jess my darling what on earth has happened? I saw you going off in a car with a strange man and I've been so worried about you.'

Alex, who was now standing behind Rosa, pulled a face of mock horror at the comment, causing Jess to look away before Rosa had the chance to notice the exchange.

'It's Alex from the pub, Rosa. Remember? And he's really not *that* strange,' she said, laughing. 'I slipped on the stairs and twisted my ankle, that's all, nothing to worry about but thank you for caring.' And then looking past Rosa, added, 'Alex has been wonderful. He stayed with me the whole time, but now he has to go and see if he has any customers left in the pub!'

Not seeming to notice Jess's praise, Rosa looked Alex squarely in the eyes and said, 'Yes well good, good, but off you go now young man, too many cooks are not needed in *this* kitchen.'

Alex turned his head away and Jess knew he was trying to stifle a giggle, as indeed she was.

'Men!' Rosa exclaimed, clicking her tongue, whilst rolling her eyes in an exaggerated manner. She had seen Alex safely off the premises and was now fussing around Jess again in her 'Italian Mamma' way. 'I will look after you my darling and cook you the most wonderful food. You will need to keep your strength up!'

There was absolutely no point in arguing with her when she had made her mind up about something, so Jess sat back while Rosa filled the ice tray 'for later' and clattered around in the kitchen looking for likely ingredients to rustle up 'a feast'.

Good luck with that Jess thought to herself with a rueful smile, particularly after yesterday's trip to the food bank.

She reached over and picked her phone up from the table, realising she had some important calls to make. The first was to Poppy to tell her she wouldn't be home as planned and the second, which she was dreading, was to the Ward Sister to tell her that she wouldn't be back at work on Monday. The Accident and Emergency doctor had given her a pair of crutches and told her to keep the weight off her foot for a few days, but that realistically she wouldn't be able to return to work for at least a week.

Poppy didn't answer her phone so Jess left her a message explaining briefly what had happened and then bracing herself, plucked up courage to ring the ward. Unusually, Sister Greenwood answered the phone and Jess began explaining in far too much detail about her mishap.

Sister had that effect on people. On the ward, it was secretly known as the 'Greenwood Effect', turning the most sensible and intelligent of people into gibbering wrecks. Sister was probably only in her mid-forties but in her ways seemed much older. She had never been married, nor had any children and if anyone ever dared to ask her about her personal life she would reply, *I'm married to the job.*

She was also a stickler for rules and unlike most of the other nursing and medical staff at the hospital, insisted on being called by her role title rather than her name. But despite her slightly draconian ways, the quality of care under her leadership was exemplary and everybody loved working on the ward.

Jess heard a sharp intake of breath at the other end of the phone, but then, much to her surprise Sister said, 'Goodness me Jessica how awful, as if you haven't had enough going on in your life. Now you look after yourself and don't worry about anything here.'

She bit her lip as she waited in silence for Sister to add one of her infamously hard-hitting comments, but instead she simply said, 'Keep me up to date with your progress but don't come back until you're fit.'

Jess struggled to convey her thanks in even a semi-coherent way, and smiled ruefully at the fact that the 'Greenwood Effect' was still as powerful as it was when she walked onto the ward on her very first day as a newly-qualified nurse.

She had one more call to make and that was to Alex. After all the kerfuffle of the day's events she had forgotten to ask him why he had come to the cottage in the first place and she really wanted to know. Thankfully they'd exchanged numbers before Rosa had arrived, *In case you should decide to throw yourself onto the floor again* he'd joked, and as she pressed the screen to ring him she was surprised to feel her stomach do a little flip.

'Alex,' she said in the most casual voice she could muster. 'It's Jess, Jess Jones, from No. 3 Back Lane, sprained ankle...'

'Aha, I was wondering who it was when the name Jess Jones flashed up on my screen,' he replied in an amused tone.

'Ha ha, hilarious I'm sure,' she said, whilst desperately trying to control her shaky voice. What on earth was going on? Was the Greenwood effect still lingering, or was there some other inexplicable reason for her apparent and sudden babbling? 'I was just ringing to find out why you came to the cottage earlier,' she continued, steadying her voice as she spoke. 'Because I'm pretty sure it wasn't just to pick me up off the floor.' She felt rather proud that she'd managed to compose herself enough to make a joke, albeit a somewhat obvious one.

'Oh yes, I'd forgotten all about that after today's *events*. Actually it was about your garden, I was going to offer you the services of the pub's gardener. I pay him on a weekly rate but to be honest he hasn't got too much to do at the moment, so idle hands and all that.'

'You sound just like Rosa,' she laughed, who at the exact same time walked into the sitting room carrying the most enormous plate of pasta Jess had ever seen.

'Who sounds like me?' she demanded in a tone of mock annoyance. 'Are you taking my name in vain?'

'See what I mean?' Jess whispered into the phone. And then looking at Rosa said, 'It's just Alex. I think you may have competition from him though, you know with your famous sayings.'

'Never. Not on your Nelly. No way Jose. And you can tell him that from me!' Rosa replied firmly.

But by then Jess wasn't really listening. She was suddenly feeling deflated, disappointed even. She was grateful for Alex's kind offer of the gardener, of course she was, but realised also that she had hoped there may be a different reason for the house call.

CHAPTER NINE

Saturday saw a flurry of visitors to the little cottage. Marcus had spread the word about the new choir member, and several of the local parishioners had come to No. 3 to see how Jess had been since the funeral.

They hadn't expected to see her sitting with an elevated foot wrapped with an ice pack though, and it soon materialised that the church grapevine was in good working order when Marcus arrived with grapes and flowers.

Rosa, having seen the stream of visitors to No. 3 had set up something akin to a tea shop in the kitchen, bringing tea and dainty individual lemon cakes, iced with butter cream to Jess's unexpected guests. The visitors complimented her on her baking skills and Jess wondered if she always had 'just in case' cakes in the oven. Rosa shrugged off the compliments in her own inimitable way by saying, 'I believe you actually *can* have your cake and eat it,' and Jess smiled fondly at her, reminding herself how lucky she was to be the recipient of Rosa's unstinting friendship and kindness.

Later, when everyone had left apart from Marcus and Rosa, who was busying herself in the kitchen, Jess briefly closed her eyes and thought what a lovely little village Thripton was. She'd now seen first hand why Eleanor had loved it so much.

Marcus rose to his feet abruptly and apologised for overstaying his welcome. 'You must be tired Jess. I'll be on my way now, but you have my number in case you need anything at all. Day or night, promise you'll ring?'

She smiled and opened her mouth to joke that he was the third man to give her their number this week, but instead said, 'Thank you Marcus, that's really kind of you.'

After finishing up in the kitchen Rosa planted a gentle kiss on Jess's head and said she would see her in the morning.

'Honestly Rosa I can't thank you enough, whatever would I do without you?'

'Well you don't have to do without me darling, so we are both happy aren't we?'

Jess smiled and squeezed her arm. 'Yes Rosa, I would say we're as 'Happy as Larry!'

Jess's phone beeped and she saw a message from Poppy, *I'll be down tomorrow after my early shift*, it read. *I can stay overnight as I have a day off Monday, then I'll drive home later that afternoon.*

Having such a good friend made Jess smile with gratitude but not wanting to take advantage of her kindness replied, *Honestly Poppy there's really no need. I'm fine and I have Rosa and other people in the village to help if I need anything. I don't want you to have to spend your one day off on a busman's holiday.*

The reply came back as quick as a flash, *There is every need. I am your best friend and I will be there tomorrow, when I will wait on you hand and foot (pun most definitely intended!). And, of course, the fact that there is a sexy single guy, with hair you want to run your hands through, living next door to you is an added bonus!*

Jess laughed out loud and replied, *Poppy, you are a jezebel, but I still love you. See you tomorrow xx*

CHAPTER TEN

Jess was woken up next morning not by the joyful sound of the Sunday morning church bells, but instead by the significantly less melodious meowing of a cat, which was so loud it sounded as if it was inside the cottage.

She grabbed her crutches and descended the stairs as quickly as she could manage, feeling concerned about what she might find. But to her relief, the less than dulcet tones were coming from behind the back door. And outside stood a thin, scruffy-looking ginger cat with pretty dark ginger stripes, who took the opportunity to shoot past her as she opened the door. In the kitchen he meowed loudly and rubbed against her legs, in what seemed like a pleading way.

'Hello puss,' she said, and then trying hard to balance on one leg, bent down to stroke his head. His eyes were wide with anticipation and so despite telling herself that you shouldn't feed other people's cats, she opened the cupboards to see what she could find.

'Aha Mr, you're in luck,' she said, reaching for a tin of pilchards. She hadn't taken them to the food bank the other day as (a) She didn't actually know anybody who ate pilchards, apart from Eleanor and (b) She thought it would be fun to take them back to London, put them in the shared food cupboard and await the response from Poppy and Amber.

The smell of the pilchards sent the cat wild and he started

scratching at Jess's legs in an attempt to get nearer to them. Quickly decanting them into an old bowl, she watched him devour the lot in a matter of seconds, and then without as much as a second glance he scurried back out the door.

'Well thank you for visiting,' Jess called after him. 'Do call again if you'd like another free feed!'

She went to close the door behind him, but before she could do so Rosa called over the fence to ask who she was talking to. Jess told her about the cat and wasn't particularly surprised to hear from Rosa that he had been a regular visitor to her house over the past few weeks.

'Greedy boy,' Jess said, which made Rosa laugh loudly.

'*He* is actually a *she* darling, didn't you notice that she has milk? Must have kittens somewhere.'

Rosa's revelation and matter-of-fact tone made Jess gasp in horror. 'But that's awful. We must try and follow her and see if we can help.'

Rosa laughed and explained that it was probably what the people in the area called a feral cat. There were lots apparently that came from the nearby farms looking for food.

'Well I feel sorry for her. She seemed starving and with a family to feed and all,' Jess said.

'They're not silly darling, they know where to go for food. You watch, she will be back later. They quickly learn where their bread is buttered on both sides!'

Jess laughed. 'Better get some more food in then. And I will give her a name. Tigger. Yes, that's what I'll call her. Tigger, you know like Tigger from Winnie the Pooh?'

'I think you'll find *that* Tigger was a boy, darling,' Rosa replied.

'Well yes, maybe, but this Tigger has very bad manners, just like the character from the books, so it's fitting really.'

Rosa shook her head and clicking her tongue replied, 'You city girls! You are crazy!'

'I'm fast becoming a country girl though, don't you think?' Jess asked.

'I think you need maybe just a little more practise,' Rosa replied. 'In any case, don't you go anywhere, I'm going to pop round in a minute. And I was only pulling on your leg about needing more practise. You are perfect either as a city girl or a country girl.'

'Thank you Rosa, you're too kind, and let's face it, I can't really go anywhere,' she replied, pulling a face.

And true to her word, Rosa appeared at the front door of No. 3 within minutes, her gingham covered basket laden with bacon sandwiches, pastries and two tins of cat food, and as if by magic, Will appeared at the exact same time.

'What are you doing still here Jess?' he asked. 'I was surprised to see your car here when I got home late yesterday evening, hence the early morning house call.'

'And there was me thinking it was the smell of bacon that brought you round here, when all the time it was out of concern for me,' she teased.

'Jess!' Will exclaimed, in a tone of mock indignation. 'I am completely shocked by your cynicism. And frankly, disappointed as well. And just for the record you did, in fact, come a very close second to the bacon!'

She laughed. 'Come on in.'

Over Rosa's delicious breakfast, Jess relayed Friday's events to Will, with Rosa chipping in at both opportune and inopportune moments. He listened with interest and shook his head in all the right places, but then at the end of the tale she noticed a look of dismay passing over his face.

Realising the look wasn't in response to her accident, she was able to pre-empt his next question. 'And don't worry about the card. You'll be able give it to Poppy yourself, she'll be here later on.'

The characteristic lop-sided grin spread across his face, and when he ran his hand through his hair it made her smile, as she knew a certain someone who would like to give that a try at some point soon.

After Will had left, Rosa cleared up, insisting that Jess wasn't to help, but was to sit down with her leg elevated.

'I could get used to this,' Jess said as she reached for the television remote control. 'Sitting around watching daytime television I mean. Not the sprained ankle!'

'You will soon be bored of it darling. There's only so many repeats of 'Homes Under the Hammer' a person can put up with. And I should know, I've seen them all my darling, several times over. I can even sing those dreadful songs they play, from memory!'

Recalling Rosa's rendition of Kylie's, 'I should be so Lucky', Jess decided it would be wise to make no further comment on the subject.

Later that day, and just as Eleanor's grandmother clock began to strike six, Jess heard the distinctive sound of Poppy's car in the lane and started to hobble towards the front door to greet her. As she opened the door she saw Will was already hovering at the top of his garden path and so she ducked back behind the door, so he didn't think she was spying.

Within a couple of minutes Poppy was standing at the front door with two bottles of beer and a selection box.

'Poppy, you're a star and I always forget how well you know me,' Jess exclaimed, pointing at the goodies.

'Well, this is an emergency. And so knowing you as I do, I decided that beer and chocolate was the correct response to said emergency, and after all it is nearly Christmas so a selection box seemed appropriate!'

Jess laughed and thought how much she loved this girl. 'You are the bestest best friend a person could ever wish for Poppy. Do you know that?'

Poppy nodded. 'I know. I know. My halo is gleaming. Now, are you going to let me in before I freeze to death?'

'Oh God, sorry Poppy. Come in and get warm. No Dave this time?'

'No, I told him I was only going for one night so he would have to manage on his own. And when I said goodbye to him, do you know what his reply was?'

Jess shook her head and covered her eyes.

'Dickhead. That's what he said, *Dickhead*. Can you believe it? Whoever has taught him that?' she asked.

'It's not a word *I* use,' Jess replied, trying to stifle a giggle. 'And I can't imagine Amber saying it either.'

'No, well me neither. But it's such a horrible thing to call someone. Especially me. His mum.'

'His *mum*!' Jess repeated laughing.

'Metaphorically speaking obviously. Anyway, enough about Dave and his potty mouth. Tell me all about the last few days, it seems I can't leave you on your own for five minutes,' she said rolling her eyes.

Jess opened a bottle of beer and a Curly Wurly, while Poppy sipped tea from one of Eleanor's dainty tea cups, easily resisting the temptation of the opened selection box.

'You're becoming a bit of a regular at the local Accident and Emergency Department,' Poppy joked. 'You'll have Social Services knocking on your door if you're not careful!'

'It's been quite a week,' Jess replied, rolling her eyes before relaying some of the other events to her friend.

'Well it's not over yet,' Poppy interrupted. 'Will is coming in a few minutes to take us both to the pub.'

Wanting to give them an opportunity to be on their own for once, Jess replied that she was really tired and was hoping to have an early night. Poppy looked a little perplexed but nodded and took the spare front door key from her friend.

'And Poppy, don't go all monosyllabic on him, or coy or anything else 'un-Poppy' like. Be yourself and he will love you.'

'I'm not sure I want him to love me.' she answered quickly. 'That's not on my current life plan, and by the way I'll start waiting on you tomorrow. I promise!'

Just as she was getting ready for bed, Jess's phone beeped and she saw it was a message from Alex. It read, *Was hoping you might have been at the pub with Will and Poppy. Sorry I didn't check in with you yesterday - manic at the pub and Jazz decided to choose the busiest time to have a melt down and quit!*

She smiled and then took nearly ten minutes to formulate a reply, adding and deleting words in a way she didn't recognise of herself.

Alex clearly wasn't suffering from the same problem as he replied to her text almost immediately, *I'll see you very soon but let me know if you need anything. PS the gardener is coming at the end of the week, Thursday/Friday.*

Jess awoke the next morning to the sound of Poppy banging around in the kitchen whilst simultaneously shouting, 'Quiet you silly moggy.'

Feeling excited about her return visitor, she joined her friend downstairs and told her about Tigger. 'She's half-starved Poppy and Rosa says she has kittens somewhere.'

Clearly feeling guilty, she watched Poppy unlock the back

door and then laughed as Tigger shot passed her friend and started rubbing round her legs.'

'See, she knows who looks after her, don't you Tiggs?' she cooed as Tigger meowed loudly, and then with one leap jumped up onto the worktop.

'Shoo,' Poppy said. 'Can't you see I'm preparing a veritable feast here and it's not easy I can tell you!'

Jess laughed and knew a bowl of food would be all that was needed to remove Tigger from the worktop. And then with the bowl licked clean, the cat went straight to the back door and clambered up the fence into Rosa's garden, meowing at her back door as loudly as she had before. The girls looked at each other and burst out laughing.

Sitting down at the table they tucked into scrambled eggs on toast whilst Poppy began telling Jess all about her evening.

'First things first,' Jess interrupted. 'What did the card say?'

'Oh Jess, it was so sweet. So, on the front it said, *Just wanted to say* and then when I opened it up, it said, *You make me smile*. And it was signed with two kisses!'

Jess smiled at her friend and realised that she hadn't seen her this animated for a long while.

'And guess what?' she continued excitedly, breaking Jess's thoughts. 'We talked. We actually talked and I managed to string several coherent sentences together! Honestly Jess you would have been proud of me!'

'Ha ha, that's great Poppy. I'm so happy for you. I really am.'

'Oh yes, and Will is making us both lunch next door today, and I mean *both* of us,' Poppy announced firmly.

'Ah that's kind of him. And something for me to look forward to rather than sitting with my leg up watching daytime television. Rosa was right. There's only so much of it you can take!'

Poppy laughed. 'Yes I can imagine, and you haven't even had to endure that much yet!'

'I know,' Jess said with a grimace. 'But I already know the television schedule! Anyway, changing the subject before I start reciting it to you, does Will not have to work today then?'

'No he has his final clinic appointment hopefully, and then the boss, who by the way is his mum, said he can work from home for a while doing paperwork.'

'That's great. Working from home I mean, not his mum being the boss,' Jess said with a giggle. And as she sipped her coffee she found herself hoping that maybe Will had invited Alex for lunch as well.

Later on, whilst getting ready for lunch next door, Jess quickly realised that trying on multiple outfits was not an option, so settled for jeans and a jumper, taking extra time with her hair and make-up just in case.

At twelve thirty, she hobbled up the garden path with Poppy walking closely behind her, *In case you were to topple backwards,* her friend had said

Inside No. 5, Jess immediately felt guilty at her disappointment when she saw the table was only laid for three people, but told herself that (a) Will probably hadn't even invited Alex anyway and (b) Even if he had, he was probably needed in the pub, what with Jazz's untimely departure.

Will was busy in the kitchen, 'Proving that men can cook too', so Jess and Poppy took the opportunity to take stock of the sitting room, sitting close together so they could whisper their observations without Will overhearing.

The room seemed to have a feminine touch, with lots of pastel colours and an abundance of the most gorgeous cushions, portraying country scenes. The fire place was decorated with candles and pretty tea lights, some of which were lit, giving the small room a subtle smell of vanilla and engendering a warm cosy feel.

Suddenly Poppy let out a gasp and whispered, 'Why is there a picture of someone who looks just like me on the windowsill?'

'Crikey,' Jess said. And then turning her shocked face back to Poppy added, 'That must be Holly, you know Will's ex I told you about? Good heavens Poppy, she could be your twin!'

The pretty blonde girl had her head tilted slightly to one side and her twinkling eyes seemed to be looking directly at them. The photo was displayed in a pretty silver frame with the word *love* engraved on the bottom part.

At that moment Will joined them in the sitting room and announced that lunch was served. The girls hurriedly tried to compose themselves before joining him at the small table.

'This looks amazing Will,' Jess said quickly, trying to give Poppy some extra time to recover from the shock of the photograph.

'Oh it's nothing. Just a simple home-made butternut squash and sage risotto. It's mainly in Poppy's honour, but I know your favourites as well Jess and I've made a chocolate mousse to follow,' he replied with a grin.

Concerned that Poppy still hadn't managed to utter a word since they'd sat down, Jess continued to make small talk with Will, in the hope that her silence wouldn't be too obvious.

But then to her dismay, Poppy pushed her chair back from the table and said, 'I'm so sorry but I'm really not feeling well. I think I need to go next door and lie down.'

Back at No. 3, Poppy cried her heart out. Jess tried to comfort her whilst desperately thinking of reasons why he may have a picture of Holly on show after everything that had happened.

'But it's not only that,' Poppy wailed. 'He's clearly not over her, which is why he's honing in on me. It's obvious. He's trying to replace her with a *look-a-likey!*' She wiped her eyes and managed a weak smile. 'I need to get on with sorting out my travel plans to help take my mind off things.'

Jess nodded reassuringly, and in an attempt at humour said, 'Good idea. And not meaning to sound selfish, that will be *my* holidays sorted for the next however many years.' And then at a loss to know what else she could say to comfort her friend, she picked up a packet of buttons and a bar of dairy milk from the selection box and ate the lot.

Poppy had packed her overnight bag and left soon after, apologising for not helping out as much as she'd intended to. Jess had hugged her and reassured her that she was absolutely fine and that she hoped to be back in London the following weekend.

She sighed and flicked on the kettle, eyeing Rosa's leftover chocolate cake.

You really shouldn't, especially after eating the selection box items, she told herself. But then reminded herself that chocolate was actually good for stress and so cut herself a large slice.

She was now down to using one crutch but it was still tricky to carry more than one thing at a time. She was on her second trip to the sitting room with the gorgeously gooey chocolate cake in her hand, when the doorbell began chiming in a frenetic fashion.

She wasn't at all surprised to see Will standing on the doorstep, but was taken aback by his untidy state. His hair was wet with sweat, and he was panting furiously.

'Good heavens Will what on earth has happened?'

Struggling to speak between gasping breaths, he explained that he had heard Poppy's car leaving the lane and he'd run after her, following her through the village, waving frantically in an effort to get her to stop. When she hadn't, he'd then run back hoping Jess could shed some light on her swift departure.

Guess I'm not as fit as I thought I was,' he said, with a weak smile.

Jess fetched him a glass of water from the kitchen and offered him chocolate, which in her eyes was the solution to most problems.

'I couldn't possibly eat anything. There's this enormous lump in my throat,' he said. 'I just need to know what's happened and why Poppy left in such a hurry. She didn't feel ill at all, did she?' He dropped his gaze to the floor and Jess felt a surge of sympathy for him.

'Okay. Okay. I'll explain everything Will, but I'll warn you that I'm not sure it's going to make any difference to the outcome.'

He frowned and sat on the edge of the chair, hands tightly clasped together.

'Right, first things first. Poppy really likes you, and to be honest I've not really seen her quite so smitten before. My best friend, who I know better than anybody, has changed from an eloquent and quick witted girl to a gibbering mess when in your company, so I'm pretty sure my evaluation is correct.'

Will's creased brow softened a little and his cheeks flushed red. 'So what on earth has happened?' he urged.

Jess sighed and moved awkwardly in her chair. 'It was the picture on your windowsill, you know the one of Holly. It was the doppelganger thing. It freaked her out Will, well both of us to be fair.'

She saw his brow furrow again as he looked at her with puzzlement, and then as if someone had flicked a switch in his head, he suddenly began laughing with what seemed like emotional relief.

'Oh God. The picture...the photo...the one you're referring to is not one of Holly! It's a photo of Anna, my sister. We're very close and she's off seeing the world, so I keep her photo on the windowsill where I can keep an eye on her,' he said in a voice that sounded an octave higher than usual.

Jess sat in stunned silence, unsure of whether to laugh or cry. She had, after all, put the idea in Poppy's head by jumping to conclusions, so now she needed to sort out the mess she had made.

'Oh God Will. I'm so sorry. I've really messed up. It's all my fault, but don't worry I will put in right. I Promise.' The words had all come tumbling out in a rush, but when she finally brought herself to look at him again she was relieved to see her was smiling.

'It's okay,' he said quietly. 'To be honest there is a resemblance between Poppy and Anna, but as far as girlfriends are concerned, I really don't have a particular type. In fact, if anything Holly looks rather more like *you* than Poppy. Not that I've seen her for a while of course,' he added quickly.

She wasn't quite sure what to make of his last comment, but decided that the best thing to do was to say nothing at all. *Less is more, Jess.*

After a few minutes thinking time she had come up with a plan. 'Right, I will text Poppy and ask her to ring me as soon as she gets home. She won't see the text until she stops, but at least she will be alerted to the fact that she has a message to read. Then I'll explain the misunderstanding and ask her to ring you so you can talk face to face, so to speak. That way it'll cut out the middle man. That's me by the way.' She realised she was gabbling again, but nevertheless looked up at Will expectantly.

'Okay. It doesn't exactly sound like a genius plan, but if it works I'll be happy,' he said.

Nodding, Jess picked up her phone and sent a message to Poppy.

Within a few seconds her phone beeped and Will sat forward expectantly in his chair.

'Sorry. It's just Marcus about choir practice,' she said pulling a face. The message read that it was choir practice on Tuesday evening, and he had thought that as she was still at the cottage he could pick her up in the lane and take her to the church. She felt a nervous lurch in her stomach, but replied that she would look forward to it.

Great. See you just before 6.30pm. The reply from Marcus was almost instantaneous which made her feel even more nervous.

Will let out a deep sigh and got up to leave. Jess patted his arm and reassured him that all would be fine. 'Remember, I know Poppy almost better than I know myself,' she said in the most upbeat tone she could manage.

He nodded and showed a slight glimpse of his lop-sided grin before letting himself out the front door, closing it firmly behind him.

'Come on Poppy, hurry up,' she said out loud. 'Or I'm going to be forced to eat another chocolate bar!'

After what seemed like ages, Jess's phone burst into its tuneful ring. 'Poppy! Thank goodness,' she said in an unusually high-pitched voice.

'What on earth's happened Jess. I was worried when I read your text.'

In the background Jess could hear Dave squawking, *There's somebody at the door, there's somebody at the door,* and the familiar sound of his rantings made her feel strangely homesick.

'Poppy, it wasn't Holly after all, it was Anna, Will's sister.'

'What? Who was? Jess, you're not making any sense,' Poppy replied calmly.

'The photo, you know, the one on the windowsill. It's Will's sister. She's away travelling. She's called Anna and they're very close. And apparently Holly looks more like me than you.' She immediately cursed herself. Why had she said that bit? She realised she was practically shouting down the phone at Poppy, who was trying to interject with an odd *'but'* and *'you said…'*

'Look Poppy it's all my fault and I'm so sorry for all of this, but honestly Will is absolutely distraught, he even chased your car half way through the village.'

'I know,' Poppy wailed. 'I just couldn't face him, so I put my foot down and managed to leave him behind by the pub!'

'Never mind that now. Just phone him right away, as soon as I put the phone down to you. Promise me Poppy?'

To her relief Poppy replied, 'I promise. I'll phone him right away.'

Jess sank back into the chair and let out a huge sigh of relief.

Half an hour later, her phone beeped with messages from both Will and Poppy and at last she was able to manage a smile. All was well it seemed and *misunderstandings were now understandings.*

How very droll, she replied to Will and then unable to contain her relief and happiness, she celebrated by eating the rest of the chocolate cake that she'd left earlier, when the drama had unfolded.

Later in bed her phone beeped again and she reached over to the old pine bedside cabinet to pick it up. Anticipating a further message from either Will or Poppy or maybe even Alex, she was surprised to see Marcus's name on the screen. *Sorry for the late message,* it read, *but I was just wondering if you might like to come for a drink at the pub after choir practice?*

She sat up in bed and re-read the message. Did he mean just the two of them? Was he asking her to go for a drink or a *drink drink?* There was, of course, a difference between the two. Friends had a drink, more than friends had a *drink drink.* Everybody knew that. Or perhaps all of the choir members went to the pub after choir practice? He was probably just being friendly, inclusive. Or maybe, horror of horrors, he felt sorry for her. *Stop it* she told herself. It's a drink, an innocent drink. That was all. Most likely nothing in it at all.

She tapped a reply into her phone. *Lovely, thank you Marcus,* and pressed send. And then turning the phone onto silent, slid down the bed and tucked the duvet around her. But although her eyes felt heavy, she had trouble drifting off to sleep as the same thought kept going round in her head. If *she* thought it might be a date, then would Alex think the same? And she realised that what he thought was important to her.

Tuesday morning eventually arrived and although Jess felt as if she'd hardly slept, she couldn't wait to get up. She'd had such strange dreams with everything and everybody being muddled up. She'd guessed it was a result of yesterday's dramas, but every time she'd fallen back to sleep the dreams took up where they'd left off, but in an increasingly haphazard and bizarre way. Anna had returned from her travels and turned out to be Holly after all. Marcus declared undying love for her at choir practice, and Alex turned out to be married to Jazz.

Thank heavens for daylight she thought, pulling on her dressing gown and heading for the kitchen, where she was greeted by the now familiar sound of Tigger meowing at the back door.

'Think yourself lucky you're a cat,' she said, stroking her head and Tigger purred loudly in appreciation at both the food and the affection. Cats were really quite therapeutic, she decided.

After breakfast, she decided she would continue to sort through Eleanor's clothes and at least get them packed into the car ready to take to the charity shop, when she could drive again.

Her ankle was improving daily and she could now get a shoe on, even if it was only one of Eleanor's wide-fitting slip-ons. Her mother had actually had quite dainty feet, but for some reason had always chosen to buy extra width shoes. But now, Jess found herself grateful for her mother's strange idiosyncrasy.

Rosa popped round late morning with more cake. This time it was the most exquisitely decorated coffee sponge. Jess made some freshly brewed coffee and just as they were about to sit down Alex arrived with a box of chocolates and a boyish grin. She noticed Rosa stiffen and shake her head.

'I've brought chocolate,' he said, holding out a very large box of soft centres.

'Thank you Alex. Chocolate is always welcome. That's very kind of you.'

'How are you managing to negotiate your way around the cottage? It must be rather tricky,' he asked.

'No shit Sherlock,' Rosa interjected, with a sharpness that Jess didn't recognise of her.

'Rosa!' she exclaimed, and then turning to Alex attempted to lighten the situation by saying, 'Rosa's trying to be more English. Aren't you Rosa.'

She was relieved that Rosa had registered that it was a statement rather than a question and had said nothing further.

'Would you like some coffee Alex?' Jess asked.

He nodded and smiled disarmingly at both her and Rosa, before sitting down at the table.

She realised that she hadn't really looked at him that closely before, but decided he was actually very easy on the eye. His dark hair was cut neatly with a sharp edge at the nape of his neck and he had probably one day's worth of stubble which gave him a strong look. And when he smiled his perfectly straight teeth made him look younger than he probably was. He was of slim build and not overly tall, but then again she was so short that men's heights had never really been an issue. Today he wore jeans and a jumper in marked contrast to the flamboyant shirts he normally wore in the pub.

'I'm going to choir practice tonight,' Jess announced in an attempt to interrupt the awkward silence around the table. 'Marcus is picking me up on his way through so I don't have to hobble down the lane.'

Alex smiled and started to make a joke about their bet, but before he could finish Rosa interrupted. 'Do you know who Marcus Edwards is?'

Jess looked at her in surprise. 'Yes, he's one of the church wardens. He was here the other day Rosa.'

'Yes, yes, *I* know who he is, but do *you*? He is very well known around here. He is a painter you know and very good, as I understand it. And he lives in a mansion!'

Alex winked at Jess and said, 'Will is a very good painter as well, you know.'

Jess noticed his face was absolutely deadpan. Rosa gave him a cold stare. 'Marcus Edwards is not a painter and decorator. He is an artist. A professional artist painter. You know, like Leonardo da Vinci!' And then looking directly at Jess added, 'And a very legible bachelor as well, or so I'm told'.

'A *legible bachelor*,' Alex teased after Rosa had left. 'I guess that makes him an easy to read single man.' And then to her surprise he added, 'Is that what you're looking for Jess?'

She felt her cheeks flush and she looked away momentarily. But then feeling a sudden rush of courage, looked back at him said, 'I'm not sure. But maybe, just maybe. It would have to be the right *legible* bachelor though!'

She watched his face break into a broad smile and found herself hoping that it was a smile of satisfaction at the answer to his question.

'By the way, I'm sorry about Rosa's behaviour towards you. I'm not sure what's got into her!'

'I think she just feels protective towards you Jess. It's actually rather endearing. And as for her sayings, or misayings should I say, they are absolutely priceless!'

Just before six thirty that evening, Marcus pulled up outside the cottage in what looked like a very stylish, if rather old sports car. Jess, leaving her crutch in the hallway, limped up the garden path to meet him and smiled as he jumped out of the driver's seat and opened the passenger door for her. Despite the semi-darkness she could see it was no ordinary car. It was kind of sleek and shapely and the engine seemed to purr.

'Nice car,' she commented in a sort of non-committal way as (a) She knew nothing about cars, so *nice* seemed like a middle of the road type of word and (b) It might be vintage or whatever you call old cars and she didn't want to offend him by not making any sort of comment.

Marcus laughed. 'Thank you,' he said looking pleased. 'Some people might think it's just an old car and technically it is, but actually it's what's known as a classic car. It's a 1990 Jaguar XJS to be precise.'

And even though Jess knew nothing about cars, she was taken aback by the incredible beauty of the interior with its glossy wood dash, immaculate leather seats and thick pile carpet in the foot well. 'Wow,' she exclaimed after she had settled herself into the passenger seat. 'It's absolutely amazing Marcus. Just beautiful.'

At the church, Marcus introduced Jess to the other members of the choir, some of whom she'd already met when they'd visited her at the weekend. They were all so welcoming and friendly that her nerves quickly disappeared as she took her place in the choir stalls with them.

Henry, the choirmaster, was Marcus's father and although he seemed like a formidable character Jess thought that, like Marcus, he had a kindly looking face. And the similarities didn't end there. He and Marcus had the exact same mannerisms and gestures and she couldn't help but smile.

Henry briefly outlined the format of the concert, which to her relief was the Christmas Story, meaning at least she would know the carols and songs. And then looking directly at her he boomed, 'So Jess, welcome to the choir. May I ask what your voice range is?'

'I'm a... um...I'm a soprano,' she stuttered, feeling as if she was back at school and standing in front of the headmaster.

Henry beamed at her. 'Marvellous. Absolutely marvellous. In that case I have the perfect solo part for you!'

She coughed nervously but by now her mouth was so dry that even though her jaw was moving, there was no sound coming from her lips. She realised that even if she could have protested, it most likely would have been futile. So instead she smiled lamely and nodded while reaching in her bag for a stick of chewing gum in the hope that it would stimulate some saliva.

Later, on the way to The Plough, Jess teasingly admonished Marcus for getting her involved in the choir in the first place.

'A solo. A solo...on my own, with nobody else...' she groaned.

'Yes. That is generally what happens with a solo,' Marcus replied light heartedly and although it was fairly dark inside the car, she was sure he was grinning.

'Well I just hope I can live up to Henry's high standards and expectations,' she said.

'Well from what I've heard tonight you will exceed them Jess,' he replied. 'And to be honest the bar isn't set that high anyway!'

His last comment made her laugh out loud. 'Well that's a vote of confidence if ever I heard one,' she said.

'I'm sure you know what I mean, having experienced the choir this evening in all its glory. I'm really not being unkind, just truthful,' he replied earnestly.

She knew exactly what he meant, but as a newcomer to the choir thought it best not to pass comment on that particular subject.

'So, is the pub a regular meeting place after choir practice? she asked. She felt rather pleased with herself for seamlessly moving the conversation round to the topic that (a) She was keen to get an answer to and (b) That would help to avoid her having to comment on the calibre of the choir.

'Not that I'm aware of,' he answered. 'Unless the others normally go without asking me that is, but I guess we'll soon find that out!'

She took a deep breath. So maybe it was a kind of date then. *Keep calm Jess*, she told herself.

'Good evening', Alex said, smiling broadly at the two of them. 'Twice in a day, must be a lucky one for me.'

Jess realised the last comment was aimed at her and she smiled back at him.

Marcus looked a little puzzled but smiled as well. 'What would you like to drink Jess?' he asked.

'I'll have a *half* of real ale please,' she replied, grinning as Alex deftly moved his hand from the pint glasses to the half pint ones.

'Alex,' she said in a high-pitched voice that even she didn't recognise, let alone understand. 'Have you met Marcus?'

Alex leant over the bar and offered Marcus a hand, which he shook warmly.

'And can she really sing?' he asked, tipping his head in Jess's direction.

Marcus smiled and looking directly at Jess said, 'Yes she can, and like a lark as well!'

Sitting at her favourite table, Jess found the conversation with Marcus easy and undemanding. And quickly realised she was rather enjoying his company. They chatted about village life, the church, the choir and their jobs.

And as Rosa had said, he was an artist, specialising in water colours and he lived at Barrowick Hall. He didn't look much like an artist though she thought. Not that she knew any artists so that didn't really make any sense. But she imagined an artist would wear loose clothing, covered in different colour paints and perhaps have a long flowing beard. Now that *really* didn't make any sense. It was quite ridiculous, as Marcus was dressed entirely suitably for a casual evening out and perhaps he did wear loose paint-splattered clothes when he was creating his masterpieces.

And as for beards, well they were very strange things in her opinion. She'd once read that they were supposed to symbolise strength, courage and even virility. But for her, manliness did not come in the shape of ever-growing facial hair. In fact, quite the opposite. She found them a complete turn off. Heavens knows what may be lurking in the mass of hairy undergrowth. Yuk.

She immediately tried to erase the images from her mind, and instead turned her thoughts back to the pleasant conversations the two of them were engaged in. And apart from anything else, the smooth-faced, softly spoken, neatly groomed man sitting beside her was a *friend*. She was out for a drink with him. Not a *drink drink*.

'But believe me, Barrowick Hall is nowhere near as grand as it sounds!' he was now saying. 'It suits my current situation though and I have always lived there, so c'est la vie,' he continued, shrugging his shoulders. 'Anyway, that's quite enough about me. Tell me more about being a nurse, Sister Jones,' he said with obvious interest.

Jess laughed. 'Well for a start off its Staff Nurse Jones, not Sister. You've promoted me. But thank you anyway!'

He relaxed back in his chair while she relayed some tales from her nursing career but despite his relaxed demeanour she could tell he was listening intently. At times he smiled, at times he looked at her with surprise, but at all times he showed his obvious admiration.

'And you actually *like* the job?' he asked with a look of amazement as she brought the topic to a close.

'No. No, I don't *like* it. I *love* it. And I know that surprises some people, well quite a few actually, but how many jobs are there that you can come home each day and know that you've made a difference to someone's life? It may be something quite small or on occasions something quite big. And I guess that's what makes it so worthwhile Marcus. It really does.'

Feeling relaxed in his company, Jess went to the bar to buy a round of drinks. Jake came over to serve her but Alex quickly dismissed him in a fun way, but in a way that she knew meant he wanted to serve her.

'So how is your evening going?' he asked casually, whilst pulling a half pint of beer.

'Very well actually,' she said smiling. And then quickly added, 'I think I've made another friend, which considering I hardly knew anybody around here until very recently, is actually really nice.' She'd made sure to put the emphasis on the word 'friend' and was sure she hadn't imagined seeing Alex's shoulders relax.

Back at the table, Marcus suddenly sat forward in his chair. 'I've had a brilliant idea!' he said.

'I remember your last brilliant idea,' Jess replied laughing. 'And look what that got me, a solo part in the concert!'

'Yes, sorry about that. But this idea really is brilliant. Why don't I pick you up tomorrow and take you to Barrowick Hall? I can show you some of my paintings and you can see for yourself how 'ungrand' my wing of the hall actually is. If there's even such a word as 'ungrand'?'

His enthusiasm was obvious and Jess found herself happily joining in with his gentle banter.

'Your wing!' she exclaimed. 'Well that certainly doesn't sound *ungrand* to me. But thank you Marcus, that would be lovely.' And then smiling at him added, 'Should I dress for the occasion?'

'Most definitely not,' he replied pulling a face. 'Unless of course by *dress* you mean putting on some clothes, in which case the answer should probably be yes!'

She felt her cheeks flush and picking up her glass took a large gulp of beer. *Probably yes* he'd said. *Probably.* Was she reading too much into what was most likely just a throwaway comment or was he, in fact, flirting with her? And more to the point, was she flirting with him? And if she was, then that was most definitely not part of the plan.

Back at the cottage Jess put the kettle on and debated whether or not she was right not to invite Marcus in for coffee. She hadn't wanted to give him the wrong idea, but equally she hadn't wanted to appear rude. He seemed to be a really nice genuine sort of guy but definitely not her type. Eligible, legible or anything else.

Sipping the freshly made coffee she decided that the answer was probably lying in one of the soft centres of the chocolates Alex had brought round earlier. But try as she might she couldn't find it in the strawberry cream, or the cherry liqueur or even the coffee cream. She would just have to keep on looking.

CHAPTER ELEVEN

Next morning the Tigger alarm was sounding bright and early and Jess laughed as the cat carried out her usual routine of scoffing a bowl of food in the cottage, before climbing up and over the fence into Rosa's garden for second helpings.

Marcus was coming to pick her up at ten thirty so after breakfast and a shower, she pulled on a pair of loose-fitting jeans and a casual jumper and awaited his arrival.

Her phone beeped with a text from Poppy saying she had managed to swap a shift so would be coming to the cottage on Saturday morning, but would have to go home Sunday evening as jury service was starting the following day. She'd relayed the same information to Will who had apparently replied, *Can't wait,* followed by several heart symbols, and Jess smiled with relief that the mistake over the photograph was now a distant memory.

Marcus pulled up in his Jaguar at exactly ten thirty and Jess, seeing it for the first time in daylight, was taken aback by its sheer elegance and beauty. The bodywork gleamed in the autumnal sunshine, so much so, that she could actually see her reflection in it. 'It's amazing Marcus,' she declared. 'And even more gorgeous in the daylight. It's a thing of beauty that's for sure.'

Obviously pleased with her comments, he beamed and then

doffing his imaginary cap replied, 'Why thank you M'lady. Please climb aboard and I'll whisk you off to pastures new!'

She settled herself into the comfort of the leather passenger seat and then smiling at him said, 'Thank you kind sir.'

As they pulled onto the imposing driveway to Barrowick Hall, Jess gasped with delight. 'It's wonderful,' she exclaimed. 'And what a beautiful building.'

The long shingle driveway was lined with perfectly sculpted trees and in front of the grand house was a circular lawn that could have doubled as a bowling green.

'So,' Marcus was saying. 'To the left is my wing and to the right is my parents' wing. The middle bit, which is the biggest part of the Hall by the way, is currently being used as a wedding venue.'

Jess was speechless. It was probably Georgian she thought and perfect in its absolute symmetry.

'Come on, let's go inside,' Marcus said grinning as she stood practically rooted to the spot.

He led her to the side door of his wing and then put his hand up as if to say stop. 'Just remembered I forgot to ask you if you mind dogs?' he said. 'He's friendly.'

Jess laughed. 'I love dogs. What's his name?'

'He's called Brutus,' Marcus replied.

'Brutus! Blimey!' she said, putting her hands to her face in mock fright. And although it was done to tease Marcus, she had to admit that she felt a little nervous about being confronted by a huge beast of a dog.

But she needn't have worried, as when Marcus opened the door the 'beast of a dog' she had imagined turned out to be the tiniest Chihuahua she had ever seen and although he yapped incessantly at first, she quickly realised it was in excitement rather than anger. And soon he was sitting on her lap curled up in a tiny ball, breathing rhythmically and making very cute snoring sounds.

She looked around the kitchen admiringly. The room was classically elegant with large sash windows allowing the light to fill the space and the tall ceilings gave it a distinct air of grandeur. The kitchen was cleverly fitted out with a mix of contemporary and traditional styling, quite minimalistic in its design and it worked perfectly. Eleanor would have loved it Jess thought. And so did she. There were no messy worktops or clutter like she was used to in her London home. No dirty dishes in the sink or empty beer bottles by the back door, waiting patiently for someone to take them to the bottle bank.

'Ungrand' Marcus had called it. Ungrand. Hardly. But she sort of knew what he meant. Perhaps more understated than ungrand. Beautiful in its simplicity. And she guessed he'd been used to living in the entire house at some point in the past, so everything's relative, she reminded herself.

'Why is he called Brutus?' She asked, pointing to the tiny ball on her lap. They were sitting in two identical leather wing-back chairs positioned either side of the gleaming cast iron Aga and sipping the most heavenly hot chocolate complete with floating cream and marshmallows.

'It's a strange one I guess but I see myself as a kind of Brutus character really, you know from Julius Caesar. Apart from the assassin part,' he added laughing. 'So not really thinking that I could change my name to Brutus, I gave it to him instead!'

She wasn't sure if he was joking or not, but she nodded and said, 'I see. Well at least I think I do anyway.' She didn't want him to know that she had initially thought the name was something to do with the dog being a brute rather than a character from a Shakespearean play. Or that she knew little about either Brutus or Julius Caesar.

Marcus laughed again. 'I'm a complex character, rather like Brutus. Best not to try and make any sense of it!' And then jumping to his feet added, 'Come on. Let me show you some of my artwork.'

Jess gently removed the dog from her lap and putting him on the floor said, 'Et tu Brutus?' and although she thought it was probably not in the right context, she nevertheless felt pleased that at least she could recite one line from said play, even if it was one that everyone knew.

Marcus smiled and nodding said, 'Yes and you Brutus. Come on let's head to my studio.'

The wide sweeping staircase led to a galleried landing with several doors, one of which opened into the art studio. The room had lots of windows which overlooked the manicured grounds, and once again Jess was in awe of its beauty. Her eyes scanned the room in amazement. Nothing, but nothing could have prepared her for the vast array of the most stunning artwork she'd ever seen in her entire life. Not, of course, that she knew anything about art, nor had she visited many art galleries, but Eleanor always used to say that *art is a very personal thing.* Meaning what one person likes, another doesn't, so surely that meant that everyone was capable of being an art critic?

'Marcus!' she exclaimed. 'These paintings are absolutely amazing. You are super talented!'

'Yes I am rather good aren't I?' he replied with a wink.

'And modest with it!' she said, rolling her eyes.

'Seriously though,' he continued. 'I just about make a living from it but the wedding venue supplements the upkeep of this place.'

Jess walked slowly around the large room, viewing each picture in turn and asking questions which she hoped didn't sound too ridiculous. 'I've just had a thought,' she said. 'Would you be able to paint a picture of my mother's cottage for me? Well the little terrace of cottages I suppose I mean. It would be lovely to have a sort of living memory once I've sold it and I'm back living my real life.'

Marcus put an arm around her shoulder. 'It would be an honour to do that for you and obviously I will give you mates rates.'

It was a friendly arm. She could just tell. Something casual that one friend would do to another. Which, thankfully, made the previous evening a drink, not a drink drink. And in any case why on earth had she started to think that every man she met might fancy her. It was quite ridiculous.

'Seen enough?' he asked, after she'd walked around the room for a second time.

She laughed as Brutus gave a short bark as if in reply to his question. 'Sounds like he has,' she said before following Marcus down the stairs and back into the kitchen.

'So you think my paintings are ok then do you?' he asked.

'Okay? They are more than okay. They are brilliant. Well in my opinion, which is what you asked for so...' She was gabbling again. Over-explaining as usual, and so to cover up her self-consciousness and in an attempt at humour, added, 'And not a Mona Lisa in sight.'

'A Mona Lisa?' Marcus replied laughing. 'Did you expect one then?'

'Well no, not really. It's just something Rosa said. You remember Rosa, she was at the cottage serving tea and cakes last weekend? She likened you to Leonard da Vinci!'

'Of course, I remember her well and I'm flattered, but my paintings are rather different to the great man's work. I would say I'm more of a Van Gogh!'

Jess laughed. 'You need to keep a check on that modesty you know. But yes I can see similarities between your work!'

'Any particular ones?' he asked teasingly.

'Okay. So I've been rumbled. I wouldn't know a Van Gogh from a Da Vinci from ...well from any other artist come to that. But what I do know is that I love your paintings and art is personal. And if I'm absolutely honest, personally, I don't even like the Mona Lisa!'

'Well don't worry. I won't tell Leonardo. It'll be our little secret!'

he said earnestly.

Jess smiled. She was becoming rather fond of her new friend. He was funny, talented, clever and very easy to talk to. And what was more, Rosa was right as usual.

'Now, changing the subject, and I'll warn you this is probably going to sound a bit strange,' he ventured. 'Would you mind coming to say hello to my mother and father. You've already met Father and honestly compared to Henry, Flora is an absolute pussy cat. And to be totally honest with you, it would make my mother's day.... actually it would make her year. For me to turn up with someone of the opposite sex I mean. But anyway that's a story for another day… maybe.'

She noticed that he had looked away from her as he'd made the last comment and although he was still smiling, it seemed to be an almost wistful smile, rueful perhaps. She was good at reading non-verbal signs. She was well-practised and what she saw now, in the man standing in front of her, was a kind of vulnerability, thinly veiled by a teasing exterior.

She smiled at him reassuringly. 'Of course Marcus. I would love to say hello to your mother and father.' And in a different situation she would have gone on to make a joke about being used as a pawn in a strategic game, but this was not that sort of situation. There was more to it. She was quite sure of that.

Over in the West Wing, Henry and Flora were just sitting down for lunch and insisted that she and Marcus joined them. Jess knew immediately that it wasn't optional and so she smiled and thanked them both. It felt more like a court appearance than a lunch, not that she'd ever been in court of course, with questions being fired relentlessly from both parties, *What do you do for a living Jess? What do your parents do? Where do you live?*

Marcus interjected whenever possible, looking apologetically at

Jess, who was sitting opposite him at the large somewhat formal table.

'This salad is lovely Mrs Edwards,' Jess said and Marcus winked at her probably realising she was trying to change the subject.

'Oh please Jess, do call me Flora, everybody does,' she replied.

'That's probably because it's your name Mother,' Marcus replied in a monotone voice, and Jess was sure that both he and Henry were trying to stifle a chuckle.

'Flora,' Jess continued trying to regain her composure. 'Barrowick Hall is absolutely incredible and Marcus is a very talented artist. You must be very proud.'

She looked over at Marcus who had raised his eyebrows in what may have been surprise, or perhaps even pride, at the fact that she had managed to handle his mother's boldness.

'Absolutely my dear. We're both very proud aren't we Henry?' Flora replied, looking across at her husband who was nodding in agreement. 'His professional life is most certainly something to celebrate.'

Jess was sure she had emphasised the words *professional life* but she was not giving anything away in her facial expressions. She was smiling warmly at Marcus and he, in return, was smiling back at his mother.

After lunch, and while Flora was clearing away, Jess whispered to Marcus, 'Less of a pussy cat, more of a tiger me thinks!'

Marcus rolled his eyes and apologised for what he called Flora's *outrageous behaviour*. 'In her defence it's what she does when she *likes* people, if that's any consolation?'

Jess laughed and said it probably wasn't, but that she was used to dealing with a wide range of different people in her job so it wasn't exactly something new to her.

And then, before Marcus could say anything else, Flora joined them in the drawing room with an enormous silver tea tray.

He rolled his eyes again in an apologetic way as Flora said, 'Marcus darling, would you do the honours please.'

Jess sipped the tea and accepted Flora's offer of a brightly coloured macaroon, more out of politeness than want or need. The dainty bone china tea cups reminded her of Eleanor, but that was most definitely where any similarities ended. Eleanor was gentle, kind, creative and warm. Whereas Flora seemed starchy, prim and not cold exactly, but not warm either. More sort of cool or maybe lukewarm to be fair.

She quickly reminded herself not to make rash judgements. It wasn't a good trait; she knew that, but before she could reprimand herself Flora's voice interrupted her thoughts.

'So Jess, do you like dogs?'

She glanced at Marcus and then nodding enthusiastically replied, 'Yes I love dogs and Brutus is absolutely gorgeous.'

'Oh no, no, I didn't mean Brutus. I meant Sheeba and...' she said.

She shot Marcus a questioning glance, but needn't have worried as he'd already closed his mother down and was beginning to explain the whole saga.

It transpired that Sheeba was Henry and Flora's Labrador, who'd had what Flora referred to as 'a liaison' with a Spaniel from the farm next door. The result was a litter of ten puppies which were now three weeks old.

Flora was shaking her head in what looked to Jess like embarrassment or even shame, as Marcus told the tale of how Sheeba had escaped through an open window and went 'looking for love'.

'Don't get me wrong Jess, they are beautiful puppies and Sheeba is a very good mother, but ten of them and mongrels at that...' she trailed off and Jess suddenly saw a glimpse of vulnerability, a soft spot perhaps, in her seemingly tough outer shell.

She smiled sympathetically at Flora and said, 'I would really love to meet them if that's okay with you?'

Marcus got up from his chair and said, 'Come on I'll take you to see them, but I warn you you'd better go in with a hard heart, as they really are quite adorable.'

And he wasn't wrong. The puppies were all asleep and they looked like a mound of soft, cuddly toys. Marcus picked up the nearest one and gave it to Jess to hold.

'Wow! He or she feels so soft and look how vulnerable and helpless they are. They are just so gorgeous Marcus,' she exclaimed.

Sheeba lifted her head and was viewing her with concern, so stroking her head gently and telling her not to worry, Jess placed the puppy next to her and stood back while she sniffed it and then began licking it vigorously.

Back in the drawing room Jess had a sudden thought. 'Marcus…and Flora of course, I may be wrong but these puppies could be what's commonly known as 'designer dogs'. They are a sort of hybrid dog, there are lots out there and they are very popular. There's even one called a 'Jug', she said laughing. 'Which I think is a cross between a Jack Russell and a Pug.'

Flora looked at Jess in surprise. 'Good heavens. A Jug? Whatever next!'

'I know. But seriously people love them. I assume that both dogs would have to have to be purebreds, but I guess it's at least something you could look into,' she said.

It was now Marcus's turn to look at her in surprise. 'Really? Designer cross breeds?' he said. But he was smiling now and sitting forward in his seat. 'We only want to find good homes for them, so if this is something that might help then I will certainly look into it,' he said enthusiastically.

Flora was smiling as well now and looking at Jess said, 'Thank you my dear and it's been really lovely meeting you.'

Perhaps she *had* judged her too harshly. Or perhaps Marcus was right when he'd said it would make his mother's year if he took a female to the Hall. There was more to it she was sure, although she couldn't quite put her finger on it.

Outside on the driveway, Henry, who had gone into the garden while they were looking at the puppies, reappeared with a bunch of freshly picked flowers.

Handing them to Jess he said, 'And don't forget to practice your solo.' Then turning to Marcus added, 'We have our very own Christmas Star this year.'

Jess thanked him for the flowers, but decided that no comment was the best course of action on his 'Christmas Star' remark. That way, she hoped she could put it out of her mind as quickly as possible.

On the way home, Marcus thanked her for her company and apologised again for his parents overbearing behaviour. 'They just can't help themselves you see. It's ingrained behaviour I suppose you'd call it,' he said pulling a face.

'No apology needed. I enjoyed it. It was fun,' Jess replied, and she really meant it. It had been fun.

Back inside the cottage and on her own again, Jess realised her ankle felt much better and although it was still a bit swollen, she was sure that she would be fit for work the following week.

She picked up her phone and rang the ward to let Sister know she would be back on Monday morning. Sister reminded her that she would be on her feet all day and that she must be able to wear the regulation footwear.

Feeling the 'Greenwood effect' engulfing her again, she managed to stutter a response of, 'Yes Sister, see you next week then,' before quickly pressing the red button to end the call. She leant back into the comfy sofa and felt a contented smile spreading across her face. Life was ticking along quite nicely at the moment she thought, even if she hadn't got as much done in the cottage as she should have.

CHAPTER TWELVE

The next morning, Alex arrived with Jim the pub's gardener, who looked more like he should be sitting in the garden with his feet up, rather than working in it.

'Thank you for coming Jim,' Jess said smiling. 'Can I get you a cup of coffee? I've just put the machine on.'

He gave her a quizzical look and replied, 'Young lady, it's nine o'clock in the morning, so if it's all the same to you I'll have a very strong mug of tea made with two tea bags, a splash of milk and three heaped teaspoons of sugar.'

Alex rolled his eyes in Jess's direction. 'He's a bit of a traditionalist but he's a really good worker!' he said in a whisper.

Jess rolled her eyes back at him and handed Jim a large mug of steaming tea, not daring to mention that she only had decaffeinated.

'Let me show you the garden,' she said, leading him out through the back door.

He looked around and after several minutes of muttering and head shaking, declared it was an easy job, and set to work at the pace of a man several decades younger. *Never judge a book by its cover,* she told herself.

Back inside the kitchen, she asked Alex how much she owed him for the loan of the gardener.

Placing his hand under his chin in a sort of exaggerated

'thinker's pose' he replied, 'Well, you can't really put a price on Jim's work. It's sort of inestimable. And as you can see he's a one off. So my thinking is, that if you agree to come out to dinner with me this evening, then we can call it quits.'

She felt her stomach do the familiar flip it did when he was around, but keeping her composure and even managing a smile, she said, 'Thank you, that seems like a very reasonable deal to me.'

That evening, Alex picked her up in his van which was emblazoned with the pub logo. Even though it was dark, the moonlight made it seem as if the decal was illuminated. She smiled to herself at the contrast between this and Marcus's mode of transport, but she knew how differently she felt about going out with Alex. Tonight she hoped this *was* a drink drink and not just a drink.

'I've booked a table at one of my favourite restaurants in town,' he said. 'I hope that's okay, only I thought you may not know that many places around here?'

'Perfect,' she replied, hoping that she had dressed appropriately. She had limited outfits at the cottage and her extended stay had only served to compound the situation. She had eventually decided on a pair of black jeans teamed with a long tunic, and had dressed it up with some of Eleanor's stunning jewellery. As was usual, her hair looked amazing and the way it shone gave her the extra confidence she needed to compensate for her own misgivings about her shape.

The restaurant was a gorgeously authentic Italian place that served some of the most fantastic food Jess had eaten in a long time. The conversation flowed easily between them, partly because they'd found out a bit about each other during the time they spent in Accident and Emergency, but mainly because there was a definite spark between them which made flirting an absolute necessity.

'I'm guessing you've found a replacement for Jazz?' Jess asked.

'Otherwise I assume we would have been eating at the pub.'

Alex laughed. 'Actually, I've had an amazing bit of luck. A girl I used to work with before I came to The Plough was looking for a new job and the rest is history really. She's very experienced in the pub trade and it's as if she's been there forever. Jake is there tonight so he is showing her the ropes, and I'm on standby in case it all goes tits up!' he said. 'Probably should have told you that before we ordered our food thinking about it,' he added. 'And on reflection, using the phrase 'tits up' probably isn't great on a first date!'

She felt her heart rate quicken. 'First date,' he'd said. Did that mean he hoped there was going to be more or was he just stating a fact as, after all, it *was* a first date. Right, *Stop it* she told herself, *keep calm and breathe!*

'No matter. About ordering the food I mean. I would have refused to leave until I'd finished every last morsel anyway, so it's neither here nor there!' she said with a grin.

She should have left it at that but instead added, 'Oh and I didn't mean only about the food when I said 'no matter'. I meant it about you using the phrase 'tits up' as well. It's fine with me. I say it all the time!' She was gabbling again. Saying too much. Agh. Such an annoying trait.

But she relaxed when she saw that he was laughing now, and then taking her hands across the table he said, 'I think I could get to rather like you Jess, Jess Jones from No. 3 Back Lane, with the sprained ankle…'

She immediately felt a warm glow spreading over her face and realised that she must be as red as a beetroot. 'Okay, okay, so I have a tendency to over explain things,' she said with a wry smile. But then, as his hands gently squeezed hers, she felt the heat diminishing from her cheeks, and she realised this was a moment. And a potentially important one at that.

The food was amazing and Jess surprised herself when she changed from her usual all chocolate dessert to something more authentic and grown up.

'Tiramisu Madam,' the waiter said, as he casually placed the dessert in front of her as if it was something ordinary. Something that had come out of a packet or a tin, like a chocolate brownie or a rice pudding (staple desserts in her London household).

But it wasn't something ordinary. It was extraordinary. It was a vision. Because the dessert she was just about to ruin by cutting into it with a dessert spoon, had been somehow magnificently and skilfully shaped into 'The Leaning of Pisa'.

'This is amazing! How is that even possible?' she exclaimed. 'Look at it Alex. It defies gravity!' She realised that she had launched into another one of her gibbering outbursts, but guessed he was getting used to them now as he was looking at her in amusement whilst nodding in agreement.

And it tasted as good as it looked. She'd had a moment's thought that maybe she shouldn't eat it. After all it was a work of art. But the thought had only been a fleeting one, and after taking a picture of the coffee sculpture with her phone, she sank her spoon into the creation and savoured every last bit.

'Shall we have coffee back at The Plough?' Alex asked, as the waiter cleared away the dessert bowls.

Jess smiled at the sight of the two perfectly clean bowls, neither of which showed any signs of having previously been the bearer of a dessert. Alex had chosen a vanilla panna cotta, which wobbled perfectly and was complimented with semi frozen berries, delicately dusted with icing sugar in the pattern of a single leaf. Another work of art. It had been an amazing meal and an amazing 'first date'.

'Yes, that would be lovely,' she replied, feeling her stomach do the now familiar Alex-generated somersaults, and then crossed her fingers in the hope that she hadn't sounded too eager.

Back at the pub the smell of smokey wood and the sound of convivial chatter felt invitingly familiar to her, and she smiled again as Alex took her by the hand to introduce her to the new member of his bar staff.

'Velvet, this is Jess,' he said. 'Jess, this is Velvet. She is literally something of a life saver. My 'knight in shining armour'. Or' knight- ress' I suppose you could say!'

Velvet pulled a face. 'Well not literally. I'm actually neither of those things. Not in the true sense anyway,' she said good naturedly. 'And before you feel you have to comment on my name, as everybody seems too, I think it's ridiculous as well! Most people just call me 'V' but Alex has always insisted on calling me Velvet,' she added, raising her eyes towards the ceiling in an exaggerated fashion.

'Well actually I rather like it,' Jess replied honestly. 'It's unique... although I'm guessing that could be a double-edged sword.'

Velvet nodded and a wry smile passed over her lips. She was a stunning looking girl Jess observed, although she wasn't sure that a thirty-odd year old could be classed as a girl anymore. She always referred to herself and her friends as girls, but actually society would probably view them as women, even if they didn't view themselves in this way. Anyway, it was an irrelevance she told herself, girl or woman she was a beauty, with masses of deep copper-coloured curls piled up on top of her head and tiny ringlets that framed her lightly freckled face. She had what magazines would describe as an hourglass figure and she had accentuated her small waist perfectly with a wide belt. Jess sighed, she would swap her 'pear' for Velvet's 'hourglass' any day of the week.

'Could you please bring two coffees to Jess's personal table Velvet,' Alex was saying and Jess shook herself back into the moment.

'Penny for them,' Alex said with a sudden look of concern.

'Oh it's nothing really, there's just been so much going on over the last couple of weeks it's sometimes hard to process it all.' And although that was true in part, she didn't want Alex to know that the main reason was the insecurities she had around her body image. It seemed so shallow.

After the pub had emptied and Jake and Velvet had cleared up and left, Alex locked the door and leaning against it said, 'Although it's a good feeling when the door closes at the end of the night and everything's shipshape, I do find it can be too quiet at times and even a bit lonely. You can get fed up with your own company you know.'

'Yes,' Jess said nodding. 'I think I can relate to that. I've found it too quiet at the cottage at times, having been used to living with two other girls.'

She picked up the empty coffee cups and took them to the bar, then turning to Alex said, 'Perhaps we're all lonely at times and looking for something that's missing from our lives.'

He nodded and then joining her at the bar took hold of her hands in his. 'Yes maybe we are Jess. But I think I may just have found the answer.'

She felt her heart skip a beat and her breathing quickened as she looked into his eyes expectantly. His face moved closer to hers until she could feel his warm breath on her skin. And then looking into her eyes he declared, 'I'm going to get a dog!'

'A dog! A dog! Or course. What a great idea!' she replied in a high pitched slightly hysterical tone that could be likened to a siren from an emergency vehicle. And then desperately trying to compose herself, she somehow managed to add, 'I may be able to help you out on that score as Marcus's parents have the most gorgeous litter of puppies, which I think would be perfect for you and the pub.' It was a good save she thought. Particularly as she wasn't renowned for her ability to think on her feet.

Trying to hide the disappointment that she had been trumped

as the answer to his loneliness by a dog, she began explaining the tale of the puppies to him. He was shifting from foot to foot in an excited manner and seeing him so animated made her realise she must have done a good job in covering her disappointment.

'When do you think I can see them?' he asked.

'I can ask Marcus tomorrow if you like?' she said smiling now. 'But there is a condition.'

'Anything. Just name it,' he replied excitedly.

She placed her hands on her hips and looked at him in surprise. 'Are you psychic or something? Because that's exactly the condition. I get to name the puppy!'

There was a brief but friendly stand off as they both looked at each other. But then grinning from ear to ear he offered an extended hand which she shook firmly.

'Deal,' he said.

'Deal,' she replied nodding.

CHAPTER THIRTEEN

Friday morning brought the familiar loud wailing from outside the back door. Jess drew back the curtains to see overcast skies and then descended the stairs as quickly as she could manage, to let Tigger in for her breakfast before the rain started.

'Come on in Madam Tiggs,' she said opening the back door as wide as it would go.

She stood back and waited for Tigger to shoot past her, as was her usual routine, but today she didn't come rushing in as if her life depended on it. In fact, she didn't come in at all. Instead she remained in the garden meowing loudly until Jess put her head out of the door to see what all the fuss was about.

But nothing could have prepared her for the sight she was confronted with. She gasped with delight as Tigger stood a few feet away from the back door next to two of the most adorable kittens, both of whom were trying desperately to hide underneath their mother's body.

Tears sprung to her eyes as she stepped out of the door and bent down to get a closer look. But the kittens weren't having any of it. They both spat and hissed wildly at her. Their hair stood up on their backs and their ears flattened.

'Sorry sweeties,' she said softly before slowly getting to her feet. She retreated back into the kitchen, leaving the door ajar while she opened a tin of food for them. She watched from the window as Tigger moved towards the door, with the kittens scurrying alongside her.

Jess coaxed her into the kitchen and smiled with relief as the tiny kittens followed closely behind her. They were identical in colour to their mother, with the same perfect dark stripes and their eyes were as blue as the ocean. They looked very young but to her relief, after a few seconds, they were all eating greedily from the bowls of food Jess had put down for them, and reaching for her phone she turned it onto video mode to capture the joyous moment.

Unlike other mornings, Tigger didn't go straight to the back door when she'd had her fill, but instead rubbed around Jess's legs purring softly. The kittens became a little bolder, venturing a few feet away from the safety of their mother, but soon scurried back at the slightest sound, taking refuge under her body. Tigger licked them with her rough tongue and they purred with obvious pleasure. Jess smiled at the delightful sight and said out loud, 'Thank you for bringing them Tigger. I will call them Ginger and Spice. Not very original I know, but I'm not very good at thinking on my feet!'

A few minutes later Tigger went to the back door with the convoy following closely. She meowed loudly and as Jess opened the door she was sure the cat's eyes momentarily met hers before she strolled up the garden and squeezed under the fence, followed closely by her offspring. Jess had an uncomfortable feeling that she wouldn't see them again, but at least she had the video for posterity.

After breakfast she phoned Marcus and explained that Alex might want one of the puppies. He sounded delighted and told her they could come up to the Hall later that morning and have what he called 'pick of the litter'. She phoned Alex straight away and she could hear the excitement in his voice.

'I'll pick you up at eleven o'clock then,' he said, and before Jess could say anything else he was gone, probably grinning from ear to ear and halfway to the pet shop to buy a dog bed.

Jess showered and then took stock of her temporary wardrobe again. Unsurprisingly, it hadn't improved since the last time she looked and she certainly had nothing that Alex hadn't seen before. Sighing, she pulled on a pair of tight black leggings and a jumper, reminding herself they were going to look at a puppy rather than going on a date.

She was just about to head back downstairs, when it dawned on her that black leggings and hairy dogs were not a good combination. She sat back down on the edge of the bed and endeavoured to peel off the leggings, which now seemed to have become firmly fixed to her legs.

'Gotcha!' she announced as the first leg surrendered to a sharp tug. But just as she was wrestling with the second leg, trying to ease it over her slightly swollen ankle, the doorbell chimed and in her haste to finish the job and get to the door, she tripped on the dangling leggings and fell to the floor with a loud thud.

'Damn, damn,' she groaned loudly. 'I'm making rather too much of a habit of this falling over business.'

Struggling to her feet, she looked out of the window to see a young girl walking back up the garden path pushing a buggy. She flung the window open and the wind caught it, nearly pulling it off its hinges. 'Damn,' she said again and then muttering, 'More haste, less speed,' wondered whether she should go to church to repent her repeated blaspheming. She would do it at choir practice, kill two birds with one stone!

'Hello? Sorry, I am in, but I was just finishing a battle with some very stubborn leggings,' she called through the open window. *There you go again*, she told herself, *over explaining*.

The girl turned round and the wind whipped her dark hair

across her face.

'Hi,' she called back, pushing the hair away and waving up at the window.

'I'll come down,' Jess called back to her, and pulling on her dressing gown made her way to the front door.

'I hope this isn't a bad time?' the girl asked apologetically. 'It's just that I heard you'd joined the choir and I wanted to introduce myself. I sing in the choir too but I couldn't make it last week. This one was ill,' she continued, pointing to the buggy.

Jess assumed there was a baby in there somewhere, but with the rain cover on and various blankets underneath it was difficult to tell.

Jess smiled. 'Come in, please come in,' she said.

The girl pushed the buggy into the small hallway and extracted the baby from the bundle of covers, deftly removing its hat and all-in-one suit with her free hand. She took her own coat off, shook her hair and smiling warmly at Jess said, 'Hi again, I'm Nora and this is Mabel.'

The baby chuckled loudly in response to her mother's voice.

'Hello beautiful girl,' Jess said looking at the baby. And she *was* beautiful. Perfect skin, big blue eyes and just a few tiny wisps of fair hair.

Over coffee the pair chatted like old friends. Nora told Jess she was married to Josh and lived at the other end of the village on the road that led to Barrowick. Mabel was six months old and was an absolute delight, but although she loved living in Thripton, there was a distinct shortage of people under forty.

In turn Jess explained a bit about Eleanor and how she came to be having an extended stay in the cottage.

'Poor you. Sounds like you're having a bad time at the moment. So sad to lose your mum and at such a young age as well,' Nora said. She paused for a few seconds. 'I hope this doesn't sound too insensitive, but I'm also kind of glad that your unfortunate circumstances have enabled us to meet,' she added.

Jess nodded and smiled. 'Me too. Listen, any chance your husband could look after Mabel tonight so we can have a drink at the pub and continue our chat?'

'That's the best idea I've heard in a long time,' she laughed. 'And yes he'd be happy to, I know he would.'

'Great. It's just that I have to go out shortly. I'm going to see a man about a dog. Literally. It's a bit of a long story but I'll tell you all about it tonight,' Jess said.

'I'll look forward to it,' the young girl said laughing.

Alex hadn't been able to wait until eleven o'clock and arrived in his van fifteen minutes early, tooting his horn at the top of the garden path. Jess, now wearing a pair of jeans in place of the fateful leggings pulled on her coat and headed up the garden path to join him.

'Patience,' she admonished whilst climbing into the passenger seat.

'Sorry,' he replied with an apologetic grimace. And then the familiar boyish grin spread across his lips, causing her stomach to do its equally familiar flip.

Once they were out of the lane, she sent a text message to Marcus to let him know they were on the way and when they arrived he was waiting out the front for them.

'Have you forewarned Alex?' he asked, pulling a face. 'You know about my parents I mean.'

Jess laughed and replied, 'They're pussy cats, the pair of them, you just have to know how to tame them. Oh yes and talking about pussy cats, look what happened today.' She took her phone from her pocket and replayed the video of Tigger and the kittens to them.

Both men agreed they were very cute, but she could tell their minds were on a different kind of cute animal, so putting the phone back in her pocket she followed Marcus and Alex to the West Wing.

Marcus introduced Alex to Flora and Henry, who in turn complimented them on Barrowick Hall. Flora smiled with pride and Jess realised he'd already tamed one of the pussy cats. Marcus nodded knowingly at her and then took them into the room where the puppies were being kept.

'Goodness,' she exclaimed looking at the two men. 'They seem to have grown in just two days.' But she quickly realised neither was listening, as Alex's eyes had glazed over as he gazed adoringly at the puppies, while Marcus was busy trying to persuade Sheeba to let him pick one of them up.

'Are you thinking of a dog or a bitch?' Marcus asked, holding out the most gorgeous chocolate coloured pup, complete with white flash on its chest.

Alex took the pup in both hands and held it close to his chest. 'I was thinking of a dog, as that's what I'm more used to.'

Marcus took the pup back from him and tipping it over in a somewhat unceremonious fashion, declared, 'This one's a boy!'

Alex laughed. 'I'm sold already,' he said. 'They're gorgeous. I definitely want one!'

Marcus put the puppy back into the pen and then passed him three other puppies one at a time, while Sheeba watched on warily.

'Come through and have some coffee and I'll tell you a bit about the parents,' Marcus said. 'And I mean the puppies' parents by the way, not mine!'

Jess laughed. 'I did wonder for a minute,' she replied teasingly.

'Don't even get me started on that one,' he said rolling his eyes. 'Anyway Alex, Jess may have told you that she thought the puppies may constitute hybrid dogs, so I have been doing some research into this and it all seems quite positive so far. I do want to stress though, that the welfare of the puppies is our primary concern and finding them what I believe is called their forever homes, is the most important thing to us all.'

Alex nodded in agreement. 'Absolutely,' he said. 'Couldn't agree more.'

Flora was waiting for them with freshly brewed coffee and a plate of dainty fairy cakes. As they sat drinking their coffee, Marcus told them that he had spoken to the farmer who owns the sire and he was able to confirm that the dog has a full pedigree and clear health test papers.

'He is also an excellent working dog with a great temperament to boot,' Marcus said.

'Perfect,' Alex said grinning.

'The poor farmer didn't know about the puppies so it's been quite a surprise for him. He knew there had been some sort of 'liaison' as Mother calls it, but he didn't know about the resultant litter,' Marcus continued.

Flora stiffened in her chair. 'Well sometimes it's a case of least said, soonest mended,' she said looking directly at Marcus.

'Not in this case,' Marcus replied firmly. And then turning back to Alex added, 'He has also expressed an interest in having at least one of the puppies himself, so Mother's proverb is certainly not true in this case.'

Jess sensing the growing tension between Marcus and his mother, turned to Flora and asked, 'And does Sheeba have the necessary paperwork Flora?'

'Most definitely my dear. I brought her from a reputable dealer and she is Kennel Club registered and properly health checked. It's just a case of locating the papers,' Flora replied.

'And best of all is that the mix of breeds is already recognised as a designer breed,' Marcus added with raised eyebrows.

To Jess's relief the tension between mother and son seemed to have passed and Henry's timely entrance into the room helped the situation enormously.

'I've just come off the phone to one of my great friends who is a senior partner at the local vet practice,' he announced. 'And he is going to pop round this afternoon and give the puppies the once over, and is happy to advise us on anything else we may need.'

Jess shook her head in astonishment. The whole family were definite doers she thought and all of this in just two days. But before she could open her mouth to praise them on their efforts, Flora looked directly at her and said, 'We have *you* to thank for this Jess, I'm so glad Marcus met you. And what's more, you are the first lady friend he has ever brought home!'

She felt her cheeks redden and wasn't quite sure whether to look at Marcus or Alex. But to her surprise, and before she could make a decision, her thoughts were interrupted by Henry, who added, 'And so am I, Songbird. So am I.'

Alex, as if picking up on the awkwardness of the situation piped up, 'Could I have another look at the puppies please Marcus, then I think I should make a decision on which one.'

'Of course,' Marcus replied, getting to his feet and looking decidedly relieved at Alex's intervention. 'I have some different colour rubber collars to help with identification, so once you've decided we can put a collar on him and he's yours.'

It was an easy decision for Alex and Jess wasn't at all surprised when he chose the first puppy he had held, with its soft chocolate brown coat and white flash. Marcus put a blue collar around its neck and the pair shook hands as if sealing a deal.

Back outside, Alex, as if suddenly realising he hadn't asked about the cost of the puppy said, 'Marcus, I think I've forgotten something quite important. How much are you charging for the puppies? Not that the cost is important to me as I've one hundred percent made my mind up, but I'm sure it's important to you.'

'It's not something we've really discussed yet,' he replied and Jess could tell it was a genuine answer. 'But in any case there is no cost to you, just promise me you will give him a fantastic life.'

Alex smiled and putting an arm casually around Jess's shoulders said, 'That's very generous of you. Thank you Marcus. And you can absolutely count on him having the best possible life, can't he Jess?'

She wondered if he'd meant he hoped that she was going to be a part of his life, or was he asking her to assure Marcus that he could give the puppy a good life?

Either way the answer was the same, so she smiled and nodded in agreement but secretly hoped that he'd meant the former.

On the journey home Alex reminded her that she now had the job of deciding on a name for the puppy.

'I already have,' she replied with a smile. 'But I'm going to keep you in suspense until tonight. I'm coming to the pub with a girl from the village.'

'I'll look forward to it,' he laughed and she really hoped he was telling the truth.

Back at the cottage, Alex declined an invitation to go in explaining that he had an interview to conduct for a new member of kitchen staff.

'Good luck then,' she said and then added, 'Does he or she have an unusual name? It seems to be part of the essential criteria to working in the pub!'

He laughed. 'Of course, it's in the job description!' And with that gave her a peck on the cheek and he was gone.

After lunch, and with her ankle feeling practically back to normal, Jess decided it would be a good time to take the clothes she had loaded into Rowan to the charity shop. She drove slowly up the lane and practised an emergency stop to test out her ankle, before pulling out onto the village road and into the nearest town.

The charity shop worker seemed delighted with the clothes and said she was astonished at the perfect condition they were in. Jess completed a form so they could claim back the tax and left the shop feeling very satisfied that at least some good would come from Eleanor's wardrobe.

As she walked back to her car, she passed a shop that had a gorgeous plum coloured knitted dress in the window, modelled perfectly by an ultra-thin mannequin. Next thing she knew she was in the shop over-explaining to the familiar-looking, but totally disinterested shop assistant, that it probably wouldn't look anywhere near as good on her as it did on the mannequin, but that she would like to try it on anyway.

As she pulled the dress over her head and down over her body, the wool material clung to her skin. She smoothed it down, took a deep breath and closed her eyes briefly before springing them open and taking a look in the full length mirror. The image looking back at her made her gasp. It actually was fantastic. The dark colour helped disguise her hips and complimented her dark hair and eyes perfectly. And to her surprise the clingy nature of the dress accentuated her figure perfectly.

'I'll take it,' she said triumphantly to the shop assistant, who managed to put her phone down long enough to tell it was seventy five pounds. Jess felt her jaw drop almost to the floor but really she *had* to have it didn't she? She was meeting Nora at the pub later and she couldn't possibly let Alex see her in the same clothes again. It was an essential purchase. A bit like chocolate was, but more expensive of course. She took a deep breath and handed over her debit card, crossing her fingers tightly behind her back, praying that it wouldn't get declined.

'Bag?' the girl asked, and as Jess looked up from the card machine she suddenly realised why she was familiar. It was Jazz, the girl who used to work at the pub.

'It's Jazz isn't it?' she asked, smiling brightly. 'We met at The Plough.'

'Yeah,' the girl replied, showing no more interest than she had done previously. 'And before you ask, there's no discount because you know me! So do you want a bag or not?'

'No thank you,' Jess said, trying hard to keep a cordial tone. 'I'm trying to save the planet.'

For the first time the girl looked directly at her. 'And what planet might that be?' she asked.

Could that possibly have been a reference to what Poppy had said to her in the pub that evening regarding the types of red wine? Surely not.

Dismissing the thought and without making any kind of response, particularly as it may, just may have been extremely sharp witted, she tucked the dress under her arm and left the shop in absolute astonishment at the girl's bad attitude but with gratitude that her card purchase was successful.

Back on track to her car, Jess suddenly had a brainwave. She needed to make a couple more purchases, but this time they were for Alex. She would get him a book about caring for a new puppy and also a small edible item that would give him a hint at the puppy's name.

But first she needed to find a cash point to see if she had enough money in her account to cover the cost of the purchases and have a few pounds left for meeting Nora. It was payday the next day so she didn't have to survive for long but her overdraft was already nearing its limit. Smiling with relief at the figure on the screen, she withdrew thirty pounds, made her two purchases, and with a spring in her step walked back to her car.

Back in the lane and before going inside No. 3, Jess knocked at

Rosa's door to show her the video of Tigger and her offspring. Rosa threw her arms up in delight and then clapping her hands together exclaimed, 'So that's why she didn't come for her prawns this morning. She probably knew the kittens wouldn't be able to climb the fence.'

Ignoring the comment about the fence, Jess said, 'You feed her *prawns?*'

'Of course darling, they are her favourite,' Rosa replied.

'They're mine too,' Jess said laughing. 'But I can't afford to have them for breakfast! Actually, thinking about it, I wouldn't really want them for breakfast. But honestly Rosa you're such a softie.'

She beamed at Jess. 'I assume that is a compliment my darling, in which case you can come in for tea and cake.'

'I won't thank you Rosa, I have a few things to do and I'm meeting a girl from the village in the pub later, she sings in the choir.'

'How lovely darling, I'm pleased you have settled in so well here.'

Smiling, Jess reminded her that it was only a temporary arrangement and that on Sunday she had to return to London and back to her real life. She saw the smile fade from Rosa's face and so quickly added that she would have to come back regularly, as there was still lots to do next door.

'I've got used to you being around Jess and I like it. As I always say, better if you know the devil.'

Jess squeezed her arm. 'Thank you Rosa, you have been a fantastic support through what have been some very difficult times for me.'

Smiling again now, Rosa replied, 'I know how hard it's been for you my darling, but just remember when life gives you lemons...

'Yes, I know Rosa. Make lemonade,' she said, finishing the sentence for her.

'No, no my darling. Not lemonade. Make a very large gin and tonic!'

Upstairs in the bedroom of Eleanor's cottage, Jess hung her new dress on the outside of the wardrobe and stood back, admiring its simplicity and style.

She glanced at her watch and realising that she still had to get herself something to eat, have a shower and get ready for meeting Nora (and seeing Alex), she needed to get a move on. She hurried downstairs to the kitchen and looking in the near empty fridge, resigned herself to the fact that it was beans on toast again. The upside was though that she still had some chocolate left which would count as a dessert.

Her excitement and anticipation for the evening ahead was causing her stomach to perform somersaults that would have made an Olympic gymnast proud, so she never would have been able to eat a proper meal anyway.

Before leaving for the short walk to the pub, Jess had one last look in Eleanor's long mirror and, for once, she didn't see her pear-shaped figure first. In fact, she didn't see any of her physical appearance first. What she saw instead was a happy, smiling young woman who looked like she was beginning to enjoy life again. And she was. It was unexpected and surprising, but it felt good.

She was first to the pub so she got the small package for Alex out of her handbag and handed it to him over the bar.

'What's this?' he asked with surprise.

'Well open it and you'll see,' she replied smiling. She had found some soft tissue paper imprinted with the words 'just for you' in Eleanor's sideboard and some brightly coloured tape, and although it wasn't up to her mother's standards of presentation it was, at least, wrapped.

Alex carefully removed the tape and as he undid the tissue paper his face lit up at the sight of the book.

'It's only a paperback I'm afraid and probably a bit basic, but it's a start.'

'It's very thoughtful, thank you,' he replied and she could tell he was genuinely pleased.

And then, as he removed the rest of the tissue paper, the real surprise dropped out onto the bar. He looked a little perplexed as he picked up the packet of Rolos.

'It's a clue,' she said excitedly. 'To the puppy's name I mean. Well it's not really a clue exactly. It's the actual name!'

Alex looked at her and for a heart stopping moment she couldn't read his face.

'Listen,' she said, wanting to spare any awkwardness. 'The whole naming thing was a bit tongue in cheek really. You know a sort of joke. He's your puppy and you should choose his name...' But before could finish the sentence he'd joined her from behind the bar and was hugging her tightly.

'Rolo. I love it. It's the perfect name, just perfect,' he said.

He called Jake to pull her a pint of beer, indicating it was on the house and then leaning towards her whispered, 'And can I just say Jones you are looking particularly lovely tonight!'

She felt herself colour profusely and her heart seemed as if it was pounding out of her chest. But somehow she managed to mutter, 'Thank you,' and breathed a sigh of relief as Nora joined her at the bar. 'Nora! Hi,' she said in a slightly over-enthusiastic tone. Actually, she thought looking at Alex again, he did have a sort of Hugh Grant look about him, apart, of course, from the hair.

Feeling a little calmer now she said, 'Alex, this is Nora. Nora sings in the choir and has the most adorable baby. Nora, this is Alex. Alex runs the best pub in Thripton and is about to get the most adorable puppy.'

Alex laughed and nodding in appreciation said, 'Very clever Jones,' giving her a clear indication that his previous remark about how she looked was, as she had thought, a nod to her Bridget Jones style introductions on the evening when she was in the pub with Poppy and Will.

'Ah,' Nora commented. 'Man about a dog?'

'Yep,' Jess replied laughing.

Jake poured Nora a glass of white wine and Jess led her to her favourite table by the fire. But to her dismay it was displaying a reserved sign. She turned to the bar to see that Alex was watching her closely and then grinning he called over, 'It's reserved for you two. I hope that's ok?'

Jess smiled and nodded her appreciation, and the pair settled into the comfortable tub chairs that she'd now become quite familiar with.

Nora exhaled deeply and took a large swig of wine. 'I really needed that!' she said relaxing back into the chair.

'Hard day?' Jess asked with a sympathetic smile.

'I shouldn't complain really as Mabel is the most special thing that has ever happened to me, but sometimes it's hard when you're on your own all day with someone whose conversation is limited to 'ba ba' and and 'ga ga' and who continually blows saliva-soaked raspberries in your face!'

They were both laughing now and Jess was grateful that it was so easy to talk to Nora who was, after all, practically a stranger.

'So tell me more about you,' Jess said, taking a sip of the glorious-tasting ale. 'Well, only if you want to of course.'

The other girl pushed her thick dark hair away from her face revealing her make-up free skin and Jess suddenly realised that she was much younger than she had initially thought. She told Jess she had been married to Josh for just over two years and Mabel's arrival had been what they both described as an 'unexpected pleasure'.

'What did you do before Mabel arrived?' Jess asked, hoping this might help age her without having to ask her outright.

'I was...well still am actually, a community phlebotomist,' she replied. 'I've been working as a vampire in different settings since finishing my A levels, so basically four years.'

That made her about twenty-two years old Jess thought. A whole ten years younger than she was and already married with a baby, a house and a career. She had a sudden feeling of dread that life was passing her by, but fortunately before she could spend too much time self-pitying, Alex appeared with more drinks and some outrageous flirting that Nora acknowledged with a wink and widened eyes.

'So what's the story with you and the outrageously flirtatious publican?' she asked teasingly.

'Well, we've only recently met actually. But I think there's a spark between us that's for sure,' Jess replied, feeling her cheeks redden.

'A spark?' Nora repeated, pulling a face of surprise. 'More like a flame. No actually a roaring fire!'

'Is it that obvious?' Jess asked, breaking into a grin.

'Very,' she replied. 'Now tell me more!'

It was only nine thirty when Nora reluctantly announced that she should be making a move, as Mabel would be waiting for her comfort feed before settling for the night.

There's the reality check, Jess told herself. At least she could stay out as late as she liked and didn't have anybody relying on her for absolutely everything. Small mercies she thought, small mercies. She walked to the door with Nora and the pair hugged each other warmly.

'See you at choir practice next week via Skype,' Jess said laughing, before covering her face with her hands.

Nora nodded and laughed. 'Looking forward to hearing your solo. The First Noel as I understand it!'

Jess pulled a face of mock horror. 'Oh God don't remind me. I haven't even done any practice yet.'

The pair looked at each other and then as if instructed to do so by Henry and in perfect harmony and unison, belted out the first line of the carol!

Smiling openly now at the success of the evening, Jess returned to her favourite chair and was joined by Alex, who was now clutching a mug of steaming coffee.

'You're putting me to shame,' she said laughing whilst pointing to her pint glass.

'No good drinking away the profits,' he joked and she nodded in agreement.

'Hey guess what?' she said, suddenly remembering her earlier encounter with Jazz.

'No sorry I can't!' he replied with a grin.

'It was rhetorical. You're supposed to sit forward in your chair expectantly and wait for me to continue,' she said, rolling her eyes.

'Ah. You're forgetting a very important fact. I'm a man and apparently we're from Mars!' he replied shrugging his shoulders.

'Well next time you go there could you bring me back one of their lovely chocolate bars. The super-size one obviously. Now be quiet and just humour me or is that what you're already doing?' she said, suddenly feeling self-conscious, but nevertheless proud of her unusually quick-witted response.

He put his coffee mug on the table and moved to the edge of his seat. 'I'm all ears.'

'Okay. Good. Well I popped into a clothes shop in town today and who do you think was working there?'

'Well considering you only know about three people around here it shouldn't be too difficult to guess,' he joked. 'Oh yes and one of them is Jim the gardener, who I can't imagine was in a clothes shop in town. So that makes it two,' he said grinning.

'Actually I'll have you know that I know lots of people around here. Granted they're mainly people of a *certain age* but we mustn't stereotype now must we?'

Alex rolled his eyes. 'Okay, you win. I have no idea. Do tell me who you saw.'

A smile of satisfaction passed over her lips as she said, 'It was Jazz and I can tell you her customer service skills haven't improved much since leaving here!'

She watched as Alex leant further forward in his chair and then picking up a spoon he began stirring his coffee, as if deep in contemplation.

'Oh dear,' he finally replied with a sigh. 'I had high hopes for that girl. I really did.'

Jess looked away in an effort to hide her surprise. That was not the response she was expecting. Not at all.

CHAPTER FOURTEEN

The next morning Jess was up early as Poppy had said she would be there by ten o'clock and she definitely needed to do a bit of tidying and cleaning before her friend arrived. But the alarm she had set wasn't needed as she was woken up by an incoming text message. She smiled when she saw it was from Alex, *Fancy coming shopping this morning for puppy essentials?* it read.

Her stomach turned its usual excited flutter as she tapped in her reply, *Just need to wait for Poppy to arrive as I'm not sure what her plans are. Although I think I have a fairly good idea! xx*

She clutched her phone tightly until it beeped a reply and sighed with relief when she saw it said, *No problem - I can wait!*

She went into the kitchen and filled the kettle before opening the back door just in case Tigger, Ginger and Spice should put in an appearance. Sipping her tea, she considered the previous evening and decided on balance it had been a success, even though she had a slightly uneasy feeling about Alex's reaction when she'd mentioned seeing Jazz in the clothes shop. Although the change in his demeanour had been subtle, there had most definitely been a change, and it had played on her mind making her toss and turn in bed for ages before she finally asleep. But on the other hand, she told herself, he'd texted her early in the morning about the shopping trip so perhaps she was reading more into it than was actually there.

Trying to shrug off her negative thoughts, she showered and dressed in clothes suitable for a trip to the pet shop and carefully applied some natural looking makeup. She tied her hair up into a high ponytail to give herself what she thought might give an, 'I'm a down to earth animal lover' kind of impression, which of course she was, and then set about tidying the cottage ready for her best friend's arrival.

Poppy arrived just before ten o'clock, looking as fabulous as ever in casual jeans, a thick knitted jumper and heels that Jess could only dream of being able to walk in even before her trip down the stairs.

Poppy kissed her on the cheek and then standing back said, 'Jessica Jones you have a definite twinkle in your eye! Help me get my stuff in and then I want to hear your news.'

Jess rolled her eyes and slipped her arm through Poppy's as they walked back up the garden path to her car.

'Good heavens,' she exclaimed, peering inside the car. 'I thought you were just coming for the weekend!'

Poppy laughed and grabbing some of the bags replied, 'I couldn't quite decide what to bring, so basically I've just brought everything!'

Back in the cottage, Jess had just poured some coffee when the familiar chime of the doorbell interrupted their lively chatter. Opening the front door her eyes widened with surprise at the sight of Rosa, Will and Alex all standing on the doorstep.

'Goodness. Is this some sort of deputation,' she exclaimed?

'Oh no darling,' Rosa replied, holding out an enormous bowl of food, 'It's a prawn linguine!'

Inside the cottage, Alex explained that he was next door helping Will carry a very heavy bath up a staircase not designed for such an item, and everyone laughed as he described how they carried it up on their backs, wearing it like a tortoise shell.

Will owned up and said he was on the doorstep because he couldn't wait to see Poppy, and Alex chipped in that he had just tagged along for the ride. Swiftly adding that he was speaking metaphorically of course.

Rosa reminded Jess to put the linguine in the fridge and then gave her strict instructions on how to reheat it later. 'I know you love prawns Jess, but they can be very dangerous creatures you know!' she said with a serious look on her face.

They all laughed at Rosa's seemingly unwitting humour and as quickly as she had appeared, she left again calling out, 'Ciao, Ciao darlings.'

Alex breathed an exaggerated sigh of relief at the sound of the front door closing.

Jess rolled her eyes at him and said with a grin, 'I think she's warming to you!'

'Well I didn't get any deathly stares today so that's an improvement for sure,' he replied laughing.

'Look at the pair of them,' Jess said signalling to Poppy and Will who were sitting together on the sofa, deep in conversation, with eyes only for each other.

Alex smiled, 'So puppy essentials shopping is on then?' he asked.

'I think that would be fine in the circumstances,' she replied smiling.

'Pick you up in an hour then,' he said and her heart skipped a beat as he leaned towards her and gave her a kiss on the cheek.

Will left soon after Alex and Poppy told Jess that they were going to look at tiles together for the bathroom he was refurbishing.

'That sounds like an important job,' she said teasingly.

And Poppy suddenly looking very serious said, 'I think it just might be.'

In the pet shop, Alex produced a shopping list as long as his arm.

Dog bed, food bowl, water bowl, collar, lead, toys, treats, food, shampoo, brush, comb…the list was endless.

'Rolo is going to have everything he needs,' he declared as if he was pre-empting Jess's next comment.

She laughed. 'So I see. And more than he needs by the looks of it. I'm not entirely sure who is the excited puppy here, you or Rolo!'

'Very funny! But I would have thought that was blatantly obvious!' he replied grinning, as the merchandise started to pile up in the shopping trolley.

'Yes very obvious,' she agreed. 'I hadn't realised it was possible to fill a trolley in a pet shop!' She watched in amusement as he added more and more to the pile.

'It's the bed that's taking up most of the room, remember,' he said. 'But I think we should head for the tills before I'm tempted to get myself a second trolley!'

'Good idea,' she replied, leading the way to the front of the shop.

At the till Jess covered her eyes in mock horror when she saw the three-figure sum on the till screen.

'Many of the purchases are one offs so they don't really count do they?' Alex said, directing his question to the girl behind the counter.

'I'm not getting involved in any domestics,' the girl replied good-naturedly. 'But getting a puppy is very exciting isn't it? Except for the toilet training and the broken sleep of course!'

'Oh yes. I'd forgotten about those bits,' Alex said with a grimace.

'You'll be fine. Good practice at parenting!' the shop assistant said with a wink.

'Oh we're…we're not….um…'Jess stuttered.

'Thinking about that at the moment,' Alex said, finishing the sentence for her and even managing a broad smile.

Outside, Jess felt the fresh air hit her hot cheeks and hoped it was helping to return them to their normal colour. 'Honestly some people have no filters!' she said, keeping her focus on pushing the trolley across the busy car park so she didn't have to look directly at him.

'True. But I thought it was rather...' He stopped short of finishing the sentence when his phone began ringing loudly. He looked at the screen and then handing her the keys to the van, walked off in the opposite direction, answering the call with a cold sounding 'Hello.'

She watched as he paced backwards and forwards, gesticulating with his hands and shaking his head in what looked to her like an unfriendly exchange of words.

'Everything okay?' she asked, when he returned to the van where she was waiting for him, having loaded the purchases into the back and returned the trolley.

'Yes, yes, um sorry, I need to get back to the pub,' he replied.

They sat in relative silence on the drive home and although Jess was desperate to know what he was going to say before he was interrupted by the phone, she knew it was not the right time. He clearly had something more important to deal with but she had no idea what.

Partly to break the uneasy quiet and partly in the hope that he might open up to her, she ventured, 'I'll get out at the pub and walk back to the cottage if that helps? Sounds like you have something urgent to deal with.'

But without even looking at her he replied, 'Thank you,' and parked in the pub car park, leaving her to return to the cottage with nothing more than a *goodbye*.

Later in the afternoon, Poppy arrived back with breaking news of how Will had put his arm around her shoulders in the DIY store and then, in the car park, they'd had their first kiss. She told Jess it had sent what felt like an electric current through her body and that she couldn't wait for the next intimate moment.

Jess smiled at her best friend and then said teasingly, 'And what about the tiles?'

Poppy rolled her eyes, 'Yes and they're lovely as well! Oh and I nearly forgot, I've been trying to phone you as we were thinking we could all do something together tonight, that is if Alex isn't working?'

Jess put her hand to her pocket and realised her phone wasn't there. 'I know I had it in the van as I looked at it on the drive back to the pub, it must have slipped out of my pocket. I'll pop back there now and retrieve it and I can ask Alex about tonight at the same time.'

She didn't want to mention to Poppy about the phone call Alex had taken as she didn't even know what it was about herself. And in any case it was probably something and nothing.

Poppy picked up her bag and with her usual sharp wit said, 'I'll tag along with you then and not for the ride either!'

At the pub Jess had a look around but quickly realised that Alex was nowhere to be seen. Walking towards the bar she saw Velvet carefully drying glasses, holding each one up to the light before polishing methodically again.

'Hi V, nice to see you again. Is Alex around please? I think my phone must have dropped out in his van this morning.'

She noticed that Velvet looked a little flustered. 'Jess. Hi. Um, Alex is upstairs actually and he said to only disturb him if it's something urgent.' She gave a half smile and then rolling her eyes added, 'I'm never really sure what constitutes urgent to be honest.'

Jess smiled reassuringly at her. 'Well I guess it's not exactly urgent, but I can't ring him as I haven't got my phone and in any case his number is in the contacts list on my phone, the same phone that I haven't got, if that makes sense? It's all very well having your whole life on your phone, but when you mislay it, it's nothing short of a disaster!'

Velvet laughed and Jess could see that she seemed relieved at her response.

'Will will have his number,' Poppy suddenly piped up.

'Ah yes of course. Quick thinking as usual Poppy. We can ask Will to try him a bit later,' Jess said.

'Always happy to be of service,' Poppy replied smiling.

'By the way,' Jess said looking at Velvet. 'This is Poppy, my best friend and clearly the brains of the outfit. Poppy, this is Velvet who likes to be known as *V*.'

The pair exchanged pleasantries and then Velvet introduced them to the new person behind the bar, who had been busy emptying the glass washer, ready for the 'polisher'.

'Jess and Poppy, this is Sandra.'

She was a middle-aged, well-rounded woman with short brown hair and the sort of face that made you instantly warm to her. She smiled broadly and held an extended arm to both of them across the bar.

'Alex was advertising for a kitchen person, but as I have previous bar experience I'm going to be doing a bit of both depending on how busy things are, which actually suits me really well.'

And it will suit the pub really well too, Jess thought, nodding and smiling in Sandra's direction.

'Are you having a drink ladies?' Sandra asked.

'No I think we'll get off thanks,' Jess said. But just as they were about to leave, they heard voices coming from the back of the pub and a woman appeared in the bar area, closely followed by Alex.

'Who's that?' Poppy whispered to Jess, who was standing stock still and looking in the direction of Alex and the mystery woman.

'I have absolutely no idea,' Jess whispered back. 'But I intend on finding out!'

The woman was probably in her early forties, slim, of medium height, and had the most incredible plum coloured hair which lay perfectly around her shoulders. Her make-up was quite heavy for the daytime, Jess observed, but nevertheless she looked extremely stylish in knee length boots and a tightly belted leather jacket edged with sheepskin. *Bet she wears matching underwear as well*, Jess thought to herself.

'Jess…and Poppy as well…um… what are you doing here?' Alex stuttered. His eyes were wide as he looked from Jess to the mystery woman and then back at her, in what she could tell was an obviously uncomfortable manner.

'I think I may have dropped my phone in the van,' she replied calmly. 'We were just leaving actually and I was going to ask Will to call you later when you were…' she trailed off and then looking at the woman standing next to him added, 'When you were less busy.'

He didn't reply but instead walked towards the door with the woman and during a brief exchange in whispered tones, Jess was sure she'd heard him say, 'See you soon'.

He returned to the bar and without even a mention of the awkward situation that had just ensued, smiled brightly at Jess and said, 'Right let's look for that phone then.'

Poppy shot Jess a look of surprise but neither said a word as they followed him out to the car park, where sure enough the phone was sitting on the passenger seat of the van.

Jess took a deep breath and thanking him, linked arms with Poppy and said, 'Let's go and get a cup of tea in the tea rooms. Bye Alex.'

Without looking back, the girls left and walked purposefully across the village green in the direction of the tea rooms.

'Bugger,' Jess said when they arrived at the door. 'It's all very well acting as if you don't give a damn, but if I ever suggest walking across a wet and boggy grassy area again Poppy, please slap me!'

Poppy laughed. 'Well let's just hope they have chocolate cake, as that is what is needed in emergency situations like this.'

The tea rooms were delightfully quaint with distressed furniture pieces, all painted in a delicate dove grey. The different sized tables were covered with pretty tablecloths depicting cupcakes that looked good enough to eat, and the chairs were dressed with large hessian bows. The tea cups, tea pots and plates were cleverly mismatched and the array of cakes looked absolutely gorgeous.

But even the thought of a large slice of cake couldn't lift Jess's mood. Not even chocolate cake. Poppy ordered her a piece anyway, saying they could always ask for a doggy bag if she couldn't face it.

What she really needed right now was to find out who the woman was with the amazing plum coloured hair. Why was she upstairs with Alex? And why was he going to see her again soon? She was just about to ask Poppy what she made of the situation, when the door to the tea room opened and Alex walked in.

Poppy immediately made a less than subtle excuse to leave and Jess mouthed, 'Thank you,' to her as she headed for the door.

'Can I sit down?' Alex asked.

Jess noticed his furrowed brow and how the corners of his mouth were unusually turned down. 'Of course,' she replied. And although she tried to smile at him, she could feel her stomach churning. And it was not in its usual excited flip floppy way. It was more like a washing machine churn.

He looked up from the tea that she had poured for him and then giving her what seemed like an apologetic look said, 'I need to explain about just now Jess. It's really important to me.'

Her eyes narrowed and she tried to steady her voice mentally before saying, 'It's really important to me too Alex. I must admit I feel a bit confused.'

He nodded. 'I know. I'm sorry.'

She felt herself relax a little. He was going to explain. He was sorry. It would all be fine.

He looked across the table at her and taking a deep breath in said, 'The person you saw me with in the pub just now is Angela and that was who phoned me when we were at the pet store.'

Jess said nothing, but kept her eyes firmly fixed on his face.

'She's... well, she's my wife,' he said. 'But......'

She gasped and shuffled uncomfortably in her seat. She swallowed hard before interrupting with, 'Your wife! Well I didn't see that one coming. And you said she *is* your wife. Not *was*?' She was surprised at how calm and steady her voice sounded. She'd even tried to make light of the situation, although she wasn't quite sure why. But inside she felt anything but calm. In fact, she felt a bit sick. She hadn't wanted to appear hysterical or over dramatic as (a) They hadn't known each other very long and (b) He'd never actually said he *didn't* have a wife. *On second thoughts,* she told herself, *scrap point b, as it was quite an important thing not to have mentioned.* Perhaps it would have been better if she had been hysterical.

'I know and I'm sorry. I should have told you but although she is legally my wife, we will actually be divorced fairly soon. She's a complex person and I only really see her or speak to her when there's problems. It's a complicated situation.'

Jess shook her head as she tried to make sense of what he was saying. She picked up her tea cup, but realising her hands were shaking, put it back down in the saucer and clasped her hands together.

Alex cleared his throat. 'And that's only part of the story I'm afraid. You see Jazz is my step daughter which is why I contacted Angela after you told me she was working in a shop in town, and not making a very good job of it. I'd left her a message saying I needed to speak to her. She returned my call while we were in the car park of the pet store, telling me she was on her way to the pub.'

The pair sat in silence for a few minutes before he said, 'Please say something Jess, even if it's just 'F off' or throw your cake at me or anything really.'

She took a few deep breaths in an effort to slow her pounding heart and then looking at him said, 'We hardly know each other Alex, we've literally just met, you don't need to explain yourself to me.' But although the words that came out of her mouth sounded grown up and pragmatic, the real words spinning around her head were a crazy mix of fear, confusion and empathy, sprinkled with a dash of hope and expectation.

He fidgeted in his seat and wringing his hands leant towards her. 'I really like you Jess and although, as you say, we hardly know each other, I do want to get to know you. I wouldn't do anything to risk that not happening. I would have told you about Angela and Jazz when the time was right. I promise I would have.'

Jess considered his words carefully and looking at his face she could see it was etched with worry and concern, clearly some of it was for her but also it was likely that some of it was for other two women, and this was to be admired.

Her face softened and holding out a hand across the table said, 'I believe you Alex. And just for the record the feelings you mentioned are mutual.'

He took her hand and suddenly his face relaxed and the now familiar grin returned. 'I'm a lucky man. I know that. And I hope we can continue this 'getting to know each other' stuff a bit later today.'

The relief was palpable and although she wasn't entirely sure who was creating the relief-filled atmosphere, she was pretty sure it was both of them.

She smiled, 'Oh yes that reminds me, I was supposed to ask you if you wanted to do something with Will and Poppy this evening.'

'In the circumstances I think it would be good for us to have some time alone. What do you think?' he asked.

'I agree,' she replied. 'Tell you what then, why don't we all have supper at the cottage, after all we have a very large dish of pasta waiting for us, and I can forewarn Poppy that they need to make themselves scarce once we've finished?'

'Brilliant plan,' he said smiling with relief, and then putting his hand in his pocket handed her a tiny box.

'I nearly forgot something as well. Something very important,' he said suddenly looking very serious.

Jess took the box from him. 'Oh, what's this?' she asked.

'Open it and you will see' he replied.

Opening the box, she could hardly contain her delight at what she saw. Because sitting on the plush velvet cushion was a single Rolo.

'It was the last one in the packet. And you know how the saying goes...' he said trailing off.

'Yes Alex, I know how the saying goes,' she answered as a single tear rolled down her cheek. 'Chocolate is my specialist subject, remember? And what's more this particular last Rolo has made me very happy,' she said.

Back at No. 3 Jess retold Alex's story about Angela and Jazz to Poppy who sat quietly throughout.

'Remember Jess, we are strong, independent women. We don't need men to make our lives complete.'

She laughed and said, 'I know that Poppy. Well, in your case more than mine. But I believe him and I really like him. And besides, he's just given me his last Rolo so I feel it's only right that I give him a chance!'

Poppy smiled. 'Well that's true I guess, especially when viewing it through your chocolate-tinted spectacles.'

Jess laughed. 'Oh yes and another thing. You're not exactly practising what you preach Poppy!' she said laughing.

'True again,' Poppy replied, laughing herself now. 'I do hope though that Will hasn't got any skeletons in his closet, not ones that come out anyway!'

Later that evening, the four friends sat down for supper together at No. 3. All agreed the prawn linguine was a triumph and that everybody needed 'a Rosa' living next door to them. Alex had brought a bottle of wine from the pub and even though Jess didn't normally drink wine, she felt she may need some Dutch courage for when Poppy and Will had gone.

'Did Rosa make a dessert?' Will asked.

'Unfortunately not,' Jess replied. 'But don't worry, I have something that, in my opinion, is even better!'

Poppy rolled her eyes as Jess returned from the kitchen and put a large block of milk chocolate on the table.

'You're very honoured,' Poppy said looking at Will. 'She doesn't normally like to share her number one love!'

Jess smiled and as she broke a few squares off the bar, she realised that chocolate may just have some competition.

With supper finished and the dishes cleared away, Poppy and Will made a perfectly executed departure, with Poppy winking encouragingly at Jess before pulling the door closed behind her.

Alex was sitting on the sofa now and he took Jess's hand as she sat down next to him.

'I just want to say sorry again for the awkward situation in the pub with Angela,' he said.

'I know Alex. And it's okay. Really it is,' she replied, squeezing his hand gently.

He sat forward and poured them both a glass of wine. She watched as he took a large mouthful of the drink before beginning to explain that he and Angela had been married for five years and separated for about two. He told her that Jazz had been about nine years old when they first met and that they'd always had a good relationship, but after he and Angela had separated, Jazz had rebelled and blamed her mother for everything, including failing all her school exams. When she turned eighteen, Angela had asked if he would consider giving her a job in the pub, as she was drifting from one job to another and in need of guidance. He looked at Jess and sighed. 'And the rest you know,' he said with a grimace.

The pair sat in silence for a few seconds before Jess said, 'I think it's my turn to apologise now. Had I even had an *inkling* of any of this, I obviously wouldn't have made that comment about Jazz's customer service skills. Not very tactful in the circumstances.'

Alex shook his head. 'You have nothing to apologise for. You had no idea about any of this and with hindsight I really wish I'd told you before.'

Jess smiled reassuringly at him and then, and completely out of character, she leaned towards him and kissed him tenderly on the lips. In return, he cupped her face gently in his hands and kissed her back in the most exquisitely gentle way imaginable. Then he slipped an arm around her shoulders, allowing her to lay her head on his chest and it seemed the most natural thing in the world.

CHAPTER FIFTEEN

Sunday morning Jess was up and about early and she felt a definite spring in her step. Alex had left just before eleven o'clock the previous evening to close up the pub, but there was no intention, certainly not on her part, for anything different to have happened.

She switched on the kettle and opened the back door just in case Tigger and family came calling, but although she was desperate to see them all, she was also concerned that they may come when she was back in London and the cottage was empty. She didn't want them to feel abandoned, so although she felt an element of disappointment, she also felt a little relieved at their non-appearance.

Perhaps she had some sort of abandonment issues herself connected to her father's desertion, but dismissed the thought immediately as being ridiculous and climbed the stairs with a cup of tea for Poppy.

But to her surprise the spare room was empty and the bed didn't look as if it had been slept in. She hadn't expected it, although she wasn't quite sure why not. They were, after all, two consenting adults who were perfectly at liberty to make their own decisions. And they certainly seemed very keen on each other. But it wasn't really Poppy's style. She was much more reserved normally.

Back in the kitchen she heard a key turning in the front door and went into the hallway to meet her friend.

'Poppy! Thank goodness! Where on earth have you been? I've been so worried about you, I've just phoned the police to report you....' but before she could finish the sentence she broke into a fit of uncontrollable laughter, unable to keep a straight face any longer.

Poppy, whose face was initially a picture of confusion, smiled with relief at Jess's laughter, before scolding her and poking her gently in the ribs.

'Jessica Jones you're embarrassing me,' she said laughing now. 'And I only did it for you as you'd warned me to make myself scarce,' she added.

'Oh right,' Jess said, gasping for breath, as she desperately tried to extinguish the fit of giggling that had become all-consuming. 'You only did it for me! Now stop fibbing and tell me all,' she added as she led her friend to the table. She placed a cup of tea in front of her and said, 'Now spill. And I don't mean the tea! I want to know everything, every last detail. Well perhaps not quite everything thinking about it!'

Poppy laughed. 'It's really not what you think. We had a lovely evening. We watched a film and then we fell asleep on the sofa. Will woke me around three, but I didn't want to come back here as I thought I might frighten the life out of you, creeping around in the middle of the night! So we cuddled up again on the sofa and that's all. That's it. Every last detail! And now I need a shower as Will's bathroom isn't exactly in a finished state,' she said pulling a face. 'Oh yes and I should also say that it was absolutely heavenly - sleeping with Will I mean,' she added with a wink.

As Poppy disappeared upstairs, Jess's phone beeped and she smiled at the sight of a text message from Marcus. *Safe journey back to London Jess*, it read. *Look forward to our Skype date on Tuesday.*

'On God. The choir solo!' she exclaimed in horror. 'I still haven't done any practice. Poppy quick, you need to come back downstairs immediately.'

'Right, don't panic. Why don't you warm up your voice now and give me a quick rendition,' she said enthusiastically?

'Okay. Right. Good plan,' Jess replied with a weak smile. She began warming up and then sang the first verse of The First Noel.

'Wow, Jess. I'd forgotten how fantastic you are,' Poppy exclaimed. 'You will blow them away. Now sing a bit more for me, it sounds so amazing.'

Jess breathed a sigh of relief and sang another couple of verses for her friend, who clapped enthusiastically at the end. She took a mock bow and then looking at Poppy said, 'Can I ask you a really serious and important question?'

'Of course. Anything at all,' she replied, her face suddenly straightening.

'Was the singing good enough to warrant a couple of squares of chocolate?'

'It was good enough for the whole blooming bar,' Poppy replied laughing and disappeared into the kitchen to fetch the bar from the fridge.

In the afternoon Poppy disappeared to say goodbye to Will and Jess took the opportunity to return the pasta bowl to Rosa.

'The pasta was fantastic Rosa but most importantly *you* have been fantastic. I don't know what I would have done without you over the past few weeks - well months actually.'

Rosa hugged her tightly. 'I will miss you so much my darling but I know you will be back soon as there's someone here you will want to see I think.'

Jess gave her a knowing nod and hugging her back said, 'You're a very wise woman Rosa.'

'Yes I am darling. I know how much you love that ginger cat!'

Jess wasn't entirely sure whether it was a tongue in cheek comment or not, but it didn't matter to her at all, she loved Rosa for all her funny sayings and foibles but most of all she loved her for being her guardian angel.

After leaving Rosa's cottage Jess walked up the lane to the pub to say goodbye to Alex. His face lit up as she walked towards the bar, and sitting together at her favourite table he took her hand and said, 'I'm going to miss you Jess Jones. When will I see you again?'

She laughed at the obvious song cue and began to sing a few lines. But she couldn't have anticipated what was to happen next as, to her surprise, Alex joined in and he was good. Really good.

A couple sitting on a nearby table began clapping and Jess blushed as she remembered that they were in a very public place with an audience, thankfully though an appreciative one.

'Alex Blake, you dark horse. I'm going to tell Marcus about you and then you will have to join the choir as well!' she said teasingly.

'Not a chance,' he replied laughing. 'Have you forgotten I have a busy time coming up, what with being an expectant father and all.'

She pulled a face, 'I think that's stretching it a bit, but yes you are going to be busy that's for sure.'

'I'm hoping *we* are going to be busy,' he said smiling.

She noticed his cheeks redden and he quickly changed the subject.

'Anyway, fatherhood aside, I've never really liked singing but I've always wanted to learn to play the guitar, so you never know one day we could do a duet.'

She rolled her eyes in an exaggerated fashion. 'That could be fun, but getting back to where this conversation began, my days off this week are Friday and Saturday and then I'm on a night shift on Sunday. So I could, if you wanted me to, come on Friday morning and stay until Sunday lunchtime?' She looked at him expectantly and felt a sudden rush of shyness, but was relieved to see he was grinning now from ear to ear.

'I'll be counting the days,' he said.

And with her growing self-confidence she replied, 'I would have hoped you'd be counting the *minutes*, but I'll take days for now anyway.'

He smiled. 'And now, I'm afraid, I need to get back behind the bar before Velvet sacks me,' he joked. And then, he brushed her cheek with the back of his fingers and gently stroking her hair added, 'I'm counting the seconds already.'

CHAPTER SIXTEEN

Later that afternoon, Jess and Poppy arrived back at their London home to be greeted by a very excited Dave. On hearing their voices he shrieked, 'Hello, hello, there's somebody at the door,' and added in several shrill wolf whistles for good measure.

'Hello Dave,' Jess said laughing. 'I've missed you.'

He was ruffling his feathers so frantically that Poppy said she was worried he was going to 'fall off his perch', so she opened the door and let him out.

Jess put her bags down and gave a deep sigh. 'Back to reality I guess,' she said, with a look of resignation.

'Same,' Poppy replied simply.

Minutes later Amber arrived home and, grabbing hold of Jess, hugged her tightly. 'I've missed you. It's way too quiet around here without you.'

Dave hopped onto Poppy's shoulder, squawking loudly and Amber added, 'Well apart from his Lordship of course.'

As Amber let go of her grip, there was a loud familiar knock on the door and she went to let James, her boyfriend, in.

'Hello you guys, welcome back,' he said smiling.

'Never mind the pleasantries,' Amber interrupted. 'Did you remember my hair dryer?' Then looking at the other two girls and pointing to her hair said, 'He's had it in his flat since we got back from holiday which is why my hair looks like this.'

'Oops!' James replied with a sheepish grin. 'I've forgotten it again.'

Amber turned to him and pulled a face. 'James you thick head!'

Dave bobbed up and down on Poppy's shoulder and shrilled, 'Dick head, Dick Head!'

'Of course. 'Thick Head', that's what Dave was trying to call me. It wasn't 'Dick Head' after all. I knew he would never have called me something like that!' Poppy said, stroking the excited bird who was still perched on her shoulder.

Jess laughed and explained what had happened to Amber and James.

'Oh dear. Sorry about that Poppy. It's my pet name for James and to be honest I don't normally use it in earshot of others, well not *people* anyway. Even though it's a term of endearment it could be construed incorrectly,' she said with a half grimace.

'Oh yes, and I call Amber 'My Precious', James announced proudly. 'It's a play on words, you know what with her name and all that.'

'And he does a very good Gollum impression when he says it,' Amber added, smiling lovingly at James. 'You know from Lord of the Rings.'

Jess shook her head at the bizarreness of the whole conversation that had just ensued. 'You two, honestly, you're completely bonkers,' she said laughing.

She watched as James winked at Amber and then disappeared into the kitchen. He returned moments later with a bottle of Champagne and four heavy china mugs.

'Blimey this is an unexpected welcome home!' Jess said with a look of surprise. But she already knew by the look on Amber's face and by the way she was practically jumping up and down now, that the champagne was not in her honour.

'Ta dah,' Amber yelled at the top of her voice as she revealed a dazzling diamond engagement ring. 'James asked me on holiday,' she said excitedly. 'Didn't you James?'

He nodded and grinned but Amber continued without waiting for him to speak, 'And I want you two lovelies to be my bridesmaids!'

Jess and Poppy both screamed in unison with excitement, which in turn made Dave hop off Poppy's shoulder and hop deftly back into the safety of his cage.

James half filled the mugs with champagne and Jess said, 'Please raise your mugs to the future Mr and Mrs...err...actually James I don't even know your surname!'

'Oh, thinking about it neither do I!' Poppy said, looking apologetically at James and Amber.

'That's shocking,' James replied with mock horror. 'Anyway, it's Stone,' and then pulling a face added, 'Which is going to make poor Amber the butt of a few jokes.'

Amber opened her mouth to respond but before she could, Jess gasped and said, 'Oh yes! Amber Stone! Well it could be worse I guess. Imagine if your first name really *was* Precious, that would make you Precious Stone!'

'Well I think it has a nice *ring* to it anyway. Amber Stone I mean, not Precious Stone,' Poppy said, emphasising the word ring and they all fell into fits of giggles, ably assisted by the champagne.

'Okay okay, that's enough of the name jokes,' James said. 'Poor Amber, I think she's a little bored with that joke. My real surname is Smith, not Stone. I just couldn't resist the Amber Stone gag, especially in the circumstances!'

Amber gave him a playful cuff round the ear, and James grinned sheepishly as he pulled her towards him and kissed her on the cheek.

'I actually rather like Amber Stone but then again amber is not actually a precious stone, it's a tree resin which takes millions of years to form, so basically that makes it very special, just like me!'

Dave began bobbing up and down frantically again, before dropping his head and squinting in the direction of James squawked, 'Dick head!'

'That bird needs speech therapy,' Amber said, taking another large swig of champagne. 'That's my intended you're dissing, you bird-brain!'

Jess smiled to herself as it dawned on her that in some ways it felt good to be home and back to the chaos of her normal life.

CHAPTER SEVENTEEN

Next morning, Jess travelled to work with Amber, and before going onto the ward she sent a quick text to Poppy wishing her luck for her first day on jury duty.

Poppy replied immediately with, *I'm nervous, no actually I'm terrified!!!*

Jess sent a quick text back reassuring her she would be fine and then popped her phone in her locker as per Sister's rules.

Back in the familiar surroundings of the hospital ward, Annie was the first patient Jess saw and she smiled at her as she called out, 'Jess, you're back! I've been looking out for you every day.'

She was Annie's key worker, which meant she was responsible for overseeing her care and this was a part of the role she loved. Advocating for her patients was hugely important to her and once, when one of the doctors had called Annie a 'bed blocker', she had leapt to her defence reminding him that (a) Annie was a human being and not an inanimate object and (b) It was not her choice to be languishing in a hospital bed. To his credit he had nodded his acceptance of her comments and from that day on the pair had developed an increased mutual respect for each other.

'Morning Annie,' she said, taking the elderly woman's hands in hers. 'Any news?'

Annie needed a complex package of care to be able to return

home and so far it had proved incredibly difficult to arrange.

Annie shook her head and Jess could see the sadness in her eyes.

'Once we've had the nursing handover and I've done my medication rounds, I will catch up on what's been going on and we can have a chat,' she said, squeezing her hands reassuringly.

She joined the rest of the nursing team at the handover and thanked her colleagues for their messages following her accident.

Sister smiled at her and said, 'It's good to have you back Nurse Jones, particularly as Nurse Clements has her court appearance this week!'

Jess wasn't sure if that was one of her usual unmindful comments or whether it was an attempt at humour but, whichever it was, you could hear a pin drop in the room. This was the Greenwood Effect in all its glory Jess acknowledged.

Just before lunch, Jess sat at Annie's bedside and told her she may have some good news. 'It's not a hundred percent confirmed yet, but we may be able to get you home on Wednesday,' she said touching her arm. 'The rest of the team have been working hard to make it happen while I've been off.'

Annie beamed at her and replied, 'Just to have that little bit of hope is wonderful, but I understand it's not always within your control my dear.'

Jess nodded, realising that despite her age and frailty she was a very perceptive woman. And even though she needed continuous oxygen and help with most activities of living, she still had a definite twinkle in her eye. She had a spark. A strong spirit.

'I'm going to do my very best Annie and let's both keep everything crossed as well, as a kind of extra insurance policy.'

Annie smiled again. 'If I can go home I will be so happy Jess, but do you know what? I'm going to miss you.'

Jess smiled and touching the elderly woman's arm said, 'And I will miss you too Annie. We all will.'

At lunchtime, Jess went to her locker to collect her phone. As she checked the screen, her heart sank. No messages. Not one single message. None. Nada. Zilch. Shoving the phone into her uniform pocket she headed for the staff canteen and bought two chocolate bars.

Now that is entirely your fault Alex Blake, she said to herself as she joined some of the other staff from the ward. She would never normally have bought two chocolate bars for lunch. One maybe, but definitely not two. Well okay, occasionally she would have done, but not as a rule.

Just as she started unwrapping the second chocolate bar, she heard her phone beep. Her heart skipped a beat as she fumbled amongst pens and tissues and pulled it out of her pocket. She held her breath as she checked the screen. Poppy. It was just Poppy. Then immediately felt guilty at the feeling of disappointment, as after all Poppy was her best friend. Whereas Alex, well he was a new arrival on the scene, albeit a very nice one.

She read the message from her friend, *It's not as glamorous as you might think. I haven't even made it into court yet and probably won't today by the looks of it!*

Jess tapped a reply which she hoped would cheer her up, *Sister reminded everyone that you were appearing in court today. She made it sound more like you were a criminal than a juror!!*

Poppy replied with a hilarious meme that made Jess laugh out loud, and then putting her phone back in her pocket she polished off the second chocolate bar, telling herself it was for therapeutic reasons.

It was a busy afternoon and Jess was an hour late finishing her shift, but in her eyes the satisfaction she felt compensated for the lateness. She was so lucky, she reminded herself, to have an amazing job that enabled her to go home after work knowing she'd made a difference to someone's life.

And with a feeling of fulfilment, she made her way to her locker and took some deep breaths as she opened the door and removed her phone from the top shelf. Feeling a wave of anticipation mixed with a sprinkling of trepidation, she peered at the screen through half closed eyes before letting out an excited squeal. Not *one* message from Alex, not *two* messages from him but *ten*, ten whole messages from her nearly Hugh Grant look-alike! She pumped the air with her fist before making her way through the hospital corridors, reading and re-reading each text with a big grin and a fast beating heart.

CHAPTER EIGHTEEN

At six o'clock on Tuesday evening, Jess logged onto her laptop in preparation for her Skype meeting with the choir. Poppy, Amber and Dave had been banished to the kitchen earlier on while she did a few scales and exercises to help warm up her voice, and then at exactly six twenty five Marcus was on line.

She stifled a giggle as Henry began shouting instructions to her as if he was trying to communicate directly without using the technology. And directly behind him, Nora was waving frantically whilst mouthing, *Hi Jess*. It looked like a scene from a comedy show rather than a rehearsal for a Christmas carol concert she thought.

But despite the initial chaos, the rehearsal went really well and at the end of it Poppy and Amber joined in with the congratulations on her solo part. And then, just before signing off, Marcus said he had a surprise for her. And what a surprise it was when Alex appeared on the screen having been in the church from the start, out of view but listening to proceedings.

Later in bed, Jess thought back on the last couple of days. They had been good, very good and she was able to close her eyes and fall into a restful sleep.

But the ups always seem to be followed by the downs, and the very next day she had to break the bad news to Annie that her planned discharge was on hold again.

'I'm not giving up easily,' she told her. 'We're very nearly there, just one piece of the jigsaw missing and I'm hoping that will be found by tomorrow.'

Annie, as always, was full of praise and thanks, and Jess was always humbled at how grateful and gracious people were even when things were not going according to plan. She felt like screaming herself so goodness knows how Annie was really feeling.

Before her shift finished, she let Annie know that she was on a late shift the following day but that she'd asked another member of the nursing team, Kitty, to follow up on the discharge in the morning.

'So fingers crossed and if you've gone before I come on shift, I wish you all the very best and enjoy your time at home.'

'Thank you Jess. I'll never forget you, well everyone, but especially you I mean,' and then she held both of her hands in the air showing Jess her tightly crossed fingers.

Back at home Jess switched on the kettle and changed out of her uniform. Poppy arrived home half an hour later saying she was now on a case but although she wasn't allowed to talk about it she said it was a fascinating experience.

'So,' Jess teased. 'Sister was right then, Nurse Clements really has appeared in court!'

The pair were still giggling when Amber joined them in the kitchen, clutching a selection of wedding magazines and various wedding venue brochures.

'Right, you two are my right-hand men, so to speak and so this evening we are wedding planning,' she announced.

'How exciting,' Jess replied. 'Let's get lots of snacks and some drinks and have a girls' night in.'

She grabbed her coat and told the other two girls she would go to the shops for essential supplies and laughed as Poppy called after her, 'Don't forget the healthy stuff!'

She turned and rolled her eyes at her friend and before pulling the door closed behind her answered, 'Of course Poppy. Chocolate is already on the list!'

The evening had been fun, Jess reflected as she climbed into bed well after midnight. But what they had also discovered was that getting married was a serious business with so many things to consider that they now felt completely bewildered.

Eventually, Poppy had suggested that it might be better to organise one thing at a time, perhaps starting with the venue which might then help set the scene for the rest of the day, and Jess had tactfully suggested that James might like to be included in the planning. Amber had laughed and said he would be much happier for her to do all the background work first and joked that he was a man after all!

Next morning, Jess didn't wake until ten o'clock and immediately checked her phone. She smiled at a, *Good morning* text message from Alex and tapped a reply which read, *Morning, can't wait until Friday* and then feeling unsure of herself changed it to, *Morning, looking forward to Friday* and pressed send before her habit of overthinking things took hold.

The house was quiet and on occasions she welcomed the peace, not often, just sometimes and this morning was of those times. She enjoyed a relaxed breakfast and then soaked in the bath for a good half an hour with no interruptions, apart from the odd squawk from Dave. Then after a quick scoot round with the hoover and a flick of the duster, she left for her late shift.

Arriving on the ward, she was delighted to see the empty bed space where Annie had resided for far too long. She smiled to herself and then finding Kitty and pointing to the empty space said, 'Well done Kits, we did it then!'

She noticed immediately that Kitty wasn't smiling back at her and, in fact, her face was etched with sadness.

Leading Jess into the nursing office she said, 'I'm so sorry Jess, it's not good news. Annie died suddenly during the night.'

Jess felt warm salty tears spring to her eyes as she rummaged in her pocket for a tissue. Kitty put a supportive arm around her waist and reminded her that they'd all done everything within their power to help Annie achieve her wish, and although Jess nodded, she felt suddenly overwhelmed with sadness at the injustice of the situation.

In the nursing handover, Sister shared the news of Annie's death to the team, as she always did with any patient who had died on the ward, and thanked everyone for their hard work and excellent care that had been provided to her.

'As Annie's key worker, would you like to add anything Nurse Jones?' she enquired kindly.

Jess took a deep breath and said, 'We failed her. It's as simple as that. She asked for nothing apart from being able to return home and we...actually I, failed her. And worse still I said to her that if she had gone when I came back on duty, that I wished her well. But I didn't mean that sort of *gone.*'

As she heard her own words, she realised they sounded melodramatic but nevertheless it was genuinely how she felt. At that moment she felt overwhelming sadness.

Sister looked directly at her and with a kind smile said, 'No Jess, *you* didn't fail her and neither did anyone else in the team. If anything, it was the *system* that failed her.'

Jess nodded and although she knew in her head that Sister was right, it didn't stop her heart from aching with sadness.

After handover, she helped Kitty prepare what had become

affectionately known as 'Annie's bed', for a new patient who was being transferred from Accident and Emergency.

Kitty, holding onto one side of the crisply starched sheet, looked across the bed and said, 'The wheels on the bus may have fallen off Jess but it still needs to keep moving.'

Jess gave her a half smile and said, 'I know Kitty and I promise I am now back in professional mode now.'

'You were never out of it Jess, you are the best nurse I know and I've learned so much from you. Don't ever stop being you.'

CHAPTER NINETEEN

On Friday morning Jess was up early and packing for her trip to Suffolk, she told herself that travelling light was not an option when you were in a new relationship, if indeed, that's what it was.

She carefully folded and shoe-horned more and more clothes into what was nothing more than an overnight bag, and then heard Poppy shout upstairs that she was leaving for court and that she'd be in Thripton first thing Saturday morning.

'Don't forget to bring the spare key for the cottage just in case I'm otherwise engaged,' Jess called back and then added, 'Although I'm sure you could find somewhere else to go if you did forget.' She heard Poppy laugh and then heard the front door close.

Realising she was not going to be able to squeeze anything else into the already bulging bag, she loaded Rowan ready for her trip and then sent Alex a quick text to say she was on her way.

A message came back almost immediately, *Call in at the pub first xx* and smiling with satisfaction she left the hustle and bustle of London once again, for the quiet of the countryside.

When she arrived at the pub Alex was standing in the car park.

'Everything okay?' she called through the open window of the car.

'Yes everything's fine. I was just..er...emptying the bins,' he replied. And then with a sheepish grin added, 'Actually that's not strictly true, if I'm honest I was hanging around the car park waiting for you!'

She felt a rush of happiness which seemed to envelope her whole body and in response she jumped out of the car and straight into his open arms. He hugged her tightly as if he never wanted to let her go and she realised then how good it felt to be loved again, well potentially at least.

After coffee at the pub, she headed to No. 3, knocking on Rosa's door first.

'Jess,' she shrieked with delight. 'I'm so happy to see you. Come in my darling, I have just taken a cake out of the oven!'

Following her into the kitchen, Jess looked around with a smile and remembered why Eleanor used to call it a 'proper' kitchen. There was kitchenalia everywhere and the open-fronted cupboards were brimming with food, crockery and pots and pans. And importantly, there always seemed to be a heavenly smell emanating from the oven making it almost impossible to say no to what was on offer.

Pointing to the cake, Rosa told her it was an apple sponge and any resolve Jess may have had about eating less 'naughty foods' quickly disappeared.

Rosa cut two slices of the gooey aromatic warm sponge and served it on pretty plates, handing Jess a tiny fork. She poured some coffee and they both sat at her little table in silence while they devoured the soft, sweet bake.

Putting her fork down on the now empty plate Rosa said, 'No sign of the Ginger Whingers I'm afraid!'

Jess, who still had a mouth full of cake, coughed and spluttered with laughter. 'Rosa, you are so funny,' she exclaimed. 'But *Ginger Whingers* is a bit harsh, they weren't really whinging, they were starving!'

'Starving, my eyes,' Rosa responded with a tut. 'You can bet that nearly every house in the village has been feeding them. And you know how the saying goes about love and cupboards? Well in my opinion cats love cupboards more than they love people, if you know what I mean.'

'I do Rosa, but I'm not sure I agree with you about the 'cupboard love' bit and also you used to feed Tigger with prawns so you're in no position to talk!'

They were both laughing now, but Jess at least felt somewhat reassured that her little cat family would be fine even if she wasn't going to be lucky enough to see them again.

Inside No. 3, Jess unpacked her bag and then texted Nora to tell her she was back in Thripton, and to pop round if she was at a loose end.

Within half an hour the doorbell rang and she was delighted to see her new friend with Mabel snuggled close to her, in what seemed to be the most complicated baby sling imaginable.

Nora stepped inside the hallway and started to unwrap the complex arrangement while Jess looked on in admiration. Mabel giggled and gurgled in the most endearing way and she wasn't surprised to feel a sudden rush of what she assumed must be maternal feelings.

She took the baby from her, holding her tightly to her chest and then removing her snowsuit, hat and mittens, breathed in the wonderfully intoxicating smell that all babies seemed to have. She sat down on the floor with her and noticed that she was wearing the cutest dungarees, over a beautifully embroidered top which Nora proudly announced she had made herself.

'What the whole outfit?' Jess exclaimed.

Nora laughed and replied, 'Well you needn't sound quite so surprised! My mum is a really good seamstress so she taught me from a very early age. I've made lots of her clothes and what I haven't made my mum probably has,' she added.

Jess smiled and squeezing her arm said, 'You're very talented Nora, surely you could make a living out of it?'

She nodded and agreed that maybe one day it was a possibility, but that she would need a bigger house with enough space for a dedicated, baby-free sewing room.

Jess laughed and tickling Mabel said, 'You would be a fantastic help wouldn't you gorgeous?' and in reply the baby giggled infectiously.

After Nora and Mabel had left, she sat down with pen and paper and started to make a plan for clearing the cottage in a more methodical way. Alex was working in the pub at lunchtime and in the evening but she was going to join him later on.

Deciding that she'd done enough planning, she showered and applied slightly heavier makeup than usual, hoping her look would transition seamlessly from daytime to evening (as per the lesson she had seen on daytime television. She knew it would come in useful for something, despite Rosa's warnings). And then, after her usual multiple outfit changes, she decided on a tartan mini skirt with thick black tights and a black skinny ribbed crew neck jumper. She was pleased that she was able to complete the outfit with heeled boots now her ankle swelling had completely disappeared, even if they weren't the killer heels that Poppy would have worn. She took a final look in the full length mirror and smiled with satisfaction as she opened the front door and made her way on foot to the pub, ever grateful for the lower heels.

As she opened the door to the pub, she felt her stomach flip and she paused to take some deep breaths to slow her quickening heartbeat.

Alex immediately came round from behind the bar and pulling her towards him, kissed her gently on the forehead.

She smiled up at him before removing her coat and on seeing her carefully chosen outfit he stepped back and said, 'Wow, you look amazing, just amazing.'

He signalled for her to sit at the bar on one of the high stools and added that by sitting there he would be able to look at her from all angles.

His eyes suddenly widened as he grimaced. 'I'm sorry, that kind of came out wrong. What I meant was that I'll be able to see you from anywhere in the pub, not…well you know…' he stuttered, whilst, at the same time, blushing a crimson colour.

'Actually, I was quite happy with you wanting to look at me from all angles,' she replied honestly and then suddenly feeling self-conscious, she looked down at the floor.

'That's great then. We're singing from the same hymn sheet,' he said with a tone of relief, and then lifting her chin, kissed her on the lips.

This was going to be a nice evening.

CHAPTER TWENTY

Poppy arrived next morning and Jess joked that she'd give it less than five minutes before Will arrived.

At the sound of the door bell ringing, Poppy looked at the kitchen clock and said, 'Wrong! It's actually been six minutes,' and the pair both began giggling uncontrollably.

'I think this might be euphoria or perhaps hysteria we're experiencing,' Jess said when she'd managed to stop herself laughing.

'Well if it is, then I think I rather like it,' Poppy replied, walking to the front door.

'Me too,' Jess agreed. 'So let's just make the most of it.'

'Make the most of what?' Will asked as he slipped off his shoes inside the hallway.

'Friendship,' Jess answered quickly. 'We should always make the most of friendship.'

Will shrugged. 'Sounds good to me, although I'm not really sure that men have friends like women do. We have mates. It's kind of different somehow.'

'Everybody needs friends Will, good friends I mean. Friends who are always there when you need them. Friends who become your family. Like Jess. She's my best friend. The sister I never had.'

'Okay this is all getting a bit deep for me now,' Will said.

'That's the whole point Will. Deep is the opposite to shallow.

Never forget that,' Poppy said.

'Right then, you two get off to wherever you're going,' Jess said in an effort to change the subject. After all they weren't even talking about friendship, it was just a ruse, but Poppy could be quite intense if you got her onto a subject she was passionate about.

Later that morning Alex picked Jess up in his van as he'd arranged with Marcus for them to go and see Rolo.

'He's huge!' Jess exclaimed sitting on the floor, while the puppy climbed all over her. 'And also very beautiful.'

He squeaked loudly in response to her gentle strokes and she joked that he sounded more like a guinea-pig than a puppy.

Marcus told them that all the puppies were now sold and that they were donating all the money to the church.

Jess smiled up at him from her sitting position and said, 'Marcus you are one of the kindest men I know.'

'Well they've turned out to be such an unexpected pleasure that we've come to think of them as a kind of gift from God,' he replied smiling. 'So it just seems right that we should give something back.'

Alex shook his hand warmly and patting him on the back said, 'You're a good man Marcus and thank you again for Rolo. I can't wait to get him home.'

CHAPTER TWENTY-ONE

The next few weeks flew by with lots of trips backwards and forwards between London and Thripton.

Rolo had arrived in his new home and had made his presence felt in more ways than one. He picked up everything, chewed most things and cried like a baby at night. But he was absolutely gorgeous. She loved him as much as Alex did and in return the ball of fluff loved them back, unconditionally. He was always so pleased to see them, he always brought them a little present; usually something they had inadvertently left lying around and his tail could wag for England. She now understood the phrase 'man's best friend'.

And then there was work, choir practice and house clearing, although the latter was definitely on the back burner Jess thought, as she looked around the cottage on Bonfire Night. It didn't really look a lot different from her first visit but it was now like her second home so it needed to be comfortable she regularly reminded herself, more in an effort to assuage her conscience than anything else.

She also had to remind herself that the cottage was a financial burden and realistically she needed to start thinking about putting it on the market with a view to a Spring completion, but she also knew that it was going to be very hard. The cottage whispered Eleanor's name from every corner and somehow it felt like she would be leaving her memory behind by selling it.

And then, of course, there was Alex. Lovely, kind, gentle Alex. Would it mean leaving him behind as well? There was so much to consider, but consider she must, and in the very near future.

That evening Alex had organised a Bonfire Night party at the pub. It was a clear, crisp evening and the stars twinkled brightly, helping to light the way on the short walk to the pub.

Jess had dressed warmly for the outside event and just before leaving the cottage had accepted that, on this occasion, being warm was more important than looking good and had pulled a beanie hat over her hair.

Alex was already outside in the pub garden when she arrived and he kissed her tenderly saying, 'You even look good in a woolly hat Jones.'

She smiled and kissed him back. 'Thank you, but I'm quite sure I don't,' she replied with a grimace. 'Where's Rolo? 'Do you think he'll be okay with the fireworks, I'm a bit worried about him?'

He nodded and laughing replied, 'He's upstairs in the kitchen but I think you may have misunderstood tonight. It's actually a non-firework Bonfire Night party. No fireworks at all, absolutely none, not even a sparkler! I hate the damn things and they cause so much distress to animals that I thought I'd buck the trend and do something different. We have a bonfire, lots of lovely Bonfire Night themed food and drink, and some crazy games.'

She looked at him with admiration and then thought perhaps she should pinch herself to make sure all this was real, because sometimes it seemed like it was too good to be true. But instead she simply said, 'That's fantastic Alex. A silent firework party, amazing. But I'll just pop up and check on him if that's okay, even though I haven't really got a good excuse now!'

'Good idea,' he replied. 'And would you mind popping him to the yard for a toilet break while you're at it?'

She prodded him fondly in the ribs and in return he pulled her beanie hat down over her eyes. They were both laughing now and as she walked towards the front door of the pub she pinched herself anyway, just to be sure.

The evening was a huge success. It seemed as if the whole village had turned out, as well as lots of people from Barrowick. Everybody joined in with 'Pin the tail on Guy Fawkes' and 'Hunt the Marshmallows', which entailed dipping your whole face in an enormous bowl of flour to search them out.

Nora and Josh had brought Mabel for a short while, all tucked up in her buggy and Jess's heart melted to see them all together, a vision of a blissfully happy little family.

Poppy and Will popped in for a while on their way into town for a 'posh meal' and Poppy had giggled and whispered to Jess not to wait up for her.

Long after midnight when the pub was once again looking clean and tidy, Alex put an arm around Jess's shoulders and moving his face close to hers so she could feel his warm breath on her face said, 'Stay tonight.'

She realised it didn't need an answer and also knew it was exactly what she wanted, so taking hold of his hand she happily followed him upstairs.

Next morning she woke up to the distant sound of the church bells that she'd come to love. She rolled over and put an outstretched arm to Alex's side of the bed but quickly realised he was no longer there.

Sitting bolt upright, she looked around the room for something to cover her modesty but realising that there was nothing within easy reach, she flopped back onto the pillows, covering her eyes and groaning loudly.

Moments later there was a gentle tap on the door and in walked

Alex carrying a tray of tea and toast, followed closely by Rolo who, try as he might, was unable to scramble onto the bed.

She laughed, but suddenly feeling shy again, pulled the duvet up towards her shoulders.

'Morning gorgeous,' he said, planting a kiss on her head and then passed her a towelling robe confirming to her that he was not only kind and funny and handsome and clever, but perceptive as well. This really was too good to be true she told herself. More pinching was needed.

After breakfast, Jess walked back to the cottage and wasn't surprised to find that it was empty. She sent Poppy a text message to say she was leaving at two o'clock as she was on a night shift, and then went upstairs to pack her bags.

On her way out of the village she made an unscheduled stop at the pub and breathed a sigh of relief when Alex practically ran from behind the bar and swept her up into his arms.

'I've missed you,' he declared and she beamed at him whilst relishing in the warm fuzzy feeling that had swept over her.

'I've only been gone for a couple of hours,' she replied laughing.

And then with a deadly serious look on his face he said 'Seven thousand, two hundred and three seconds to be precise.'

Back in London she reflected on how her life and life in the shared house had changed quite dramatically over such a short period of time. She and Poppy were like ships that passed in the night, with both of them spending the majority of their mostly different days off in Thripton, and Amber who was entirely immersed in wedding planning had seemed oblivious to their absence.

She'd even noticed that Dave seemed to have picked up on the changes as he had become noticeably less talkative, which although at times was a positive, she didn't like to think of him being unhappy.

'I think you need cheering up,' she told Dave. 'I'll speak to Poppy.' The bird lowered his head and peered at her, but made no response.

The following week Jess's days off fell on a Tuesday and Wednesday and she was pleased to be able to tell Marcus that she would be at choir practice in person.

Alex had joined her, sitting quietly at the back of the church and again was full of praise for her performance. The concert was really coming together now and she was looking forward to the actual event.

Sister had kindly agreed that both she and Poppy could have their days off together for the weekend of the concert, even saying she might attend herself. Jess had pulled a face in Poppy's direction as she really couldn't afford for the Greenwood Effect to strike during her solo, but then in true 'Greenwood style' Sister had added that she would probably have to work as two of her key staff would be off.

Jess had breathed a sigh of relief, managing she'd hoped, to disguise it as cough and Poppy as sharp as ever skilfully changed the subject.

CHAPTER TWENTY-TWO

Towards the end of November, Jess arranged for an estate agent to come and value the cottage with a view to putting it on the market. That morning it had chosen to pour with rain and the heavy skies made the cottage look a little dark inside.

She hoovered and tidied, switched on all the lights and lit some candles. She wasn't quite sure why she felt so anxious as the estate agent wasn't going to buy the cottage himself, but she guessed it was because she wanted him to see it for what it was - a beautifully styled, characterful cottage that had been loved and cherished. Eleanor's cottage.

At eleven o'clock the doorbell chimed and Jess opened the door to Jamie, the estate agent, who to her surprise was a 'she' rather than a 'he' as she had been expecting.

'Oh!' She exclaimed. 'I was expecting a man...sorry...that's what assumptions do I guess.'

The smartly dressed woman smiled and replied, 'Please don't worry, this name has been the bane of my life. And it gets worse,' she said holding out a business card. She rolled her eyes before adding, 'I'm Jamie James. Pleased to meet you and thank you for inviting me to value your home today and to give you an overview of the current market.'

Jess immediately felt at ease in her company. 'Please come in Jamie, would you like some coffee?'

While she put the coffee on, the estate agent walked around each room making notes on a 'tablet' and asking lots of questions.

Back in the sitting room she smiled at Jess and commented, 'It's lovely, absolutely beautiful and I'm sure we will have a lot of interest if we market it at the right price.'

Jess was surprised at her sudden feeling of disappointment, not at the comments but at the fact that it may sell so easily. She needed to sell it, she knew that, but it was Eleanor's and now it was hers; emotionally hers, and that was the hardest part.

Jamie discussed various options with her, and then with no pressure at all, left her to consider her next move, saying she would phone in a couple of days' time. Jess was grateful for her seeming sensitivity and was glad she had turned out to be female.

Later that day she relayed the details of the estate agent's visit to Alex who nodded in a supportive way, touching her arm gently when her voice began cracking with emotion.

'Perhaps you should wait until after Christmas to put it on the market?' he suggested before adding, 'New Year, new start and all that?'

'Maybe,' she replied. 'In any case, I guess I could start gathering the necessary papers together in preparation. I've never sold a house before but knowing how organised my mum was I'm hoping everything will be easy to find.'

He put a protective arm around her shoulders and nestling her head into his chest she could feel the comforting rhythm of his heartbeat making her feel safe and loved.

'Let's go for a walk,' he suggested. 'Be good to get some fresh air and it'll help clear your head.'

'Lovely idea,' she agreed. 'And it's even stopped raining just for us.' How was it that he always seemed to know what to say?

They walked hand in hand across the fields towards Barrowick and Alex said he couldn't wait until Rolo was big enough to go for a 'proper' walk.

Jess nodded in agreement, 'How is he getting on with his lead practice?'

He put his free hand over his eyes and with a despairing look on his face replied, 'Absolutely hopeless. He's practically chewed through it already!'

That evening the pair sat upstairs in Alex's lounge with a pint of beer from downstairs and a selection of nibbles.

'Talking about Christmas...' Alex ventured.

'Were we?' Jess interrupted, raising her eyebrows.

'Well I know it's a bit of a tenuous link but I mentioned it earlier when we were talking about you putting the cottage up for sale,' he replied.

She laughed. 'Okay, I'll give you that one. Do continue,' she said teasingly.

'Well it was just about your plans really. I would love us to spend Christmas together, unless you have other plans of course?'

Jess smiled and replied, 'This will be my first Christmas without my mum so I think it would be lovely to spend it with someone who cares about me and also to be in Thripton. Unfortunately, though, I'm working Christmas Day.'

'Snap,' he replied, pulling a face. 'So perhaps we could make Boxing Day our Christmas Day? And just for the record, I more than care for you Jess, I'm falling in love with you.'

He loves me. He said he loves me. Well he actually said he's 'falling in love' with me but it's the same difference surely?

And suddenly she felt deliriously happy and despite the ringing bells and singing bird sounds that had filled her head, she managed to murmur, 'And I'm falling in love with you too Alex.'

After a few seconds of silence, he grinned and said, 'I can stop holding my breath now then! And are we good for Boxing Day?'

'We're more than good. We're...we're...fantastic!'

Next morning Jess received a text message from Poppy to say that she was on her way to Thripton with Dave in tow. *I'll explain all when I get there xx* the message read.

After a leisurely breakfast with Alex, she headed back to No. 3 and shortly afterwards heard the sound of Poppy's car trundling down the lane.

Will was already waiting at the top of his path for her and when Jess joined him, he laughed and said they looked like a guard of honour.

Poppy climbed out of the car and hugged them both, beaming from ear to ear. Jess was pleased to see that Dave was now dancing up and down on his perch and wolf whistling loudly. She laughed and said, 'He seems chirpier!'

Poppy groaned. 'That's a *cheep* pun,' she said. 'But yes, he seems very excited to be back in Thripton. He's going to be staying with Will for a while. I'm pretty sure you were right when you said about him being lonely at home, so we're going to see how he is at Will's as, let's face it, I am here as much as I am in London and Will's going to be working from home two days a week.'

Jess shot Will a look of surprise and teased, 'How does that work then, decorating from home?'

He rolled his eyes and explained that he was going to be taking over the invoicing and some of the book work, 'In preparation for when you take over the business' he said, repeating his mother's words and mimicking her voice in an overly exaggerated fashion.

Poppy shook her head and admonished him, 'Will, your mother doesn't sound anything like that. Now help me get Dave inside.'

Jess left the two of them to unload Poppy's car and went back inside No. 3. But within ten minutes Poppy was on the doorstep. 'Didn't expect to see you quite yet,' she said with a grin.

'Would you believe it?' Poppy replied, throwing her arms in the air. 'Typical man, he's bought his mum a birthday present and a card but hasn't bought any wrapping paper.'

Jess laughed. 'Come on in and I'm sure you realise that you've come to the right place,' she said, pointing to the large oak sideboard that dominated the small sitting room. 'In one of those sections is a veritable stationery shop!' She knelt down beside the sideboard and opened one of the doors, then began pulling out reams of brightly coloured paper, shiny metallic paper, soft pastel tissue paper, gift bags and sticky tape.

Poppy stood and watched open mouthed. 'Good heavens,' she said. 'I see what you mean. Has that cupboard got a false back or something?'

Jess laughed and replied that some of it was left over from the memory boxes Eleanor had wrapped as she recognised the paper, but that much of it was simply Eleanor's creative collection.

And then, while Poppy sat on the floor next to her sifting through the pile of paper, Jess put her arm back in the cupboard and pulled out a small black metal box which she had noticed was tucked in a corner right at the back of the cupboard.

'It's locked,' she said looking at Poppy in surprise, whilst tugging determinedly at the lid. She grabbed her phone and shone the torch light into the cupboard, hoping she might find a key. But there was nothing. And then shaking the tin vigorously declared, 'Nothing rattly, so no jewels or ancient coins or...'

'Keys,' Poppy interrupted.

'Keys?' Jess said. 'Why keys?'

Poppy laughed. 'When we were kids we had these little boxes which we would put our so-called 'treasure' in, then we would lock them and put the key in another box and then hide both boxes.'

Jess looked at her friend with exaggerated amazement, causing Poppy to reply, 'Well we were only kids after all.'

Poppy took the box from her and gave it a shake. 'Papers,' she declared. 'Definitely papers. Which could, of course, amount to treasure!'

Jess smiled. 'More likely some ancient premium bond certificates or national health service cards. I found quite a lot of stuff like that in the file in the attic.'

Poppy frowned and said, 'Let's try and break into it. Knowing Eleanor there'll be some suitable tools in the shed.'

Jess sighed and clambering to her feet went outside to the shed, returning a few minutes later with a variety of likely implements. But all to no avail. The lid remained stubbornly closed.

'Smash it with a hammer,' Poppy said in an excited voice.

'Poppy, whatever's got into you?' Jess said laughing.

'Sorry, it's just quite exciting. You know, finding a locked box. Takes me back to my childhood.'

'Well I'm not smashing it with a hammer, that is for sure. I was planning to pop into the pub on my way home so I'll ask Alex if he can open it. I'm sorry to have to say that this is a blue job.'

Poppy frowned. 'Well I don't agree with you, but in any case let me know as soon as you've managed to open it. I need to know whether or not there's treasure inside.'

Jess grinned and then walking to the door with her friend said, 'Of course Poppy, you'll be the first to know. See you back at the house in a day or two.'

The two girls hugged each other and Jess watched her friend disappear into next door, clutching several pieces of wrapping paper and a roll of tape.

'Treasure indeed,' she said out loud, smiling to herself at Poppy's excited manner. It was so unlike her, but childhood memories had a habit of causing high emotion. She knew that herself only too well.

Later on at the pub, Alex prised the lid open with surprising ease using a screwdriver and an element of physical force. Jess decided she would be a little economical with the truth when she told Poppy how easy it had been to break into the box.

Her heart skipped a beat as she lifted out a small pile of discoloured and slightly tattered opened envelopes, all of which were addressed: *Eleanor Jones, c/o Grace Martin, Flat 17, Acacia Court, Broad Street, Shoreford, Kent* and marked *very personal*.

Very personal. What did that mean? 'Personal' was enough surely? It meant for the person it was intended. So what did 'very personal' mean? She didn't know, but what she did know was that it made her feel uneasy, uncomfortable, but she wasn't sure why. Her breathing quickened and her throat suddenly felt tight. Her mind was asking her questions that she didn't know the answers to, and so tucking the envelopes back into the box she forced a half smile at Alex and keeping her tone as light as possible said, 'I think I'll take these home and read them later.'

He nodded but said nothing. And she was relieved he hadn't commented. He knew. He understood that she needed to look at the papers on her own. He was perceptive. Instead, he simply put an arm around her waist, walked out to Rowan with her and kissed her goodbye tenderly. 'Text me when you're home,' he called through the half opened window and she blew him a kiss in reply.

Back in London, Jess placed the box on the kitchen table before filling the kettle. Amber had sent her a text message to say she was staying at James's, meaning she had the house to herself. No reason not to look at the contents of the envelopes then, she told herself. But something, and she wasn't sure what, was making her procrastinate. She was definitely stalling, but she didn't know why.

An hour later and after two cups of coffee and an unnecessarily long soak in the bath, she sat at the table and gently lifted the envelopes from the little box. Taking a deep breath, she carefully removed the contents of the first envelope from the small pile. It was a short letter written in neat handwriting on a single sheet of lined paper and began with, *My dearest Eleanor* and was signed *Yours Anton.*

She felt the familiar feeling of panic rising in her chest and she stood up in an attempt to allow more air into her lungs. She tried to calm her feelings by reminding herself that she hadn't even read the contents but nevertheless she had an overwhelming sense of deep unease.

She looked up at the kitchen clock and realising she'd been sitting at the table for over an hour and was not much further forward, gathered the envelopes up and put them back in the box. She switched off the kitchen light and headed upstairs.

But after tossing and turning for what seemed like half the night, she pulled on her dressing gown and found herself sitting back at the kitchen table, wrestling with her subconscious over the contents of the little black box. She was on an early shift so she needed to get some sleep but would opening the envelopes help or hinder her fear-induced insomnia? Reminding herself again that she didn't have any concrete reason for feeling as she did, she made herself a cup of coffee, which definitely wouldn't help with sleeping, and removed the envelopes again from the box.

Taking a deep breath, she removed the top letter from its envelope for a second time and scanned the page. Her vision suddenly became blurry as the words screamed out at her, *I've always loved you. I long to hold you. I can't wait to see you. We are meant to be together.*

The letters were dated, but not with a year. Reeling, she opened another envelope and then another to discover they were all written in a similar vein. Each letter began with *My Dearest Eleanor* and were all signed *Yours Anton*. Her stomach churned and her head was spinning. They were love letters, that was obvious, but who was Anton and what did this all mean?

Sleep did not come at all that night and Jess left for work feeling exhausted both mentally and physically. And things were only to get worse when on the ward her puffy eyes and furrowed brow didn't go unnoticed for long by Sister.

'Nurse Jones, a word in my office please,' she ordered, immediately after the nursing shift handover.

Jess took a deep breath and knocked on the door. Sister pointed to a chair, but it was not just *any* chair. It was *the* chair. The chair where you sat when Sister wanted to talk to you. Jess sat on the edge almost holding her breath.

'Nurse Jones,' she began. 'We seem to have a problem...'

But before she could finish, Jess felt large salty tears rolling uncontrollably down her cheeks and then she was sobbing, gut-wrenching rasping sobs that brought Sister round from the other side of her desk and holding her head against her body she gently stroked her hair.

'There, there Jess, let it all out,' she said in such a gentle and caring way, that it made Jess sob even harder.

As the crying began to dissipate, she watched Sister leave the office momentarily, before returning with a cup of hot sweet tea. She slid the engaged sign across the door and pulled up a chair next to her.

Jess managed a weak but grateful smile as she sipped the comforting tea and then, as if Sister was a close friend, began explaining about the letters.

Sister sat quietly, nodding and making comforting noises in all the right places and then in the softest of tones said, 'It seems to me that you have a lot to think about and maybe some things you need to sort out, so may I suggest you take a few days leave? And before you say anything, we will be fine from a staffing point of view.'

Wiping her face with a tissue, Jess nodded gratefully. 'Thank you for being so understanding and for listening and I think a few days off would really help.'

And then to her surprise Sister passed her a slip of paper and said, 'This is my personal mobile number, promise me Jess that you will ring me day or night if you need anything. And just remember, things are often not as bad as they first seem.'

Jess felt some of the tension slowly begin to ease and as she stood up from her chair she nodded her appreciation to Sister, not daring to speak in case the tears came again. Then she walked through the ward, keeping her head low and headed for the locker rooms.

On leaving the hospital she didn't go straight home, preferring instead to go to her favourite coffee shop where she ordered a double espresso. She'd never actually tried espresso before but hoped it might help with the overwhelming emotional tiredness she was feeling. She took a large gulp of the dark syrupy liquid, shuddering and grimacing as its surprisingly bitter taste pricked her throat on the short journey to her stomach.

She reached in her bag and pulled out her phone to ring Alex and then put it down on the table not knowing quite what she was going to say to him. *Hi Alex, I think my mum may have had an affair,* or *Hi Alex, my mum may not be as perfect as I always thought she was.* It all sounded too ridiculous and, of course, she may just be jumping to conclusions in imagining something that had never actually happened. Then with caffeine-fuelled clarity she knew this was something she needed to face on her own, at least until she knew exactly what it was she was facing.

Within the hour, having told both Alex and Poppy by text messages that she had something important to do with regard to the box, she found herself in her car driving to the address on the envelopes, with the little black box of secrets perched on the seat next to her.

Alex had perceptively replied, *You know where I am if you need me* and Poppy, who knew nothing more than that the box contained letters rather than her hoped-for treasure replied, *How exciting.*

Jess felt a pang of guilt that she hadn't told either of them more about the contents of the letters but she wanted to see if she could find out more herself first and in any case she just wasn't emotionally strong enough at this point in time.

In a little over an hour and a half her phone announced that she had reached her destination. Parking in the street, she got out of the car and clutching the box, walked towards the small block of flats called Acacia Court. The road was a mix of houses, some semi-detached and some in a terrace, with the block of flats perched towards the end. It looked strangely out of place she thought and was in definite need of redecoration. The front gardens of the nearby houses looked largely uncared for and the street itself looked drab and unloved.

As she reached the main doors to the flats, she felt her heart rate quicken and her mouth and throat felt dry. She swallowed hard and taking some deep breaths pressed the intercom buzzer for No. 17. Within seconds she heard a woman's voice say, 'Hello', but when she opened her mouth to answer she found she had been rendered temporarily speechless.

'Who's there?' came the voice again. 'Hello?' And then to her dismay she heard a click and realised the one-way communication had been terminated. She stood rooted to the spot for several seconds before she felt the familiar trickle of warm tears on her skin. She knew she couldn't press the buzzer again. She wasn't sure why, she just knew.

Wiping away the tears she turned to walk away, but as she did so she heard the door open and a familiar sounding voice say, 'Did you want something love?'

In front of her stood a woman probably a bit older than her, wearing a grey tracksuit and an enormous pair of novelty slippers. Her hair was scraped back into a tight pony tail and her face was make-up free.

She took a deep breath. 'I'm so sorry, for a minute I just couldn't speak...I'm...I...I'm looking for Grace Martin.'

The other woman looked at her questioningly and Jess knew immediately she needed to tell her more. Opening the black box, she removed the envelopes and passed them to the woman. 'The letters inside the envelopes were sent to my mother, Eleanor Jones, to this address,' she said, trying to steady her voice.

The woman looked at the envelopes and then looking back at Jess held the door open in a silent invitation to step inside.

'Thank you,' Jess said quietly. 'I'm Jessica Jones but everyone calls me Jess.'

The woman gave her a half smile and replied, 'I'm Isabella Martin but everyone calls me Izzy. Grace is my Mother.'

Jess nodded and on the way up to the second floor flat explained about finding the letters, deliberately keeping the content as vague as possible.

Izzy shrugged nonchalantly and without looking at her said, 'I don't know anyone called either Anton of Eleanor, neither have I heard my mother mention either of them.'

She sounded dispassionate Jess thought, but then why wouldn't she be? It wasn't her life, nor was it her problem and, after all, it wasn't as if they even knew each other.

Inside the hallway Jess bent down to remove her boots.

'No need,' the other woman remarked with what seemed to be

an amused grin. 'There's much more to worry about in here than a bit of dirt from outside!'

Jess nodded, wondering what on earth she might be confronted with, before following her through a doorway and into the sitting room. In one corner of the room close to the television, a frail-looking older woman with a long white untidy plait sat in a tatty wing back chair. She looked unwell Jess thought but despite her frail looks, her skin was smooth and she was probably younger than she appeared at first sight.

'Mum, this is Jess. Jess Jones and she wants to ask you about someone you may have known a very long time ago.'

Jess immediately noticed that Izzy's tone had softened and her lips were parted in a gentle smile

Looking away from the television, the woman viewed Jess through narrowed eyes and then, as if some kind of realisation had suddenly struck, her eyes widened and she let out a slight gasp.

'So you came. You finally came. I wasn't sure you ever would my dear. Please come and sit down. We have a lot to talk about.'

The older woman moved her gaze to her daughter and said, 'I think some tea might be in order,' and without speaking, the other woman nodded and disappeared into the kitchen which was situated directly off the sitting room and closed the door behind her.

Jess opened the black box and showing Grace Martin the contents said, 'I found these the other day. My mother, Eleanor Jones, died earlier in the year.'

The older woman inhaled sharply before turning away from her to look out of the window, as if to gather her thoughts. And then turning back she gave her a look of consternation and her deep exhalation forced a loud sigh from her lips. 'So you know about Anton then?' she asked quietly.

Jess shook her head. 'I know nothing of this Anton. The letters have come as a complete surprise. Well a complete shock to be honest.'

'I see,' Grace replied nodding. 'I see.'

'Please tell me Mrs Martin. Did my mother have an affair with this man? With this Anton?' she said, desperately trying to fight back tears.

The older woman gave her a sympathetic smile and leaning forward took hold of her hand. 'Please call me Grace my dear. And I *will* tell you everything I know, but you must prepare yourself for some surprises, shocks maybe.'

Jess nodded and took a sip of tea from the heavy china mug that Izzy had put in front of her. It was too milky for her taste but she was grateful for anything that would help lubricate her dry mouth and throat. She noticed the two women exchanging a knowing look and then the younger woman left the room without a word.

'So,' Grace began, taking a deep breath. 'I have lived here for what seems like forever and many years ago Anton lived in one of the flats on the floor below. We were both young then and neither of us had anything much really but we became good friends and we shared whatever we did have. Isabella was very young, I was a single mother and I suppose I leaned on him for support. Anton had been through some difficult times himself and I did some cooking for him and a little bit of housework. Do you see?' she asked. 'We helped each other. It's what people did in those days.'

Jess nodded and she really did understand what Grace was saying, but what she didn't understand was what on earth all of this had to do with Eleanor.

She took another sip of her tea but before she could speak, Grace continued, 'I can see you're wondering what this has to do with Eleanor?'

Jess felt her cheeks redden and she looked away momentarily to avoid Grace's gaze. 'Well yes, I have to confess I am a bit confused.'

The other woman smiled knowingly. 'I'm just setting the scene my dear. It's important, you will understand why.

Jess nodded.

'But then something changed. Anton met a young lady,' Grace continued. 'Or to be precise he *re-met* a young lady and rekindled an old relationship. And that young lady was Eleanor.'

Jess gasped and she was sure that Grace must have been able to hear her heart thumping. 'So my mother did have an affair then, with Anton.'

It was a statement rather than a question but Grace nodded nevertheless. 'I know this must be hard to hear Jess, but please let me continue as it's important that you know the whole story.'

Jess nodded again. She wasn't sure she wanted to hear anymore, but she'd indicated for Grace to continue so she now had to listen.

'You see they loved each other, *really* loved each other but it was so hard for them. Eleanor was so scared of hurting her husband and disappointing her family that their relationship was incredibly difficult. Anton often worked away and they had to catch a few moments together whenever they could. They made each other happy Jess, really happy and I was very fond of both of them.'

Jess stood from her chair and walked towards the door, suddenly feeling unable to breathe. 'I'm sorry I need to get some air,' she said quickly and then descending the stairs two at a time, stumbled through the main door to the outside. Leaning against the wall of the building she desperately tried to control her breathing by inhaling through her nose and exhaling through pursed lips. It was raining now and the gentle raindrops felt cool against her face and mixed readily with the tears that were now flowing freely down her cheeks. How could this be true? How could this be happening to her? Her mother, her own mother. It was impossible, it was a lie surely.

'You okay?' came a woman's voice from nearby.

The question made her jump and she looked up to see Izzy

who was now wearing a rain jacket and holding an umbrella, but surprisingly was still wearing the novelty slippers. It was a comical sight, and under different circumstances Jess would have found it funny but considering the news Grace Martin had just shared, her sense of humour had long since gone. 'Yes I'm okay,' she answered weakly. 'I've just had a bit of a shock, that's all.'

The other woman nodded and reaching into her jacket pocket pulled out a packet of cigarettes and a lighter. She offered the packet to Jess who shook her head and then with a shrug, the other woman lit one herself and inhaled deeply.

Jess was grateful that she had, at least, directed the trail of exhaled smoke away from her, as she already had an unpleasant sick feeling rising up to her throat.

After a few moments of deep smoke-filled inhalations the other woman asked, 'You coming back in? These slippers are not taking kindly to this weather, look the colour is running from the unicorn's hair! Guess that's what happens when you buy stuff from the pound shop. Mind you they were more than a pound which is something I don't really understand in a pound shop.'

And then Jess did laugh, not really at Izzy but more at the absurdity of the scene in front of her.

Back upstairs in the flat, Jess apologised to Grace for her sudden exit. 'I'm rather good at not facing things, running away, putting things off. You know, that sort of thing.' She realised she was probably saying too much, over explaining, but on this occasion it somehow seemed important.

The older woman smiled kindly and patted the seat next to her and Jess sat down again. 'Would you like me to continue?' she asked quietly, touching her arm.

Jess nodded and then took a deep breath as if bracing herself for what was to come.

Grace told her how when Anton was working away, he would send letters to Eleanor at her address and Eleanor would collect them from the flat. 'Sometimes she would read them out loud and they were beautiful, they were true love letters,' she continued.

Jess dabbed at her eyes with a damp tissue and said, 'And then what?'

Grace sighed and looking at Jess said, 'And then she told me she was pregnant.'

Jess gasped and clapped a hand over her mouth. The other woman reached out a bony hand and took Jess's other hand in hers.

'She wasn't sure if Anton was the father or whether it was her husband. But in any case when she told Anton, he just couldn't cope. He ended the relationship and he never saw Eleanor again and neither did I.'

Jess looked at the older woman and she could see real sadness in her eyes as she spoke those last words. She sat in silence trying to comprehend the enormity of the revelations she had just been confronted with, but it was too much, much too much. Her life had been completely turned upside down in a matter of hours and she knew she desperately needed to talk to Alex, she needed him to hold her and tell her everything was going to be okay. Standing up from the chair she said, 'I just need to make a phone call if that's ok?'

Grace pointed to the kitchen and Jess nodded and closed the door behind her. Within seconds she found herself blurting out the story to Alex, the words interspersed with gulping sobs.

'Text me the postcode. I'm on my way,' he replied in his usual calm and reassuring manner, and suddenly she felt an overwhelming sense of relief. She returned to the sitting room and told Grace about Alex.

'I'll find a coffee shop and wait there for a while, I've taken up enough of your time already,' she said.

'Whatever is best for you my dear. You'll find various shops if you head towards the sea,' Grace replied softly. 'But please come back when your man arrives. It's important.'

Jess nodded and picking up her bag and coat left the flat and building feeling totally drained.

Within a few minutes she had parked along the seafront. Pulling up her hood, she walked along the path with her hands in her pockets, the wind and the rain pounding her face. Could this really be true? And if it was, how could Eleanor have done this to her and then let her find out about it in such a traumatic way? Was it just careless or had she wanted her to know?

So many unanswered questions, so much to think about. Her head felt like it was about to explode as she opened the door to a small coffee shop along the street, but shaking the rain off her face she somehow managed to smile at the waitress and order a double espresso.

She sat in the window and watched the droplets of rain slide uniformly down the glass as if they were in some sort of sequence. The inside of the window was slightly misted and she was pleased that it partly obscured her from the gaze of people walking past. She drank the coffee down in one gulp and then ordered another. She felt weary and emotionally drained but she knew she needed to keep her mind alert.

'I'm sorry but we're closing shortly.' It was the voice of the girl who had brought her the second espresso and her abrupt tone cut through Jess's thoughts and the silence that surrounded her. She hadn't realised she'd been sitting there for over an hour already and it was now dark outside. She smiled politely at the girl and after paying the bill, walked back along the sea front and to her car. She hadn't bothered to put her hood up on the way back and her hair was now damp and frizzy but it didn't matter, she told herself, nothing mattered. Absolutely nothing.

She checked the time and then decided to drive around for a while to try and warm herself up before going back to Acacia Court. But the familiarity of her beloved Rowan and the warmth and quiet of the cab was suddenly interrupted by the loud ringing of her phone and her mind was quickly brought back into sharp focus. She pulled over to the side of the road and switched off the engine, crossing her fingers that it was Alex. But instead of seeing his name, the screen simply displayed the word 'Call'.

'Hello?' she answered, her voice shaking with emotion.

'Good evening. Am I speaking with Miss Jones?'

'Yes,' she replied, and then immediately realising the nature of the call, rebuked herself for answering it.

'My name's Samantha and I understand you may have recently been involved in an accident?'

She felt a sudden mix of anger, hurt and sadness coursing through her veins and taking a deep breath replied, 'Yes, apparently so. But it wasn't a recent accident. It was, in fact, thirty three years ago.' She was surprised at how steady and even her voice sounded and then ending the call without waiting for a reply, she drove back to Acacia Court to wait for Alex.

Almost another hour passed before Alex pulled up in his van and parked directly behind her. In her hurry to see him, she practically fell out of the car and cursed to herself as she stumbled towards the van in the most ungainly manner.

Alex was already out of the driver's seat and he wrapped his arms around her, kissing her hair and saying, 'It's okay baby, I'm here now.'

And as she buried her head in his chest she cried, 'I thought she was perfect, the perfect mother. How could I have been so wrong?'

She felt his arms tighten around her as they stood in silence on the quiet street and in the darkness of the evening and with the falling rain, she felt as though she was acting out a scene from a film rather than one from her own life.

Back in the upstairs flat, Jess introduced Alex to Grace and Izzy and he gratefully accepted the offer of a cup of tea. Jess nudged him as he looked around the flat with a distinct lack of subtlety and he shot her an apologetic glance which she was sure Izzy had picked up on.

'So,' Grace was now saying, 'Would you like me to continue?'

Jess gave her a weak smile and then taking hold of Alex's hand, nodded as a way of reply.

The older woman explained that Anton had continued to live in the flat below for several years and then eventually he'd met another 'lovely lady' and moved away to make a fresh start. And then looking into Jess's eyes she said, 'But he regretted not finding out if the baby was his. If *you* were his. He *bitterly* regretted it and when he moved away he wrote a letter for you just in case you should ever come looking. I have the letter here.' She held out an envelope which bore the writing that Jess had come to recognise as Anton's.

She shook her head and half pushing Grace's hand away said, 'I don't want it. I don't want anything from him. I already have a father...' and then as she trailed off, she reminded herself that the reality was somewhat different.

Grace nodded. 'I understand my dear, I really do. But perhaps you should take it with you as maybe one day you will want to read it. I don't know what it says but I've always hoped that one day I would be able to carry out Anton's wishes.'

Alex squeezed her hand reassuringly, and leaning forward Jess took the envelope from the other woman's hand. She looked at the envelope and then taking a deep breath asked, 'Did he ever look for me?'

Grace shook her head. 'No my dear, not as far as I know. It was too hard you see. He didn't know if you were his child and he didn't know if your father knew anything about his relationship with your mother. There were just too many unknowns. Too many complications.'

'Do you still keep in touch with him?' Jess ventured, not really knowing why she was asking.

'I did my dear, mostly just at Christmas but I'm so sorry to say that he died last year.'

Jess nodded and tucking the envelope into her handbag stood up from the chair, signalling to Alex that it was time to leave. She realised she felt no emotion at hearing the news of Anton's death, she just felt numb, numb from the realisation that her life may have been built on a lie. Taking the older woman's hand she summoned the strength to thank her, and with Alex close by her side walked out through the flat door before allowing the tears to flow once again.

'Let's stay the night somewhere nearby,' he suggested. 'It's a long drive home for both of us and I don't like the thought of you being on your own.'

'What about the pub and Rolo?' she asked. 'And I have nothing with me either.'

He kissed her hair and told her he already had Velvet on stand-by. She would close up the pub and stay the night in the spare bedroom. 'And what's more,' he added, 'I've brought a few essentials, you know a toothbrush, a comb, chocolate...'

Jess managed a grateful smile. 'Thank you Alex,' she said wiping her face with a soggy tissue. 'And I'm sorry to land all this on you, I just didn't know what else to do,' she added.

'No thanks needed. And I'm glad you did,' he said opening the door to her car. 'I'll come with you and pick my van up tomorrow.'

In less than an hour Jess was soaking in the biggest bath she had ever seen, filled to the top with the most deliciously warm vanilla-scented bubbles, in a hotel room that under any other circumstances she would have been thrilled to stay in. There was an enormous four poster bed complete with soft cream-coloured organza drapes and canopy, and gorgeous silky bedding in a pale duck egg blue. It was incredibly beautiful but of no real interest to her in the circumstances.

When they'd arrived at the closest hotel to Acacia Court, the receptionist had told them they only had the honeymoon suite available, and when Alex had replied 'perfect', Jess had (a) Been too tired to argue and (b) Was acutely aware that he'd said yes to the room for all the right reasons and she had no intention of throwing it back in his face. He'd handed over his credit card to the surprised receptionist and then ushered her upstairs before running her a bath. And now as she lay back and relaxed in the warm water, she thought how amazing he was and it brought a smile to her lips.

Half an hour later she was sitting on the bed wrapped in a soft fluffy white towelling robe. She sighed and said, 'It's been a long day.'

Alex nodded and kissed her gently. 'You get into bed my lovely and I'll see if I can get us something to eat.'

She smiled weakly and replied that she didn't think she could eat anything and he nodded in a way that she knew meant he understood. Removing the robe, she slid under the soft silky sheet and rested her head back on the plump pillow. He lay on the top of the covers beside her and stroked her hair with a soft rhythmic motion and feeling the stress melt away, she closed her heavy eyelids and fell into a deep slumber.

CHAPTER TWENTY-THREE

When Jess woke the next morning Alex was already up and he'd arranged for room service to bring breakfast, which was served on a huge silver tray. She had slept surprisingly well in the circumstances and in the cold light of day perhaps, she thought, things seemed marginally less bad than they had done the previous evening. Not better, but less bad. She thought back to when she was a child and how she was scared of the dark and remembered how she'd felt so protected by her father. And even now as an adult, everything seemed much worse when it was dark.

She sighed and taking a sip of the freshly-brewed coffee and a mouthful of soft buttery croissant said, 'I think that maybe I should open the letter...the one from Anton...before we head back, just in case there's any other...you know...questions...or...for Grace I mean.'

Alex nodded. 'Whatever you think is best Jess, I'm here for you, you know that don't you?'

She nodded and smiled gratefully at him. 'No time like the present then,' she said reaching in her handbag and pulling out the envelope. It was addressed to *Eleanor's child* and seeing the words made her shudder even though, of course, she was still Eleanor's child, the memory had been somehow tarnished.

She slid her finger under the already slightly lifted edge of the envelope and then gritting her teeth tore it open with unexpected venom. The sudden force of her index finger caused something from inside the envelope to fall onto the floor. And as she bent down to pick it up she realised it was a photograph. And she knew immediately it was a photograph of Anton. Her mouth dropped open and gasping she said, 'Oh God Alex, it's like looking in the mirror!'

He moved closer to her and took hold of the hand that was clutching the photograph and then it was his turn to gasp. 'But this man is…he's mixed race Jess.'

She nodded. 'I know. But look at the likeness. I'm pretty sure he is my biological father.'

They sat staring at each other for several seconds in a state of confusion, before Jess unfolded the letter and taking a deep breath began reading it out loud:

Writing this letter to you is the hardest thing I have ever done and I'm sure will ever have to do in my entire life. You are probably wondering why I even am writing it and I suppose you could say it's just in case. And by that I mean just in case you should ever come looking for me, or just in case Eleanor should ever tell you about me or just in case you find out about me by accident. But as I write this I have no idea what you have been told or even IF you have been told anything which makes it even harder to write. So I am going to assume you know nothing of me or of the situation we found ourselves in and so I will start at the beginning.

Eleanor and I first met when we were young. She was only 17 and I was 24. Things were difficult right from the start for lots of different reasons which I will try my best to explain. My father James Johnson came to this country from Jamaica when he was only 16 with his parents via a government invitational scheme which brought immigrants from the Caribbean to help rebuild the parts of the United Kingdom which had been ravaged by war. I'm sure you will have heard about it.

My father met and married a British woman called May and I was their only child. When I was in my early twenties my father decided he wanted to go home as he called it but I didn't want to go with them as you see this country is my home. My mother was very torn but eventually she agreed to go as well. It was very hard without them but I had some good friends and I trained as a lorry driver and managed to rent a room in a shared house. And then my life changed as I met your mother. At last I was happy again. We laughed a lot, we danced, we sang and we had fun. We were young and in love. But sadly our happiness was short lived as Eleanor's parents were dead against our relationship saying that she was too young but we both knew there was more to it than that. I'm afraid they did not like the colour of my skin. We tried so hard to stay together but it could never be.

And then by chance we met again some years later. Eleanor was married by then but I had never found anyone else to take her place. You see I'd always hoped she would come back to me. And then although we both knew it was wrong we started seeing each other again. I had a flat and a steady job but there was so much pressure on us and so much deceit, it was almost doomed from the start. And then when Eleanor told me she was pregnant, I was scared, really scared and I suppose I was a coward as well. I panicked, no excuses, but I have regretted deserting her and not finding out about the baby - about you - every single day of my life. I want you to know that I loved her more than words can say and I let her down. I have to live with that.

You may be wondering why I didn't look for Eleanor or for you but I knew it had the potential to cause such devastation for everybody involved, it would not have been fair. There are so many unanswered questions and perhaps some will always remain unanswered but I want you to know that I will always love you regardless of whether you are biologically mine or not because you are part of Eleanor and she was my first true love.

I am leaving this letter with my dearest friend Grace Martin in the faint hope that one day for whatever reason you may come looking for me at Acacia Court. I need to move away as there are just too many sad memories here for me. But I'm lucky that I have met a wonderful woman who knows everything about me and accepts me for who I am.

I will continue to think of you every single day of my life and I am so very very sorry if I have caused you unnecessary pain.

Yours

Anton Johnson

Jess folded the letter neatly into its previous creases and placed it back in the envelope and then looking at Alex said, 'I may be a totally different person from the one I thought I was.'

He nodded, 'I know what you mean Jess, but you are still *you*. You are still Jess. You always will be. You...'

'What did you see when you first saw me?' she interrupted.

'I saw a funny, kind, caring and if I may say so, rather cute person, who I liked from the first moment I met her,' he said, taking her hand.

'Yes but what did you actually *see*? I mean did you see a white person or...' she trailed off, shaking her head.

'I saw *you* Jess. I didn't see a colour, I just saw you,' he answered truthfully.

She nodded, 'But it doesn't change the fact that I may not be the person I thought I was. Yes, I'm still me, I'm still Jess, just not the Jess I thought I was.'

'I understand,' Alex replied with obvious sincerity.

'But you don't. What I mean is you can't. Can't understand I mean.' She looked at him and saw his face had dropped and she suddenly felt guilty. It wasn't his fault. He was kind and thoughtful and he was only trying to help. She knew that. 'I'm sorry Alex. That wasn't fair,' she said in a softer tone. 'I can't really explain how I feel. It's not about my colour. That isn't what matters. It's..I suppose, well

I suppose I'm trying to convince myself that Thomas is my biological father. I was raised by two white people, as a white person. When I was a little girl people would say I was the spitting image of my father, of Thomas. So how can I possibly be someone different? It just doesn't make any sense. But also it's about other people knowing things or perhaps thinking things about me that I didn't know or hadn't thought about myself. Hugely important things. Does that make any sense?'

'Perfect sense,' he answered. 'I just don't know what else to say Jess. It's such a lot to take in, it's as if it isn't real, you know like something out of a film.'

She nodded, staring at the picture of Anton. 'Yes it is but as the protagonist of this particular film I need to face up to the consequences.'

'Just remember though Jess that at the moment you don't know the truth. It's all 'ifs', 'buts' and 'maybes'. So perhaps the best thing to do is to wait until you know for sure, and whatever the truth is I will be there to help and support you, if that's what you need,' Alex said.

CHAPTER TWENTY-FOUR

Having eventually persuaded Alex that she was fine and that he should go back to the pub, Jess dropped him off at the flats to collect his van and then hoping she hadn't been spotted, drove off to look for a thank you gift for Grace.

Spotting a florist shop along the seafront, she found a parking space and walked along the path, looking out to sea and filling her lungs with the misty sea air. It would be lovely to live by the sea she thought; to walk along the front and hear the lapping of the waves; to breathe in the aromatic sea air and in the summer to feel the soft sand between your toes. She would need a sturdier pair of straightening irons though as the sea mist was playing havoc with her hair. And then, as if realisation had suddenly struck, she ran her fingers through the damp, frizzy curls and exclaimed, 'My hair! Of course!'

Her mind was whirring as she stepped inside the florist shop. But the sight of the beautiful array of flowers managed to bring a half smile to her face. She stood still and drank in the deliciously heady smell of the fragrant flowers. But although she was surrounded by beautifully arranged and colourful displays, she quickly realised that she didn't know anything about flowers and certainly had no idea what sort Grace might like or even if she liked flowers at all. Deciding that she was probably over thinking things again, she chose a pretty brightly coloured hand-tied bouquet and headed back to her car.

She felt compelled to go back and see Grace. It was a given. Not only because she had more questions but also because she wanted to thank her for the intuitive, understanding and sensitive way in which she had imparted such difficult news to her. The poor woman had been caught up in the middle of an impossible situation and it was obvious it had been a burden to her. None of this was her fault but Jess hoped that she could find peace in knowing she had been able to carry out Anton's wish.

At the flats she was about to press the buzzer for No. 17 when Izzy appeared at the door, dressed in a bright pink velour tracksuit and the same unicorn slippers as she was wearing the previous day. Opening the door wide in an invitational way, she said, 'Saw you coming from the flat window.'

It was a statement that didn't need a reply but it made Jess wonder if she had seen her drive off earlier. But then the flowers were an explanation for that, so she simply smiled and followed her up the stairs to the flat.

Grace was sitting in the same chair as the previous day and as Jess walked towards her she said, 'Morning Grace,' and held out the flowers for her.

'There was no need my dear,' the older woman replied with a smile. 'But thank you and Gerberas are my favourite flowers.' She looked at Izzy and added, 'Could you find a vase for these lovely flowers please?'

Izzy rolled her eyes and taking the flowers into the kitchen said, 'I suppose you want tea as well?'

Jess smiled. 'Thank you Izzy.' Then thinking it sounded as if she was dismissing her in a kind of 'That will be all' style quickly added, 'That's really kind of you. I'd love one.'

Sitting next to Grace now, Jess suddenly felt a strange affinity with her although she wasn't quite sure why. 'Grace, I have read the letter and seen a photograph of Anton. I'm pretty sure he is...was... my father,' she ventured, swallowing hard.

The older woman looked away briefly and then touching her arm replied, 'I know this must be such a shock to you Jess but he was a good man, a really good man and he loved you even though he didn't even know you. He would have been so proud to have known he had such a beautiful, strong and clever daughter.'

Jess felt the familiar tears pricking her eyes, but she managed to smile gratefully at the other woman and then taking a deep breath asked, 'Do you think I look like him Grace?'

The older woman looked into her eyes and nodded her head. 'Yes my dear you do, with a few obvious differences.'

Jess realised that she'd been pretty sure of the answer but nevertheless had wanted to hear it from someone who knew Anton. Suddenly feeling overcome with emotion again she said, 'Thank you Grace. Thank you for being so kind and for spending so much of your time with me.' She wanted to hug her, to hold her close, perhaps because she was the link between her and Eleanor and her biological father.

The other woman touched her arm again and replied, 'It's been good for me as well my dear. It's given me peace to know that I've been able to fulfil Anton's wishes and I'm so happy to have met you.'

Jess nodded. 'Yes I understand. I really do.' She stood up and walked over to the window. 'There's just one more thing Grace. Do you have an address for Anton's wife? I'm not sure yet, but I think I may want to meet her in the future.'

Grace nodded and getting to her feet retrieved a small address book from a nearby cupboard.

'Don't worry about writing it down,' she said. 'I'll take a picture of it with my phone.'

The older woman smiled and pointing to an entry which read *Melissa Johnson (Anton)* replied, 'You youngsters, what would you do without those blessed contraptions!'

Jess laughed and then without any awkwardness the two women hugged each other as if they were long lost friends. And in a strange way that's what they were; they had a bond; a connection that would last forever.

On the drive back to London Jess thought about the last forty eight hours and was surprised at how calm she was now feeling. She wished she'd asked Grace what she'd meant when she had said, 'With obvious differences', in response to her question about whether she looked like Anton. Had she meant her skin colour or was it just a reference to the gender difference perhaps? She knew it wasn't really that important but she was grappling with her own identity and other people's opinions had suddenly seemed relevant.

What was important though, was that she knew exactly what she had to do next and although it wasn't going to be easy, she reminded herself that she was in charge of her own destiny. And it was somehow very calming to be in control, to know the next steps.

CHAPTER TWENTY-FIVE

Back at home Jess phoned Alex; Sister Greenwood and Jamie James, who had tried to phone her on several occasions about selling the cottage. She made herself a cup of strong, sweet tea and devoured two chocolate bars, informing her hips that it was essential for her emotional wellbeing. And It was, because she felt better almost immediately and although she knew it was most likely to be because of the sugar rush, the outcome was the same.

She still had another day's leave plus her two days off and so had told Alex she would be in Thripton by late afternoon. There was also choir practice that evening which would take her mind off the events of the last few days, if only for a couple of hours and it would be especially lovely to see Nora.

Packing her bag, she practised her Christmas solo and realised she was actually quite looking forward to the concert, and despite recent events was looking forward to Christmas as well. And she knew, in particular, that she needed a distraction from the other part of her life that was unravelling at speed in front of her eyes.

Later that afternoon she had a feeling of relief and calm as she arrived in Thripton. She was beginning to love the quiet of the countryside and the friendliness of the locals and that's exactly what she needed at the moment.

She called in on Rosa who, as always, gave her a warm welcome. 'Jess my darling what a lovely surprise, come in and have tea with me.'

Jess smiled and kissing her on the cheek followed her into the kitchen. As always the worktops were laden with baking paraphernalia, but Jess's eyes were drawn to the wire tray where the most deliciously smelling savoury tarts were cooling off in a kind of invitational 'eat me' manner.

'Are you tempted by my savouries?' Rosa asked, beaming at her.

She nodded, 'I am Rosa, but I ate two chocolate bars at home so I really shouldn't be eating anything else at the moment. I had what I call a 'snaccident'.'

Rosa laughed. 'A snaccident. I will remember that. But you know my darling, there's another very good saying which is, a little bit of what you fancy will do you good and that's how I've always lived my life.'

Jess laughed and sitting down at the table found herself tasting a tomato, cheese and onion tartlet while giving Rosa the abridged version of the letters from Anton and her meetings with Grace Martin.

Rosa sat spellbound, not even taking a sip of her coffee but once Jess had finished speaking, she put a comforting arm around her shoulders and gently kissed her hair. It was just what was needed; no advice; no solutions; just comfort and support. She was a very wise woman.

Just before six thirty, Alex knocked on the door of No. 3 and walked down to the church with Jess. Marcus's face lit up when he saw them and he came over immediately and hugged them both. Alex took up his regular position at the back of the church while Jess joined the others in the choir stalls.

Henry called them to order in his usual indomitable way and

when Nora nudged her they both had a fit of the giggles, which they were then asked to explain.

'It's like being back in school,' Nora whispered and Jess nodded, skilfully disguising another giggle as a cough.

Later that evening in the pub, Alex was full of praise for the rehearsal and declared that the drinks were on the house. Sitting next to Nora, Jess leaned forward and quietly asked her if she could pop round to the cottage the next day as she had something important to tell her.

'Goodness, that sounds intriguing,' she whispered, her eyes widening with interest.

Jess nodded in agreement. 'Be prepared for a surprise. And probably lots of tears as well.'

'Crumbs Jess, are you okay?' she asked.

'Yes. It's just been a difficult couple of days but I'll explain all tomorrow.'

After the pub had closed, Jess sat upstairs with Alex and Rolo. She made two cups of hot chocolate and slipped Rolo a dog biscuit which he swallowed with one gulp, leaving no evidence of the late night treat.

Sipping his drink Alex asked, 'Are you staying tonight?'

'If you'll let me,' she replied.

He pulled her closer, kissing her gently which she knew was his answer and she kissed him back with passion, knowing it would lead to gloriously satisfying love-making. And that was what she needed, to be wanted, to be held and caressed with the kindness and tenderness that only Alex could provide her with.

Next morning after breakfast, Jess kissed Alex goodbye and headed back to the cottage. Nora was coming around eleven o'clock and she was looking forward to sharing her story with another female of a similar age and outlook. She had already given Poppy a brief insight when she spoke to her by phone but it wasn't the same as sitting down in a face to face conversation. She needed the solidarity of another woman; the companionship; the sisterhood and that was not taking anything away from Alex or Rosa for that matter. She had been bowled over by Rosa's understanding. And Alex had shown her nothing but empathy and support, but she also needed the support of a like-minded person with whom she wasn't romantically involved. Somehow he was almost too close to her. She needed someone who was more detached and Nora would be that person, she was sure of it.

Nora arrived with Mabel, looking as angelic as ever as she slept in her pushchair. After gently removing the rain cover, blanket and her fluffy jacket, she left the pushchair in the hallway and tiptoed into the lounge behind Jess, whispering that it would be much easier to talk without any 'Goo goo' noises.

'Let's go in the kitchen then,' Jess said. 'That way we're less likely to disturb the little cherub.'

Norah smiled and raising her eyebrows said, 'I'll remind you of that when she's awake and shouting the place down!'

Jess poured them both a cup of coffee and they sat at the kitchen table, Nora practically on the edge of her chair. After taking a large swig of the strong coffee, Jess began filling Nora in on how she'd found the letters from Anton and the subsequent visits to Grace Martin.

Nora was aghast at the revelations but the understanding and empathy she showed reinforced to Jess that she was fast becoming a really good friend. And she felt a sense of catharsis at being able to recount the story. She knew she *needed* to tell her story, and probably re-tell it many times. She needed to say it out loud, to try and make some sort of sense of it all.

'So I'm assuming you need to talk with your father then?' Nora asked, as Jess sat back in the chair and finished the rest of her coffee.

'Yes I do but I'm just trying to figure out how. I haven't spoken to him for so many years and worse still I ignored him for a long time when he tried to contact me. And then out of the blue I'm going to contact him with the most shocking news he's ever likely to hear.'

Nora nodded, 'Yes, it definitely needs some thought, but having Mabel has made me realise that there is nobody more important or precious than your own children. I'm sure he will want to see you Jess and if you need moral support I will gladly come with you.'

Jess thanked her and then got up from the table to check on Mabel, who to her amazement was wide awake but perfectly content sitting in the pushchair, gurgling and chuckling to her hands as if they were telling her something of great importance.

'Shall I get her out?' she called through to Nora.

'Yes please,' Nora answered and then Jess smiled as the other woman was suddenly standing right next to her.

'See what I mean?' she said with an apologetic look. 'Parents have this overwhelming desire to protect their children. It's sort of innate I suppose. Your child trumps everybody. You'll see.'

Jess nodded, 'I hope you're right Nora. I really do.' And then picking the baby up, lifted her above her shoulders and in return Mabel giggled and blew raspberries at her. She laughed and passed her to Nora saying, 'She is so gorgeous, you are very lucky.'

The other woman smiled back and said, 'I know, she is my absolute world.'

Jess looked at them both giggling and making strange noises at each other and realised that she not only owed it to herself to contact her father, but that she owed it to him too.

A little while later, she walked up the lane with Nora and took a turn at pushing the pushchair which, she realised, was rather pleasurable. When they reached the pub she hugged Nora and waved to Mabel who chuckled in response. 'See you soon,' she called after them as they disappeared along the road and Nora turned and waved enthusiastically.

Inside the pub Alex was busy serving, so Jess sat down at her favourite spot close to the fire. She took her phone out of her bag and put it down on the table. Staring at it, she could almost hear her mind working overtime. Should she phone her father or send him a text message? Phoning would be harder, certainly for her, but was texting the coward's way of doing things? Or was it perhaps justified as it would, at least, act as a sort of warning shot for him and he could then take his time in deciding whether to answer it or not? Too many questions with no clear answers she realised, and putting the phone down on the table, she sat back and exhaled deeply through pursed lips.

She was deep in thought when Alex arrived at the table with a pint of beer for her. 'Alex Blake it's the middle of the day, what are you trying to do to me?' she admonished teasingly.

'It will clear all those muddled thoughts,' he replied smiling, as if he was able to read her mind.

'I do hope so,' she answered seriously. 'I really cannot continue to vacillate.'

Alex looked into her eyes and replied earnestly, 'No you can't, it's really not good for you.' And then, unable to keep a straight face added, 'Actually I have no idea what that word even means!'

Jess laughed and looking up at him realised she loved the man standing in front of her, the person who always seemed to have a way of easing awkward situations with the right amount and type of humour, and the fact that he was rather handsome as well was an added bonus.

After swallowing a mouthful of beer she picked up the phone

and looked up her father's number in her contacts list, but just as she was about to press the button to ring him, the door of the pub door swung open and in walked Jazz. She looked at Alex, who was now looking directly at Jazz, who in turn was scanning the pub. As she spotted the two of them at the table, she began walking purposefully towards them. But as she reached them, Jess noticed her face had softened and her cheeks were flushed. She stood in silence for several seconds and then looking from Alex to Jess and then back to Alex said, 'I'm glad I've caught you both together. You see, I owe you both...I owe you...an apology. I'm truly sorry for the way I've treated you Alex, particularly as you've always been so good to me.' And then turning to Jess added, 'I'm sorry I can't remember your name, but I know I've been rude to you on more than one occasion. I've got a sharp tongue my mother would say.'

Jess managed a smile and resisted the temptation to say that her mother was right. Instead she offered the girl a seat and a drink as a sort of unspoken acceptance of her apology.

'Excuse me a minute ladies, but my bartending skills are required,' Alex said, leaving the two women sitting together.

Jazz sipped her mineral water through a straw and explained to Jess that she had left the clothes shop by 'mutual agreement' which, perhaps unfairly, Jess took to mean that she had been asked to leave.

After a few minutes of small talk, the younger girl leaned towards Jess and whispered, 'What do you reckon the chances are of Alex giving me a job back here?'

Jess almost spat her beer back into the glass but managing to regain her composure answered, 'I really don't think that's for me to say.' She stopped short of adding that if she were a betting person she wouldn't put any money on it.

Jazz shrugged her shoulders and standing up from her chair said, 'I'll get my mother onto it,' and then left with a curt goodbye and something of a forced smile.

On her own again at the table and with nobody nearby, Jess picked up her phone and pressed the button to ring her father. She could feel her heart thumping and her throat felt as if it was being constricted by something, but she took some deep breaths and a gulp of beer for Dutch courage.

And then after only one ring she heard the familiar voice of her father saying, 'Jess? Jess is that you?'

She exhaled and replied, 'Yes Dad it's me,' and then her voice cracked and she found that she couldn't utter another word.

But then, as if by magic, Alex appeared at her side and taking the phone from her trembling hands, explained to Thomas Jones that his daughter would like to see him and when he fell silent too, Alex was able to give Jess a nod of affirmation.

CHAPTER TWENTY-SIX

The following day Jess was on her way back to Kent but this time it was to see her father. Both Alex and Nora had offered to go with her, but she felt she needed to go on her own. Neither of them had met her father before and she was conscious that, as she hadn't painted him in a particularly good light, it was only fair that she didn't expose him to any of their potential preconceptions.

She wasn't entirely sure where he lived but he had sent her a text message with his address and when her thoughts were interrupted by her phone app announcing that she had reached her destination, her heart skipped a beat.

It was a quiet residential street with rows of ordinary and almost identical looking semi-detached houses and No. 24 was no exception. The front garden was neatly kept and two newish silver cars were parked on the driveway. Jess had never met her father's mistress, as she had always referred to her as, neither had she wanted to but the sight of the two cars made her realise that she now faced that stark reality.

Turning her phone onto silent she walked slowly up the driveway to the front door and taking a few deep breaths rang the doorbell. Loud barking and raised voices followed and then the door opened wide and Thomas Jones stood in the hallway. She felt the familiar thumping of her heart and the constriction in her throat that was now so commonplace it had almost become comforting.

Apart from looking a little older with more grey hair, she noted that he hadn't changed very much at all. His tall, broad stature filled the doorway and, as always, he was what Eleanor would have described as, 'Well turned out'.

'Hi,' she said with a faint smile and then watched as Thomas's face changed from one that was etched with concern, to one that showed obvious relief.

'Please come in Jess. It's so good to see you,' he said quietly, before showing her into the lounge. Would you like tea or coffee?'

But without answering the question she found herself blurting out, 'I found some letters from a man called Anton. Did you know about him Dad? Did you know about Anton?'

She looked at his face and saw it had taken on a grey colour and the worry lines had dramatically reappeared. This was not what she had rehearsed on her journey to Kent. She had promised herself she was going to be calm and measured; to let him speak; maybe to explain or perhaps just to listen to what she had to tell him. But she had blown all that in an emotional outburst and now she was sobbing uncontrollably in front of the man she knew as her father, but who she hadn't spoken to for well over ten years.

She watched him leave the room momentarily and then return with a box of tissues and a glass of water. She smiled gratefully at him and then wiping her face, took a deep breath and tried to compose herself. 'I'm sorry, it's been a very difficult few days for me but I really didn't intend on having a meltdown.'

Thomas nodded, 'It's okay, I understand. And in answer to your question, yes I did know about Anton. How about I make us a hot drink and we have a proper talk?'

Jess nodded her agreement and felt grateful for his calmness and honesty, and although she knew it was going to be hard for her, she also realised how hard it was going to be for her father as well.

Within minutes Thomas had returned with two mugs of coffee, pushing the door closed behind him to drown out the sound of the barking dog.

'If you want to let the dog in it's fine by me,' she said, realising it was more a comment to help break the ice than her actually wanting to see the dog.

Thomas made a face and shaking his head replied, 'He's rather on the large side and has the sort of coat that he seems to think looks better on others than on himself! And in any case Sally will take him out shortly so peace will be restored.'

Sally...Sally. Jess repeated the name in her head realising that it was the first time she had heard him say it. She had never seen her, never heard her voice and after the initial shock of her father's revelation, had locked the 'offending woman' away in the back of her mind, deciding she would never think about her again.

The pair sat sipping their coffee in silence for several minutes before Thomas sat forward in his chair and said, 'I'm just trying to... to...decide I guess on the best way of moving things forward.'

In response Jess moved to the edge of her seat and put her cup down with a bang, spilling some of the dark liquid onto the table. Breathing in sharply she replied, 'Dad, you are not chairing a business meeting nor are you dealing with a customer. You are speaking to me, Jess, your daughter.' And then before she could stop herself added, 'Although that, I have recently discovered, is in considerable doubt.' She immediately regretted the latter comment and cursed herself for not biting her tongue but for some reason she couldn't bring herself to apologise.

Thomas pulled a tissue from the box on the table and Jess gritted her teeth behind her lips which were clamped firmly together. And then to her dismay she realised that the tissue was not for mopping up the coffee as she had thought, but for wiping the tears that were now trickling down his cheeks.

She got to her feet and moved towards Thomas's chair. He immediately stood up and without any awkwardness they hugged each other, clinging on tightly, their faces streaked with tears. It felt so good she thought, realising just how much she had missed the feeling of her father's strong arms around her.

'Dad,' she said, choking back the tears, 'Why don't we just open up our hearts, you know...let it all out. It's going to be tough for both of us but it's the only way we are going to get through this and be able to.. you know, move forward.'

Thomas smiled weakly, nodding in agreement and seemingly grateful for her attempt to recover the situation and with a hint of humour as well. And then looking into his eyes, she realised that despite his stature, he suddenly seemed so much smaller and vulnerable somehow and she felt more tears pricking her eyes.

Sitting next to each other now, she listened as her father recounted the day Eleanor had told him that she was pregnant. 'I remember it so clearly, just as if it were yesterday,' he said quietly. 'I was ecstatic, we both were. We laughed and cried and I remember picking her up and swinging her round, which with hindsight probably wasn't one of my better ideas.'

Jess touched his arm and he put his hand over hers, squeezing it gently.

'We made so many plans for our little family, I was on cloud nine, I'd never felt so happy. And whenever we talked about names, it was always going to be Jessica for a girl.' He took a deep breath and continued, 'And then, one day, my world fell apart.' He sighed and shaking his head added, 'It was the hardest day of my life.'

She looked at her father and gave a reassuring nod. 'And then what happened?'

He took a deep breath and continued, 'And then Eleanor told me about Anton...about the affair and worst of all about the fact that she couldn't be sure I was the baby's father.'

Jess bit her lip and fought back tears as she listened to her father's emotional account of the revelation.

'But I loved her Jess and I had already fallen in love with the baby she was carrying. I'd already fallen in love with *you*,' he trailed off and got to his feet. 'I'll get us some more coffee,' he said with a weak smile. 'I think we're going to need it.'

With her father in the kitchen, Jess wiped her eyes and tried to gather her thoughts. As she sat in quiet contemplation, she found her eyes scanning the room. She had been careful not to look too closely while Thomas had been in the room as it somehow would have felt intrusive, but now looking around she felt more than a pang of guilt. But she wasn't meaning to be nosey, she just wanted to try and get some sort of snapshot of his life since he had left them, to try and visualise what his life was like and who the important people were *in* his life.

The furniture was comfortable but far from new and the carpet was worn in places, but the room had a homely feel, helped by the many photographs that decorated the walls. They were, of course, mainly pictures of people she didn't know, although Thomas was in many of them and a woman who she assumed to be Sally. But her eyes stopped suddenly on the photograph hanging in the middle of one of the walls, as if in pride of place. It was a large print of her graduation ceremony with Thomas and Eleanor standing proudly on either side of her and she immediately felt her shoulders relax and some of the tension began to dissipate. She stood up and moved closer to the photo. She touched the edge of the frame, it was made from a beautiful heavy gilt material and she could see it had been professionally mounted. And it brought a smile to her lips. A smile of relief and gratitude.

When Thomas returned, Jess saw that he was carrying a tray complete with cups and saucers, milk jug, sugar bowl, cafetiere and a plate of biscuits. She guessed that Sally must have returned from walking the dog and had prepared the refreshments, but was grateful to her for her seeming discretion.

'It's beautiful isn't it?' Thomas enquired. 'Your photograph I mean.'

Jess nodded, 'Yes Dad, it really is.'

He placed the tray on the table and moving towards her, put an arm around her shoulders.

'I look at it every day you know and as I move around the room your eyes seem to follow me and although it may sound strange, I've found so much comfort in that. It's as if you're somehow with me.'

'It seems strange to see us all together,' she said. 'I'm assuming you know Mum died earlier in the year?'

Thomas nodded. 'Remember Betty?' he said with a slight grimace.

'Ah, enough said,' Jess replied, pulling a face which matched her father's grimace.

'I desperately wanted to get in touch with you after Eleanor died. I argued with myself for weeks afterwards but I finally decided that if you needed me then you would contact me,' he said.

Jess nodded. 'It's okay. I understand.'

And then they both smiled and she hoped it was a father/daughter connection that would help them both on the road to reconciliation.

She poured them both some coffee and then asked, 'Is it okay if I ask a couple of questions Dad?'

He nodded and she noticed him swallow hard as if bracing himself for what was to come.

'Do you know for sure who my biological father is Dad? Is..I mean *was* Anton my father? You see I've seen a photograph of him and I think I look like him. And so does Grace and Alex come to that.' She wasn't sure why she had brought the two of them into the equation as he wouldn't know who they were, but somehow it seemed to give the statement legitimacy.

Thomas looked away briefly and then taking a deep breath nodded, 'Yes Jess, we had a DNA test and sadly for me it showed there was no chance of you being my biological child.' And then in little more than a whisper he added, 'You said *was*, I assume he has died then?'

She nodded her confirmation but said nothing more, not that there was anything more to say really. Anton was dead. She would never get to meet him. She would never know her biological father. She would never hear his side of the story. And now her mother was dead as well. It was if they had conspired against her.

She got to her feet as she felt anger rising up through her body. 'So why the hell didn't you tell me? Why did you and my mother think it was okay to keep something so momentous from the very person who would be affected the most? Why Dad, just tell me why?' She realised she had almost spat the words out and she could see the look of shock on his face. She slumped back down onto the sofa and covered her face with her hands, the overwhelming feelings of anger not allowing the tears that had once again gathered like dark heavy clouds to flow and release some of the pent up emotion.

Thomas jumped to his feet in response to her sudden outburst and was now pacing the room, shaking his head and wringing his hands. 'I'm so sorry Jess but please let me try and explain.' His voice was calm and soft and she noted that it didn't match his body language at all. He had always been a gentle person and she was never more grateful for this than now. She knew only too well that anger was a pointless emotion but she just couldn't seem to help herself.

He moved closer to the sofa and asked, 'May I sit next to you?'

She nodded and was relieved that he had not sat down right next to her but had perceptively given her space by leaving a gap between them both.

After a few moments of silence in which it seemed he was gathering his thoughts, he said, 'I wanted to tell you. I had always wanted to tell you right from an age when you would have been able to begin to understand but Eleanor was adamant that you must be protected from knowing.'

Jess shook her head in disbelief and replied bluntly, 'That's easy to say now my mother is *dead* and she can't have the chance of answering the same question, nor can she defend herself.' She wasn't sure why she suddenly felt the need to protect Eleanor but was relieved that she hadn't gone one step further and called him a liar, as when she looked at him she saw his face was contorted in a grimace of pain and she immediately felt sorry for her caustic comment.

The momentary silence was broken by the sound of the lounge door opening and in the doorway stood the figure of a petite woman with short dark hair, dressed in jeans and jumper.

'Sally, it's okay...we're okay. Nothing to worry about,' Thomas said.

Jess noted his tone was gentle and calm and he was smiling reassuringly at the woman in the doorway. In return she smiled back at him and without saying a word she withdrew and closed the door gently behind her.

Jess immediately felt a pang of guilt and looking at Thomas apologised for raising her voice.

'Sally has...she has what you might call a *nervous disposition*,' he said and she noticed he'd looked away when he'd spoken the words.

'I'm so sorry. It was wrong of me to raise my voice, especially in your house,' she said regretfully and he nodded at her in what she hoped was acceptance of her apology, rather than agreement with her statement.

They sat in silence for a few moments before Jess spoke again.

'Did you know Anton was mixed race?' she asked. But before he could answer she felt compelled to continue. 'And *that* is what is also so hugely significant. Do you see? I'm not only a different person to the one I thought I was, I have a completely different background and heritage to the one I thought I had...a totally different identity. Did you not think how important that might be to me and how it changes everything?' Her voice was calm and steady now as she looked directly at her father.

Thomas inhaled sharply and replied, 'Yes I did, which is just another reason why I always wanted to tell you. Perhaps it would have been easier if you'd looked...you know...looked...'

'Looked what Dad? Less white?' she interrupted.

'No, no. That's not what I meant. I simply meant more like Anton I suppose. It might have pushed Eleanor into realising it was the right thing to do.'

'But I do look like him, Dad.'

'Maybe now, but people always used to say you looked like me when you were a child and perhaps in my subconscious it was what I believed or at least wanted to believe. Everything I've told you is the truth Jess, that's all I can say and there are no words to explain the regret I feel in not telling you.'

She sighed and looking at her father replied simply, 'I know Dad, I know.'

On the drive back to London she felt like her head was about to explode. She kept going over and over the conversations she'd had with Thomas, trying to make sense of them but try as she might nothing seemed to make any sense. It was a betrayal and it was clear that her parents had let her down in the most spectacular way. Her whole identity was in question, her very being and she suddenly felt alone, somehow detached from everyone and lonely, so very lonely.

The shrill sound of her phone ringing suddenly jolted her mind back into the present moment and she cursed herself for changing the ringtone. She pulled over and looked at the screen. It was Alex. Dear, sweet Alex. Just seeing his name on the screen lifted her mood and reminded her that she wasn't alone. She had Alex. And there was Poppy and Amber and her friends at work and there was Rosa, Nora and Will. No, she wasn't alone at all but at the same she knew that wasn't enough. She needed to know her roots, her family origins and she realised at that moment that it would have to start with Anton's widow, Melissa.

'Alex, hi,' she said as brightly as she could manage.

'Jess are you okay? I was worried when you hadn't phoned.'

She gasped, remembering that she'd promised to phone him when she'd left her father's house. 'I'm so sorry. I just wanted to get away when I came out of my dad's house and I meant to stop down the road but...well never mind the excuses, I'm sorry if I worried you.'

She heard him laugh at the other end of the phone and relieved, she added, 'Alex Blake, you are the best boyfriend anyone could wish for. I'll phone you as soon as I get home.'

And as she put her phone back in her bag and re-started the engine she realised she felt a slight glimmer of optimism at what the future might hold. This was just another new chapter in her life. That was all. Nothing more. And life had a habit of throwing her curved balls, she should have realised that by now. All she had to do now was to learn how to catch them.

CHAPTER TWENTY-SEVEN

Back in London, Jess was relieved to see Poppy was at home. They hugged each other and Jess said with a grimace, 'Got a spare couple of hours Poppy, I've got so much to tell you?'

Poppy smiled and replied, 'I'll put the kettle on and see if we have any 'emergency chocolate' in the fridge.

'Chocolate is essential,' Jess replied. 'And after what I've got to tell you, I think you will need some as well Poppy!'

She made a quick phone call to Alex to let him know she was home safely and explained that Poppy was there so she would ring him later with the next instalment of her 'life story'. She realised she was making light of it so he wouldn't worry too much but she also realised it was the right thing for her as well. Somehow she thought she would find it easier to tell Poppy first, maybe because they had always told each other everything or maybe because their relationship was different to the one she had with Alex. She wasn't entirely sure, but whichever it was she was comfortable with her decision, reminding herself again that she was the protagonist in this particular story.

The two women sat together on the sofa and Jess suddenly realised how quiet it was without Dave.

'Before I begin telling you my tales, how are things with you and Will and Dave of course?' she asked.

'All good thanks,' Poppy replied smiling. 'Very good, in fact, and Dave is back to his old self. Unfortunately, Will has taught him some new phrases and he now says *watch out* or *lock the door* whenever his mother comes round or anyone else come to think about it!'

Jess laughed. She felt genuinely pleased that Poppy seemed so happy with Will and although her friend had said she wasn't looking for 'Mr Right', she thought that maybe she had found him in what were quite unusual circumstances.

She broke off a couple of squares of the 'emergency chocolate' and mixed it in her mouth with the warm tea. 'I really do think that chocolate is a very underrated cure-all,' she said looking seriously at Poppy.

Poppy shook her head. 'I don't think you're going to win a Nobel prize for that one,' she said, raising her eyebrows.

'Maybe not, but I'm going to keep up my research anyway, you know, just in case,' Jess said with a grin.

She sat back into the cushions, tucking her legs up onto the sofa and then half turning to Poppy began explaining first about the letters, then about her meetings with Grace Martin and finally about seeing her father.

Poppy sat quietly, occasionally asking a question for clarification on something, but Jess was relieved that mainly she just listened as she poured her heart out, and it was really very cathartic.

'So there you have it,' Jess concluded, and then looking at her watch added, 'My new and unforeseen life story in less than an hour!'

Poppy puffed her cheeks out and exhaled loudly before replying, 'Good God Jess, I don't know what to say. It's an incredibly sad story for so many people but especially, of course, for you. And to find out in the way you did must be utterly devastating.'

Jess nodded. She absolutely knew that Poppy would understand how she felt and she was ever grateful for having such an amazing friend. And then, in an attempt to lessen the emotional tension in the room she said, 'And to be honest Poppy, when people talk about sorting out a deceased person's affairs, I had no idea it was going to be quite so literal!'

'Ah, sardonic humour. Always useful in these sort of situations,' Poppy said, hugging her friend tightly. 'You going to be okay tonight, only I'm on a night shift?'

Jess smiled at her friend. 'I'll be fine. I need to plan my next move in this game of discovery and that requires some thinking about.' She knew that now the Pandora's Box was open, there was no closing the lid until all the secrets were out. 'The genie's out of the bottle Poppy. And it's not going back in.'

A few minutes after Poppy had left for work, Jess heard the front door bang and Amber appeared in the doorway laden with shopping bags.

'Christmas shopping?' Jess asked, and her friend rolled her eyes in reply.

'It's great to see you Jess,' she said excitedly. 'How's tricks?'

'Good thanks Amber. How are things with you, wedding plans in full swing?' She loved Amber dearly but really couldn't face going through the whole story again that evening and she knew that wedding talk would shift the focus away from her.

Amber raised her eyes to the ceiling. 'Well, I now have five bridesmaids, would you believe? You and Poppy, my sister and two little kids who I don't even know but they are my mum's best friend's daughter's children, apparently. I think I'll just hand over the reins completely to her!'

Jess laughed and replied jokingly, 'Who, your mother's best friend?'

And then Amber began laughing too. 'It's ridiculous. But that's my mother for you. And there's more to tell, so do you fancy a beer?'

'Have you forgotten who you're talking to? Of course I fancy a beer! You go ahead and I'll join you shortly. Just need to make a call.'

After phoning Alex and filling him in on how things went with her father, Jess pulled on her coat and walked the short distance to the local pub to meet Amber. She had deliberately kept some of the detail from him as she wanted to tell him in person and then if she cried he would be able to take her in his arms and protect her from herself. She loved him and realised how much she missed him when she wasn't with him which added another dimension to this game of discovery.

Amber had already bought the drinks and was sitting in a quiet corner of the busy pub. Jess thanked her and took a large swig of the beer, exclaiming, 'Perfect, just what I needed,' and then steered her friend into more wedding talk.

'My mum wants us to get married in church, but to be honest I'm more comfortable with a register office or a venue. And she's already chosen the style of wedding dress and the colour scheme!'

Jess looked at her friend's face and quickly realised it wasn't what she wanted at all. 'Amber, why don't you and James decide what you want and then remind your mum that it's *your* wedding and you are going to do it your way?'

Amber made a face and replied, 'If only it were that simple Jess. But you see I can't do that as my mother is paying for the whole thing. So that's the deal. She pays and she organises!'

'Difficult one then,' Jess admitted. 'But surely organising something doesn't mean making all the decisions?'

'It does when you're my mother,' Amber replied, with seeming resignation.

Next morning Jess slept in. She hadn't heard Amber go off to work or Poppy come back from her night shift and was surprised when she looked at her phone and saw it was ten o'clock. She'd been awake part of the night, planning the next move in her game of discovery and then when she had eventually fallen asleep, she had slept fitfully, tossing and turning and dreaming about the strangest situations that were impossible to interpret.

Downstairs in the kitchen she made herself a strong cup of coffee and opened a text message from Alex. She smiled as she read that Velvet had decorated the pub ready for Christmas and he had sent some photos of the enormous tree next to the fireplace and of the beams decked with yards of garlands and twinkling lights. It looked amazing but although she was looking forward to seeing it in person, Christmas was the last thing on her mind at the moment. She hadn't even started any present shopping, she reminded herself, but until she had executed her next move she couldn't even begin to think about it. Instead she sat down at the table with a pen and writing pad and recalled her middle of the night plan to write to Melissa Johnson and ask her if she would be prepared to meet her. In his letter Anton had said that Melissa knew everything about him, so she hoped that hearing from her wouldn't be a complete surprise. She knew, though, that it was going to be a hard letter to write.

She was still sitting at the table at lunchtime when Poppy appeared in the kitchen. The table was littered with balls of paper that she had torn from the pad, screwed up and tossed aside. Some of the sheets contained just a few words, while others had several lines. But they had all eventually suffered the same inevitable fate.

'Hi Poppy,' she said. And then pointing at the table added, 'Sorry about the mess.'

Poppy raised her eyebrows and said, 'Next part of your plan by any chance?'

Jess nodded glumly in response.

'Can I help at all? Fresh pair of eyes and all that.'

Jess smiled gratefully and unravelled some of the sheets of paper so she could show Poppy her failed attempts so far.

'It's just an observation but perhaps you're trying too hard. Why not just start with a short letter introducing yourself and asking if she will meet you? If Anton really has told her everything then she won't be too surprised,' Poppy suggested.

Jess smiled at her friend and exclaimed, 'That's exactly it Poppy. You're a genius and I love you for it!'

Poppy laughed and said, 'Pleasure. And now if you'll excuse me, I'm going back to bed with a superfood salad and a kale shake.'

Jess pulled a face of mock disgust and kissed her friend on the cheek.

An hour later and clutching the finished letter tightly in her gloved hand, Jess walked to the post box along the street and pushed the letter and her hand into the box as far as they would go. Then with a sudden surge of relief that she had done what she'd set out to do, made a spur of the moment decision and jumped on a tube to Oxford Circus to make a start on her Christmas shopping.

The cheerful crowds and the Christmas lights and decorations lifted her mood and she was soon loading gifts into a basket in her favourite department store. She chose a gorgeous vanilla and pomegranate scented candle for Amber and a superfood recipe book for Poppy. For Nora she found the most exquisite hand-painted glittery Christmas bauble and for Mabel a wipeable book full of colourful animals all wearing different style hats. And for Rosa she found a beautiful bone china cake stand which she hoped would quickly be stacked with delicious cakes. Now that was a 'win win' she told herself with a smile. And it was a good start towards Christmas and had served to take her mind off the Pandora's box at least for a short while.

CHAPTER TWENTY-EIGHT

The following week Jess was on her way back to Thripton again. She had heard nothing back from Melissa Johnson so far but she was working on the premise that no news was good news. She hadn't seen Alex for almost a week either and she felt a flutter of excitement as she neared the village. It was also what Henry had described as a 'full dress rehearsal' for the Christmas concert that evening and she had packed a pair of black trousers and a red top as instructed by the choir master.

Nora had sent her a message to say she had made herself the 'obligatory uniform' and Jess was amazed at how her friend could have found time to do this with Mabel demanding so much of her time and attention. She really was incredibly talented and Jess wished there was some way she could help her realise her dream of starting up her own business.

As she pulled into the pub car park she was suddenly struck by a brilliant idea. She practically leapt out of the car and ran inside the pub, scanning the bar area for any sign of Alex. Velvet waved and disappeared into the back and within seconds Alex was round the pub side of the bar. He hugged her as if he never wanted to let go and it felt so good. Strangely she felt like she was back home.

She lifted her head from his chest and said, 'Alex, this is going to sound a little bit random but I think I may have had a good idea.'

Looking directly at her and keeping a completely straight face he replied, 'Actually I have known you to have good ideas before, perhaps you're being a bit hard on yourself!'

She pretended to pummel his chest with her fists and laughing said, 'Very funny. Now shut up and listen. You know the outbuilding in the car park, what's it like?'

He raised his eyebrows and replied, 'Well you couldn't live in it if that's what you're thinking?' And then after pausing for a few seconds added, 'Please tell me that's not what you're thinking?'

She laughed. 'No of course not. I already have two places to live and that's a big enough burden. I was thinking about Nora. She's a fantastic dressmaker and would love to start up her own business but she couldn't do it from her own home as it's just too small.'

Alex smiled and hugged her again. 'Jones, I completely agree it is rather random, but if it would work for Nora then she is welcome to clean it up and make use of it.'

She grinned and replied, 'Really? That's fantastic. I'll put it to her tonight after the dress rehearsal. Are you coming?'

He kissed her hair and replied, 'I wouldn't miss it for the world and I'm particularly looking forward to seeing you in your choir outfit!'

Henry was on top form at the dress rehearsal that evening and as usual called them all to order in a way that made Jess and Nora jump with fright.

'From the top,' he bellowed, which made Nora dissolve into a fit of nervous giggles and brought Marcus running to her with a glass of water.

Jess looked towards the back of the church to where Alex was sitting and he signalled an encouraging 'thumbs up' and then she was singing her heart out, filling the magnificent building with the crystal clear vocals that Nora had previously told her made her hairs stand on end. It was the only thing she was really good at it and she loved the fact that it actually made other people happy. And then the whole choir was singing and it sounded spectacular, majestic even and at the end Jess noticed Henry had tears in his eyes.

'Job done,' she said to Nora and Marcus. 'We're ready.'

At The Plough Jess complimented V on her Christmas decorating skills. It really did look amazing, the log fire was roaring, tiny fairy lights twinkled all around the pub and the tree looked spectacular adorned with dozens of different sized gold and silver baubles. Pure white lights hung from the branches like tiny stalactites and surrounding the bottom of the tree were piles of different shape boxes posing as presents, all wrapped in colourful metallic paper and finished with ribbons and bows. It was mesmerising, and the pub even had that lovely Christmas smell of cinnamon and mulled wine.

A little later she managed to get Nora on her own and told her about her idea for the outbuilding. 'It could be perfect Nora, I'm sure between all of us we could make it into a lovely little sewing room and there's already electricity in there.'

Nora sat in silence for a few seconds and then Jess saw a solitary tear trickle down her cheek. 'I'm overwhelmed Jess, what a fantastic idea and an amazing opportunity. I just don't know what else to say except thank you and of course Alex. I love you both.'

Next morning Jess was woken up by the ringing of her phone. Alex was already up and she could hear him having a full blown conversation in the kitchen with Rolo. She smiled as it sounded so adorable even though it was rather one way. She leant over and grabbed her phone from the bedside cabinet and saw Poppy's name flashing on the screen. 'Hi Poppy, is everything okay?' she asked.

'Hi Jess, yes everything's fine but a letter has come for you in a handwritten envelope and I think it may be from Melissa. I'm coming to Thripton later today and I just wondered if you wanted me to bring it?'

Jess felt her heart quicken as she replied, 'Yes please Poppy, even if I am scared stiff of what it might say.'

She put the phone back on the bedside table and groaned, pulling the duvet up over her head. It would have been quite easy just to hide in bed today and not open the letter but she knew in her heart that she needed to know what Melissa had to say, and also Nora was popping round to have a look inside the outbuilding so she needed to get herself moving.

'Morning,' Alex called from the kitchen. He'd heard her talking on the phone and had 'released the beast', who had apparently been dying to come and see her since hearing her voice on the phone.

'Hello Rolo,' she said rubbing his ears. He leapt onto the bed and licked her face, before rolling on his back for her to rub his belly.

'Cup of coffee,' Alex announced, kissing her on the head.

'Thank you,' she replied smiling up at him. 'It was Poppy on the phone, she thinks there's a letter from Melissa, she's going to bring it later today.'

He nodded and squeezed her arm. 'I'm here for you Jess, you know that don't you,' and she smiled in response, knowing it was a statement rather than a question.

An hour later she was inside the outbuilding of the pub with Nora and Alex. Nora walked around the empty space and gasped with delight. 'It's much lighter than I imagined it would be and there's plenty of space for a sewing table and cupboards and drawers. It's perfect.'

Jess smiled at Alex who in response joked, 'That's great Nora, at least it'll stop Jess moving in!'

Nora shot Jess a questioning look. 'It's just his attempt at humour Nora, ignore him, he thinks he's funny!' and then she kissed him on the cheek before he disappeared back to the pub. 'Time for a coffee or do you need to get back for Mabel?' She asked.

'Yes please, coffee would be lovely. I have plenty of time as I've left Mabel watching television with my mum,' and then looking at her watch added, 'It'll be Teletubbies time now!'

Jess had already created a mental picture of Mabel and her Grandma watching television together and it brought a smile to her face. 'Is that her favourite programme?' she asked Nora.

'Yes, she absolutely loves it, although I'm not sure Mabel is quite as keen!'

Both women dissolved into fits of laughter as they linked arms and walked across the car park to the pub. It was just what Jess needed before having to face up to the letter from Melissa.

After lunch she walked from the pub to No. 3 to wait for Poppy. She stood outside the cottage and thought about how much she'd always loved it. Ever since she had plucked up courage to return after Eleanor had died, she'd realised just how much being there had made her feel closer to her mother.

But today as she opened the front door, it somehow felt different. She felt cheated and deceived by the person she loved the most in the world, and disappointed, yes that was the word, disappointed that the very person she respected and admired the most had destroyed the memories of her life that she had always thought of as perfect.

She quickly wiped her eyes as she heard Poppy's Beetle coming down the lane. She didn't want her to see that she was emotional even before she'd even seen the letter.

She walked up the garden path and opened the car door for Poppy, greeting her with a hug. Poppy reached in her handbag and pulled out the envelope and holding it out towards her she said, 'Would you like me to come inside while you open it?'

Jess nodded in response and smiling weakly, linked arms with her best friend and walked back down the garden path.

She felt the contents of the sealed envelope and realised it was thicker than just a sheet of paper. Suddenly feeling a wave of hope, she tore the envelope open and a small package fell out onto the table. She looked at Poppy with wide eyes and picking up the package, passed it to her. 'Could you open it for me please?'

Poppy took it from her. 'Of course I will Jess, but it looks as though there's a letter in the envelope as well, do you think you should perhaps read that first?'

She took some deep breaths and nodding to her friend removed the folded letter and read the first page. And then breathing a sigh of relief and looking at Poppy said, 'She wants to meet me and apparently there's a surprise in the package for me. She wants to meet me Poppy, I can't tell you how important this is to me.' And then she was crying again but this time the tears were ones of relief.

The two women hugged each other tightly before Poppy said, 'Would you like me to open the package?'

'I think I can do it now that I've read the letter. Thank you Poppy, what would I do without you?'

She took the package from her friend and carefully removed the tape which was securing the flat package. It was a photograph, carefully packaged between two pieces of rigid card. A photograph of a man she recognised as Anton, flanked by two identical looking young men dressed in graduation caps and gowns. A little note was attached to the bottom of the picture which read, *Your father and your twin brothers.* She stared at the photo in disbelief, feeling a surge of emotion coursing through her veins and when she looked at Poppy she saw that she too had tears trickling down her face.

With perfect timing and as if pre-planned, Rosa appeared at

the door with the most spectacular looking triple layered chocolate cake. The three women sat round the kitchen table and Jess filled Rosa in on the developments.

Jess watched as Rosa's jaw dropped in astonishment and then throwing her arms in the air, she declared, 'Good heavens my darling, just look at those two handsome boys. You have two for the price of one, you are a very lucky girl Jess. Two brothers and twins as well. That's very special you know.'

Jess sat in silence contemplating her words and then she quickly realised that those few words spoken in Rosa's own inimitable way, may just have helped change her mind set regarding the situation she had unexpectedly found herself in.

She looked at the photograph again and then smiling at her said, 'Yes Rosa you're right. I *am* lucky and perhaps I can now start to look at this as the beginning of a new chapter rather than the end of the book.'

Back at the pub Jess showed Alex the letter and the photograph of her father and brothers.

'Wow,' he exclaimed looking at the image. 'This is incredible and the likeness with you is obvious. How do you feel?'

'Well, thanks to Rosa I think I actually feel quite positive about it. I'm looking forward to meeting them...assuming they want to meet me,' she said suddenly, feeling a pang of doubt.

Alex gave her a reassuring squeeze and she felt the uncertainty fade as he replied, 'Who on earth wouldn't want to meet you?'

Later on as Jess was getting ready to head back to London, Alex's phone rang and she saw his face change. He was talking in hushed tones and she could tell it was not a friendly conversation, partly by the look on his face and partly by the way he was pacing around the kitchen. *No, no. I can't do that* and *that's unfair* were the only words she could pick out from the conversation and not wanting to look as if she was listening in, she left the room with Rolo following close behind her.

After several minutes Alex joined her in the sitting room. Rolo jumped up to greet him, wagging his tail frantically as if he'd been missing for half of his life.

His face softened as he patted the dog's head and then flopping down on the sofa next to her said, 'The damn cheek of the woman. And to think I was actually married to her.'

Jess pulled a face. 'Oh dear, what did she want?'

He sat forward on the sofa and replied, 'She only wants me to give Jazz another chance at working in the pub. Apparently it was my fault it didn't work out last time because I didn't give her enough training and support.'

She gasped, suddenly remembering that she'd completely forgotten to tell him what Jazz had said to her when she came into the pub to apologise. 'Alex I'm so sorry, with everything that's been going on I forgot to tell you that Jazz asked me if you might give her another job. I didn't comment but when she left she said she would, and I quote, 'Get my mother onto it.'

Alex rolled his eyes, 'Absolutely typical,' and then with a worried expression quickly added, 'Jazz I mean, not you obviously. She has a way of knowing which buttons to press and just for the record there's absolutely no need for you to apologise, it's a wonder you can even remember your name with everything that's been going on.' He immediately put his hands to his head as if realising the irony of his words.

Jess took his hands and smiling said, 'Please don't think you have to be guarded with me, I love the funny things you say. They are what makes *you you* and you should never change. It's who you are and I happen to love who you are.'

He kissed her hair and replied, 'Thank you.'

In the car park Alex put her bags into the back of the car and tapping the roof said, 'Safe journey Rowan, remember there's precious cargo on board.'

She smiled and then before kissing him asked, 'What will you do about Jazz?'

'I'm not sure,' he answered. 'I need to have a think.'

On the drive home Jess's thoughts kept returning to the phone call between him and Angela. She couldn't shake off the nagging doubt she had that there was something he wasn't telling her. Something didn't quite make sense. He had already given Jazz a chance and she had messed it up but it seemed that Angela had some sort of hold over him, otherwise surely he would have just said an outright 'no' to her request. Her thoughts were interrupted by her phone ringing and she somehow knew it was going to be Alex.

A couple of miles down the road she pulled over in a side street and took her phone out of her bag. The screen flashed 'missed call' and as she opened the call log she smiled when she saw that it *was* Alex and that he'd left a message. She pressed the voicemail button and her heart melted when she heard his voice saying, *Jess, I forgot to tell you how much I love you before you left...so...well that's it really...I love you...okay, bye then...oh yes and text me when you're home, love you.*

She played the message twice more before she set off again and then tucked away her previous thoughts about Angela to the back of her mind.

CHAPTER TWENTY-NINE

With just over two weeks to Christmas, Jess realised she still had a lot to do. In between going to work she still had Alex's present to buy; all of the presents to wrap; cards to write; the Christmas concert; helping Poppy and Amber to decorate the house; the ward Christmas meal and of course the possibility of a meeting with Anton's wife and maybe even her brothers. But although she felt mild panic at the thought of all of this, she also felt a sense of anticipation and eagerness at the thought of meeting and finding out more about her new found family and about herself.

Buoyed by her nervous excitement, she picked up her phone and tapped in Melissa's number. The voice at the other end of the phone was soft and friendly and Jess felt a surge of relief. 'Hi, this is Jess...Jess Jones...Anton's daughter...' and then she trailed off not knowing what else to say.

'Jess, how lovely to hear your voice. It makes it feel real somehow. I was so happy to get your letter. We have so much to talk about don't we?'

And then the conversation between the two strangers flowed naturally and easily and as she ended the call she knew that she had made the right move.

The following days were so busy that the time passed by like a whirlwind. Jess hadn't even managed to speak to Alex every day and though they'd exchanged several hundred text messages, she realised how much she missed actually hearing his voice.

But now it was time for her to set off to Thripton again and she was full of excitement and nervous tension as apart from seeing Alex, it was the Christmas concert the following evening. Rowan was packed ready to go with bags and presents and she smiled to herself as she carefully placed Alex's present on the front seat. It had taken a lot of research and quite a lot of money but she knew it was the perfect present for him, and she set off on the journey to Thripton singing along to Christmas songs on the radio at the top of her voice.

'So what made you decide to wait until after Christmas to go and see Melissa?' Alex asked later that evening after the pub had closed.

Jess frowned and replied, 'It was just impossible to set a date what with work and the concert and Christmas so close, so rather than put her in an awkward position I suggested we wait until after the festivities. And of course with her being in Manchester it's not exactly close.'

He nodded, 'Sounds sensible but I bet you can't wait.'

'I'm desperate to go but it gives me a bit of time as well to, you know, gather my thoughts. And to be honest, these last few weeks have been so full of shocks and surprises, I don't really think I can cope with any more just at the moment!'

He pulled her close and kissing her gently replied, 'Well I hope you can put up with just one more surprise seeing it's Christmas next week?'

'I'll try my best,' she said grinning at him. 'Changing the subject, have you made a decision about Jazz yet?' She tried to keep her voice as casual-sounding as possible as she knew from his text messages that he was still struggling with it all but although she had tried hard to keep the nagging feeling at the back of her mind, it just wouldn't stay there.

As she looked at him, she became immediately aware of the sudden change in his demeanour. So taking his hand she asked, 'What's wrong Alex, you can tell me anything you know?'

He sighed and keeping hold of her hand answered quietly, 'It's something I find really hard to talk about. I'm not intentionally keeping anything from you Jess, it's just painful for me and it makes the decision about giving Jazz another chance a really hard one. Come on let's go to bed and perhaps in the morning things will be a bit clearer.'

She nodded and smiled sympathetically and then followed him into the bedroom, not making any further comment.

At breakfast the following morning, Jess was aware that Alex was quiet and distant, as if he was deep in thought. He was definitely more of a morning person than she was and he was usually up first, but last night he had slept restlessly, tossing and turning and mumbling in his sleep and so she had got up and made him a cup of tea, bringing it into the bedroom where he had drunk it gratefully.

Rolo sat by his side at the table and he ruffled his head gently repeating, 'good boy' absent-mindedly and picking at his toast. It was so unlike him and she could feel her stomach churning as she watched him across the table.

And then as if sensing her concern, he looked up from his half eaten breakfast and taking a deep breath said, 'She tried to take her own life. Jazz I mean, and Angela has always blamed me for it. And even though the rational part of me knows it wasn't my fault, I have been wracked with guilt ever since.'

Jess got up from the table and put an arm around his neck, cradling his head with her other arm as he wept openly. 'It's okay. It's okay, just let it all out,' she soothed. 'You'll feel better for it.'

He clung to her tightly as his throaty sobs gradually began to quieten and his shoulders started to relax. 'I'm so sorry, I didn't mean this to happen, especially not on such an important day for you,' he said quietly.

She looked at him questioningly and then realising he must have meant the Christmas concert, she smiled and kissed him on the cheek. She didn't want to burden him with how she had been feeling as this was about him, but nevertheless she felt a sense of relief that however bad the situation was, at least she knew *what* it was. And he was ready to talk which she felt was a big part of helping him work through the situation and hopefully to find a solution.

Later that day Jess went back to the cottage to get ready for the concert. She carefully applied extra makeup to her eyes which made them sparkle in the light and straightened her hair until it was glossy and sleek and fell perfectly onto her shoulders. After pulling on the 'choir uniform' as she and Nora had come to call it, she sprayed herself lightly with some shimmer spray and headed down to the church for a last minute rehearsal as per Henry's strict instructions.

Several choir members were already in the church and Jess was impressed at how incredibly smart everybody looked. The men were all dressed in dark suits with red bow ties that complemented the women's outfits perfectly and she felt a flutter of excitement as she walked towards the choir stalls.

The church itself looked stunning. It was lit by dozens of battery-powered candles which flickered gently and gave the church an air of calm and peace. The enormous Christmas tree had been dressed with hand-made decorations, designed and made by the local school and Sunday school children and was finished with shimmering silver lametta tinsel, each delicate individual strand hanging with vertical perfection. And the church flower arrangers had used masses of holly, mistletoe, ivy and fir to make garlands and wreaths, adding large sprigs of rosemary and thyme to their creations, giving the whole church a gorgeous Christmassy aroma.

The rehearsal went like a dream and Jess looked excitedly towards the church doors as the audience started to file in and take their seats. Alex was one of the first in and she was pleased to see that he had collected Rosa on the way. She smiled to herself as Rosa led him by the hand up the aisle and pointed to a pew right near the front. And Poppy and Will were not far behind, managing to squeeze in the pew next to them.

Rosa had mellowed considerably towards Alex recently and when Jess had asked her what had changed she'd said, 'That boy looks at you in the same way as *you* look at chocolate cake, so I know he must love you and that's all that matters to me.'

Nora nudged Jess enthusiastically as Josh, Mabel and her mother found seats towards the front as well, and when Mabel saw her she shrieked with excitement, bouncing up and down on Josh's knee.

At exactly seven o'clock the vicar began addressing the audience in a light-hearted and humorous way that made Jess think how much more appealing the church would be to the masses if more vicars were like him. He had managed to strike a clever balance between humour and seriousness in getting across the importance of the Christmas Story, and in turn it had set the scene for the evening perfectly. She took some deep breaths and cleared her throat as quietly as she could before taking up her position by the pulpit, and then smiling at the audience in front of her waited for Henry to give her the cue.

'You were amazing my darling, just amazing,' Rosa enthused at the end of the concert. 'Wasn't she Alex?' she added, poking him sharply in the ribs.

He let out a mock cry before taking Jess's hand and saying, 'You were incredible, honestly you're so talented. The whole concert was just fantastic.'

She smiled modestly feeling her cheeks flush, and then Marcus appeared with a tray of mulled wine and taking a glass from him she took a grateful swig.

Rosa had baked several batches of mince pies and she revelled in the praise and compliments which came from all angles.

Jess laughed as she heard her telling people that mince pies used to be illegal in England, so best eat two or three just in case it should ever happen again. 'Rosa, where on earth do you get these stories from?' she said rolling her eyes, but before she could answer Will appeared, and grinning told her that it was a legend from Oliver Cromwell's time so may in fact be true.

'That man of yours knows everything. The works of Shakespeare, Goldwynisms and now legends. Whatever will be next? she whispered to Poppy.

But Poppy wasn't listening. She was transfixed as she listened in admiration to Will, who was now re-telling the mince pie legend to the fascinated group who had gathered around him.

A little while later, Nora and Josh brought Mabel over to say goodnight and with her coat now removed, Jess could see that she was wearing the most gorgeous red velvet dress, edged with white satin ribbon and tiny poms poms which hung uniformly around the hemline.

'Is this one of your creations?' she asked in amazement, pointing to the gurgling baby.

'Yes,' Nora replied smiling with pride. 'This is Mabel, but you've met her before!'

Her response made Jess laugh out loud. 'And what a beautiful creation she is too,' she said and then tickling Mabel's tummy added, 'Your mum is being modest but she is very clever you know.'

'I played a small role in it too,' Josh said with a look of mock indignation.

'Really?' Jess replied with a wink. 'I didn't realise you could sew as well Josh!'

After most of the congregation had left and making sure Rosa was safely back at home, Jess and Alex walked hand in hand back to the pub. It was a clear and frosty evening and the dark night sky was scattered with stars that gleamed and glittered like diamond dust.

She sighed and said, 'The sky is so beautiful here, there's so much light pollution in London, that we just don't seem to have skies like this.

'Well I'm more than happy to share my skies with you, and anything else come to that,' Alex replied and as he pulled her close and they kissed under the stars, she felt a lovely warm feeling sweeping over her.

As they neared the pub they could hear excited voices and Christmas music spilling into the grounds and Jess saw Alex beam as he pulled open the door to reveal that it was packed to the rafters. Lots of people from the church had stopped off there on their way home and the atmosphere was electric.

Alex helped Velvet and Jake behind the bar, as Sandra brought out plates of food from the kitchen, smiling and chatting affably with the customers. He really had struck a brilliant balance with his staff choices Jess thought, and she could see that bringing Jazz back into the mix might upset the equilibrium. She reminded herself though that it had to be Alex's decision and she would support him in whatever he decided.

Her thoughts were interrupted by Marcus's voice behind her, 'Jess, I've been trying to catch you on your own all evening. Have you got time to pop up to the Hall tomorrow, preferably on your own? It's important.'

'Of course, I'll pop in on my way back to London if that's okay?' she answered, smiling reassuringly whilst at the same time getting the distinct feeling that there was something wrong. Why did he want to see her on his own? But it wasn't only his spoken words. His demeanour was somehow different as well, and it was that that had stopped her from asking any questions.

'Perfect,' he said with a faint smile. She watched him for a few moments as he carried on mingling and chatting with the visitors who had been at the church. But she also noticed that he kept looking over to a corner of the pub where a youngish man was sitting on his own at a small table. She hadn't seen him before, but there were a lot of people in the pub that evening who she didn't know so that wasn't really surprising. But what *was* unusual was that he seemed to be entirely on his own.

The last customers left the pub at past midnight and Alex had let all the staff go home soon after, declaring that he would do the clearing up. Pulling on an apron, Jess began clearing tables and filling the glass washer with dozens of empty glasses, while Alex was in the cellar or the 'engine room' as he often referred to it as.

On hearing Rolo moving around upstairs, she popped up and brought him down into the pub where he ran around gratefully picking up any bits of food that had dropped onto the floor.

'You'd better not be ill,' she warned as she chased around after him, desperately trying to get to the spillages before he did. And then with all the grace of a baby elephant, she fell headlong across the pub floor having caught her foot on the leg of a chair, and face planted in a spectacular move that would have scored top marks had there been a panel of judges around.

Rolo bounded over to her and licked the sides of her head in an attempt to get near to her face, and when Alex came up from the cellar a few seconds later she realised the scene must have looked very comical.

He helped her to her feet and they both fell about laughing. 'If you were trying to beat Rolo to the scraps and I can assure you that it won't work!' he said. 'And honestly if you're hungry then I can easily make you something to eat,' he added teasingly.

'Shut up,' she replied, wagging a finger while desperately trying to keep a straight face as she pretended to admonish him. 'That was not one of my finest moments I will admit, but it's nice to see you laughing so a slight dent to my pride is well worth it.'

'Falling over is fast becoming one of your specialities, but really there's no need to do it on my account.'

'Very funny,' she said brushing down her apron.

'I love you Jess Jones,' he said smiling. 'And tomorrow I will talk some more about Jazz and Angela because with you, I know I can.'

Next morning Jess made sure she was up first so she could take Alex breakfast in bed. She had woken a couple of times in the night and was relieved to find that he was sleeping soundly, the gentle rise and fall of his chest and the rhythmic feel of his soft breath on her skin allowing her to fall back to sleep with ease.

'Good morning,' she whispered, gently kissing him on the lips. 'Breakfast is served.'

He stretched his arms above his head and smiled up at her. 'I could get used to this,' he said. 'And I don't mean the breakfast in bed either,' he added, taking the laden tray from her. 'I'm so happy when you're here Jess, really happy,' and then taking a bite of the thickly buttered toast added, 'Actually perhaps I could get used to breakfast in bed as well!'

'Unfortunately I have to go soon. I promised Marcus I would call in on him on my way back home,' she said. 'Alex, do you know who the man was who was sitting in the corner of the pub last night on his own?

'The man Marcus was sitting with towards the end of the evening?' he asked.

'What?' she exclaimed. 'I didn't see Marcus sitting with him. Why didn't you tell me?'

He laughed, 'Well to be fair, I didn't know you wanted to know until now!'

'So who is he?' she pressed.

'I've no idea. Never seen him before. Well apart from at the concert that is,' he said shrugging.

'At the concert!' she repeated, practically shrieking now. 'He was at the concert?'

'Yes, he was sitting just behind us. Nice singing voice as well,' he replied. 'Anyway, why the sudden interest in the tall dark stranger?' he added with a wink.

'Oh nothing really, I just felt a bit sorry for him, you know sitting on his own. Everyone else in the pub seemed to know most people, especially Marcus and his family, but he didn't seem to know anyone. Except for Marcus it seems.'

She slid into bed next to him and resting her head on his chest said, 'Anyway enough about Marcus, tell me about Jazz and Angela. But only if you want to.'

'Yes I do want to Jess,' he replied. And then she listened while he talked about their relationships; the not so good times; the bad times, but also the good times. *The ugly bits are quite ugly*, he'd warned her. And they were. They really were.

CHAPTER THIRTY

After leaving the pub Jess made the short journey to Barrowick Hall. Marcus greeted her with a hug and Brutus vied for her attention by circling her legs and yapping frantically. She laughed and bent down to pick him up. 'Hello Mr, how are you?' she enquired of the tiny animal who licked her face with excitement.

Marcus grinned, 'I'm sure he prefers you to me,' he said. 'Come with me, I have something to show you.'

'How exciting, but before you do I have something for you,' she said, handing over a sealed envelope. 'It's a donation from Alex for the charity we supported at the Christmas concert.'

Marcus thanked her and taking the envelope promised to pass it to Henry who he said was co-ordinating the donations and the thank you letters. 'It's his controlling side you see,' he said pulling a face.

She planted a kiss on Brutus's head and returning him to the floor followed Marcus to his studio where she could see the outline of a painting on an easel covered by a sheet. She gasped, 'Is that the cottage underneath there?' she asked eagerly. 'With everything that's been going on I'd almost forgotten about it.'

Marcus pulled a face of mock surprise and teased, 'You mean while I've been slaving over a hot easel, you'd forgotten I was even doing it?'

She laughed and replied, 'Of course not, you know exactly what I mean so stop trying to make me feel bad, you naughty man!'

He laughed as well then and pulling the sheet from the easel declared, 'Ta-da!'

She stood looking at the painting in absolute awe. 'Marcus I can't believe it. It's incredible. It's as if I'm actually standing outside the cottage right now. And the frame is beautiful, it sets it off perfectly. Really, it's just wonderful.'

He smiled and replied, 'Thank you and I'm glad you like it as it's your Christmas present and I don't have a plan B!'

She shook her head, 'No, no I couldn't possibly accept it as a present. It's a work of art - well obviously - but you know what I mean. I commissioned you to paint the cottage Marcus and I want to pay you for your time and talent.'

Taking her hand and leading her to the kitchen he smiled faintly and answered, 'I'm not going to argue with you, it's a present and that's all there is to it.'

He'd said it in such a way that the conversation was immediately shut down. She knew there wasn't going to be any further discussion on the matter. But it wasn't only what he had said, it was the unspoken words; the look on his face; his demeanour. There was something different about him today, just as there had been in the pub the previous evening. It was subtle but she had seen it. Felt it even.

'Marcus, I...' she began

'Jess, sorry but I need to speak. What I mean is I need to talk to you,' he interrupted.

The words were rushed and his tone had a sound of urgency. She looked at him with alarm and was shocked to see his face was suddenly etched with concern as he rubbed the unshaven skin with his hands. She nodded. 'Of course,' and sat down on one of the chairs next to the Aga.

He swallowed hard and then perching on the edge of the other chair said, 'You've become a good friend to me Jess. I feel I can talk to you and trust you and that's quite unusual for me. And that's why I want to tell you something. Something very important'. He looked away momentarily and then continued, 'You see I've been living a lie for most of my life and I just know I can't do it any longer.'

She leant forward and touched his arm, 'What is it Marcus? What's wrong? You can tell me anything you know.'

He nodded. 'I know. And that's exactly why I'm telling *you* Jess. I need to unburden myself I suppose. To share my secret. A secret that's overshadowed my whole life. I just hope that when I've told you, you won't think differently of me.'

She nodded reassuringly at him. She knew from the many difficult conversations she'd had in her nursing career that now was not the time to speak. It was the time to listen and to hear. He needed to speak, to share his story and she was privileged that he'd chosen her to do that with.

He took a deep breath and continued, 'So I'm just going to say it. You see I'm...I'm...not the person you thought I was Jess. I'm different. I'm gay.'

She gave him a moment to compose himself and then taking his hand said, 'Why would I think any differently of you? *You* are *you* Marcus. And that is who I like. You. Nothing else is of any consequence.' She saw tears rolling down his cheeks now and as she gently brushed them away she added, 'Did you think any differently of me when I told you about my biological father? When I told you I was a different person?' It was a rhetorical question but she knew that the analogy would be one that would resonate with him and as she had hoped the worry lines began to fade as he relaxed back in his chair.

'I don't want to spend my whole life regretting things I've either done, or worse still regretting things I haven't done. Do you understand what I mean Jess? Am I making any sense?' he said.

'I do Marcus and yes you are making perfect sense. Regret is such a negative emotion I always think. It's wearing and damaging.'

'It's my 'go to' emotion,' he said with a wry smile. 'I torture myself with it, but I know I need to change that. As Kurt Vonnegut said, Of all the words of mice and men, the saddest are it might have been.'

Jess nodded. 'How true.' And then smiling at him added, 'Do you have to have a library of sayings up your sleeve to live round here?'

'Absolutely. It's essential,' he replied. And then squeezing her hand added, 'Thank you Jess. I feel a little unburdened already. I've made a start at least, but it's scary.'

She nodded again. 'Remember that everyone has their own insecurities and vulnerabilities. On the outside people seem different. They have different opinions; different strengths and weaknesses; different traits and characteristics. But on the inside they're basically all the same. *We* are all basically the same. Because no matter what persona you or me or anybody else portrays, we all have one thing in common; our skin, everybody's skin is thin. So you see we are all vulnerable. Mostly though we try to hide it, to shield ourselves but it's really okay to admit when you feel fragile, to recognise that your skin is thin. And when you do, those very people, those *everybodies* will help and support you because really they are just the same as you. They know. They understand.'

Marcus stood from his chair and hugged her tightly. 'How does one so young get to become so wise; so clever; so knowing?' he said, smiling softly at her.

She smiled back at him. 'Well perhaps you *can* put an old head on young shoulders after all,' she replied with a wink.

'Ah, I can see you're beginning to get the hang of living round here already!'

She smiled again. 'Seriously though, I too have my own

insecurities and I guess they have helped me to learn things about myself. I overthink things, over-complicate things and over-explain things. And my 'go to' emotion is to shed tears. I cry at everything. But I know that. I recognise my vulnerabilities. I recognise that my skin is thin and it helps, it really does.'

On the drive back to London Jess went over the conversations she had had with Alex earlier that morning about Jazz and Angela, and the ones she had just had with Marcus. It was good, she realised, to have things to think about other than her own situation, but she felt huge sympathy with both men. It was clear from what Alex had told her that Angela was using a kind of emotional blackmail on him regarding Jazz, and she was shocked to learn that she had done a similar thing with Jazz's father, although she was a much younger child then so perhaps the results weren't quite so catastrophic.

Alex seemed to be starting to accept that he couldn't take responsibility for what had happened to Jazz and he'd also realised that talking was very therapeutic. And with him filling in some of the detail, she realised that she had probably judged Jazz too harshly and had even found herself suggesting that maybe he should give her another chance. But whatever he decided to do she would support him fully as he was kind and generous of spirit and she loved him for it.

Marcus's situation, although different, had some definite parallels. He too had kept something monumental and life-changing to himself, trying to keep it tucked away in the back of his mind until it could stay there no longer.

She sighed at the tragedy of the situation. He'd told her that he had hidden his sexuality from everybody apart from the two men he'd had a 'romantic liaison' with, but now he had met somebody he was serious about he knew that he neither could, nor wanted to hide it any longer. 'Ah the man in the pub last night,' she'd said, and he'd nodded in confirmation.

She'd desperately wanted to say to him that there was nothing to hide and that being in love was something to celebrate, to shout from the rooftops, but she'd stopped herself knowing the reality was somewhat different. Knowing that that was far too simplistic. But he had started to talk and she hoped that was the first step on the road to him finding eventual peace of mind and happiness.

Back in London, Jess carried the painting into the house and stood it on a chair in the kitchen. As she removed the protective padded wrapping that Marcus had carefully secured around it, she was joined by a curious Amber who had just returned from another Christmas shopping trip.

With the painting revealed, Amber clapped a hand to her mouth and exclaimed, 'Wow, that is absolutely amazing, really stunning. Bet that set you back a pretty penny.'

Jess smiled and replied, 'It's a present from Marcus, remember I told you about him, he's the artist who lives in the Hall.'

Amber nodded and then said teasingly, 'Blimey that's very generous of him or is there more to it than that? And then with a loud gasp added, 'Do you reckon he fancies you?'

Jess felt a stab of pain at the irony of her friend's comment, but not wanting to betray any confidences managed a wry smile and replied, 'No I'm not his type, we've just become good friends that's all, and in any case I already have a gorgeous man who loves me thank you.'

Amber pulled a face and pretended to throw up in the sink while making realistic gagging noises, causing Jess to laugh out loud and tell her that she had missed her true vocation in life.

CHAPTER THIRTY-ONE

The next day after her early shift, Jess set off to pay her father another visit in Kent. She had spoken to him several times by phone since her last visit and the conversations although relatively short had been cordial. She was grateful that he never pushed her, never questioned her and thankfully was just like he'd always been, her gentle, kind and loving father.

As she pulled up outside his house she noticed there was an extra car on the driveway and she hoped she wasn't interrupting anything. But reminding herself that this wasn't a cold call, she walked towards the front door suddenly feeling a flutter of anticipation at the thought of seeing her father again.

'How have you been Dad?' she asked.

Thomas Jones grinned broadly and she immediately noticed how much younger he looked when his face was relaxed and smiling.

'And why are you grinning at me?' she continued affably, her eyes looking at him questioningly.

'It's just so wonderful to have you sitting here, calling me Dad again and just being *you*. That is why I'm smiling Jess. You've made your old man a very happy old man.'

She shuffled closer to him on the sofa and rested her head on his shoulder. 'I've missed you Dad,' and as he put an arm around her shoulder she felt safe and content, just as he'd always made her feel as a child.

'I have a little Christmas present for you Dad, I didn't really know what to get you...' she trailed off, looking down awkwardly at her hands which were clasped so tightly around the present that her knuckles had turned white.

Thomas took the bag from her and removed the pretty package from inside. Smiling he said, 'Thank you my darling, it wouldn't matter if it was a packet of sweets, it's what this means to me that's important and it means everything.'

She looked up at his face and she saw his eyes were glistening with tears and suddenly she felt as close to him as she had done all those years ago.

After tea and cake, Jess watched as Thomas walked towards the window before beckoning her to join him. 'I have a Christmas present for you as well,' he said, and she watched in surprise as he furrowed his brow and tightened his shoulders. 'Come over here and look out the window, you will be able to see it,' he said pointing in the direction of the driveway. 'Sorry it's not wrapped,' he added, his face relaxing slightly.

Jess peered through the window for a few moments before the realisation struck her that the extra car on the drive was, in fact, her Christmas present. She gasped in disbelief, unable to speak.

'Before you say anything please let me explain,' Thomas was now saying. 'You see I have bought you a birthday and Christmas present every year since I left, each year hoping that we would be reunited so that I could give them to you. But now we are together again and after a lot of thought, I have decided it would be best to donate them to charity as I think it's important not to spend too much time looking back because the past is something that can't be changed.'

She could hear his voice was trembling and she squeezed his

hand tightly.

He took a deep breath before continuing. 'But what you can do is move forward and I hope that we can look to the future together, not with regret but with expectation and anticipation.'

She nodded and without saying a word hugged him tightly, knowing that she never wanted to let him go again.

Outside on the driveway Jess sat in her new car and smiled up at her father. 'It's fantastic Dad, just perfect and I'm going to call him Rowan Too,' she said grinning.

Thomas laughed and said apologetically, 'It's not as new as I would have liked but it's got a good warranty and it's only had one previous owner, so hopefully it will serve you well for a few years.'

She started up the engine and revved it a few times. 'I have no idea why I did that,' she said as she climbed out of the car, 'But that's what people always seem to do!' and then they both laughed as they walked back to the house with their arms tightly around each other.

Inside the hallway she looked at her father and said, 'Dad, I would like to meet Sally if that's okay? Well that's if she wants to meet me of course.'

He nodded and although she thought she saw a flicker of relief pass briefly over his face, she could also tell there was something more troubling him.

'Come into the lounge and we can have a chat first,' he said and as she followed him she felt her stomach tighten into knots of nervous tension.

She watched Thomas closely as he inhaled deeply and then looking in her direction said, 'Sally has not been a well person for many years. You may remember I made reference to it when you were here last time?'

She nodded, remembering he had said she was of a 'nervous disposition'.

'Well the reality is that she has quite a severe mental health illness and although it's relatively well controlled now, I have to protect her, especially from stressful situations which are one of the triggers.'

She saw the pain in her father's eyes and suddenly felt an overwhelming urge to protect him. But knowing that wasn't possible nor was it probably needed, she replied, 'That must be really hard for you both.' And then immediately cursed herself for making what sounded like a banal platitude, when in reality it was said with the utmost sincerity.

Thomas took her hand and said, 'It's okay. We have a strong relationship and we've coped with it well. It's part of who she is and I wouldn't change her for the world.'

Jess smiled and squeezed his hand, realising how lucky both she and Sally were to have such a wonderful man in their lives.

'Were you always going to leave her Dad? Eleanor I mean?' She wasn't sure if it was the right time to ask the question but it was something she really needed to know.

'Yes, for a very long time. I thought I could live with what had happened but I couldn't and in hindsight I probably left it too long,' he answered truthfully.

'There was probably never a right time though Dad and what I know now is that it wasn't about me, well not directly anyway. I suppose what I mean is that it wasn't my fault and I feel unburdened just by knowing that.'

Thomas looked shocked. 'None of this was your fault Jess. We should have told you. I should have told you. And by leaving in the way I did, I made it about me. And that will always haunt me.'

'We've all made mistakes Dad, so as you said let's try and leave the past in the past. We have been reunited in the strangest of circumstances, so let's look to the future and only change the things we can.'

Chapter Thirty-one

Thomas nodded. 'I'll go and ask Sally to join us.'

She smiled reassuringly at him and then within seconds he reappeared with the person she had always imagined in her mind to be some kind of scarlet woman; a harlot; a home-wrecker. But looking at her now, all she saw was an ordinary woman, just an ordinary woman, who even after all these years was looking up lovingly at her father. And although it made her sad to think that she had wasted so many years on hating someone she didn't even know and for blaming her for breaking up her perfect family, she knew now that it wasn't the case at all. The woman standing in front of her was actually the very person who had loved her father so much that she had waited for him and it was obvious that their love was enduring.

Jess deliberately kept the conversation very casual, with questions about the dog and holidays and hobbies. She noticed that Sally regularly looked at Thomas for reassurance and in return he squeezed her hand encouragingly.

After about 15 minutes she thought that it was time for her to leave. She didn't want to overwhelm Sally, but it was a good start, a really good start.

She kissed her father goodbye and after a fleeting moment of awkwardness the two women then hugged each other warmly. She thanked them again for the present saying, 'I'll be back after Christmas to collect him. Alex can bring me and then you can meet him too.'

And then as she walked down the driveway she turned round to see them standing close to each other smiling and waving, and she felt a wave of relief and happiness sweep over her. Smiling to herself she thought that perhaps it wasn't only problems that came from the Pandora's box.

Once she was back at home Jess phoned Alex, excitedly relaying the evening's events to him whilst apologising for the late phone call.

'Wow,' he exclaimed. 'A car. That's fantastic and it's a good job I decided not to get you that Porsche after all. Seriously though, it's great that you've made it up with your dad and met with Sally and I'll look forward to meeting them both.'

She laughed and replied, 'Well Porsche or no Porsche, I have a feeling it's going to be a really good Christmas.'

'Me too my darling, me too,' he answered. 'Night night, sleep well.'

CHAPTER THIRTY-TWO

Christmas morning was bright and crisp and a flurry of snow made a stunningly picturesque winter scene. The ward was full of the sound of excited chatter from staff, patients and visitors alike and although Jess would have loved to have been spending the day in Thripton, she recognised there was something lovely about making Christmas as special as possible for people who were also away from their homes and often their loved ones as well.

Much to everyone's amusement, Sister pushed the tea trolley around wearing a Santa hat and the rest of the nursing staff were allowed to wear either a pair of Christmas earrings or an elf hat, although many had taken advantage of her 'relaxed rules' and worn both.

The hospital's charity arm had brought in colourfully wrapped gifts for the patients and Jess overcame her nerves and spoke on the local radio station about working at Christmas. It was a lovely shift, a sort of escapism for everyone, if only for a day.

After work Jess walked back to her car which was already packed ready for her to drive straight to Thripton. Due to the lack of public transport she had driven into work, being able to take advantage of the relaxed parking restrictions and quiet roads, and she was grateful to be able to get straight off to the place that she now thought of as her second home.

Originally she had intended to drive there first thing on Boxing Day morning, but neither she nor Alex could wait that long to see each other, and as Amber and James were away and Poppy was at Will's, it would have meant she would have been on her own on Christmas evening.

She arrived in Thripton in record time due to the unusually quiet roads and despite a gentle covering of snow, she was relieved they were easily passable.

Her heart skipped a beat as she drove slowly past the pub. The roof was partly covered in a soft layer of glistening snow and as she breathed in the aromatic smoke which curled from the chimney, it made her feel like she was on the set of a film. She was desperate to stop at the pub so she could see Alex but she needed to go to the cottage first to see Rosa, Poppy and Will and to collect his presents.

As she turned into the lane she noticed there was a little more settled snow on the road but somebody had kindly brushed it to the sides of the lane, and as she pulled up outside the cottage she had a feeling of excitement and anticipation.

After collecting Rosa's present from the cottage, she knocked on her door and Rosa squealed with delight at seeing her standing on the doorstep.

'Merry Christmas. Come on in my darling, come and meet my sister, I've told her all about you.'

Jess laughed and followed her into the cottage, placing the gift bag down in the hallway for Rosa to open after she'd gone.

'Jess, this is my sister Maria. Maria, this is my Jess.'

The other woman stood from her chair and kissed her. 'You are even more beautiful than I imagined my darling and my sister loves you, so I do too.'

Jess felt herself blush. 'Thank you. Rosa is always talking about you but she didn't tell me that you were practically her double!' she said, looking from one sister to the other.

Maria laughed and looking at her sister said, 'Well strictly speaking she is *my* double as I am two whole minutes older than her.'

Jess felt her jaw drop. 'You're twins?'

'Of course darling, didn't Rosa tell you?'

Jess shook her head and wagging her finger at Rosa said, 'I can't believe you didn't tell me that, even when you saw a photo of my twin brothers you didn't mention it. But anyway, how amazing. I always wanted a twin sister myself and, in fact, when I was at junior school I had an imaginary one called Emma-Louise!'

The sisters both laughed and Jess realised that they even sounded the same.

'The news about your twin brothers was *your* news my darling, it was about *you* not me so that would not have been the right time to start talking about myself. And anyway I've never been one to blow my own...'

'Trumpet,' Maria announced triumphantly. Finishing one of her sister's infamous sayings on her behalf had Rosa clicking her tongue loudly, before they both laughed in unison and identically.

'We always do that to each other, don't we?' Rosa said, putting an arm around Maria's similarly rounded shape.

'We do, but never mind all that now. We have V.I.P. in our company.' And then turning to Jess asked, 'Would you like some Christmas cake my darling? And perhaps a cup of Christmas cheers?'

Jess stifled a giggle at the realisation that Maria even had Rosa's endearing way of getting sayings slightly wrong. And even though she was keen to get to the pub to see Alex, she was thoroughly enjoying the company of these two delightful women and a small piece of cake would be very welcome.

Next stop was Will's house and after collecting Poppy's present from

No. 3, Jess knocked on his door and heard Dave screech, 'There's somebody at the door.'

Poppy pulled the door open wide and held a sprig of mistletoe above her head.

'Happy Christmas Bestie,' Jess said laughing, planting a kiss on her friend's cheek. She held out the present and although she knew she wasn't in the same league as Eleanor when it came to gift wrapping, she was rather pleased with what she'd done with Poppy's present. She'd wrapped it in pretty metallic gold paper and tied it up with shimmering gold ribbon, like an old fashioned parcel wrapped with brown paper and string. And it looked stunning.

'Wow, that looks so pretty,' Poppy exclaimed. 'I hope you saw my present for you. I left it on the kitchen table but then forgot to tell you.'

Jess smiled. 'I did thanks Poppy. And actually I was very bad as I opened it on Christmas Eve!'

'That's so typical of you,' her friend replied teasingly, rolling her eyes.

Jess pulled a face. 'I know, but in my defence I would have been short of time on Christmas morning. Well that's my excuse anyway. And thank you. You always get such brilliant presents.'

Will appeared from the kitchen, wiping his hands on a tea towel. 'Happy Christmas Jess,' he said, kissing her on the cheek. 'Can I get you a drink?'

She opened her mouth to answer but was beaten to it by Dave who squawked, 'Beer, beer,' and followed it with an ear-splitting wolf whistle.

'Hello Dave,' she said laughing. 'I can see you're enjoying Christmas!'

Dave dropped his head and peering at her screeched, 'Lock the door.'

She pulled a face. 'Can I have my beer first Dave? Would that be okay with you?'

'Silly bird,' Will said apologetically. 'You're supposed to save that one for my mother. Remember?' he added looking at Dave, who was now ruffling his feathers proudly.

After a quick Christmas drink with Poppy and Will, Jess collected Alex's presents from the cottage and put them in the boot of her car.

'Happy Christmas you gorgeous girl,' Alex called out as she opened the pub door, and then practically running from behind the bar, he lifted her off her feet and kissed her squarely on the lips.

She laughed. 'Happy Christmas to you too. Now close your eyes while I bring your presents in.'

She was relieved to see that the pub was quiet and even though Alex had let Velvet leave early, she hoped there wouldn't be too much clearing up to do before they could lock the door and retire to the peace and comfort of the upstairs.

As she opened the door at the top of the stairs Rolo was sitting on the other side and he greeted her with his usual exuberance. He followed her into the kitchen clearly realising that at least one of the bags contained food, his nose in the air and tail wagging furiously. She slipped him a dog biscuit before putting the contents of the bags out of his reach and then took Alex's presents into the lounge and placed them on the floor by the small artificial Christmas tree she had brought from her mother's cottage. She had also found a box at the cottage that contained the most beautiful tree decorations and Alex had bought a string of tiny soft white lights which complemented the decorations perfectly.

She had wrapped Alex's main present, a guitar, with some corrugated cardboard to disguise the shape and covered it with a deep red metallic paper with coordinating ribbon and looking at presents around the tree she felt a flutter of excitement at the thought of him opening them.

She went back downstairs and was pleased to see that the last few customers had left the pub. Alex was collecting the last of the glasses and she wiped the tables and bar to help speed things up.

After checking the doors were locked, Alex switched off the lights and putting an arm around her shoulders said, 'Now our Christmas can begin.' But then as he opened the door at the top of the stairs he exclaimed, 'Oh dear I think Christmas has already begun for Rolo!'

Jess peered round the door and to her dismay saw pieces of her carefully chosen metallic Christmas paper strewn around the floor. 'Rolo you naughty boy,' she admonished. But as he stood with his tail wagging excitedly and pieces of wrapping paper hanging from his mouth, neither of them could help but laugh at the sight of the crime scene and the culprit.

'Thank goodness he doesn't seem to have damaged the presents,' she said with relief as she surveyed the scene in the lounge. He had managed to partly unwrap the guitar down to the cardboard and had also opened another parcel that contained a jumper, which he was now proudly lying on. Alex retrieved it from underneath him and announced that apart from a few hairs, it seemed to be relatively unscathed and he then set about removing the cardboard from the present that Rolo had also started on.

Jess sat nervously on the edge of the sofa, holding her breath in anticipation of Alex's reaction to the guitar. But she needn't have worried, he seemed absolutely delighted.

'I just can't believe it,' he said. 'This is the best present I could ever have wished for.'

She smiled with relief and passed him a small box which luckily had escaped Rolo's attention. He gasped as he took a voucher for guitar lessons from inside the box and shaking his head said, 'You are the best Jess Jones and this is going to be the best Christmas ever.'

He disappeared into the bedroom and reappeared moments later with two of the most beautifully wrapped presents she had ever seen, and that included Eleanor's.

'Goodness Alex, did you get these professionally wrapped?' she asked teasingly. 'They almost look too good to open...almost!'

'Excuse me,' he said in mock indignation. 'I have a lot of artistic and creative flair I'll have you know, I even won a prize once for one of my sculptures.'

She looked at him in surprise and replied, 'Really? That's amazing, I had no idea you had such hidden talents. Sorry if it sounded like a put down, I really didn't mean it to be.'

He nodded and with a straight face said, 'That's okay, luckily I'm not easily offended.' And then his face broke into a wide grin as he added, 'And to be fair the sculpture was a square...well square-ish...money box I made when I was about eleven years old and I forgot to make a way of getting the money out so when it was full I had to smash it! That was the beginning and end of my creative career so I'm not sure I'm going to rival Michelangelo.'

She burst out laughing and reaching for a piece of discarded wrapping paper, screwed it up into a ball and directed it as his head. He pulled her towards him and kissed her gently before holding out the larger of the presents which she took excitedly from him. She carefully removed the metallic colour-coordinated tape from the paper, not wanting to spoil its perfection and then she let out a shriek of delight as she glimpsed the contents.

'Alex is this...is this what I think it is? It can't be. Surely?' she exclaimed, trying to remove the present without damaging the wrapping.

He laughed. 'Well I guess that depends on what you think it is. But it's not a fake if that's what you're insinuating!' he teased.

'Oh Alex, I've always wanted a Louis Vuitton handbag. How

did you know? Or have I been talking about it in my sleep!'

'Let's just say Poppy has been very helpful over the last few weeks,' he replied and she nodded knowingly whilst carefully unzipping the sumptuous, soft, supple leather bag to reveal the most exquisite interior.

'It's so beautiful, I'll be scared to use it,' she said gently stroking the outside of the bag, and then peering inside added, 'Oh there's an envelope in here, perhaps it's the guarantee?'

He shrugged and looked on nonchalantly as she opened it up, and then she let out another shriek. 'Paris! We're going to Paris?'

He smiled. 'That's why I had to get the handbag, you couldn't possibly go to Paris without a Louis Vuitton bag now could you?'

She leaned back against the sofa, puffing out her cheeks and exhaling loudly. Alex grinned and passed her the other present which was a selection of all of her favourite chocolates, and she leant over and kissed him on the cheek.

'This is an amazing Christmas. Merci Beaucoup,' she said taking his hand. 'And we haven't even had our Christmas Day proper yet.'

Later on, Jess picked up her phone, realising that she hadn't read all of her messages from earlier. She had sent messages from work during her lunch break to Thomas, Amber, Nora, Marcus and Melissa and she smiled as she read the replies.

Thomas said that he and Sally had enjoyed a quiet day and had raised a glass to her. Amber said her mother was driving her completely crazy with more wedding plans and James had become so fed up that he'd gone to the pub and had returned somewhat worse for wear, throwing up in her mother's newly decorated bathroom. Nora had replied to her message saying that Mabel loved the book Jess had bought for her and had been really excited all day. Marcus's text message was short, simply saying, *Happy Christmas Jess*, and she felt a pang of sadness at the predicament he was in. And Melissa had sent a photo of herself and her brothers sitting at the table wearing the obligatory paper hats, which brought a smile back to her face. It still seemed strange to think she had two brothers whom she hadn't even met yet.

'By the way,' Alex said as she put her phone back on the table, 'Marcus and Henry came in the pub at lunchtime but they only stayed for one and Marcus didn't seem his normal self at all.'

Jess sat quietly for a few moments as she contemplated her reply. She didn't want to lie to Alex, but Marcus had taken her into his confidence and she would never betray his trust. 'Yes, when I collected the painting he was a bit quiet. I think he has some things to deal with at the moment. I'll contact him tomorrow and see how he is then,' she replied and then steering the conversation in another direction added, 'Any chance of a beer? Correct me if I'm wrong but I thought this was supposed to be a pub!'

CHAPTER THIRTY-TWO

Boxing Day started in the most wonderfully relaxed way, with a lie-in and a leisurely breakfast of scrambled eggs and smoked salmon, complemented by Buck's Fizz made with freshly squeezed oranges.

It was another bright and frosty day and the dusting of snow glistened under the sun's rays as she and Alex walked Rolo across the fields late morning. He was delighted with the snow and charged around rolling in the light flurries that had collected in the ploughed furrows, before shaking his coat in what looked something like the action of a spin dryer.

It was the perfect start to their 'Christmas Day' Jess thought, as she walked hand in hand with Alex laughing at Rolo and from time to time managing to collect enough snow to make a small snowball to throw at one of 'her boys'. However, there was something that was never far from her mind, something that was worrying her and that something was in fact someone - it was Marcus. He too deserved to be happy, to walk hand in hand with someone in the snow, to laugh, to love and to be himself.

'Alex,' she said squeezing his hand. 'While you're cooking dinner, would you mind if I popped up to the Hall?'

'What?' he exclaimed, his face taking on a look of shock, and as she looked at him she felt a little bit sick. 'You mean you're expecting me to cook dinner?!' he added with a wink.

'Alex,' she practically yelled with relief. 'I thought you meant... actually it doesn't matter. You're such a tease. Now let's go back to the pub, I can't wait to see you in your Christmas apron!'

'Jess, what I lovely surprise,' Marcus exclaimed as he opened the door wide and beckoned her inside.

'Apologies for my impromptu visit but I was worried about you,' she said, suddenly feeling awkward and wishing she had phoned him first.

'You are always welcome here you know that and, in fact, I made a momentous decision yesterday, so your visit is very timely.'

She sat in her usual seat by the Aga and waited in anticipation as Marcus made hot chocolate; called Brutus in to see her and generally pottered around tidying and wiping down the kitchen work surfaces.

'Marcus, please come and sit down' she said. 'You're making me nervous.'

He smiled weakly at her and replied, 'I'm making myself nervous as well, but not as nervous as I will be in half an hour when I head over to the West Wing to tell Henry and Flora that I'm not the son they thought I was.' He put the hot chocolate on the table and Brutus jumped on his lap, as if sensing his sadness.

She sighed and leant forward to take his hand. 'No Marcus you are still the *same* son, you are the son they love and are proud of and that hasn't changed. Always remember that. And you too deserve to love and be loved by someone special. You deserve to be happy and fulfilled. I'm not saying it's going to be easy but you can do it. And remember those 'everybodies' we spoke about? Well they will be there to help and support you.'

He nodded and they both sat in contemplative silence as they drank their hot chocolate.

And then walking her to the door he said, 'I love you Jess...just as a friend of course!'

She laughed. 'And I love you too Marcus. But now I have imparted even *more* of my wisdom to you, I must return to the pub to check on Alex who is cooking our Christmas dinner.'

He smiled. 'Many a true word is spoken in jest Jess, but you really are wiser than you think.'

'And *you* Marcus are stronger and braver than *you* think,' she replied.

Back in the upstairs of the pub, Jess was greeted by the delicious smell of roast turkey wafting from the kitchen. 'Wow, dinner smells amazing Alex,' she said, kissing him on the cheek.

'Oh it's nothing,' he said. 'It's just a ready meal but I did get it from one of the upmarket supermarkets so it's not just *any* old ready meal,' he added with a wink.

'Well ready meal or not, Rolo seems very satisfied with it,' she said pointing at the dog, who was sitting as close to the oven as he could without getting his nose burnt.

'You've been gone a while. Everything okay?' he asked, passing her a plate of tasty nibbles.

'It will be,' she answered. 'These are gorgeous. Same posh supermarket I'm thinking?'

'Rumbled,' he replied laughing. 'But I did open the packet with considerable flair I'll have you know.'

'I called into the church after I'd been to see Marcus. I still feel angry with my mum but it was something I felt I needed to do, and in a strange way I think I've found some peace. A sort of inner peace I suppose. I need to find a way to forgive her and today I've realised that I can, it will just take time.'

He nodded, his face showing understanding and empathy and she loved the fact that he was so perceptive. 'And Marcus? You said things *will* be okay,' he asked.

'He's going through a bit of a tough time at the moment so I said a little prayer for him as well whilst I was at the church,' she said nodding.

And in his usual insightful way, he said nothing more on the subject

'Alex Blake, that was the best Christmas dinner I have ever eaten,' Jess exclaimed as she scooped up the last bit of thick gravy from her plate. 'Is there no end to your talents?'

He laughed and replied, 'Well actually no there isn't!

In response she laughed and poked him in the ribs with a plastic fork that she'd 'won' in her cracker, and then waving it in the air said, 'Eleanor will be turning in her grave. She always made her own crackers and she wouldn't be at all happy that I bought these in the bargain basement shop!'

He smiled. 'It sounds like your mum was a very talented woman.'

'Yes, she really was,' she replied and then she found herself smiling as well.

The rest of the day and evening was spent eating chocolate and watching television with Rolo firmly planted in between them, occasionally pawing at their hands to be stroked.

'I hope you don't fancy a game of chess,' Alex said, pointing at the beautifully hand carved chess set that had permanent pride of place on the coffee table.

Looking at the chess set Jess exclaimed, 'Oh! There's a figure missing.'

He pointed to Rolo. 'Yep, I found it in his bed. Unfortunately, the black King has lost his head and various other parts of his body!'

'Rolo! You naughty boy,' she said, trying hard not to giggle. And in response the dog rolled onto his back expectantly, making her laugh out loud.

She sighed. It had been the most wonderfully relaxing

Christmas and the thought of going back to London the following day suddenly filled her with dread. She sighed again as she got undressed for bed but then hearing the bedroom door click open, quickly brushed her negative feelings aside and smiled at Alex who had been taking Rolo out into the garden and checking on the pub.

He sat down next to her on the bed and taking a deep breath suddenly announced, 'So I've made a decision about Jazz. I am going to give her another chance but this time I know it's not because I feel guilty. It's because I believe she is a good person, who has probably made some bad choices, but who also needs some guidance and direction.'

Jess slid an arm around his waist. 'You are a good person too Alex, and for what it's worth I think that's the right decision.'

The following day brought considerably milder weather with accompanying fine drizzle. Any snow that had stayed on the ground had now turned to slush and as the pair stood in the pub car park, Alex looked up at the sky and said, 'It seems as if Christmas is over, what with the change in the weather and you going back to London.'

'Yes. And I need to get into the car quickly or my hair will be getting frizzy and out of control,' Jess replied with a grimace.

'Oh I see, there's me full of sorrow and longing and you can't wait to get off so you can protect your hair from the elements!' he teased. 'I feel destroyed Jess. Second fiddle to an inanimate object!'

'Stop it,' she said laughing. 'You're almost making me feel bad! And in any case, hair is not inanimate. It's a living structure, well partly living, and is made up of a protein called keratin. It also has a very important social function.'

'Okay, okay, you win. Now get into the car before it becomes fully alive. The drizzle is getting heavier and your hair is definitely getting bigger!'

She jumped into the car and put the window down, smoothing

her hair with her fingers.

'So I'll see you New Year's Eve then,' he said.

'Yes, I'm looking forward to it. I love the New Year. I'll leave as soon as my early shift has finished but I'll have to go back on New Year's Day as I'm on a night shift,' she reminded him, pulling a face of dismay.

He put his head through the car window and kissed her on the cheek and then stood waving as she drove out of the pub car park

CHAPTER THIRTY-THREE

The hospital ward was very busy between Christmas and the New Year and it helped take Jess's mind off how much she was missing Alex. She'd only seen Amber and Poppy briefly, either at the changeover of shifts on the ward or at the house when they'd grab a quick cup of coffee, usually drinking it standing up before dashing off somewhere and it made her reflect on how much all of their lives had changed in a few short months.

The one bit of cheering news was from Marcus who'd messaged her with, *You were right Jess. All is okay. Will explain all when I see you next xx*

She felt so relieved at the thought of Marcus being able to live the life he wanted and deserved to live and she'd eaten a large bar of whole nut chocolate as a way of a celebration.

Driving back to Thripton on New Year's Eve, she had the familiar feeling of happiness that she always got when she was going to see Alex and she sang along to the tunes on a radio programme that was reviewing the hits during the year.

Since Eleanor had died and since finding out about her birth father, she had taught herself how to de-compartmentalise her life and although the songs on the radio brought back both good and bad memories of the past year, she really felt that she was now better positioned to be able to cope with them. It was the inner peace that she had spoken to Alex about.

As she pulled up in the pub car park she realised it was completely empty and perplexed she hurried across to the pub to make sure everything was okay. To her surprise there was a note on the door which read, *Apologies, the pub is closed this evening for a private function.* She pushed the door but immediately realised it was locked.

She pulled out her phone from her pocket and rang Alex who quickly appeared at the door, looking flustered and breathless. 'Jess, you're early,' he exclaimed. 'You weren't supposed to be here yet!'

She looked at him in surprise feeling her pulse quicken and her cheeks flush, but trying to appear nonchalant she replied, 'Well that's a nice welcome I must say, Sister let us leave a bit early as it's New Year's Eve, but I'm kind of wishing she hadn't!'

His lips parted as he grinned at her, his eyes twinkling with mischief. 'It's supposed to be a surprise but I suppose you'd better come in as you're here!' he teased. And then as he pulled open the door she was stunned to see Jazz smartly dressed in black and white, laying a table with crisp white linen and carefully placing sparkling glasses in exactly the right places. The table was laid up for eight people she noted and it took centre stage in the middle of the pub.

'Jess, it's nice to see you. Can I get you a glass of champagne?' the young girl said, with a welcoming smile.

She laughed with relief. 'This looks wonderful Jazz and yes please I'm sure I could manage a small one.' And then turning to Alex added, 'What's this all about?'

He explained that the locals had told him the pub had always been quiet on previous New Year's Eves and from his own experience he'd often found it problematic getting staff anyway, so he'd decided to close up early and have a small dinner party for close friends. 'And I've hired outside caterers. They're a start-up business who are going to specialise in dinner parties, so fingers crossed it'll be a nice evening.'

She shook her head in disbelief, struggling to find the words to describe how she was feeling. Instead she perched on a bar stool while she took in the surroundings and sipped the deliciously cold, effervescent champagne, which felt like a frothy citrus-flavoured sorbet on her tongue. It wasn't beer, but it was gorgeous nonetheless and she had to admit that it was the perfect aperitif. She just knew it was going to be a lovely evening and she couldn't wait to find out who the other guests were.

Upstairs, Jess pulled a tight fitting black dress over her head. 'Lucky I brought a suitable outfit with me,' she said, looking at Alex.

'I quite liked you in the one you had on before,' he said with a wink. 'You know the sort of flesh coloured one!'

She laughed and giving him a gentle shove said, 'Yes, yes I get it. Now get yourself ready and I'll pop downstairs and see how Jazz is getting on.'

But as she descended the stairs she became aware of raised voices and although muffled ,she could tell they were both female voices. Moving to the bottom of the stairs as quietly as she could, she stood still hoping to be able to hear more of the on-going conversation. It was obvious that one of the voices belonged to Jazz but she didn't recognise the other one. *Please don't let it be one of the caterers*, she said to herself, her shoulders stiffening with tension.

She could hear more clearly now and realised it was partly because both women were now speaking in raised voices.

'Do not protect him,' the unknown voice was saying in a hostile tone. 'He's caused nothing but pain for both of us, especially you and I intend to make him pay in whatever way I can.'

'No, that's not fair, he has helped me more than I could ever expect and in return I've been a cow. A real cow. Now I want to try and make amends regardless of what you say or think.'

Jess took a deep breath, straightened her dress and holding her head up in an attempt to make herself look taller, marched purposefully into the bar area. And there in the middle of the pub stood Jazz and Angela, either side of the table.

Jazz was standing with her hands placed firmly on her hips and her mother was standing opposite with her arms folded resolutely in front of her. It was an unpleasantly confrontational scene Jess thought and it was obvious that Alex was the subject matter.

She steeled herself and looking Angela squarely in the eyes asked, 'Can I help you?'

The other woman flashed her a look of annoyance and practically spat, 'I'm trying to have a private conversation with my daughter if you don't mind. Could you leave us alone?'

Jess felt her cheeks redden and her throat and mouth were dry. But taking a deep breath she replied, 'Firstly, the conversation you were having was far from private considering I could hear you from the staircase, and secondly I do mind actually as the pub is closed for a private function and *you* are not on the guest list.' Well I suppose you might be she thought to herself as the guest list was another one of Alex's surprises, but in any case that was just semantics surely.

For several seconds there was an uncomfortable silence in the room. It was a sort of standoff situation, Jess realised. And then from behind them came the sound of Alex's voice and as Jess turned round she saw the steely resolve in his eyes. 'Angela you are not welcome here, not just tonight but any other night or any other time come to that. Please don't cause Jazz or yourself any more embarrassment, just leave.'

Jess held her breath as Angela stared in disbelief at Alex and then without looking at any of them again, turned on her heel and walked out of the pub, pulling the door closed firmly behind her.

She exhaled with relief and then looking at Jazz realised that she had tears rolling down her face. Signalling to Alex to make himself scarce she put an arm around Jazz's shoulders. 'Would you prefer not to stay this evening?' she asked her in a gentle tone. 'I'm sure it would be fine with Alex considering the circumstances.'

The young girl wiped her face and with a weak smile said, 'Thank you, but I want to stay. I owe it to Alex and to you, and actually I owe it to myself as well. And I'm so sorry for my mother's behaviour.'

Jess smiled reassuringly at the young girl and squeezing her arm said, 'Good for you and really you shouldn't have to apologise for other people's behaviour. You can only be responsible for your own and from what I've seen so far this evening, yours has been exemplary.'

Half an hour later the first guests arrived and Jess was delighted to see it was Poppy and Will. Her best friend looked stunning in a short clingy black and silver dress paired with the most amazing red patent ankle boots. 'Are they Prada boots?' she exclaimed with a gasp.

Poppy nodded and explained that Will's sister Anna had helped him choose them for her for Christmas. 'When I wore them to Rosa's she made one of her infamous comments about only the devil wearing Prada and even Maria started looking for my horns and tail. Honestly that pair could make a good double act!' she said laughing.

Jess nodded in agreement and then hugging her friend tightly said, 'You told me you were going out this evening you naughty girl!'

Poppy laughed and with her usual sharp wit replied, 'Well I wasn't lying was I? I am going out. Out out in fact!'

Jess laughed as she desperately tried to think of a suitable reply but before she could come up with anything remotely funny or clever, the door opened again and Nora and Josh walked in, clutching boxes of party poppers and indoor sparklers.

'No Mabel?' she asked in mock surprise.

'No, my mother-in-law wanted to watch a programme called 'In The Night Garden' on CBeebies, so she insisted on babysitting!' Josh said with a grin.

Nora giggled as she took a flute of champagne from the silver tray that Jazz was holding in front of them, and Jess smiled to herself as she watched the young girl chatting amiably with the guests.

Well that's six of us, she thought. Who could the other two be? Rosa and Maria? Unlikely. Amber and James? Even more unlikely. But she didn't have to ponder long as within minutes the door opened again and in walked a man she had only seen once before, on the night of the Christmas concert, closely followed by a beaming Marcus.

'This is Charles,' Marcus announced proudly, pointing in the direction of the other man as if there was more than one person in the room needing an introduction.

Jess noticed that the poor chap had flushed almost crimson and was looking decidedly uncomfortable. She opened her mouth desperately trying to think of something to say to divert attention away from him, but before she could Jazz had perceptively intervened by holding out the silver tray. 'Welcome Charles. Would you like a glass of champagne? It's rather delicious...or so I've been told.' She was smiling affably at him and then continued to engage him in small talk until the others began chatting amongst themselves again.

Very impressive, Jess thought and she was beginning to see why Alex was keen to give her another chance. She most definitely had potential.

Before she had a chance to speak with Marcus and Charles the catering team emerged from the kitchen to introduce themselves to the guests and Jess smiled as they told the group their story. They were a husband and wife team, Jason and Kelly, who had both worked in Michelin star restaurants in the past, but had decided to quit in order start up their own business doing what they described as 'Posh dinner parties' in people's homes or at small venues.

'So tonight just for fun, we would like you to help us think of a name for our new venture,' Kelly was saying, while handing out paper and pens to each couple. 'And then we can all have a giggle after dinner when we read out the suggestions.'

'Fabulous,' Poppy exclaimed excitedly. 'I love a competition.'

Jess pulled a face. 'It's not fair. You and Will have a distinct advantage, you're both too clever by half!'

'Don't worry darling,' Alex chipped in with a grin as wide as his face. 'I have a cunning plan.

I'll pretend to be the perfect host by mingling amongst the others and then I'll be able to listen into their ideas and we can steal the best one for ourselves!'

'Good plan,' she agreed, nodding enthusiastically, whilst desperately trying to keep a straight face.

Marcus grinned and shaking his head said, 'I'm afraid that plan, Mine Host, is flawed. Not for the reasons you may all be thinking, but for the reason that it's not possible to be the perfect host, as perfection does not exist...'

Jess saw him turn to look at Charles who, smiling back at him said, 'But what you can be is perfectly imperfect..and that is what matters.'

Will and Poppy looked at Marcus and Charles admiringly and Poppy clapped enthusiastically, encouraging the others to join in.

Josh raised an arm in the air as if signalling for the applause to stop and then looking directly at Alex announced, 'Well this is all very philosophical and thought-provoking I'm sure, but basically Alex the bottom line is that you are not allowed to cheat, so think up your own ideas!'

'Josh!' Nora exclaimed.

'What?' he said, shrugging his shoulders, which in turn made the group all laugh and Jess knew it was going to be a lovely evening. It was the perfect mix of old friends and new, of different characters with different backgrounds and contrasting views. It was a perfect group of perfectly imperfect people and it made her heart swell with happiness.

Jason cleared his throat to get their attention. 'So for the important bit, the menu. We have grilled scallops with black pudding and a ginger veloute, followed by beef Wellington served with roasted potatoes, vegetables and a red wine jus. And to finish we have the most delicious rose panna cotta with plum and lavender shortbread. But first we would love you to try some of our delicious canapes and feedback on all parts of the menu will be gratefully received.'

They all clapped in appreciation and then continued to chatter noisily as Jazz helped serve the canapes.

'You're doing great,' Jess whispered to her as she smiled and chatted with the other guests.

'Thanks, I'm really enjoying it. Your friends are lovely. You're lucky you know.'

Jess looked around at the small gathering and smiled at Jazz. 'Yes I am.'

At last Jess managed to get Marcus on his own and he told her that the conversation with Henry and Flora had gone somewhat better than he'd expected. 'My mother didn't seem in the slightest bit surprised and said she just wanted me to be happy. She even said, and I quote, 'Well at last the elephant in the room has started to move! My father, on the other hand, did what he always does by disappearing into the garden and then coming back a couple of hours later. It's as if he needs some thinking time, you know time to process things before he can make any sort of comment.'

Jess nodded. 'And what did he say when he came back?'

'Well you will never believe it Jess. He said something like, 'Before you can love another person, truly love another person, freely and without boundaries, you have to learn to love yourself Marcus.'

She smiled. 'He's a good man Marcus and a very insightful one it seems.

'Yes he is but never in a million years did I see him saying anything like that. And because of what he said I now think I can begin to love myself because I'm free Jess, liberated from the very chains I put around myself and that wasteful regret that you spoke about has gone. Assigned to the past where it belongs.'

She felt a lump rising in her throat and unable to speak she took his arm and led him to his place at the table.

She carefully positioned herself between him and Charles in the hope that (a) It might protect Charles from too many questions and (b) It would give her a chance to get to know him. She reminded herself that she too should not ask too many questions but she needn't have worried as he was now much more relaxed and spoke openly about his job as a lawyer, his love of art and his delight at meeting Marcus.

After the first course, Poppy gently tapped her fork on the table and pushing her soft blond curls off her shoulders said, 'Excuse me everyone, but Will and I have an important announcement to make.'

Jess and Nora both gasped with excitement and in perfect unison, causing Marcus to chuckle and Alex to roll his eyes in an exaggerated fashion.

Poppy, unfazed by the other women's excitement and in true Poppy style replied, 'And no ladies, you don't need to get new hats. Will and I are going travelling in the New Year with first stop Australia to meet up with Anna, Will's sister, who has been travelling for a while now. But I'll be back for Amber's wedding of course!'

Jess felt her cheeks flush at the mention of Anna's name and was relieved when the others burst into spontaneous applause, sparing her glowing cheeks any attention.

As the applause died down, Marcus said, 'A wedding? Are they looking for a venue by any chance, as it just so happens that I know the perfect place?'

'Actually that might just be the perfect plan, or the perfectly imperfect plan,' Jess said grinning.

'Never a truer word or words,' Poppy agreed.

'I'll speak to Amber tomorrow,' Jess said.

Lots of excited chatter about travel plans and the best countries and places to see followed and Jess was pleased to hear Charles joining in enthusiastically. She could tell as well that he was a well-travelled man with a lot of knowledge and stories to tell. Definitely a good match for Marcus.

Jason, Kelly and Jazz served the main course and everybody tucked into the succulent beef and beautifully crisp roasted potatoes, and for the first time in several hours the room fell quiet as they savoured the delicious food.

Jazz continued to top up the wine glasses at regular intervals and Marcus complimented Alex on his choice of red wine which really was the perfect pairing, even though secretly Jess would have preferred a pint of beer.

After the caterers had cleared away at the end of the main course, Nora tapped her glass with her dessert spoon. 'I too have an announcement to make.'

Jess raised her eyebrows in Nora's direction and she laughed before saying, 'I know what you're thinking Jess and no there's not going to be a little brother or sister for Mabel, well not for a while anyway. But I just wanted to let you all know that my business loan has been approved and I can start work on setting up in my new sewing home in the New Year.'

Jess noticed Josh was gazing admiringly at Nora and then more spontaneous applause erupted around the table with lots of excited and congratulatory chatter quickly following.

Jess touched the panna cotta with her spoon, it wobbled gently and looked like a work of art having been decorated with the most striking purple edible flowers and the tiniest pieces of gold leaf. It almost looked too good to eat but eat it she would as soon as she too had made her own announcement. Alex looked at her in surprise as she got to her feet and cleared her throat. 'It seems like it has been a night for announcements and so continuing with that theme I have one of my own to make. My life has changed dramatically over the past year and in particular over the past few months. I feel like I'm a different person and I suppose in reality I am a different person, certainly to the one I thought I was and I have a whole new family to meet and get to know. But also I have a whole new and different life here in Thripton and what with Poppy going off on her travels and Amber getting married it seems a good time to think about leaving my London life behind and starting a new one here.'

She held her breath, hardly daring to look across the table at Alex. She had rather sprung it on him she realised and perhaps it wasn't what he wanted. She hadn't actually considered that.

Plucking up courage she looked in his direction. He was grinning from ear to ear. He was actually grinning. It was what he wanted as well. She relaxed her shoulders and grinned back at him. 'I love you,' she mouthed.

Alex stood up and looking directly at Jess said, 'I too have an announcement. I want the world to know I love you Jess Jones from No. 3 Back Lane. And just for the record this has not only been the best Christmas ever but also the best New Year.'

Poppy led the cheering this time and blew a kiss across the table to her best friend.

As the excitement died down Marcus stood up. 'Well I certainly can't follow any of that but what I would like to do is to propose a couple of toasts. The first is to Alex for a wonderful evening.' He looked around the table approvingly before finally resting his gaze on Charles and added, 'And the second is to New Year, new beginnings.'

Everyone got to their feet and chinking glasses shouted, 'Alex and New Year, new beginnings.'

After dinner Alex brought Rolo downstairs to join in the celebrations and after methodically checking every inch of the floor for any food spillages, he turned his attention to the guests and greeted them with his usual exuberance. Marcus proudly introduced him to Charles and relayed the story of the unexpected litter and Jess could tell he was a dog lover, as when Rolo rolled onto his back for a tummy rub, Charles knelt on the floor next to him and seemed happy to oblige.

'Nora, I've hardly had a chance to speak to you since Christmas. Did you have a lovely time? What did you get for Mabel?' Jess asked.

'Well you'll never believe it. Well actually you probably will,' she said covering her eyes.

We got her a ginger kitten. Well two to be exact. They are the cutest little things imaginable. So soft and fluffy. They couldn't be separated you see...' She pulled a face and Jess laughed.

'Are you sure you got them for Mabel?'

Nora laughed. 'It's good to bring children up with pets. Helps them learn to be kind. And anyway she'll grow into them!'

'You don't need to convince me,' Jess teased.

'But yes, I do love them as well!' Nora said

Jess let out a gasp as realisation suddenly struck. 'Nora, I don't suppose they're feral kittens from one of the local farms are they?'

'Yes they are. How did you know?' her friend replied with surprise.

'I used to feed them. Well half the village did according to Rosa. I even gave them names!'

'No way!' Nora said laughing. 'What a coincidence. What did you call them?'

'Ginger and Spice,' Jess replied, pulling a face. 'Not very original I know, but I had to think on my feet and that's definitely not my forte.'

Nora laughed. 'I've named them Cotton and Bobbin. You know, to keep with a sewing theme.'

'Fabulous,' Jess said hugging her friend.

'You two talking about those little monsters?' Josh said, suddenly appearing at Nora's side.

She giggled. 'You love them Josh, you know you do.'

Josh pulled up the sleeve of his jumper to reveal several fresh and rather sore looking scratches. 'They're the children of Satan,' he said.

'They're beautiful. Just a little playful,' Nora said, giving Josh a firm nudge. 'And guess what? Jess reared them up. She's been feeding and nurturing them,' she added.

Jess laughed. 'They're very beautiful but I don't think I can really take any credit for how they've turned out. We have to give that credit to Tigger.'

'Tigger?' Josh said.

'She's their mother. I named her Tigger as she has the most beautiful stripes,' Jess replied.

'You two honestly, you're as bad as one another. In fact, you're like sisters from another mister,' Josh said grinning.

Norah let out a gasp. 'Josh, that's so insensitive and very inappropriate in the circumstances.'

Jess smiled at both of them. 'It's fine, honestly. You can't go around watching what you say all the time.'

'He never watches what he says,' Nora said, rolling her eyes in Josh's direction. 'You should hear some of the things he says to my mum!'

'Well I'm certainly not offended or upset or anything else come to that!' Jess said. 'And I'm so happy that the kittens have a lovely new home. Perhaps I could be their godmother!'

'Well that's funny you should say that, as on a serious note Josh and I had planned to ask you to be a godmother. But not to Cotton and Bobbin. To Mabel.'

Jess felt her jaw drop and tears spring to her eyes. 'Really? I'm overwhelmed. I would be honoured to. Thank you both so much. And I will take my duties very seriously.'

The three of them hugged each other for a few moments before Jason tapped a spoon on the table to get everyone's attention. 'Please could you divide into your couples now and try to come up with names for the catering business,' he said.

Poppy and Will sat as far away as possible from the others with their heads close together, speaking in hushed whispers and when Alex crept up behind them both and pretended to listen in Poppy let out a blood curdling scream which sent him scurrying back to where Jess was sitting. He put his arm around her shoulders and whispered, 'You've made me very happy tonight Jones, very happy.'

She laughed and planted a kiss of his cheek. 'Now get your thinking cap on Alex Blake, I want to win this one!'

'Your half hour is up,' Kelly announced. 'Who would like to go first?'

Jess laughed as Poppy's hand shot up in the air as she shrieked, 'We would!'

Kelly laughed as well. 'Go ahead please Poppy.'

'Our suggestion is *Moveable Feasts*,' Poppy said proudly.

Jess gasped in amazement. 'I told you, that pair are geniuses or genii or whatever the plural of genius is!'

Kelly and Jason nodded their approval and thanking Poppy moved onto Marcus and Charles. 'Our contribution is *Fine Dine-In*,' Charles said, taking care to spell out the name so everyone understood the play on words. 'And we also have a strapline which we believe is important, as it will give the potential customer a little more detail.'

'Objection your honour,' Nora yelled. 'That was *not* part of the remit. You must stick to the brief Charles.'

'Overruled,' Marcus announced in response and everyone fell about laughing.

Next it was Jess and Alex's turn. 'Ours is also a play on words,' Jess said, trying to compose herself after Nora's hilarious outburst. 'We think the company should be called *Let's Cook*. You know...Let Us Cook.'

'Yes, yes we get it,' Will said rolling his eyes and Jess shot him a glance of mock annoyance for his interruption.

Jason shook his head in disbelief. 'These ideas are absolutely brilliant. You lot are very talented. So last and certainly not least is Nora and Josh.'

The pair looked at each other and in unison said, '*The Posh Nosh Company*. And we realise it doesn't necessarily depict a cooking at home company but that, of course, could be explained in the strapline,' Nora added, winking at Charles.

Charles laughed and clapping his hands at her wit said, 'Touché Nora. Touché.'

'Thank you all for those great suggestions,' Kelly said. 'We will now retire to the kitchen to consider our verdict.'

Jazz cleared her throat and piped up, 'Would it be okay if I had a go please?'

Jess noticed her cheeks were pink and guessed it had taken courage for her to speak up in front of everybody.

Handing Jazz a piece of paper and a pen Kelly answered, 'Of course.'

Jazz scribbled on the paper and folding it neatly, handed it straight back to Kelly who unfolded the piece of paper and raising her eyebrows passed it to Jason.

Jess's stomach did a slight lurch as she recalled Jazz's caustic comments in the clothes shop, and she really hoped she wasn't going to blot her otherwise pristine copy book.

'You read it out Jazz,' Jason said, handing the paper back to her.

Jess noticed she took a deep breath before saying, 'My suggestion is *The Galloping Gourmets*.'

There were a few seconds of stunned silence before everyone started clapping and cheering, saying how brilliant her idea was and then without any further consultation, Kelly announced Jazz as the winner. And the proud smile that crossed the young girl's face was priceless.

Just before midnight, Jazz handed out the party poppers and sparklers and did a sterling job in getting the group to join in a countdown to the New year. She was growing in confidence by the hour, Jess thought. After a couple of renditions of Auld Lang Syne and a lot more chinking of glasses, the group began to disperse, all well fed, happy and some slightly worse for wear.

As Alex closed the door to the last of the guests Jess noticed that Jazz was still busying herself with the last of the glasses, even though Alex had told her not to worry and that he would do them in the morning.

'You get yourself off now Jazz and thank you for this evening, you did a great job,' he said.

She gave him a half smile in response and then looking from him to Jess asked, 'I was wondering if I could stay here tonight? It's just that I think my mother will be easier to handle in the morning. I don't need a bed, the sofa or even a chair would be fine - I can sleep anywhere!'

Jess looked at her with concern. 'I'm sure that would be fine wouldn't it Alex? But is there anything else you need to tell us?'

'No not really', she replied. 'It's just that I'd prefer to face her when she's sober and maybe had time to reflect on her behaviour. Although that may be wishful thinking.'

Jess shot Alex a worried look but she could see from his face that the revelation was not a surprise to him. Not wanting to discuss anything further in front of her, she took Jazz upstairs and showed her to the spare bedroom.

Later in bed Alex put his arms around Jess and said, 'Well I think that went rather well.'

'It was a fantastic evening. The best, and thank you for inviting Marcus that was really thoughtful of you,' she murmured sleepily. She could tell he didn't want to talk about the situation with Angela and Jazz at that time, so she said nothing more.

Next morning Jess woke to the sound of noises coming from the kitchen. She pulled on her dressing gown and went to investigate, wondering if Rolo had managed to open a cupboard in the hope of searching out some food. But to her surprise it was Jazz who was dressed and was preparing scrambled eggs on toast and tea for the three of them.

'Morning,' she said, smiling at Jess. 'I've taken Rolo out for his morning wee but I haven't fed him as I wasn't sure what he eats.'

Jess laughed. 'Anything he can find usually but seriously that's fine, I'll do it in a minute. This looks lovely, thank you Jazz. I'll go and wake Alex up.'

Jazz had left for home straight after breakfast, having declined Alex's offer of a chaperone. 'I'm fine,' she'd said brightly. 'Mum will have calmed down by now and most likely she'll apologise. That's the usual way of things anyway.' She'd hugged them both and told Jess how pleased she was that she was coming to live in Thripton and then hopping onto her scooter disappeared up the road, leaving a trail of smoke behind her.

After more tea, Jess gathered up her belongings ready to head back to London. 'Somehow it seems easier going back today knowing that it's only for a short period of time. I need to talk to Amber, look for a job here and hand my notice in at work so lots to do, but it feels right and actually rather exciting. Oh yes and don't forget we're going to my father's on the third to pick up my new car.'

Alex nodded. 'Of course I haven't forgotten, I'm looking forward to it and I've asked Velvet to do an extra shift so I don't have to rush back.'

'Perfect,' she said and then after kissing him goodbye headed back to London via Rosa's, for the dubious joys of a night shift.

CHAPTER THIRTY-FOUR

Jess slept for a couple of hours on the morning of the third of January after what had turned out to be a very quiet night shift, and then after coffee and a chocolate biscuit she had a quick tidy around in preparation for Alex's arrival. Amber and Poppy were both at work and as none of them had been in the house much over Christmas or the New Year, a quick hoover and a flick with the duster was all that was needed.

She had decided she would take Alex to the local pub before they set off to her father's house. He'd said he wanted to see a bit of her London life, so she'd told him that the pub seemed an obvious choice as the three of them had always spent a significant proportion of their time there.

He arrived just before midday and after showing him around the house they walked along the road to the pub, arm in arm. Jess pointed out various landmarks to him and he laughed at her descriptions of the different buildings.

'We don't exactly live in the most picturesque part of London, so I need to embellish it a bit,' she said laughing.

'Well you tell a good story that's for sure,' he said.

She pulled a face. 'What do you think of the house?'

'I think it's lovely. So much space and character.'

'Yes,' she agreed. 'But that's all it is. A house.'

'I think I'm missing something,' he said.

'What I mean is, it's just a house and what I want now is a home and I have the perfect one in Thripton. Which reminds me, I must ring Jamie James and tell her I'm no longer selling the cottage.'

'Ah I see,' he said and his whole face seemed to smile.

'Come on, let's step the pace up. I can smell the beer from here!'

Inside the pub Jess bought them both a drink and ordered her favourite lunchtime meal for them both. 'Lunch is a surprise,' she said, biting her lip and wrinkling her nose.

'I think, by the look on your face it's going to be *surprising* rather than a surprise,' Alex said.

'Semantics,' she replied rolling her eyes.

Ten minutes later lunch was served and Jess rubbed her hands together as the barman put the enormous plate on the table.

'It's an all-day breakfast pizza,' she declared excitedly. 'Look. Sausage, black pudding, bacon, hash browns, mushrooms, tomatoes and double fried egg in the middle. And all on a thick-crust pizza base. What more could you possibly want?'

'Wow. It actually does look amazing,' Alex said.

'It tastes even better than it looks and more importantly it doubles as the perfect hangover cure as well,' she said.

'Now that most definitely makes it perfectly imperfect,' he said with a grin.

'Most definitely,' she nodded.

That sat in silence while they tucked into the pizza, until the quiet was disturbed by a man's voice. 'Jess? Jess? Is that you?'

She knew the voice. She knew it so well. Her pulse quickened as she turned her head to see Daniel standing behind her. Daniel, who she hadn't seen since the day she left him at the zoo. And now here he was, as large as life and was not on his own either.

'Jess, it *is* you. How lovely to see you. Meet Claire and our beautiful daughter Phoebe!' he announced. 'Phoebe, say hi to Jess.'

She watched as the child looked at her for a few seconds before poking her tongue out and screwing her eyes up, as if in protestation at the request from her father.

She forced a half smile, and congratulating herself on not spitting the pizza she had just put in her mouth directly at him, replied, 'How sweet. And this is Alex.'

Fortunately, Daniel had taken the obvious hint that she didn't want to make small talk with him and had moved on to find a table on the other side of the pub.

'Who was that?' Alex asked.

'Nobody important,' she replied, and even though Eleanor had been right, he clearly had changed his mind about having children, she knew now for certain that he would not have been the right man for her.

Later that afternoon they journeyed to Kent and pulling up outside Thomas and Sally's house, Jess pointed excitedly to Rowan Too who was parked on the driveway, the paintwork gleaming in the winter sunshine.

'I bet Dad's been out there cleaning and polishing him,' she said. 'Come on let's go in, I want to show you off to my Dad.'

Thomas and Sally were waiting at the door for them and Thomas extended an arm to Alex, who shook hands with him.

'I'll get the keys for the car,' he said to Alex. 'Then you can give it the once over. You go inside Jess, we won't be long.'

She followed Sally inside and feeling a little nervous at being alone with her for the first time, began telling her about the journey in such minute detail that when she stopped for breath she noticed the other woman looking at her in surprise.

'You sound a bit like me Jess,' she said softly, reaching out to touch her arm.

Jess looked at her and saw she was smiling now, and she

suddenly felt a rush of empathy and affection for the woman who she'd always thought of as the perpetrator. Because she knew in her heart now that she was a victim too. They all were.

After about ten minutes, Thomas and Alex joined them in the sitting room and they all sat and enjoyed the afternoon tea that Sally had clearly spent a lot of time and effort preparing.

As she'd carried in the plates of sandwiches, homemade cakes and delicate pastries, she'd explained in some detail that as it was half way through the afternoon it was too late for lunch, but too early for dinner, so after much deliberation she had plumped for afternoon tea. And then she'd looked at Jess and given her a knowing wink saying, 'See what I mean Jess?'

Thomas looked questioningly from Sally to Jess but she had simply laughed and replied, 'I do Sally, but at least you'll know all about the pitfalls of the journey to London should you decide to go and I will know the right circumstances in which to serve afternoon tea!'

The other woman smiled. 'Very true Jess and very useful information in fact.'

Thomas had shrugged his shoulders and made a remark about cryptic comments but Jess could tell by the look on his face that he was pleased to see the women were getting on so well.

After they'd all finished eating, Jess said, 'Dad, I have a couple of things to tell you.' She didn't want to cause Sally any undue stress and was relieved when she started clearing away the plates and tea cups. Perhaps she was used to removing herself from situations that might cause her harm Jess thought, but it was more likely that she was simply being tactful. 'Alex, why don't you give Sally a hand,' she added, nodding at him encouragingly and picking up on her cue he gathered some plates and followed Sally to the kitchen.

'Should I be worried?' Thomas asked and she saw his facial expression change.

She moved quickly to sit close to him and taking his hand said, 'I don't think so, but you're my dad and the things I do will undoubtedly have some effect on you which is why I want to tell you.'

She watched as his face relaxed and taking a deep breath she told him about Melissa and her twin brothers and about her move to Thripton.

He listened without speaking, occasionally inhaling sharply and Jess suddenly realised that they were both experiencing the same fears, the same uncertainty and the same pain and she hoped that them being together was as comforting for him as it was for her.

'I'm really pleased for you Jess, really I am and although I can't deny that I feel worried, I would never try and stand in your way.'

'I know Dad; I think I know how you must be feeling but I hope you can understand that I have to find out who I really am. I can't move on with my life until I have done that.'

He lifted her chin gently with his fingertips and looking into her eyes said, 'I understand completely. And I will be with you in spirit, every step of the way.'

'Thank you Dad. And now we should be getting on our way as we're travelling back to Suffolk this evening.'

Back at The Plough, Jess jumped out of Rowan Too and waited for Alex who she knew wouldn't be far behind her.

'Guess what?' she shrieked as he opened the van door and stretched his arms above his head.

'What?' he asked.

'The gear box doesn't clunk, the whole car doesn't shake when you go over fifty miles per hour and best of all the heater actually works!' she said laughing and then linking arms with him, she walked him into the pub and ordered them both a pint.

'Do you want anything to eat?' she asked Alex. 'Packet of crisps, chocolate bar?'

'Are you joking!' he said with incredulity. 'I'm absolutely stuffed. An all-day breakfast pizza and afternoon tea and all within a matter of a few hours!'

'Alex, you must know by now that you can never be too full for chocolate. It's a simple fact of physiology. The body has a very clever way of ensuring there's always room for chocolate and you can't argue with science now can you?'

'Ah, I guess I didn't know that because I'm not a nurse,' he said laughing.

'Exactly. Could I have a sharing size chocolate bar please Jake, just to prove my scientific theory to the landlord.'

'Let's take these upstairs,' Alex said. 'That way I can undo the button on my trousers. Just to make a bit more room you understand!'

Jess grinned. 'If you say so Mr Blake.'

Next morning Jess phoned Melissa to sort out arrangements for her forthcoming trip to Manchester. Her pulse was racing with nervous anticipation as she heard Melissa's soft voice on the end of the line, and she was suddenly grateful that she was blessed with such a calm and even tone.

A few minutes later she shouted Alex's name and in response he came running into the sitting room where she was sitting clutching her phone.

'Are you okay?' he said with a look of concern.

'Yes, sorry I didn't mean to yell at you like that. I think I'm a bit over-excited,' she replied laughing. 'It's all sorted though and we're going to Manchester the weekend after next.'

CHAPTER THIRTY-FIVE

The days until the trip seemed to drag by and it reminded Jess of counting down the days to Christmas when she was a child. Fortunately, the hospital ward was busy and she'd volunteered herself for a couple of extra shifts which was mutually beneficial as it helped with a staffing shortage and gave her something else to concentrate on.

She had started to make a list of questions for Melissa, but both Poppy and Amber had reminded her that it was not an interview or worse still an interrogation and it might be better just to see where the conversations led.

She was glad that Alex was going to Manchester with her but she'd told him that she wanted to see Melissa on her own. He'd seemed to understand, saying that at least he would be close by if she needed him, and also he was keen to see the football stadiums so she was sure he would have no trouble occupying himself.

At last the weekend of the trip had arrived. Jess was up early and carefully packed a bag with several choices of outfits, not really knowing where the weekend might lead them. She'd washed, blow-dried and straightened her hair and then wet it down again, deciding that a more natural look might be more suitable.

She'd also tried on various tops and dresses, having eventually settled for a soft wool jumper in warm coral, which coordinated perfectly with her dark hair and after pulling on a pair of black skinny jeans and black suede ankle boots, she jumped into Rowan Too and left for the nearby station to pick Alex up.

'Hi,' he said, kissing her on the cheek and handing her a wrapped box added, 'Just a little present for you.'

'What!' she exclaimed. 'We've just had Christmas.'

'I know,' he agreed nodding. 'But this is more of an *essential*. A practical present shall we say.'

She grinned and tore the paper from the package to reveal a satellite navigation device complete with a holder, ready to set up in her shiny new car.

'Oh Alex, this is brilliant. Thank you so much,' she said, kissing him squarely on the lips.

He smiled at her and replied teasingly, 'Well I thought it might also be useful if you get a job as a community nurse as you spoke about. You know what your sense of direction is like you'll never find any of the patients' houses!'

'Well guess what else? she said giggling. 'I'm no good at technical stuff either so you'd better get this thing set up properly for me otherwise we might end up in Scotland.'

The sat nav worked like a dream and took them straight to the door of the hotel in Manchester they had booked into for the night. After checking in, Jess left Alex to explore the city and the football grounds, and after putting Melissa's postcode into her new device, she set off for what could be one of the most important meetings of her life.

When she arrived at Melissa's house, she felt the familiar nervous tension return and she closed her eyes briefly, taking some deep breaths to help calm her nerves. Walking along the path towards the house, it suddenly dawned on her that she had absolutely no idea what Melissa looked like and for some reason hadn't even conjured up a picture in her mind. She reached out her hand to press the bell but the door opened before she could do so, and there in front of her stood the woman who was the keeper of at least some of the details of her life that she herself knew so little about.

As the two women sat at the kitchen table sipping tea and making small talk, Jess realised there was something strangely familiar about the woman sitting opposite her. She was smartly dressed in trousers and a long tunic top and her strawberry blond hair was cut into a neat bob, showing off her fine bone structure.

Jess's thoughts were suddenly interrupted when the other woman said, 'It's really great to finally meet you Jess. It's just so strange, as Anton never knew for sure if he had another child but he always hoped that he did and he always hoped that one day that person would come looking for him.'

She nodded, desperately trying to keep the tears at bay. 'Unfortunately my mother has caused much pain to many people but I hope that those of us who are left behind can pick up the pieces and start joining them together.' And then, as she looked at Melissa again the realisation struck her that the reason for the feeling of familiarity was that from some angles the woman looked distinctly like her own mother. She looked like Eleanor

Melissa cleared the kitchen table and brought out boxes of photographs, some in albums and some loose, all marked with dates and locations and although the ink was faded on some, Melissa was able to identify them all. There were pictures of Anton, her brothers and other members of the Jamaican side of the family. They were happy pictures of family holidays in the gloriously sunny Caribbean and of rainy days at the British seaside where the boys were wrapped in towels having ventured in the sea. There were pictures of her brothers on their first day at school and of course the obligatory official school photographs which made Jess smile as she remembered her own school photos.

'Do you think you look like Anton or your brothers?' Melissa ventured.

Jess wiped a tear from her cheek and nodded. 'I can see many similarities. And it's so strange as I feel like I know who I am now and yet at the same time I know nothing about myself.'

The older woman touched her arm and smiling said, 'We will learn together my dear and this evening I would like to invite you and Alex to have dinner with us. Your brothers are dying to meet you.'

That evening, Jess was back at Melissa's house but this time with Alex in tow she somehow felt less nervous. She had tried on several outfits before settling for an above-knee knitted dress in midnight blue and thick tights which had a hint of sparkle.

Melissa hugged them both and showed them into the sitting room, disappearing into the kitchen and returning seconds later with a tray of rum punch.

'I thought we'd go Jamaican tonight,' she said grinning.

'How lovely,' Jess replied. 'But I have to drive back to the hotel so I'd better have a soft drink please.'

'No need for that, I already have it covered. My brother runs a taxi firm and I have him on standby to run you back to the hotel, free of charge of course. And then I can pick you up in the morning, that way we get to see more of you. Cunning plan eh?' she said with a wink, and suddenly Jess felt very relaxed in the other woman's company.

Moments later she heard the front door being unlocked and the sound of male voices from the hallway.

'That'll be the boys back from the football,' Melissa said and then shouted, 'In here boys, come and meet your sister.'

Jess felt her pulse quicken and she grabbed hold of Alex's hand for moral support as the door flew open.

'Jess!' they shouted in unison, and she felt a sudden rush of relief as she realised they sounded as excited as she was.

'I'm Anthony and this is my younger brother Bailey,' one of the twins announced.

'He's *so* annoying,' the other twin said with a grimace. 'I am two and a half minutes younger than him but I've had to pay for it all my life. You know the sort of thing Jess, smaller bedroom, he's in the front of the car while I'm in the back, he's allowed to stay up later than me. Need I go on?'

Melissa pulled a face of pretend shock and pointing a finger at Bailey said, 'Very funny. Take no notice Jess, he's a proper comedian this one.'

But she *was* taking notice because what she saw was heart-warming and fun and she realised she was lucky to be a part of this family. It could have been so different. It could have been so much worse and it made her hopeful for the future.

'I'm guessing the rum punch is a precursor to a full blown Jamaican meal?' Bailey said teasingly, putting an arm around his mother's shoulders and then looking at Jess and Alex added, 'Be careful with the rum punch, it's lethal. Mum always tries to get people drunk before she feeds them. It's her way of disguising her terrible cooking.'

Jess looked at Melissa and saw she was smiling. It was banter. Friendly, fun banter. And it was lovely.

At the dinner table the atmosphere was warm and friendly and they all chatted about work and hobbies as if they'd known each other for years. Jess was pleased that Alex and her brothers had found a common interest with the football, and the three men talked and laughed amiably even though they supported different teams.

The meal was spectacular and Jess, feeling emboldened by the rum punch, asked the boys what Anton was really like.

They exchanged a knowing look and then smiling, Anthony answered, 'He was amazing. Kind, funny - unlike my brother - generous and really just the best dad anyone could have ever wished for.'

She smiled. 'I wish I had been able to meet him.'

'And he wished the same Jess, he really did,' Bailey said.

She knew his response was genuine and that was so important to her. 'Thank you. That means so much.'

Over coffee and with a captive audience Jess felt ready to ask the question she had been wanting to ask all evening. 'I hope it's okay to ask this but for me it's really important. I guess it's different for you but for me I've just found out I'm of Jamaican heritage and I don't really know what that means for me. I know it makes me a different person to the one I thought I was but apart from that I'm not really sure.'

Her brothers both nodded, seeming to understand what she was trying to say.

'Yes, perhaps it is different for us as we've always known our roots and we're super proud of them but I think I speak for both of us when I say we embrace them but we don't let them define us in the eyes of other people. There are many other elements that make us who we are, that make us individuals and our roots are just one part of that. I think that's what really matters,' Anthony said.

She nodded. 'Yes I can understand that, I think. It's just so strange for me to suddenly find out I'm a different person. I'm not unhappy about it, please don't think I mean that. In fact, I'm quite excited about it and I'm keen to discover what it means for me. You know, to discover who I really am.' She had so many more questions but that was enough for tonight she decided. Probably for all of them.

'It must have been a bombshell,' Bailey said grimacing. 'It's hard to imagine but I guess they had their reasons…you know for not telling you I mean.'

'It was complicated,' Jess replied. She knew she wasn't ready to say much more. Not yet. And she was sure Melissa wouldn't either. 'Maybe I'll be ready to explain it all one day but I have to have processed it myself first and I'm getting there, I really think I am and today has helped enormously.' She looked up and was grateful to see that by their body language at least, they all seemed to understand. She smiled at them gratefully but said nothing further.

When the taxi arrived Jess hugged them all warmly and thanked them for a lovely evening.

'This is just the beginning,' Melissa said smiling. 'We have a bond now. We are a family. I realise there must be a lot of sadness for you and you have missed out on so much, but having met us all I hope you will see that we can have a happy future together.'

She nodded. 'Thank you Melissa, you've been great and yes I have had a lot of sadness to contend with but what I have learnt is that if you keep looking back then you can't move forward, so it has to be onwards for me from now on.'

And then to her delight as she walked hand in hand with Alex to the waiting taxi she heard Bailey shout, 'See you soon Sis.'

It sounded so genuine and natural that it made her beam up at Alex, who squeezed her hand tightly in response.

Back at the hotel Jess slid into bed next to Alex and as he put a strong and comforting arm around her he asked tenderly, 'How are you feeling my darling?'

She kissed him and was able to answer truthfully, 'I feel okay. No, actually I feel more than okay. The past few months have been hard but I've learnt so much. People have been so kind and it's reinforced the real significance of kindness to me and how it makes you feel when you are shown kindness. It makes you feel secure and…well… valued I suppose. And it's also taught me how important forgiveness is, both to others and for your own self-preservation. I thought Eleanor was perfect. Perhaps I have to accept that she wasn't, but maybe she was perfectly imperfect. We all are I guess. We all have flaws. And you know what? Life's full of surprises with twists and turns and ups and downs and although I haven't ended up where I thought I was going to end up, I truly believe I've ended up where I was meant to.'

'I love you Jess Jones,' Alex murmured.

'I love you too Alex Blake.' And then as his breathing changed to the soft and gentle breaths she had grown to recognise as him drifting off to sleep, she whispered, 'And I love you too Mum.'

AUTHOR'S BIOGRAPHY

Ruby Mae Winter is the author of the brand new novel Secrets, Lies and Chocolate Highs. Ruby was born and raised in East Anglia where she lives with her 'super tolerant' husband and faithful dog!

After raising her family and enjoying a long and happy career as a nurse, Ruby took early retirement to follow her dreams of becoming a published author. Her lifelong love of reading fiction and her many and varied experiences as a nurse, have proved 'invaluable' to her in helping write her debut novel.

Aside from reading and writing, Ruby loves to travel and visit new places. She also enjoys long walks in the countryside and spending time with her family and friends, who have been a never ending source of help and support to her in realising her dream.

Ruby is currently working on her new novel, so keep an eye on the website for further details.

Printed in Great Britain
by Amazon

60938701R00187